TIME WILL RUN BACK

A Novel About
the Rediscovery of Capitalism by

Henry Hazlitt

Ludwig von Mises Institute
Auburn, Alabama
2007

BOOKS BY HENRY HAZLITT:
Thinking As a Science
The Anatomy of Criticism
A New Constitution Now
Economics in One Lesson
Will Dollars Save the World?
The Great Idea
The Free Man's Library
The Failure of the "New Economics"
The Critics of Keynesian Economics
What You Should Know About Inflation
The Foundations of Morality

Originally published by Appleton-Century-Crofts in 1951 as *The Great Idea.*

Revised Edition published in 1966 by Arlington House, Inc.

Library of Congress Catalog Card No.: 66-23142

Mises Institute Print on Demand 2007

Printed in the United States of America

TO: Ludwig von Mises

For it so falls out,
That what we have we prize not to the worth,
Whiles we enjoy it, but being lack'd and lost,
Why, then we rack the value; then we find
The virtue that possession would not show us,
Whiles it was ours.

—*William Shakespeare*

PREFACE

I

If capitalism did not exist, it would be necessary to invent it
—and its discovery would be rightly regarded as one of the great
triumphs of the human mind. This is the theme of *Time Will
Run Back*. But as "capitalism" is merely a name for freedom in
the economic sphere, the theme of my novel might be stated
more broadly: The will to freedom can never be permanently
stamped out.

This book was first published in this country in 1951 under the
title, *The Great Idea*. The British publishers, however, were not
happy with the title. Of the several alternatives I submitted, they
much preferred *Time Will Run Back*; and it was published in
England under that title in 1952. I now prefer this myself, not
only because of its Miltonic origin, but because by implication
it challenges the present smugly fashionable assumption that
every change means progress, and that whatever political or economic trend is latest in time must be best.

In addition to changing the title I have changed the ending.
The original novel closed ironically; by that ending I meant to
emphasize the insecurity of all human progress. But my ending
unfortunately gave at least one or two reviewers the quite mistaken impression that I personally favored Wang's middle-of-
the-road notions over Peter Uldanov's forthright libertarianism.
I have changed the fictional ending in the new version to obviate
any such impression.

The idea of writing a novel on this theme came to me many

v

years ago. It was touched off, as I recall, by several paragraphs in Ludwig von Mises' *Socialism*, which I reviewed for the *New York Times* (January 9, 1938). But more than a decade passed before I felt sufficient sense of urgency to put the idea into effect.

The form I chose for my work made it difficult to assign credit where credit was due. If it had been written as an economic treatise, it would doubtless have been peppered with footnotes. Not only, however, would footnotes have been out of place in a novel, destroying whatever illusion I might otherwise have succeeded in creating, but by the premise of this particular novel all the economic and political writing of the past, except that of the Marxists, has been completely wiped out. My hero is supposed to perform the truly prodigious feat of recreating out of his own unaided head ideas that it has in fact taken generations of great economists to develop and refine. It would be fatuous to make excessive claims to originality in this field. I should like, therefore, to indicate here some of the principal writers to whom my own thought is indebted.

They include Böhm-Bawerk, John Bates Clark, Frank H. Knight, Ludwig von Mises, Brutzkus, Halm, Pareto, Barone, Jevons, Wicksteed, Carver and Roepke. There are doubtless still further debts that slip my mind at the moment. Most readers will, of course, recognize the metaphor of "the invisible hand" as Adam Smith's. And some will recall that the aphorism: "Despotism may govern without faith, but liberty cannot," is de Tocqueville's.

So much for ideological credits. Now as to structural. Many readers will see, in Part One of my book, striking coincidences with George Orwell's *Nineteen Eighty-Four*. These are, however, in fact coincidences. Orwell's book was published in 1949, *The Great Idea* not until 1951. I did not read Orwell's book until after I had finished the first draft of my own. I was at first disturbed by the number of coincidences, but it then occurred to me that at least the broad outlines if not all the details of the imagined future life were the common property of more than one of the recent writers who have tried to imagine that life (Zamiatin in *We* and Aldous Huxley in *Brave New World*, for example).

These writers had not been plagiarizing from each other; but all of them had, so to speak, been plagiarizing from the actual nightmare created by Lenin, Hitler and Stalin (and now prolonged by Communist regimes wherever they get into power). All that the writer had done was to add a few logical extensions not yet generally foreseen.

While Orwell, moreover, portrayed with unsurpassable power the intellectual paralysis and spiritual depravity that a totalitarian regime imposed, he left the determining economic aspect virtually blank (except for the dreadful end-results for consumers). And his book closed on a note of utter despair. *Time Will Run Back,* with its promise of material progress and spiritual rebirth, is in a sense an answer to the black pessimism of *Nineteen Eighty-Four.* Though my book begins at practically the same point as Orwell's, it ends at a diametrically opposite one. My book is also, in a sense, an answer to Bellamy's *Looking Backward* of 1888, because it turns the Bellamy situation upside down. But *Time Will Run Back* was not conceived as an answer either to Bellamy or to Orwell. It was written to state a positive theme of its own. Its fate must rest on the success with which it states that theme.

II

The question may arise in some readers' minds whether as a result of the passage of time in the fifteen years since my mock-novel was originally published, parts of it may not have become out of date. But to ask this is to misconceive the nature and purpose of the book. It is true that the people in my story are forced to rely on radio and the airplane, and do not have television and intercontinental thermonuclear missiles. But a central theme of my book is that under complete world totalitarianism (in which there was no free area left from which the totalitarian area could appropriate the fruits of previous or current discovery and invention, or in which its own plans could no longer be parasitic on knowledge of prices and costs as determined by capitalistic free markets) the world would in the long run not only stop progressing but actually go backward technically as well as economically and morally—as the world went backward and remained backward for centuries after the collapse of Roman civilization.

If my book seems out of date in a few other respects it is, ironically, precisely because of the fulfillment of some of its predictions or apparent predictions. Thus the dictator in my story is named Stalenin (an obvious combination of Stalin and Lenin). He is incapacitated by a stroke, and later he is shot. By coincidence it happened that a bare two years after my book appeared Stalin was reported to have had a stroke. And it is still an unanswered question today, because of the mystery and delays surrounding the announcements of his illness and death, and the subsequent puzzling zigzags and reversals in attitudes towards him on the part of Khrushchev and his successors, whether or not he was actually assassinated.

But other events since the original appearance of *The Great Idea* were not coincidences. Thus my book points out that a centrally directed economy cannot solve the problem of economic calculation, and that without private property, free markets, and freedom of consumer choice, no organizational solution of this problem is possible. If all economic life is directed from a single center, solution of the problem of the exact amounts that should be produced of thousands of different commodities, and of the exact amount of capital goods, raw materials, transport, etc. needed to produce the optimum volume of goods in the proper proportion, and the solution of the problem of the *coordination and synchronization* of all this diverse production, becomes impossible. No single person or board can possibly know what is going on everywhere at the same time. It cannot know what real costs are. It has no way of measuring the extent of waste. It has no real way of knowing how inefficient any particular plant is, or how inefficient the whole system is. It has no way of knowing just what goods consumers would want if they were produced and made available at their real costs.

So the system leads to wastes, stoppages, and breakdowns at

innumerable points. And some of these become obvious even to the most casual observer. In the summer of 1961, for example, a party of American newspapermen made an 8,000-mile conducted tour of the Soviet Union. They told of visiting collective farms where seventeen men did the work of two; of seeing scores of buildings unfinished "for want of the proverbial nail"; of travelling in a land virtually without roads.

In the same year even Premier Khrushchev complained that as of January 1 there were many millions of square feet of completed factory space that could not be used because the machinery required for them just wasn't available, while at the same time in other parts of the country there were the equivalent of hundreds of millions of dollars worth of machinery of various kinds standing idle because the factories and mines for which this machine was designed were not yet ready.

At about the same time G. I. Voronov, a Communist party Presidium member, said: "Who does not know that the national economy suffers great difficulties with the supply of metals, that the supply of pipes is inadequate, that insufficient supplies of new machinery and mineral fertilizers for the countryside are produced, that hundreds of thousands of motor vehicles stand idle without tires, and that the production of paper lags?"*

In 1964 *Izvestia* itself was complaining that the small town of Lide, close to the Polish border, had first been inundated with boots, and then with caramels—both products of state factories. Complaints by local shopkeepers that they were unable to sell all these goods were brushed aside on the ground that the factories' production schedules had to be kept.

Such examples could be cited endlessly, year by year, down to the month that I write this. They are all the result of centralized planning.

The most tragic results have been in agriculture. The outstanding example is the famine of 1921-22 when, directly as a result of collectivization, controls, and the ruthless requisitioning of grain and cattle, millions of peasants and city inhabitants died of dis-

*See *New York Times*, Oct. 29, 1961.

ease and starvation. Revolts forced Lenin to adopt the "New Economic Policy". But once more in 1928 more "planning" and enforced collections of all the peasants' "surpluses" led to the famine of 1932-33, when more millions died from hunger and related diseases. These conditions, in varying degree, come down to the present moment. In 1963 Russia again suffered a disastrous crop failure. And in 1965, this agrarian nation, one of whose chief economic problems in Tzarist days was how to dispose of its grain surplus, was once more forced to buy millions of tons of grains from the Western capitalist world.

The industrial disorganization has been less spectacular, or better concealed—at least if we pass over that in the initial phase between 1918 and 1921. But in spite of extravagant claims of unparalleled "economic growth," Russia's problems of industrial production have been chronic. Since factory output goals are either laid down in weight or quota by the planners, a knitwear plant recently ordered to produce 80,000 caps and sweaters produced only caps, because they were smaller and cheaper to make. A factory commanded to make lampshades made them all orange, because sticking to one color was quicker and less trouble. Because of the use of tonnage norms, machine builders used eight-inch plates when four-inch plates would easily have done the job. In a chandelier factory, in which the workers were paid bonuses based on the tonnage of chandeliers produced, the chandeliers grew heavier and heavier until they started pulling ceilings down.

The system is marked by conflicting orders and mountains of paperwork. In 1964 a Supreme Soviet Deputy cited the example of the Izhora factory, which received no fewer than 70 different official instructions from nine state committees, four economic councils and two state planning committees—all of them authorized to issue production orders to that plant. The plans for the Novo-Lipetsk steel mill took up 91 volumes comprising 70,000 pages, specifying precisely the location of each nail, lamp and washstand.

Yet in 1964, in Russia's largest republic alone, deliveries of 257 factories had to be suspended because their goods were not bought. As a result of the consumer's stiffening standards and an increased inclination to complain, $3 billion worth of unsellable junk accumulated in Soviet inventories.*

Such conditions have led to desperate remedial measures. In the last couple of years, not only from Russia but from the Communist satellite countries, we get reports of massive decentralization programs, of flirtations with market mechanisms, or more flexible pricing based on "actual costs of production" or even on "supply and demand". Most startling, we hear that "profits" is no longer a dirty word. The eminent Russian economist Liberman has even argued that profit be made the foremost economic test. "The higher the profits," he has said, "the greater the incentive" to quality and efficiency. And equally if not more miraculous, the Marxian idea that interest represents mere exploitation is being quietly set aside, and in an effort to produce and consume in accordance with real costs, interest (usually at some conventional rate like 5 per cent) is being charged not only on the use of government money by shops and factories, but against the construction costs of plants.

III

On the surface all this looks indeed revolutionary (or "counterrevolutionary"); and naturally I am tempted to hope that the Communist world is on the verge of imitating the optimistic prediction of my novel and rediscovering and adopting a complete capitalism. But several weighty considerations should warn us against setting our hopes too high, at least for the immediate future.

First, there is the historical record. This is not the first time that the Russian Communists have veered toward capitalism. In 1921, when mass starvation threatened Russia and revolt broke out, Lenin was forced to retreat into his "New Economic Policy",

*For the foregoing and other examples, see *Time*, Feb. 12, 1965.

or NEP, which allowed the peasants to sell their surplus in the open market, made other concessions to private enterprise, and brought a general reversion to an economy based on money and partly on exchange. The NEP was actually far more "capitalistic", for the most part, than recent reforms. It lasted till 1927. Then a rigidly planned economy was re-imposed for almost forty years. But even within this period, before the recent dramatic change, there were violent zigs and zags of policy. Khrushchev announced major reorganizations no fewer than six times in ten years, veering from decentralization back to recentralization in the vain hope of finding the magic balance.

He failed, as the present Russian imitation of market mechanisms is likely to fail, because the heart of capitalism is private property, particularly private property in the means of production. Without private property, "free" markets, "free" wages, "free" prices are meaningless concepts, and "profits" are artificial. If I am a commissar in charge of an automobile factory, and do not own the money I pay out, and you are a commissar in charge of a steel plant, and do not own the steel you sell or get the money you sell it for, then neither of us really cares about the price of steel except as a bookkeeping fiction. As an automobile commissar I will want the price of the cars I sell to be set high and the price of the steel I buy to be set low so that my own "profit" record will look good or my bonus will be fixed high. As a steel commissar you will want the price of your steel to be fixed high and your cost prices to be fixed low, for the same reason. But with all means of production owned by the state, how can there be anything but artificial competition determining these artificial prices in such "markets"?

In fact, the "price" system in the U. S. S. R. has always been chaotic. The bases on which prices are determined by the planners seem to be both arbitrary and haphazard. Some Western experts have told us (e. g., in 1962) that there were no fewer than five different price levels or price-fixing systems in the Soviet Union, while others were putting the number at nine. But if the Soviet planners are forced to fix prices on some purely arbitrary basis, they cannot know what the real "profits" or losses are of any individual enterprise. Where there is no private ownership of the means of production there can be no true economic calculation.

It is no solution to say that prices can be "based on actual costs of production." This overlooks that costs of production are themselves prices—the prices of raw materials, the wages of labor, etc. It also overlooks that it is precisely the *differences* between prices and costs of production that are constantly, in a free market regime, redirecting and changing the balance of production as among thousands of different commodities and services. In industries where prices are well above marginal costs of production, there will be a great incentive to increase output, as well as increased means to do it. In industries where prices fall below marginal costs of production, output must shrink. Everywhere supply will keep adjusting itself to demand.

But in a system only half free—that is, in a system in which every factory was free to decide how much to produce of what, but in which the basic prices, wages, rents, and interest rates were fixed or guessed at by the sole ultimate owner and producer of the means of production, the state—a decentralized system could quickly become even more chaotic than a centralized one. If finished products M, N, O, P, etc. are made from raw materials A, B, C, D, etc. in various combinations and proportions, how can the individual producers of the raw materials know how much of each to produce, and at what rate, unless they know how much the producers of finished products plan to produce of the latter, how much raw materials they are going to need, and just *when* they are going to need them? And how can the individual producer of raw material A or of finished product M know how much of it to produce unless he knows how much of that raw material or finished product others in his line are planning to produce, as well as relatively how much ultimate consumers are going to want or demand? In a communistic system, centralized or decentralized, there will always be unbalanced and unmatched production, shortages of this and unusable surpluses of that, duplications, time lags, inefficiency, and appalling waste.

It is only with private property in the means of production that the problem of production becomes solvable. It is only with private property in the means of production that free markets, with consumer freedom of choice and producer freedom of choice, become meaningful and workable. With a private price system and a private profit-seeking system, private actions and decisions determine prices, and prices determine new actions and decisions; and the problem of efficient, balanced, coordinated and synchronized production of the goods and services that consumers really want is solved.

Yet it is precisely private property in the means of production that Communist governments cannot allow. They are aware of this, and that is why all hopes that the Russian Communists and their satellites are about to revert to capitalism are premature. Only a few months ago the Soviet leader Kosygin told Lord Thomson, the British newspaper publisher: "We have never rejected the great role of profits as a mechanism in economic life. . . . [But] our underlying principle is inviolate. There are no means of production in private hands."*

The Communist rulers cannot permit private ownership of the means of production not merely because this would mean the surrender of the central principle of their system, but because it would mean the restoration of individual liberty and the end of their despotic power. So I confess that the hope that some day an idealistic Peter Uldanov, miraculously finding himself at the pinnacle of power, will voluntarily restore the right of property, is a dream likely to be fulfilled only in fiction. But it is certainly not altogether idle to hope that, with a growth of economic understanding among their own people, the hands of the Communist dictators may some day be forced, more violently than Lenin's were when the mutiny at Kronstadt, though suppressed, forced him to adopt the New Economic Policy.

Yet any attempt to decentralize planning while retaining centralized ownership or control is doomed to failure. As a recent writer** explains it:

*New York Herald-Tribune, Sept. 27, 1965.
**G. William Trivoli in National Review, March 22, 1966.

"If the state owns or controls the major resources of the economy, to allow for local autonomy in their utilization invites utter chaos. The Soviet planners, then, are caught on the horns of a serious dilemma. They find that their economy is becoming too complex and diverse to control minutely from above; yet they cannot really achieve the tremendous productiveness of a decentralized economy without relinquishing complete ownership or control of the nation's resources."

Henry Hazlitt

March, 1966.

PART ONE: LOST

Chapter 1

PETER ULDANOV had been waiting half an hour.

He walked to the window and looked down to the streets thirty stories below, and then his glance wandered higher to the drab buildings opposite, and out over the city, until everything melted into a misty horizon.

It was a picture of unrelieved shabbiness.

So this was Moscow! This was the capital of Wonworld!

This building itself was new, towering and shiny black. He had caught a moment's outside glimpse of it when he had entered from the taxi. But from his present point of outlook he could see nothing with the slightest charm or interest, nothing even clean and fresh-looking.

It was Peter's first day in Moscow since early childhood.

Since the age of eight he had spent his years, isolated with his mother and a handful of servants and instructors, on a small island in the Bermudas. A vivid picture of the white house with its white roof, and of the incredibly blue sea just beyond his garden, now came between him and the sordid actuality below.

Why had his father sent for him? He had not seen him since childhood. He remembered only a dark, towering man from whom he had shrunk in terror.

His father was Dictator of Wonworld, ruler of all the peoples of the earth.

The fact would have given Peter himself a tremendous distinction if it had ever been a matter of common knowledge. He took a secret pride in it, overlaid by the hatred and fear which he had caught from his mother. It was a fact, also, that threatened the chief desire of his life—to be let alone, and to work in peace at his music.

What could his father want of him now, after ten long years of silence?

He turned and looked idly at the room in which he stood waiting. The single object on the wall was a large day calendar. Leninsday, April 30, 282 A.M.

A.M: After Marx. Marx was born, under the old, bourgeois calendar, in 1818. If no change had been made in the calendar it would now be the bourgeois year 2100. It had never occurred to Peter to make the calculation. No one was interested in the old, poisonous capitalist world that had been wiped out more than a century ago.

Stalenin's private secretary, Sergei, entered at last: "His Supremacy will see you now."

Peter followed through an office which he assumed to be the private secretary's own, and then into an immense paneled room.

Behind a great desk in the far left-hand corner sat Stalenin, Dictator of Wonworld. It now occurred only as a second thought to Peter that this was his father.

The secretary bowed himself out.

The Dictator stood up, and came forward. He was grayer and more tired-looking than in his pictures, which had not been changed for as long as Peter could remember. But he had the same massive strength. His frame was big; his hair cropped close; his head, shoulders and chest solid and square as if hewn out of granite.

He put his hands on his son's shoulders, gazing at him appraisingly. Peter was surprised to discover, at this nearness, that his father was no taller than he. Peter himself was a little over six feet, but he now realized that he had unconsciously come to think of his father as being of much more than human dimensions. The enormous posters had no doubt contributed to this impression. It was almost a shock to realize that Stalenin was

2

only another man like himself. Their eyes met on the same level. Stalenin's expression, which had been grim, softened a little. "You are handsome," he said. "Even impressive. That's good. Important, too." He looked at Peter again. "They tell me that you are a first-rate pianist and composer. I'm glad to hear it. If a man shows talent even in trivialities, he is apt to show it in important things also."

Peter flushed. Music a triviality? And how did his father come to know anything about Peter's music? They had never written to each other. Nor had his mother, up to her death last year, exchanged a single letter with his father since she left him ten years ago. Who had been his father's informant?

Stalenin smiled enigmatically. "You are wondering why I sent for you?"

Peter was silent.

"For one thing," Stalenin continued, "I have decided at last to give you an education. You may not know it, but you are the most ignorant man in Wonworld."

"But, Your Supremacy, I was told I had the very best tutors—"

"I know all about your tutors. Their function was to protect you from any real knowledge of the modern world."

He went back to his desk and filled his pipe. "I lived with your mother until you were eight years old. After I became Dictator in 268—you were only five—your mother became a problem. She objected vehemently to the Great Purge of 271, which carried away her brother. That purge was absolutely necessary to the security of Wonworld. But she said she hated me and everything I stood for. She even thought you were being 'corrupted' by getting the same communist education as everyone else in Wonworld! She defied me. No doubt she expected me to torture her, make her confess treachery, have her beheaded—"

He paused. "I asked her to tell me exactly what it was she wanted. She said she wanted to go off somewhere—on an island —anyway, some place isolated from Wonworld, where she could have her son back and where she could bring him up without ever hearing about me or about the ideology or so-called glories

3

of Wonworld. . . . I agreed to this madness. I sent her off with you to that little island in the Bermudas—how big is it?"

"About three hectares."

Stalenin nodded. "I stipulated that no one was to be allowed on the island except servants to bring supplies. These supplies, as you know, were carried regularly from the main island in a small launch. Your mother wanted your place preserved, she said, as a sort of oasis in Wonworld. She asked that you be taught only the subjects selected by her. I agreed to supply the best tutors. So you were taught music, mathematics—I understand you know as much mathematics as a first-class engineer. Let's see—what else were you taught?"

"Physics, chemistry, astronomy, physiology, biology, horticulture, meteorology—"

"And sports, of course," put in Stalenin. "I'm told you swim like a professional. And that you're a first-class chess player. That impresses me most of all. It shows a sense of strategy. . . .

"Nevertheless"—he was looking at a dossier in front of him—"it's time you were told how ignorant you are of everything a modern man should know. I notice, for instance, that you are completely ignorant of history, politics, sociology and economics. Your acquaintance with our great propaganda literature is negligible. You have never been taught Marxist logic . . . therefore you cannot begin to understand Dialectical Materialism. . . . There is a tremendous lot to be done on you."

He looked at Peter closely. "So unless you can convince me that you can be taught to think right, that you can be made into a useful member of society . . ."

He left the sentence unfinished.

"You are entirely free for the next two weeks," he continued. "You will go around, see this great city, give yourself an education. You have been well supplied with ration books?"

Peter rummaged through his pockets. He pulled out ration books of all colors and sizes.

"Learn what they are all for," said Stalenin. His voice became

4

more kindly. "What do you know about that gray uniform you have on?"

"I was told to put it on this morning before I left the hotel."

"It is the uniform of the Proletarians," said Stalenin gravely. "A very honorable status. The Proletarians make up three-quarters of our whole population. It is, of course, they who really dictate. Wonworld is a dictatorship of the Proletariat. I am merely their instrument, their spokesman."

He smiled grimly. "But you must recognize the other uniforms too, so that you will know how to deal with them—and how you can expect to be dealt with. First and foremost, you must recognize the Protectors. Their uniforms are black—unless they are army officers, in which case they wear a bright red jacket. The Protectors, our top-level comrades, are about 1 per cent of all the people. Next come the Deputies. Uniform—navy blue. About one in ten of the population. They are the intellectuals, technicians, submanagers—anybody whom we consider capable of eventually becoming a Protector. Protectors and Deputies together constitute what we sometimes call the Steel Frame. They are like the commissioned and noncommissioned officers of the Army. . . . At the bottom are the Social Unreliables. Unfortunately, they are still about 20 per cent of the population. They have either committed crimes against the Steel Frame, or have shown themselves incapable of becoming good Proletarians. They are assigned to labor camps . . . or left to starve. They wear brown uniforms—wherever you can still recognize the color. In any case, you will pretend never to see them. But toward the Deputies, of course, you will maintain proper deference. And to the Protectors you will give reverence and love, as well as absolute obedience. . . . Any questions?"

"Where am I to stay, Your Supremacy?"

"You'll find an address among your cards. You will have a room to yourself—a privilege granted to few Proletarians. . . . One more thing. At least for the present you are not to tell anyone that you are my son."

"But what about my name, Your Supremacy?"

5

"Oh, give your real name when asked. Outside of the Politburo, probably no one remembers that my own real name is Uldanov; and anyone who did would probably regard your name simply as a coincidence. Anyway, a Proletarian hasn't much use for a name. Most of the time you will simply be called by your license number. Tomorrow you will apply for one. Any further questions?"

"When do you want to see me again, Your Supremacy?"

"I will let you know. By the way, tomorrow is the May Day parade. Of course you will go to see it."

Chapter 2

THE wind was blowing up swirls of dust, cigarette butts and tattered newspapers. Peter bent forward against it, constantly turning his head to protect his eyes and throat from the grit.

If Moscow looked shabby from thirty stories up, it was squalid from the pavement. The buildings were in every stage of disrepair and decay. The only relief to this drabness—if it was relief—was the omnipresent posters, displaying either enormous faces of Stalenin or exhortations to Work! Production! Loyalty! and warnings against Wreckers and Spies.

The people, too, were drab. The typical face was as devoid of expression as the back of a baby's head. The women wore precisely the same shabby gray proletarian uniforms as the men. Why had he expected anything else? Then he remembered. His mother had always worn something she called skirts. It was the first time it had ever occurred to him that she might have been in any way affected or eccentric.

What he was seeing now was the real world. His previous life on his Bermuda island suddenly struck him as a strangely insulated, even sterilized, existence. He was beginning to feel like a freak.

He found himself in front of what appeared to be a small public library. His interest quickened. Could he go in? He decided to chance it.

It was restful inside. He broused among the shelves.

"Is there anything special I can get you?"

A pretty, smiling blonde stood at his elbow. She was a Deputy, in a neat blue uniform. She had a soft, sympathetic face, and the deepest blue eyes he had ever seen.

She would understand me, he thought immediately.

"I'm the librarian," she offered.

There must be something special he wanted. Ah yes. "Where is your music department? I'd like to see the Mozart scores."

"The Mozart scores? Why, they're in the Old World Department . . . they're on the Special Privilege list!"

"What do you mean—Old World Department?"

She looked at him incredulously. Oh well, he was only a Proletarian.

"The Mozart scores," she said, as if talking to a child, "are among the small list of books held out from the Great Liberating Bonfires when the old poisoned capitalist civilization was destroyed. No book on that list can be read by anybody who does not hold a Special Privilege card. I'm not allowed to read them myself. They are in a special room behind two locked iron doors. My key opens only the first."

"Where do I get a Special Privilege card?" Peter asked.

She looked pointedly at his proletarian uniform. "Personally I never heard of anybody's holding a Special Privilege card who wasn't a member of the Protectorate, and even a Party member."

"But why shouldn't anybody be allowed to read any book there is?"

This time she looked at him more sharply. Suspicion came into her eyes. Nobody, even from a collective farm, could be as ignorant as this. Was she dealing with a member of the secret police?

"It would be a pretty state of affairs," she said mechanically, "if everybody were allowed to read the books kept over from the old poisoned capitalist civilization. Putting all sorts of subversive notions into people's heads! Only a small trained class can be allowed to read those books—only people whose minds are so disciplined that they will not be upset by every scrap of the old bourgeois ideology that they come across. Even this small class is only allowed to read these books so that they will be prepared to answer the lies that may be brought forward by malicious wreckers."

"But Mozart," Peter insisted. "What possible harm can there be in the liquid gold of Mozart?"

Surely a member of the secret police! This was a tricky question. Her livelihood might depend upon the answer.

"What possible harm? It isn't for me to say. But still, it's safer to confine every book of whatever kind carried over from the old poisoned civilization to a Special Privilege list. A very wise decision."

She was watching his eyes closely, apparently to see how he was taking this answer.

"Don't worry too much," she went on, now in a kindly tone, "about not having a Special Privilege card. We have many wonderful books." She led him along the shelves. "Here, for example, are our books giving the life story of our Great Dictator, Stalenin."

"Why is there no one in the library but myself?" asked Peter.

Her glance once more became suspicious and fearful. "The library does everything possible," she said, "to induce people to read these books. We always recommend them first. Some of them doubtless do not praise Stalenin in sufficiently high terms to satisfy readers. And then I think there is a moral laxity in the people. We need to get after that."

That answer is self-contradictory, thought Peter. What is she saying—that the books are not good enough for the readers, or that the readers are not good enough for the books?

He felt beaten. The books looked hopelessly dull. He sensed, moreover, that he was being too inquisitive. And he wanted her to like him.

"Well, these are very wonderful books," he said, "but it just occurs to me that I am going out with friends tonight, and I may mislay a book if I take it now. I'll be back tomorrow."

"The library's closed tomorrow. May Day."

"Oh yes; of course. Will you be watching the parade?"

"Naturally."

"So will I. I may see you then."

She smiled at the improbability. Suddenly she understood. Of course he would see her. He had been assigned to see her. She stared at him in open fright. Her eyes fell on his left lapel, where his number badge should have been. There was none. Triumphantly: "I'll have to see your identity card, please."

His identity card! It might give him away. But his father had assured him . . . He produced the card.

"Peter Uldanov," she read expressionlessly. She wrote down the name in a card file along with the date and the hour he had been there. "Number?"

So the name didn't mean anything to her.

"I haven't got a local number yet. This is my first day in Moscow. I'm sorry about my stupid questions. But I'd like to drop in again—often—and look at your books."

Chapter 3

IT was growing dark. He found himself in a workers' section. From up the street came the sound of marching in cadence. A column of men and women approached, four abreast. Every once in a while it would halt at a command, then start again. It came almost opposite. A hardfaced woman was in charge. "Halt! ... Numbers T349, T350, and L184!" The column stopped; two men and a woman stepped forth, saluted, and marched past him into neighboring houses. The column moved again.

Peter stopped a passer-by. "Is this a parade, comrade?"

"Parade?" The man looked puzzled, then suspicious. "That is part of the workers' army being marched home, just as on any other day!"

Peter mumbled his apologies.

He was getting hungry. Time to look for a good restaurant. He trudged endless blocks, occasionally coming on a dingy little eating place from which nauseating cooking odors oozed out.

Just as he was giving up hope, he found himself in front of a restaurant better lighted and cleaner than the others.

He was challenged immediately inside the entrance. "What are you doing here?" The waiter looked pointedly at Peter's proletarian uniform.

"Why, I thought—" Peter looked around. The tables were occupied solely by Deputies in navy blue.

He went into the next proletarian eating place that he found. It was noisy, crowded and dirty. In spite of his hunger, the stench of cooking made him feel faint. But he took his place on line as he was told. In time he came up opposite the desk of the registry clerk.

"Why aren't you at your regular restaurant?" asked the clerk.

"I'm new in Moscow."

At last a large registration book was shoved in front of him and he was told to fill in the blanks under the headings: *Name; Address; Time of Entrance; Purpose of Visit. . . .*

"Purpose of visit?" asked Peter. "Does anybody ever come for any other purpose than to eat?"

"They might come to conspire against the government by spreading false rumors," said the man at the desk.

"Would they put that down in the registry book?"

"Probably not. But then the government could get them on the additional crime of perjury."

Peter was led to a table for four. It was already occupied by three others. None of them spoke to him.

"What have you got tonight?" he asked the waiter with cheerful anticipation.

The waiter stared at him as if he had been guilty of some piece of impudence, and walked away. He came back in fifteen minutes with a dish containing some dark-gray mashed potatoes, brussels sprouts and mashed turnips covered with grease.

Was this, Peter suddenly wondered, the usual food of Wonworld? Had he been pampered up to now?

The grease on the handles of the cutlery came off on his fingers. The tablecloth was covered with coffee stains and cigarette ashes.

At intervals the waiter came over and looked at Peter's plate. "Not finished even yet?" he asked. Peter gently pushed the plate toward him. "Wasting good proletarian food?" asked the waiter. Peter nodded. He was impatient for his coffee. It would take the taste of the food out of his mouth.

The coffee was lukewarm and tasted like mud.

Peter looked about. At a nearby table a big man with bushy eyebrows seemed disturbingly familiar. Then he remembered. It was the same man he had noticed, standing on the opposite side of the street, when he came out of the library. Odd coincidence that he should be here!

He took out his ration books and began to study them. They were bewilderingly complex. He didn't know which to offer the waiter, so he pushed all of them at him.

The waiter tore out coupons from three of the books and turned them back to Peter with a new look of respect. "You are very well supplied, comrade. I see you even have entertainment coupons. You must be a Stakhanovite!"

Peter had not the slightest idea what the waiter meant, but gave a vague nod of confirmation. An idea occurred to him.

"Anything interesting to see or hear tonight?"

"What sort of thing do you like?"

"Music."

"Ah, then you should certainly hear Eliena Bolshekov sing."

"Who's she?"

The waiter stared incredulously. "You must certainly be new to Moscow. She's No. 2's daughter."

"No. 2?"

"Bolshekov! Bolshekov's daughter!"

After standing on a long queue, presenting his ration coupons and identity card, and signing in, Peter got a good seat in the balcony.

He looked around. There was only a handful of proletarian uniforms. Most of the seat holders up here were Deputies. The boxes and the first dozen rows in the orchestra were filled with Protectors and army officers.

The opera was based on an historic story set in the Dark Ages, just prior to the birth of Marx. It represented a struggle between the capitalists and the rising proletariat. The proletarians, when they arrived late to work on the railroad, or fell down from the fatigue of stoking the engine, were repeatedly flogged. Bolshekov's daughter, the heroine, took the part of a ticket seller on the privately owned railroad and was constantly flogged when she

13

failed to sell her quota of tickets, which the railroad kept marking up in price. Her voice was only a little above mediocre, but she had wonderfully shapely thighs and wore red silk tights throughout the opera.

The music was mainly noise.

Eliena Bolshekov got tremendous applause and repeated curtain calls.

On his way out through the lobby Peter caught another glimpse of the big man with the bushy eyebrows.

He found that he had been assigned to a dreary little hotel room. His baggage was already there.

Chapter 4

HE was awakened by a reveille bugle blast coming from a radio speaker built into the wall. There was no way of turning it off.

The strains of the *International* followed. Then a throaty voice began shouting commands for setting-up exercises. Five minutes later a more suave voice broadcast the news. Production of paper boxes was now running 16 per cent higher than in the preceding year. In the output of straw mattresses there had been evidence of sabotage, but the guilty ones would soon be rounded up. . . .

At breakfast Peter had to wait on another long queue.

He hurried to the Red Square. At the Gate of Communist Salvation people were already pouring in from all directions. Impressed, he stopped to watch them.

Suddenly and miraculously, he caught sight of the girl from the library! He elbowed his way over to her, fighting the human torrent.

"What a coincidence!" He grabbed her arm.

She was startled. "Is it?"

"Oh come now," he protested. "Do you think I've been following you?"

She gazed at him steadily. His naïveté half melted her suspicions and she broke into a smile. They were being jostled along by the crowd.

"May we see the parade together?" he asked.

"How can I avoid it?" she said; but her tone had changed to a good-natured banter.

They were lucky enough to get a place near Lenin's Tomb.

Ten o'clock. A great cheer came from the crowd, and a band struck up the *International*.

The ranking members of the Army and Party, marching in single file, began to fill up the temporary reviewing stand on top of the tomb. Rear rows were filled first. Army officers and Party members of increasingly high rank began to fill the rows in front.

"Watch the line-up carefully when the first row comes in," said the girl. "That's how we find out about changes in the Politburo."

"You already know my name is Peter," he replied irrelevantly, "but you haven't told me yours."

She pointed to her badge: L—92-05.

"Yes, but—" he persisted.

"Comrade Maxwell."

"You have a first name?"

She hesitated. "Edith."

The first row was filling up. A hush fell on the crowd. Politburo members ranged themselves on one side, the heads of the Army, Navy and Air Force on the other. They left a vacant place in the exact center.

"No change in the rankings," announced Edith in Peter's ear. "Bolshekov, on Stalenin's left, is still No. 2, Adams No. 3. . . ."

The music stopped, followed by a burst of drums. Then amid complete silence Stalenin, in a pure white uniform, marched to the center position, turned to face the crowd, raised his clenched fist, held it for a dramatic moment, and then dropped it smartly.

The crowd roared. The band burst into "Wonworld Forever!" The parade was on.

First came the infantry, then the tanks, and then a cloud of planes roared overhead. This took an hour.

"The parade is to be very short today," said Edith again in

16

Peter's ear. "Stalenin has an important speech to make at the end."

"Where do you learn all this?"

"Don't you read the *New Truth?*"

A fresh burst of cheers. A barelegged majorette was leading a brilliantly uniformed band. Then came row on row of male gymnasts and athletes, barrel-chested, big-muscled, faceless, each carrying a basketball, football, tennis racquet, or other symbol of his sport. Then came the women athletes, heavy and hard-looking.

Next the professions: bureaucrats with briefcases, doctors with kits, painters with palettes, journalists with notebooks and pencils.

Each group carried a banner proclaiming Stalenin not only the world's greatest citizen but the greatest in their particular line. He was the doctor who watched over all; he epitomized the scientific spirit; he knew the news before the newspapers; he was the architect of socialism, of industry, of the State; the supreme engineer; the poet of progress; he created the poetry that others could only record.

Next came the workers: bricklayers with their trowels, carpenters with their saws, plumbers with their wrenches. Rows of railroad workers with blacksmiths' hammers alternated with rows of farm workers with sickles. They swung these in reverse unison. At the top of each swing, hammers crossed sickles to bursts of applause.

Next came the floats, dedicated to the Spirit of Work, of Efficiency, of Production. Some carried enormous charts, showing the output of guns, tanks, steel, wheat, pigs, education, music and poetry. All charts showed sharply ascending curves.

But to Peter the most interesting floats were two that came at the end. The first consisted of a great steel cage. Inside was a peasant family consisting of a father, his wife, and two children—one a girl of nine or so and the other a boy of about five. They cowered in terror and shame. The float immediately behind was strewn with flowers. In the center was a raised throne on which sat a boy of about twelve, smiling, laughing and bowing from side to side. The first float was greeted by the crowd with hissing and imprecations, the second with wild cheers.

"Who are they?" asked Peter.

"Those are kulaks in the cage," answered Edith.

"Kulaks?"

"Yes; people with a capitalist mentality."

"What have they done?"

"Held back grain."

"All of them?"

"The father, anyhow. The rest ate more than their quota of potatoes from their collective farm."

"How do the authorities know?"

"He confessed."

"Voluntarily?"

"Not till the boy in the back float reported everything to the security police. That is why everyone is cheering the boy."

"Who is he?"

"He's the kulak's oldest son."

A pause.

"What will happen to the family?"

"They are to be guillotined at three this afternoon—like that other family after last year's parade."

"All of them?"

"Of course."

"What did the wife and children do?"

"They ate the potatoes. Besides, they didn't report him. . . . Didn't you read all about it in the *New Truth?*"

Next came row upon row of marching children, mainly about eight or nine years old, carrying huge bouquets of pink and blue flowers.

"The Young Pioneers!" shouted Edith. "The most honored youngsters of Moscow!"

"What did they do to distinguish themselves?"

"Most of them also reported treachery by their parents—but the kulak family you just saw must have been the worst case."

"That's why the boy was selected for chief honors?"

Edith nodded.

The parade was at an end. The bands stopped, and silence fell.

Stalenin arose. He stood for a time motionless, amid deafening bravos from the crowd. Then he raised his hand for silence, and began to speak.

He spoke of the glories of Wonworld, of the incredible progress made, of the launching of the new Five-Year Plan. He cited statistics, statistics of everything, revealing the magnificent progress made in the past twelve months over the twelve months preceding. But—and here he paused significantly—he deeply regretted to have to report that one or two lines of production had not met their quotas; and that in one or two others, quality was defective. To what could this be attributed? Only to one thing: to saboteurs, to traitors, to still uneradicated traces of capitalist mentality.

(Denunciations of the traitors from the crowd.)

They were a very small percentage, these traitors, Stalenin continued, but the future of Wonworld could not be secure until they were utterly stamped out. (Cheers.) And (with a smile) he thought he knew how to stamp them out. (Cheers and laughter.) The comrades must have noticed, by a float in the parade, how a few of them had been uncovered and were going to be dealt with as an example at three o'clock that afternoon. (More cheers and laughter.)

But then Stalenin paused a moment, and his expression assumed a more serious cast. He had a very important announcement to make. The cares and responsibilities of his office had been mounting; the demands on his time were staggering; to meet them he had to make still further sacrifices. The people must have noted that his public appearances had become rarer. This had been simply the result of increasing demands on his energies in more important directions. He had to make a decision, and he had now made it. This would probably be his last public appearance. He would not preside hereafter even at the May Day exercises.

Shouts of "No, no!"

Stalenin raised his hand. He was not deserting them: he had made this decision only in order that he might serve them still more intensely in other ways. He must hereafter leave the laying of cornerstones and the making of speeches to others. And there were others who, acting as his deputies, could do that very well: Bolshekov, Adams—he turned to look at them—need he mention every member of the Politburo? (Great cheers.)

Hereafter Comrade Bolshekov, acting as his deputy, would preside at the May Day parades and other functions, while Comrade Adams would have to assume some of Bolshekov's former powers and administrative duties. In fact—and here he assumed a jovial, bantering expression—instead of Bolshekov being No. 2 and Adams No. 3, as heretofore, it might almost be more accurate hereafter to call Bolshekov No. $1\frac{1}{2}$ and Adams No. $2\frac{1}{2}$. (Much good-natured laughter. A sick smile from Bolshekov.) And here Stalenin must take his public farewell, but only so far as public appearances were concerned, for the people would know that, silently, often alone, late into the nights, he would be working for them with the last grain of his vitality and the last drop of his blood. "Work! Work! Work!" he cried. "And Wonworld forever!"

The applause, the shouting, the crying, rose to a height never before reached. People became hysterical. Some fell on their knees. Soon the whole crowd was on its knees.

Stalenin strode off, followed by the members of the Politburo.

In a few minutes the reviewing stand was empty.

Chapter 5

WHEN they had got up and brushed the dust from their trousers, Peter turned to Edith. "What are you doing now?"

"I join my ORP, of course."

"ORP?"

"My Organized Recreation Platoon. Ours forms in ten minutes at Engels Square."

"May I walk over with you?"

"If you wish. But haven't you been assigned to any ORP of your own?"

"No—that is—not yet."

At Engels Square a number of platoons were already forming. "How long will this take?" asked Peter.

"Till four o'clock."

"Does the platoon come back here?"

"Yes."

"May I see you then?"

"I'm taking my father out. He's just recovering from pneumonia. I have a permit to take him out for an hour a day for the next week. See!" She pulled out a card.

"May I walk with you and your father?"

She hesitated. All over the square platoon leaders were shouting the command, "Fall in!" She ran toward her platoon and waved a quick good-by to him.

"All right!" she said finally. He watched her fall into line.

The platoons marched off until the square was almost deserted. But not quite. Peter looked around. Behind him was the man with the bushy eyebrows. And somewhat further away was a new figure—a short, gorillalike man with extraordinarily long arms.

"Did you have a good time?" asked Peter. Edith's ORP had returned to the square and been dismissed. He himself had put in four dreary hours.

"Oh, wonderful!" she answered. "We had lunch; then setting-up exercises; then we played organized softball; and then we were taken to see the kulak family guillotined."

They walked through blocks of drab tenements. Edith stopped in front of one. "Here we are!" she exclaimed.

She led him up three flights of stairs and opened the door to a dark room looking on a tiny courtyard. "Isn't it nice?" she asked.

Peter looked around. It was a medium-sized room into which had been crowded four beds, a number of chairs, and a couple of packing cases apparently used as bureaus. Two of the beds were in complete disorder.

"This is our part of the room," said Edith proudly, pointing to the two neatly made-up beds.

The only occupant of the room as they entered was a white-haired man, distinguished and intelligent looking. He was sitting in an invalid's chair.

"Father," said Edith, "this is Comrade Uldanov."

Her father glanced suspiciously at Peter's empty lapel.

"He just got into Moscow yesterday, father, but he expects to get his license number tomorrow."

"Uldanov . . ." said the old gentleman. "That sounds familiar." He held out his hand. "I'm glad to know you, comrade. My number is EN–57."

Peter shook hands. "My full name is Peter Uldanov."

Her father shot a questioning glance toward Edith, who gave him a reassuring one in return. "My name is John Maxwell," he said.

"Oh—you are English?"

"Yes, an engineer."

"Father was one of the chief designers of the new Lenin super-dam!"

"Where is that?" asked Peter.

"Why," said Edith, "it will be the biggest dam ever built—"

"It's still in the blueprint stage," cut in Maxwell. "The old story—shortage of labor, shortage of raw materials, and above all, shortage of ration tickets."

Peter looked around. "Do you have to share this room with other families?"

"Only with the O'Gradys," said Edith. "A nice quiet family. They have a little boy of three and a nine-months-old baby girl."

"How about privacy?" The question was out before Peter had decided whether it was tactful.

Father and daughter exchanged distressed glances. "I'm surprised that you should mention such a bourgeois concept," said Edith. "We have all the privacy that a socialist society needs. See!" She pointed to wires near the ceiling that intersected the room. There were curtains, or rather sleazy sheets, hanging from them. They had been pushed up against the walls, and she pulled them out straight. They divided the father's from the daughter's bed and both from the rest of the room.

"Snug, isn't it?" she asked.

Peter became indignant. "Couldn't they give you anything better than this?"

Another distressed glance between father and daughter. Edith looked appealingly at Peter, put her finger to her lips and shook her head, as if they were being overheard by someone not present. "How *could* you ever get anything better than this?" she said loudly and distinctly, as if speaking for an audience. "All of us will indeed get still better living quarters if we work longer hours and tighten our belts. And now let's go out for our walk!"

They helped Maxwell out of his chair and handed him his

23

cane. "Father has just recovered from a bad case of pneumonia," said Edith, still very loudly and distinctly. "The doctor prescribes walking, and I have a permit to take him out at this hour."

There was something abnormal about the conduct of these two that made Peter uneasy. When they were in the street and well past the house, Edith asked coldly: "What made you say things like that, when you knew we might be listened to?"

"But by whom?"

"You know that every room in Moscow is wired for sound reception and that the secret police may be listening at any time."

"Can we be overheard now?" asked Peter.

"Not unless we're being followed," said Edith. "That's why I waited for the privacy of the street to tell you this."

Edith's remark reminded Peter. He looked back. There was the inevitable man with the bushy eyebrows, and behind him in turn the man with the long arms.

"Well, we *are* being followed," Peter laughed. "I've been followed ever since I got to Moscow yesterday. And by the same handsome pair."

Edith and her father glanced back. Their faces became livid. Edith turned on him. "You *knew* you were being followed?"

"Yes."

"And yet you did not hesitate to lead these people to me, to my house, to put them on the track of myself and my father?"

"But they aren't following *you;* they're following *me!*"

"Don't you know that whenever the secret police suspect anyone of disloyalty, everybody he associates with is under suspicion?" Tears came into her eyes. "The least you can do now is to leave us immediately, and take your spies with you!"

Maxwell faced him with a menacing expression, but said in a low tone, "You must establish yourself as our enemy."

"What can I do?" asked Peter, bewildered.

"Anything— You are forcing yourself on my daughter, and she and I resent it—"

Peter grabbed Edith, pulled her to him, and kissed her vehe-

24

mently. He suddenly realized that he had been wanting to do it all along.

He felt Edith's hands on his chest pushing and Maxwell's hands on his shoulders pulling him away. At arm's length Edith gave him a stinging slap on the face. Maxwell shook his fist at him.

He turned and ran. When he had run half a block he glanced back. He was relieved to find that both his followers were running after him. At least, he thought, they won't bother the Maxwells.

He walked directly to his hotel.

When he had got to his room he closed the door (it was illegal, he had found, for Proletarians to lock their doors) and examined the room from base to ceiling to see whether it was wired for sound reception.

He found two tiny microphones built into the walls at diagonally opposite corners.

He sank onto the bed.

Chapter 6

STALENIN, pipe in hand, walked slowly back and forth, "I'm going to tell you something, Peter, that is known to nobody on earth except my personal physician and my private secretary. . . . About six weeks ago I had a stroke . . ."

"Oh!"

"I recovered in four days. It seemed to leave no mark. But my doctor warns me that I may have another, more serious. It may affect my heart, my brain—paralyze me—carry me off. That's primarily why I brought you from Bermuda two weeks ago. . . . I don't know whether your mother ever made clear to you the real reason for our breakup."

"You said, Your Supremacy, that she objected to the Great Purge that carried away her brother—"

"Yes, yes. But our real split came earlier. It was ideological, like all real splits. *She accused me of betraying the revolution! Me!* She insisted that the kind of communism I had put into effect was not Marxian-Leninism! It was, of course, the *essence* of Marxism and Leninism. If I had had her liquidated then and there, as I first thought of doing, she would have gone to her death convinced that she was right. I was determined to force her to change her mind, and *really* change it, before she died. And that was why I kept her alive, guarded and isolated, on that island. I was going to show her, when the job was done, the great classless society that I could bring into being. I was going to lead her through a world flowing with milk and honey. Her accusation was a monstrous lie! I was going to prove *even to her* that it was a lie! So far from betraying the revolution, it has been my supreme mission to carry the revolution to its destined fulfillment!"

His pace quickened and his excitement grew as he spoke. Suddenly he put his hand to his heart, and Peter saw that he was making a deliberate effort to calm himself. After a pause he went on:

"Time was not on my side. . . . She died too soon. And now, perhaps, *I* am going to die too soon. . . . And that is why I sent for you."

He walked slowly to his desk and shook the ashes out of his pipe.

"Since your mother insisted that *I* was not creating true communism, maybe *you* can. I'm going to let you try."

Peter was staggered. "But, Your Supremacy, I know nothing—"

"If you know nothing, it's because you were taught nothing. You were educated precisely in accordance with your mother's views. I chose the best teachers in Wonworld to teach you the subjects that she wanted you taught. And she didn't want you to be taught anything about politics or economics or history because, she claimed, you would only be indoctrinated with corrupted views. Well, let's see what you can do with the views *she* taught you!"

"But, Your Supremacy, I wouldn't have the remotest idea of where to begin! You wouldn't want me to *wreck* Wonworld, but that is precisely what I would probably do. I don't even know what my mother's principal objection *was* to your regime. She never spoke to me about it."

Stalenin looked astonished. "She never spoke to you about it?"

"She seldom talked about the world outside. She seldom mentioned your name."

Stalenin was taken aback. He walked up and down as if trying to absorb this.

An intercom buzzed on his desk. "Yes. I'll see him right away."

He turned to Peter. "It's Bolshekov. Go out through this back

27

door. The guard at the end of the corridor will show you the way down. Be back here promptly at ten o'clock tomorrow."

The next day Peter found his father in an altered mood.

"Even if nothing had happened to your mother, I would soon have faced a decision about you. Obviously you couldn't have been kept isolated on that island all your life. As soon as I passed on, you would have been automatically assassinated."

"Why?"

"First, for being my son. And second for being miseducated, and hence an ideological menace. . . . Your life is in the greatest danger."

He sank into a chair. "I can trust no one."

Peter was amazed. "Not even Bolshekov?" He remembered how many times Stalenin had publicly lauded the "loyalty" and "devotion" of Bolshekov. Hadn't he given a renewed expression of his confidence on May Day?

"I trust Bolshekov least of all," said Stalenin. "He is the greatest menace to my regime, to my life. And to yours."

"But why?"

"There was a time when I did trust Bolshekov completely. Perhaps his own ambition had not yet become overvaulting. He is tremendously able, shrewd, fearless—and a complete fanatic. There was a time when, though I was known as No. 1, the twelve members of the Politburo had no numbers. Bolshekov exposed a plot within the Politburo to assassinate me. He extorted confessions from the three members involved, and they were liquidated. I should have known that those confessions were meaningless. You can make anybody confess to anything. But I was away addressing the Wonworld Congress of Scientists at Paris when all this occurred. When I got back there was no version but Bolshekov's for me to hear. He convinced me that this plot was the result of the absence of any clear line of succession to my power. Such plots were apt to recur, he pointed out, so long as anybody in the Politburo thought he could seize power with me out of the way. I asked his suggestion for the cure. He recom-

28

mended that everybody in the Politburo be given a public number so that the resort to violent methods for succession to power would be impossible. I agreed to this. And, still more unfortunately, out of gratitude I named him No. 2. Not till I had done this did I realize what should have been obvious to me from the first—that in naming him No. 2, I had in effect publicly named him as my titular successor. Now all he had to do was to get rid of me. And that, I have found, is precisely what he is planning to do."

"But wouldn't it be a simple matter, Your Supremacy, to give him a lower number?"

Stalenin waved his pipe impatiently. "A man in Bolshekov's position cannot be demoted. Suppose I named him No. 3 or 4 or 5? This public evidence of my distrust would mean that no one would ever know whether to obey him or not. Everyone would shun him. He could not hold even minor power. He himself would know that he was doomed, and have me killed, if he had the chance, before I had him killed. No, the only thing is to arrest him, force a confession out of him, and then kill him."

"But—"

"You are wondering," continued Stalenin, "why I could not simply have him shot and then blame the shooting on enemies of the State. I have thought of that. There are one or two things to be said in its favor. For example, I could accuse others, whom I suspect of being ambitious, of having engineered the assassination. I could have confessions wrung from them, so diverting all suspicion from myself and killing several birds with one stone. You may be sure that Bolshekov has thought of doing the same thing in my case—having me assassinated, staging simultaneously a fake attempt on his own life, having other members of the Politburo—especially Adams—arrested, extorting confessions from them, and so on."

His pipe had gone out again. He walked over to his desk and refilled it.

"These things take considerable arranging," he went on. "I have increased my own bodyguard, and have agents watching

Bolshekov. No doubt he has taken similar measures in my case. He must already know about your presence in Moscow. The bushy-browed comrade who has been following you around for the last two weeks, by the way, is one of my own agents—to protect you. He has sent me daily reports. The long-armed fellow is undoubtedly a spy for Bolshekov. But I shall pretend to know nothing about the matter. Bolshekov and I must act against each other without rousing each other's suspicions. Action on either side may come any day."

Everybody in Wonworld lived in fear. Peter now realized that the Dictator himself lived in as great fear as anyone else. He had to rule by fear because he was himself ruled by fear.

"As to my public expressions of trust in Bolshekov, which seem to be puzzling you," Stalenin continued, "you must understand that these are, of course, necessary for my own protection. The more faith I show in Bolshekov in public, the more impossible it is for him to plot against me openly—and the harder it would go with him if it were ever found out that he was acting against me in secret. I keep promoting him, as you know. This not only conceals my own suspicions from him; it also encourages him to think that he can gain his ambitions without violence or treachery. My May Day speech had still another purpose. I may have a paralyzing stroke at any moment and then it would be impossible for me to show myself in public, and Bolshekov would either finish me off or take power without even bothering to finish me off. So why not announce, while I still seem to be in the prime of health, that I am making no more public appearances? Then if I make no public appearances, no ugly rumors will start—or if they start, they will not be believed. Further, I have removed at least one source of the drain on my energies and postponed a second stroke by just that much. . . . And remember, though I seemed to be placing a lot of power in Bolshekov's hands, I made it clear that he holds all this power only as *my deputy,* and that nothing can be done except in *my* name."

He smoked for a while in silence, and once more walked about the room. "You are probably wondering where you fit into all this. I don't mind telling you that your mother's accusation has rankled in me all these years. You may have gathered as much from what I said yesterday. She charged that *I* betrayed the revolution! She said that this, this Wonworld, is not real communism, not what Marx and Lenin and the great Stalin intended! But it is exactly that! It is the consummation of all that they worked for. . . . Or at least it would be, if it were not for the lazy and the slovenly and the wreckers and the spies! But she blamed *me* for all that! She said that Marx called for a classless society and promised that when socialism had been perfected the State would 'wither away.' Haven't I brought a classless society? There are no differences in classes; there are only differences in functions. *Somebody* has to direct. But how can the State wither away? Under socialism, and by the very concept of socialism, the State owns everything, controls everything, plans everything. How the hell can it wither away?" His questions were directed challengingly at Peter, as if it were he who had made the accusation against him. "Or maybe it *could* wither away, when we have killed off all the traitors. But there is no end to treason; there is no end—"

Peter saw that his father was making another conscious effort, as on the day before, to get control of himself.

"You are probably wondering," Stalenin now resumed very calmly, "as I said before, where you fit into all this. . . . During these years, as your mother's accusation has festered in me, I have thought that my life might be terminated before I could prove to her that she was wrong. And it has occurred to me that it might be at least some satisfaction to select *you* as my successor, you who have been brought up according to her ideas of what an education should be, and defy *you* to try to create true communism—since I wasn't supposed to be doing it."

"But, Your Supremacy, as I told you yesterday, I am completely unequipped—"

"Of course you are. The idea, as I originally conceived it, had no sense. It was merely an emotional daydream of revenge. It

31

began to evaporate, in fact, the moment I first saw you two weeks ago."

"I realize, Your Supremacy, that I am quite untrained for *politics;* but that doesn't mean that I am not equipped for *other—*"

"That has nothing to do with why I changed my mind. I had always thought of you as *her* son. But at my first glance at you as a man instead of a child, I suddenly realized that you are *my* son. And now I want you to succeed me, when I pass on, for a better reason, a real reason. And *that* is why, if you prove equal to it, I'm going to give you a chance to become the next Dictator. I'd like to think of the flesh and blood of Stalenin carrying on. I can understand how the old kings felt—"

"Your Supremacy—"

"When we are alone you may call me 'father.'"

"Father. . . . I don't want to succeed you as Wonworld Dictator. I know that sounds amazing, but . . . I have no reason to suppose that I would have any particular aptitude for it. I have no training for it. . . . I have no heart for it. I'd like to devote myself to music—"

Stalenin cut in with another impatient wave of his pipe. "Music may be all right as a hobby, but it's not a full-time occupation for a serious man. Besides, I've already told you—your life is in imminent danger. Do you imagine for a moment that, if anything happened to me, whoever took my place would let you live? Let you become a potential rallying point for a plot against him? You have only one choice: succeed me as Dictator or be annihilated."

Peter was silent. He said at last: "What do you want me to do, father?"

"The first thing I intend to do is to introduce you to the Politburo at tomorrow's meeting. Your presence in Moscow is bound to be known soon. Bolshekov already knows of it, though he still may not know just who you are. The best way to lull suspicion is to appear to be perfectly frank and introduce you as my son. . . . But I shall treat you with a certain contempt. That is one rea-

32

son why I have given you the status of a Proletarian. Anyway, you ought to know what it's like to be a Proletarian. The next thing for me to do is to see that you get a real communist education. You shall get the best. I will put your education directly in charge of Bolshekov himself."

"Wouldn't that give him even more opportunity—?"

"It will lull his suspicions. He has already been spying on you. Now it will not be necessary. But *you* can watch *him*, with a perfect excuse. By the way, I had almost forgotten to tell you: every member of the Politburo must be addressed as 'Your Highness.' . . . Any further questions?"

Peter had none.

"The meeting of the Politburo is at four o'clock. You will be here ten minutes before then."

At five minutes after four the next day Peter followed Stalenin through a short corridor leading from his office to another room of the same size—and found himself in the presence of the Politburo.

Eleven men in black, and one in the red coat of an army officer, were seated along a large oblong table, half a dozen on each side. At the moment of Stalenin's appearance they stood up.

"Comrades," said Stalenin, "I have a surprise for you. Let me introduce my son, Peter Uldanov!"

He took Peter around the table and introduced him to each member individually, beginning with His Highness No. 2, Bolshekov. It was only the second time that Peter had even seen Bolshekov. He was tall and gaunt—about two inches taller than Peter himself. Even more striking than his high cheekbones and prominent nose were his eyes. They were a distinct green.

Next came His Highness No. 3, Adams, a shrewd-looking Yankee below average height, thin and wispy. But there were humor and good-nature in his wizened face, and Peter liked him immediately. There was also something vaguely reminiscent about Adams that Peter could not quite identify.

He followed his father around the table. . . . No. 4, Marshal

Zakachetsky, head of the Army. . . . No. 5, André Giraud, Commissar of Provinces. . . . No. 6, Ivan Orlov, Commissar of Propaganda and editor of the *New Truth*. . . . No. 7, Nickolas Petrov, "our oldest member." . . . No. 8, Vladimir Kilashov, Commissar of State Security, and head of the secret police. . . . Peter began to lose track of the names.

He did keep track of the Soviet Republic from which each member originated. Adding his father's identifications, he counted eight Russians, one American, one Frenchman, one German, one Englishman and one Argentinian.

Stalenin took his seat at the top of the table, and waved Peter to a chair at the bottom. All sat down.

The Dictator filled his pipe and began to tell the Politburo the story of his son's life. He concealed few outward facts, but his tone was now heavily derisive.

"And so," he concluded, "when his mother died a year ago, I had to decide his fate. Should he be kept on the island for the remainder of his life, a burden to himself and an ideological menace to Wonworld? Or should he be exterminated? Or should we try, belatedly, to turn him into a Marx-fearing Communist and a useful member of society?"

A dozen pairs of eyes turned on Peter as if he were some strange, newly discovered kind of animal.

"I decided on the last, and have brought him here. I am wondering, Your Highness"—Stalenin was addressing Bolshekov— "whether I can place him in your care? Would you be able to give him a little of your own time for a while, to make sure that he gets started right? Later we could hand him over to the right teachers and have him report to both of us regularly, so that we can watch his progress—or lack of progress."

"When do you want me to begin, Your Supremacy?"

"As soon as possible."

Bolshekov turned to Peter. "Report to my office at ten o'clock tomorrow morning."

"One thing more," continued Stalenin. "I don't want this young man to get any favors whatever simply because he happens

34

to be my son. Whatever he gets or doesn't get is to depend solely on himself. You will notice that I have given him simply the status of a Proletarian. However, it might be embarrassing, during the period of his education, to have a Proletarian wandering in and out of the Kremlin offices, where he would be constantly stopped by the guards. So beginning tomorrow morning, No. 2, before he gets to your office I will see that he gets the temporary status and uniform of a Deputy."

He looked sternly at Peter. "It will depend on how rapidly you learn, whether you will be allowed to keep that status."

Chapter 7

"SO!" said Bolshekov. He looked Peter up and down. "You know absolutely no history, absolutely none?"

Peter nodded.

"Well, that can only be made up by giving you a list of books to read. But I will sketch in the general outlines, so that you can get your bearings. Our histories, like our calendar, are divided roughly into two parts: B.M. and A.M.—Before Marx and After Marx. This, for example,"—pointing to a day calendar on the wall—"is the Year of Our Marx 282, which means 282 years after His birth. Certainly you learned at least *that* in the Communist schools before you were eight!"

Peter nodded again.

"But this is the older division. Our recent writers divide history into three great periods: Ancient History, the Dark Ages, and Modern History. Ancient History is all that period, of which practically nothing is now known, that came before what was amusingly called in the Dark Ages the Industrial Revolution. Of course it wasn't a revolution at all; it was a counterrevolution. The Dark Ages begin with the birth of capitalism. There is still some difference among historians as to the exact year in which the Dark Ages began. Some of them place it at 95 B.M., which was the year in which a bourgeois named Adam Smith was born; others place it at 42 B.M., which was the year in which a book appeared by this Adam Smith. This book gave birth to, and

36

presented an elaborate system of apologetics for, the capitalist ideology."

"What was the name of the book?"

"That is no longer known; but I will come to all that in a moment. The Dark Ages represents the whole period from the birth of capitalism until its final overthrow in the series of cold and shooting wars between about 150 A.M. and the final triumph of communism in 184 A.M."

"So modern history, Your Highness—history since the complete and final triumph of communism—is now just a couple of years less than a century old?"

"Correct. Now I won't go into the details of the long and complicated series of wars that led to the final overthrow of capitalism. Soviet Russia, of course, led the forces of communism. The forces of capitalism mainly centered around what we now know as the Disunited States, which kept losing allies, both without and within. But you will get all of that from your history books, of which I will give you a list before you leave."

He made a note on a small pad in front of him.

"Yet I must impress upon you," he continued, "the one central reason for communism's success. We began with apparently every possible disadvantage. The enemy started with better arms, more technical advancement, more production, more resources. And yet we beat them in the end because we had the one tremendous weapon that they lacked. We had *Faith!* Faith in our own Cause! Faith that never for a moment wavered or faltered! We knew that we were right! Right in *everything!* We knew that they were wrong! Wrong in *everything!*"

Bolshekov was shouting. He stopped for a moment as if to let this sink in.

"The enemy never had any real faith in capitalism," he went on. "They started out with little, and began rapidly to lose what they had. Those who had once embraced the gospel of communism were willing to die for it; but nobody was willing to die for capitalism. That would have been considered a sort of joke. Finally, the best thing our enemies could think of saying for capitalism was that it wasn't communism! Even they didn't seem to think that capitalism had any positive virtues of its own. And so they simply denounced communism. But their idea of meeting the challenge of communism was to imitate it. They gave lip service to capitalism and to something that they called private enterprise or free enterprise—nobody any longer knows what these old phrases meant—but every 'reform' they put into effect as an 'answer' to communism was another step in the direction of adopting communism. For every reform they adopted left the individual with less power and the State with more. Step by step the control of individuals over resources and goods was taken away; step by step that control was taken over by the State. It was at first not 'ownership' but merely the power of decision that was turned over to the State. But the fools who were trying to 'reform' capitalism did not see that the power of decision, the power of disposal, was the *essence* of 'ownership.' So they took away from private individuals, step by step, the power to set their own prices, or to decide what to produce or how much of it, or to hire or discharge labor at will, or to set the terms of employment. Gradually their governments themselves fixed all these things, but piecemeal, instead of in one grand logical swoop. It was amusing to see them slavishly imitate the Communist Five-Year Plans by their own 'Four-Year Plans.' These were, of course, like ours, all State plans. Incredible as it now seems, these people actually seemed to believe that calling them Four-Year Plans instead of Five-Year Plans would prevent everybody from recognizing the imitation. In fact, some of them were too stupid even to know at first that they *were* imitating."

He stopped to pour himself a glass of water.

"In brief, step by step the capitalistic world accepted the basic premise of communism—that the individual, left to himself, is greedy, callous, stupid and irresponsible; that 'individualism' and 'liberty' are simply euphemisms for dog-eat-dog, the law-of-the-jungle, the-devil-take-the-hindmost—in short, euphemisms for anarchy—and that only the State has responsibility, only the State has wisdom, only the State can be just, only the State can be trusted with power. They accepted this premise, but they lacked the courage or the clarity to follow it to its logical end. They lacked the courage to see that the individual, because he is responsible to nobody, must be deprived of all power, and that the State, the State representing *all* the people, must be the sole depositor of all the power, the sole maker of decisions, the sole judge of its own—"

He pulled himself up. "I hadn't meant to get into all of this just now. But is it any surprise that the capitalist world was defeated? Is it any surprise that it kept losing supporters both from the outside and from the inside? Do you know what the American political leaders did at one time? They threw huge sums of money around the world to try to *bribe* the rest of the world not to go communist! They thought they could *buy* off faith by dollars!"

"And what happened?"

"What would you expect to happen? The other bourgeois countries found that the easiest way to get money out of the Disunited States was to hint that they might go communist if they didn't get it. Soon they began to believe themselves that their chief reason for not going communist was as a favor to the Disunited States, and that their chief reason for arming against us was not for their own preservation but again as a favor to the Disunited States! If bourgeois America wanted them to arm, they felt, it could jolly well pay for it! And they used most of the other American funds, anyway, to finance socialist programs— in other words, to move in the direction of communism!"

He grinned, then turned suddenly serious again. "Should there be any surprise that while they could bribe only a few spies among *us,* we had swarms of voluntary spies among *them*— people who gave us information gladly, of their own will; people whom we did not have to pay; people who 'betrayed their countries,' to use the phrase of condemnation that the capitalist nations tried to adopt—people who betrayed their countries exultantly, from a sense of duty, because their countries were wrong, and because they were serving a higher cause, the cause of humanity!"

Peter was deeply impressed by the passion and conviction of this man.

"Well, I hope you'll forgive me," said Bolshekov, "if I keep getting carried away from my point."

"No, no," said Peter; "all this is precisely what I need to learn. But may I ask one question? Why did the bourgeois countries fight against communism at all?"

"They fought against communism because they were 'against' communism. That was the only point on which they could agree. But they didn't know what they were *for*. Everybody was for something different. Nobody had the courage to defend a capitalism that was true to the basic premises of capitalism. Each had his own little plan for a 'reformed' capitalism. They could stave off communism, they thought, only by 'correcting abuses'; but all their plans for correcting abuses were steps *toward* socialism and communism. They quarreled among themselves as to how far they wanted to go toward communism in order to 'defeat' communism, as to how far they should embrace communist ideas in order to destroy communist ideas. I know all this sounds incredible, but I assure you it is true."

"But didn't *anybody* have faith in capitalism?"

"Not in the sense in which everybody on our side had faith and has faith in communism. The strongest among our enemies were halfhearted. They merely *apologized* for capitalism. They would say that capitalism, with all its faults—and then they would compete against each other in seeing who could admit the most faults—that capitalism with all its faults was probably as good as reasonable men could expect—and so forth and so on. And so we wiped them out."

Bolshekov made a quick movement with the flat of his hand to symbolize heads being cut off.

"But we will have to get on with our history. Having utterly defeated them, having exterminated not only their leaders but everybody who could be remotely suspected of believing in capitalism, we decided that the job would not be complete, and that we might at a later time face the same struggle all over again, unless we stamped out the whole rotten capitalist civilization, so that the very memory of it would disappear from the minds of men!"

"You mean that our ancestors stamped out *everything?* Didn't they try to separate the good from the bad?"

"The good? Separate? What could be good in a thoroughly rotten civilization? What could be good that was built on a lie? What could be good that was based on injustice, on the exploitation of class by class? What could be good in a bourgeois ideology? And as for separating— When the plague of 261 broke out in Moscow we had to shoot everybody who had it to keep him from contaminating the rest of us. Could we separate the 'good' people who had it from the 'bad' people who had it? *They had the plague!* Whoever or whatever carried the microbes of the plague was a menace to all the rest of us! And so it was with whoever or whatever carried the microbes of capitalism!

"And so we began the work of stamping out every sign and memory of the rotten capitalist civilization. We leveled all the churches. You may not believe it, but there were people who dared to question that step. They called the churches 'things of beauty,' 'architectural monuments,' 'frozen music.' You have no idea of the nonsense they talked. Architectural monuments! Monuments to superstition! Monuments to lull and drug and enslave the people! As if anything could have beauty, except a poisonous and dangerous pseudo-beauty, that was built on a lie! Then of course we slashed and burned all the religious paintings, and shattered all the religious images and statuary. Wait till you read about the ridiculous fuss that was raised in the Italian Soviet, for example, about *that!*"

He laughed sardonically. "Well, then of course we burned all the other paintings, which were simply dripping with bourgeois ideology and capitalist apologetics. We did save a few paintings— portraits of Karl Marx, of Lenin, of Stalin, and a few paintings by a Mexican called Orozco depicting the proletariat rising against their masters. But we didn't save much, fortunately.

"And then we got to the books! . . . Our ancestors thought it was more fun not to burn them all at once. Cat-and-mouse tactics, you know. Assurances of moderation, so as not to raise opposition even within our own camp at the start. The leaders of our ancestors decided to begin merely on all the capitalist economic books. No one could object to *that!* So on one fine May Day we burned the whole of capitalist economics, the whole rotten system of direct apologetics. . . . I don't think we have yet begun to realize the progress the world made on that day! Naturally we had to burn most of the answers to capitalist apologetics, too, so that nobody would be able to reconstruct from them an idea of what capitalist economics was like.

"Well then, of course, we started on what they called their literature! And here too our ancestral leaders were very clever. About two weeks after the burning of capitalist economics, they announced that the whole of religious literature would have to be destroyed, but that this would end the program for the present. So on May 17—another great day—they burned every extant copy of a book called the Bible, perhaps the book that had done more than any other to hold up the spread of communism and dialectical materialism. Of course all other religious literature, including prayer books and mountains of sermons that probably no one read anyhow—but our ancestors had to play safe—was burned along with the Bibles.

"A few months later our ancestors announced that the new Wonworld regime was unfortunately not yet safe, and would not be so long as bourgeois philosophy and ethical theories and logic were allowed to exist. So these were consigned to the flames."

"Did that mean, Your Highness, *all* the then existing philosophy?"

"Certainly—all of it except Marxist philosophy, for whatever was not Marxist was of course either unnecessary or pernicious.

"Well, then our ancestors burned all the books on politics and sociology. These of course were the worst of all. They used the words 'liberty' and 'democracy' in the capitalist and bourgeois sense instead of in the communist and proletarian sense, and created endless confusion. By liberty they meant liberty to starve, liberty even to criticize the State—can you imagine? And by democracy they meant secret elections, in which you couldn't even tell who or what a man had voted for. How could you ever detect disloyalty under such a system? By democracy, in fact, they even meant the power *openly* to organize a *recognized* opposition to the existing government! Well, thank Marx, our ancestors took care of *that!*

"The next big bonfire was that of history and biography. All these bonfires took place at intervals of a few months, and of course the next step was never announced until the Protectors got to it. The one thing to be said in favor of 'gradualism' is that it lulls and divides the opposition. You tell them always that the step you are taking completes your program, that it isn't a precedent for anything else; that they are foolish to talk of the 'principle' involved in a new step when every step is taken purely on its individual merits; and that they are downright hysterical to oppose what hasn't even yet been suggested.

"Well, bourgeois history, of course, was the worst of all. It would sometimes openly contradict dialectical materialism. It would even try to twist facts so as to lead people to think, for example, that every struggle had not been a class struggle. These historians not only pretended that the world had actually grown richer under capitalism; they talked as if the poor themselves, in America, for example, had constantly become better off— whereas, in fact, they were dying off miserably like flies."

"But how," Peter began, "did the population grow to be—?"

Bolshekov rebuked him. "You'd better keep your questions until after I've finished. . . . Well, next our ancestors burned the essays and encyclopedias—they only needed to declare a half-holiday for that—and then they made mighty bonfires of all the poetry and drama and fiction—all of it, of course, riddled throughout with bourgeois ideology—"

"Didn't they have *any* great poets or dramatists, like ourselves?"

"How *could* they have had, when these poets and dramatists either understood nothing, or were hired lickspittles trying to curry favor with the rich and powerful?"

"But didn't any of their fiction attack capitalism?"

"Oh, *most* of it did—but incompetently. In any case, it had served its purpose. It had divided, confused, undermined and disintegrated the opposition to communism. But now that the opposition was totally destroyed, what further need was there for such literature? Moreover, though most of these novelists ridiculed and hammered away at some cornerstone, or one or two of the pillars supporting capitalism, they always seemed to want to preserve some other pillar, some bourgeois or capitalist value, like 'liberty,' 'freedom of speech,' 'freedom of conscience,' or some other pernicious doctrine. They hadn't the slightest realization of how or why the capitalist values hung together.

"Then our ancestral leaders turned to music, and ordered all existing score sheets burned—with, of course, the exception of the *International,* and a few revolutionary compositions—"

"But what was wrong, Your Highness, with the existing music?"

"What was wrong with it? Ask me what was *right* about it! Of course there were not lacking people—and one or two of them were on the Politburo itself—who argued that bourgeois music was harmless. They thought that with the exception of an enormous number of bourgeois love songs, full of claptrap about sexual faithfulness, and songs about mother and home and liberty, and patriotic songs—and all this trash of course *nobody* defended—they thought that with these exceptions the rest might be left, on the ground that it didn't actually *say* anything. Fortunately they were overruled, on the solid ground that bourgeois music necessarily reflected and might perpetuate all sorts of sticky bourgeois sentiments and emotions and ways of feeling—"

"But what harm," Peter broke in, "could a pure pattern of sound—"

44

"What harm? Look at a music scale! The very symbol of bourgeois inequality, with some notes higher than other notes—"

"But don't we have inequality in our own social system? Don't we divide people into Protectors, Proletarians—"

"That is not inequality; that is merely difference in function. Let's not bring up these matters until we get to them. In any case, there is no resemblance whatever between the bourgeois inequality and class divisions reflected in the musical scale—they even had 'major' keys for the employers' songs and 'minor' keys for the workers' songs—and the necessary differences of function in a communist society. Do you know that bourgeois music even had self-confessed *dissonances?* Proletarian music can contain only the purest harmony, to reflect the unadulterated and uninterrupted harmony of the communist society!"

Peter felt that on this point, at least, *he* ought to be the instructor and Bolshekov the pupil. He suspected that Bolshekov did not know the difference between a dominant seventh and a hole in the ground. He longed to tell him how necessary discords and their resolution were to harmony. Instead, he asked mildly: "Is Mozart a communist composer?"

"Mozart? Great Marx, no! He was the worst type of bourgeois! He composed all that rubbish on commission from archbishops and emperors and such, and even from the church! So you can imagine what kind of trash it must have been." Bolshekov suddenly looked at him shrewdly. "How do *you* know about Mozart? Do *you* play Mozart?"

Peter admitted that he had. Bolshekov threw up his hands in a gesture of resignation and despair.

"Well, this proves that my feeling about it has always been right. I've always contended that on this point of music our ancestral communist leaders weakened in their resolution, that they failed to be thorough, and we are suffering from that mistake to this day.

"Here is what happened. They ordered all the music of the Dark Ages burned; and it was burned. But there was one thing they didn't count on—people's memories."

45

"Memories of the bonfires?"

"No! Memories of the music! The musicians *remembered* the music! They remembered nearly all of it! Do you know that there were orchestra conductors who remembered whole symphonies, even when these were written for scores of instruments? It was found that among them the living musicians carried in their memories the whole of bourgeois composers like Mozart, Beethoven, Brahms, Bach, Haydn! And of course the pianists remembered all the piano music; and so on."

"I am not surprised to learn that," said Peter; "but what could have been done about it?"

"They could have wiped out the melodies by wiping out everyone who remembered the melodies! They could at least have forbidden anyone to play or sing or hum them, on penalty of death, and gradually the memory would have died out. . . . But on this one point our communist ancestors were lax and weak. They compromised. They allowed people to rewrite the old scores, and even the tunes of the old songs, provided the words were left out or proletarian words substituted. They provided merely that none of these things could ever be played except by chosen members of the Steel Frame in the hearing only of other members of the Steel Frame."

"Oh, *that's* why His Supremacy allowed me to learn Mozart! And *that's* why I couldn't get at the scores in the library without a special card and key!"

"His Supremacy can never do anything wrong." Bolshekov made the sign of the S on his breast, and then looked significantly into space.

"Well, to continue. The biggest split in the Politburo itself came on the question of science. Bourgeois biology was nonsense. Bourgeois astronomy was unnecessary, except for navigation. But bourgeois medicine had cured even communists. . . . And bourgeois physics and chemistry and mathematics had helped to direct artillery fire and were necessary for the industry and engineering that are necessary for wars. . . . Moreover, all the important discoveries of so-called bourgeois science or mathematics had in any case been made by Russians—"

"I've often wondered," said Peter, "who discovered the differential calculus."

"I've forgotten myself," said Bolshekov, "whether it was Tchaikovsky or Lenin. . . . In any case, there was lengthy debate about the whole matter, and our ancestors finally decided on a selective purge of the sciences. They burned all the old books, but not until they had copied what they wanted out of them and rewritten them from a Marxist point of view."

"Supposing somebody did not turn in all his books for the bonfires when they were demanded?"

"Our ancestors simply prescribed the death penalty for anyone in whose possession any of these books was found. If they were found in any house, every member of the family in that house—and everybody in the house on either side of it—was sentenced to death. This naturally made everyone alert to see that all the books were destroyed."

"People were encouraged to spy on each other and to betray each other?"

"How else could a really thorough job have been done?"

Peter was silent. His thoughts went back to the peasant family in the May Day parade. "But what happened," he resumed, "when people had memorized poetry as they had music—or parts in plays—or stories or novels or old sayings?"

"Ah," answered Bolshekov, "here we come to the most brilliant stroke of our communist ancestors—the invention of Marxanto!"

"Didn't people always speak Marxanto?" *

"Not until after the former capitalist world had been wholly conquered! Our ancestors saw precisely the problem you have just raised. They saw that people might remember these stories and verses and pass them down from generation to generation by

* All the conversations in this book are, of course, translations from the Marxanto. Wherever Marxanto terms are literally untranslatable, I have used what seemed to me to be the nearest English equivalent.—The Translator.

47

word of mouth. And then they thought of a device that solved not one, but nearly all of their problems at a single stroke!"

Bolshekov paused dramatically.

"They invented a new language—Marxanto, and forced everybody to learn it!

"Can't you see how many problems that solved?" he went on, smiling. "The language we think in determines the very way we think. The words we use come already loaded with the meanings that decide our conclusions. Now all the ancient languages —all of them now dead and fortunately irrecoverable—were loaded almost from the beginning of time with bourgeois and capitalistic connotations, implications, emotions, sentiments, attitudes. We had already seen how much could be done to change all these by describing everything in a new vocabulary. This was the great discovery and the great triumph of our Prophet and Redeemer, Karl Marx. When he had finally maneuvered his opponents into talking in his vocabulary they were already in the linguistic trap. For everyone who used the Marxist terms— *capitalism, finance capitalism, bourgeoisie, petty bourgeoisie, proletariat, the masses, the class struggle, class antagonism, capitalist imperialism, historical determinism, dialectic materialism, utopianism, capitalist exploitation*—whoever used these terms accepted along with them the concepts that must inevitably lead him to the Marxist conclusions. Why not, then, complete and nail down the intellectual triumph by eradicating every word embodying a bourgeois concept and substituting for it words embodying the Marxist concepts?

"That is what our revolutionary ancestors did. They called together an assembly of their greatest Marxist dialecticians, linguists, lexicographers, semanticists and propagandists, and ordered them to create an entirely new language. They made a new dictionary, consisting not only of new words, but of new, precise Marxist definitions of each of those words. They replaced the bourgeois grammar of the old languages with a new proletarian grammar for the new language!"

48

"But how did they get people to learn the new language and to forget their own?"

"Ah! They were forced to issue new bilingual dictionaries in each of the scores of existing national languages. The new equivalents were given with the new definitions. Each of these dictionaries was numbered and allowed to be held for only three years. Henceforth only Marxanto was allowed to be taught in the schools. Children and adults both were given three years to learn and use the new language. Then they were forced to turn in all bilingual dictionaries, and all of these were burned. Meanwhile everything that was worth preserving was rewritten and translated into the new language. And thereafter no one could use anything but Marxanto on penalty of death!

"Now look at all that was accomplished at a single stroke! The old bourgeois languages, words, meanings and connotations were totally destroyed. People were prohibited, on penalty of death, from speaking any poetry or phrase that they remembered from the old languages—and their grandchildren wouldn't have been able to understand them anyway. Wonworld was cemented together by a single international language! And this language itself was so constructed, and its words so defined, that nobody could henceforth arrive at any but Marxist conclusions!

"We constructed a new poetry, a new science, a new logic! It meant at last a clean slate, a fresh start, a new dawn in the history of man!"

An exalted light came into Bolshekov's eyes.

"Well, I have talked too long. You are so ignorant, there is so much to tell you, and the excitement of having for the first time a grown man to whom all this wonderful history can be communicated, has carried me far beyond the hour I had set aside. Here: I must give you a list of books."

He wrote down some names rapidly on a pad and handed a slip to Peter. "Here are the three best histories—though if you begin with the three volumes of Ordanov you won't need the other two small volumes: they are merely popular condensations.

Get these from a State bookstore today. Be here again at ten to-morrow."

"Have you time now, Your Highness, to answer one question?" Peter asked, getting up.

"What is it?"

"If all the old histories of the ancient world and the Dark Ages were destroyed, in order to wipe out the very memory of these so-called civilizations, how is it that you yourself know so much about them?"

"You don't seem to understand. What I have given you is the present *official* history of that dead world. It is the history that the Protectors of Wonworld have voted to teach. When they wiped out all the old books, they had to decide what history to put in its place. What I have told you is the *agreed-upon* history."

"But did things actually happen that way? Was it actually *so?*"

"I will explain all that when we get to neo-Marxian logic. The only question to be raised about a statement is not, Is it so? but What good will it do?"

"You mean you don't actually know whether the history you have just recited is true or not?"

"What do you mean by 'true'? Truth, as you will see by the Marxanto dictionary, is just an instrument; it is simply what-ever belief works satisfactorily. Truth is whatever is good for Communism. But that opens up the whole subject of neo-Marxian logic, and we can't go into that today. Be here to-morrow at ten."

Chapter 8

STALENIN took up a pad of paper and signed his name on it. He shoved it toward Peter.

"Imitate that."

Peter did his best.

"Try again."

Peter tried.

"That's a little better."

Stalenin took a clean sheet and signed his name half a dozen times.

"Take this. Don't let anyone know you have it. But keep perfecting my signature."

"But what's the purpose of—"

Stalenin pointed significantly to his heart, and then rather vaguely to his brain. "We may have less time than I thought."

He looked appraisingly at Peter's new but ill-fitting Deputy uniform.

"That's more becoming. . . . Here is the address of my personal tailor." He handed Peter a card. "He will measure you for Protectors' uniforms, but you are not to wear them until the time is right. And now"—his tone was unexpectedly soft—"is there anything else you want?"

Peter got up his courage: "Would it be possible, father, for me to have a piano?"

"In this emergency you can't afford to waste your time drumming—"

"But only for an hour a day, in the evening? Even your organized recreation platoons recognize—"

"I'll think about it."

At the government book store Peter found that he needed special ration coupons to get the history volumes Bolshekov had recommended. It would take at least a week to get these, he learned. It suddenly occurred to him that he might borrow the books at Edith's little branch library.

He had not dared to see her since the kiss and the slap. But his new Deputy uniform, it struck him, gave him an excuse to patch things up. . . .

Her glance was hostile.

"I don't know how to apologize for kissing you—" he began.

"Oh, it isn't that. But when you knew you were being followed by the secret police, and you led them to our house—"

"But I found I was being followed, not because I was under suspicion, but because they were thinking of promoting me. Notice?" He looked down proudly at his new Deputy uniform.

He was surprised himself to hear how plausible his explanation sounded. And, he thought, it's even close to the truth.

He not only got his history books, but before he left had persuaded her to let him call the following evening.

He spent the night in his hotel room assiduously practicing forgeries of his father's signature.

Chapter 9

B OLSHEKOV motioned Peter to a chair.

"There is something," he began, "that I perhaps failed to explain yesterday. You asked how I happened to know so much about the history of the Ancients and the Dark Ages when all the records had been destroyed. I told you that what I knew was the *agreed-upon* history of those times, the history we had decided to teach. But I should have made it clear that a few specialists among the Protectors are permitted to know more about the past than the rest of Wonworld. If you think about the matter a moment it will be easy to understand why this is so. The old fallacies, the old errors, the old vicious and dangerous doctrines held before and during the Dark Ages are liable to recur. They might recur through the discovery of some old book—though that doesn't seem likely—or by a sort of spontaneous combustion. In any case we must be prepared with the answers. So a small group of scholars among the Protectors are permitted access to some things that it would be too dangerous to allow everyone to have access to. That's how you—prematurely—happen to know about Mozart's music, for example."

"You mean, Your Highness, that this is withheld from the masses?"

"You'd better not be caught playing it in their hearing! I might give you a better illustration from economics. The version of Karl Marx's *Capital* that is available in the State bookstores is, of course, an abridged and expurgated volume. It is not a mere translation into the Marxanto of Marx's original book."

"Why not?"

"Because if our communist ancestors had retained all the passages in which Marx denounced capitalism it might have been possible for someone to reconstruct from them what capitalism was actually like, and to try to restore it. It would be obviously foolish to allow any such idea to get into anyone's head. The people, left to themselves, are capable of any sort of perverse idea."

"But might not the same idea occur to a Protector?"

"There we have powerful safeguards. In the first place, the Protectors comprise less than one in a hundred out of the whole population. You will gradually come to realize how enormous are the power and prestige which that confers. No Protector risks his position lightly. In the second place, our communist ancestors were not so foolish as to permit even the Protectors complete access to Marx's *Capital* and the other sacred writings in the original. Even the special editions for the Protectors have been edited in translation—abridged and expurgated—but not as much as the editions for the masses. We must give the scholars of the Protectorate just enough knowledge to be ready with answers should any old errors reappear."

"But isn't all this, Your Highness, a class system?"

"Nothing of the kind! Nobody gets any higher income than anybody else! Nobody exploits anybody else! Never confuse a difference in *function* with a difference in class."

"What about all these differences in uniforms?"

"They simply mark differences in function. I assumed you had been told about that. The Protectors include less than 1 per cent of the population, and the Deputies only about 10 per cent. As their names imply, they are merely the instruments of the Ruling Proletariat—their spokesmen, their representatives. They act only in the name of the Proletariat, which constitutes three-fourths of the whole population."

"If the Proletariat constitutes 75 per cent of the population, the

54

Deputies 10 per cent and the Protectors 1 per cent," said Peter, "that still leaves 14 per cent unaccounted for."

Bolshekov gave him a sharp glance. "You are an excellent mathematician," he said drily. "But the 14 per cent may be disregarded. They're lucky to be alive. They are in our Correction Camps. We shall visit one some time. . . . Today I am taking you to our new workers' dormitories. They are my own project."

A limousine guarded by sentries was waiting for them, with a chauffeur and an armed guard in the front seat. They drove to the outskirts of the city and pulled up before a row of drab new one-story wooden structures with tar-paper roofs and siding.

An obsequious commissar came out to welcome them.

"Male quarters first," ordered Bolshekov.

The first building they entered consisted of a long narrow room lined with regularly spaced single iron beds on each side, as in a hospital or an army barracks. The beds were made up haphazardly, and the room was deserted except for a few attendants.

The three-man inspection party marched through. The floor was unswept, the windows dirty.

They went through still another barracks of the same sort, then through a smaller building with washstands, toilets and urinals, then through a mess hall with long tables in the center and backless benches on each side. A kitchen was at one end. The kitchen was filled with cooks, helpers, and the odor of garbage, sweat and boiling cabbage soup.

"The lunch period will begin in an hour," explained the commissar.

"Female quarters," ordered Bolshekov.

The only difference Peter noticed between the men's and women's sleeping quarters was a crisscross of overhead wires, like those he had seen in the room occupied by Edith and her father, supporting pulled-back curtains.

A woman commissar joined the party to conduct them through.

"All these are just temporary quarters, I presume?" said Peter.

"Everything on earth—except communism—is temporary," was

Bolshekov's tart reply. "I think these buildings excellent for their purpose. Of course we would like to have them bigger and better —made of steel and glass. But we simply can't get the labor and materials for all the tasks to be done. I will give you the statistics showing the enormous number of square feet of living space we have added in the last two years!"

Perhaps if you talked of it simply in terms of square feet, thought Peter, it might sound good.

"This is only for single men and women, I suppose," he asked. "When a man and a woman register permanently with each other, I assume they are assigned to quarters by themselves, where they can raise their children?"

Bolshekov gave him a glance of mingled pity and contempt. "This so-called family life you speak of is merely a relic of an ancient capitalistic institution called marriage. Such relics, unfortunately, still exist, because our communist ancestors lacked the courage to follow their new vision to its logical end. I'm making it my business to rectify this. Marx and Engels unequivocally demanded the abolition of the bourgeois family. They pointed out that it was based on capital, on private gain. They denounced the disgusting bourgeois claptrap about the family and 'the hallowed correlation of parent and child.' I have full authority by the Politburo to stamp out the last vestige of the bourgeois family—at least among the Proletarians, in all cities of 50,000 population and over. When I get through, nobody—at least among the Proletarians—is going to be anybody's property! Nobody is going to belong to anybody!"

"But, Your High—"

"In the Communist Manifesto, Marx and Engels pointed out that 'bourgeois marriage is in reality a system of wives in common.' All that the communists at most could be accused of wanting to do, they said, was 'to introduce, in substitution for a hypocritically concealed, an openly legalized communization of women.'"

"The collective use of women now means the liberation of women," explained the woman commissar.

56

"Exactly," said Bolshekov. "Commissar, will *you* tell Comrade Uldanov how the system works?"

"Proletarian men and women," she said to Peter, as if talking to a child, "are permitted to have sexual relations on Marxday and Stalinsday nights. All that is necessary is for a male and female to come together to the license bureau, not less than twenty-four hours in advance, and take out a license, good for the date stamped. The female is then permitted to close the curtains around her bed for an hour—"

"Still a concession to the old bourgeois fetish of privacy," admitted Bolshekov, "but we move by stages."

"No single couple," continued the woman commissar, "may receive licenses for more than a single month without change of partners. Prolonged registration together would lead to a tendency on the part of each partner to believe that he or she *belonged* to the other. This would lead to jealousy."

"And even keep alive concepts of private property," added Bolshekov.

"What about children resulting from—" Peter asked.

"These are taken to the public nurseries," said the woman commissar, "and brought up and educated in public institutions."

"You'll see all this some other day," Bolshekov promised him.

"The children are assigned license numbers," continued the woman commissar, "that have no relation to the license numbers of their parents. No mother is allowed to know the number of her child. That again might breed ideas of *belonging,* of private property."

"In short," said Bolshekov, "we can't afford to tolerate any 'family' loyalties in danger of being put ahead of loyalty to the communist state."

"Your Highness," said the woman commissar, "may I ask a question?"

Bolshekov nodded curtly.

"One of our histories—Valik's," she continued, "—says that the idea of separating children immediately from their parents actually originated with a bourgeois named Plato, and that all that Marx and Engels asked for at first was free love and free cohabitation; and there have been some disputes among us regarding the present official party line."

"That history is being withdrawn," said Bolshekov. "There was nobody named Plato. And there is nobody named Valik." He looked at her icily.

"That's precisely what *I've* been saying, Your Highness," said the woman commissar.

They inspected another female dormitory. In this a girl of about eighteen was just getting up from one of the beds. The woman commissar smilingly introduced her as SL-648, a Stakhanovite worker who had broken a production record one day last week. As a special reward she had been allowed this morning to stay in bed till noon.

As they talked with her the girl proceeded to change her clothes. She took off her pajama top. Peter's heart beat faster. No one else was embarrassed. The girl unbuttoned her pajama trousers and let them slip to the floor. The blood rushed to Peter's face.

Bolshekov gave her a friendly pinch on the buttocks. She smiled proudly, and leisurely put on her gray blouse and slacks.

When they were outside, the woman commissar was dismissed. Bolshekov took the man commissar aside.

"The floors and windows in the men's dormitories were filthy. Who's fault?"

"I can't say, Your Highness, I—"

"Somebody must be sent to a Correction Camp for that within the next twenty-four hours. We must have an example!"

"Yes, Your Highness."

Chapter 10

WHEREVER he accompanied Bolshekov, Peter detected the same terror in the eyes of the officials and workers, and found the same fawning servility.

For everything that went wrong, Bolshekov demanded an immediate scapegoat. He rarely allowed a day to pass without accusing someone of slackness, sabotage or treason. A few weeks afterwards Peter was always sure to read in the *New Truth* the same self-abasing "confession." It was always couched in the same stilted, stereotyped language.

The accused would then disappear.

Bolshekov took Peter through nurseries and schools. The children were taught to repeat endlessly that Stalenin was omniscient, that their parents had no claim on them, that their only loyalty was to the State, that private property was theft, that hell meant capitalism and heaven socialism.

"Do they understand what all these phrases mean?" asked Peter.

"They will when they grow up," answered Bolshekov, "and then they will be incapable of believing anything else."

At the visits to the government publishing bureau Peter learned how books were written and selected. The bureau was divided into many divisions: political propaganda, economics, engineering, the sciences, art, history, drama, fiction, and so forth. Usually the publishers decided themselves what kind of book was needed, what the correct party line and conclusions

59

should be, and who should be ordered to write it. The principal qualification demanded of a writer was fervor for the existing regime. If he also had the necessary technical knowledge, the government publishers considered themselves fortunate.

Peter thumbed through many volumes. They were all dedicated to Stalenin—who, it appeared, depending on the particular subject matter of the book, was the greatest political genius, economist, engineer, mathematician, chemist, architect, chess player, of them all.

Each writer in every field insisted that his book was written from a completely orthodox Marxist-Leninist-Stalinist-Staleninist point of view. He often contended that his predecessor had been a deviationist. Peter learned that in these cases the predecessor had already been shot for coming to the wrong conclusions.

He tried the fiction, but could not read it. It was always designed to point some moral, such as the precedence of love for the State over that of mere sexual attraction or the accident of family relationship, the need of reporting to the secret police the slightest transgression on the part of one's closest friend or sexual companion, or the duty of long hours of work.

"Reports are coming in, Peter, of another serious famine in Kansas," said Stalenin. "I'm sending Bolshekov right out there."

In the first day of Bolshekov's absence, Peter was promoted to membership in the Protectors.

"I'm turning your education meanwhile over to Adams," Stalenin said. "He is to teach you everything that an Inner Circle Protector should know."

Peter had felt drawn to Adams even from his first meeting. He had not known exactly why. Adams was far from handsome or imposing. But a probable reason suddenly occurred to him. Adams' thin, wizened face, so full of shrewdness and intelligence, strikingly resembled a small bust of Voltaire that had stood, as far back as Peter could remember, in the library of his home in Bermuda. It was this resemblance, he now saw, that had made Adams seem vaguely familiar to him. Peter was constantly reminded afresh of the resemblance by Adams' strongly anachronistic habit of taking snuff.

Adams was remarkably frank. No doubt this was partly because Peter was now to be treated as part of the "inner circle"; but it seemed to spring, also, from a certain open cynicism in Adams' nature.

"What are some of the things that have been puzzling you?" Adams asked.

Peter hardly knew where to begin.

"One thing I would like to know is just how much progress Wonworld has made since the beginning."

"Since the overthrow of capitalism?"

"Yes."

"There are two answers. One is the answer for the Proletarians—the public answer. The other is the answer for the Central Committee of the Party—what we sometimes call the *entre-nous* answer. These two answers exist for most questions in Wonworld."

"But only the second answer, the *entre-nous* answer, is the truth?"

"We do not ask in Wonworld whether a statement is 'true' or not. We only ask: What good will it do? And what good— or harm—a statement does depends on whom you are talking to. It is obviously important, for example, that the Proletarians should believe that Wonworld has made tremendous progress; but it is also important that the Central Committee should know exactly how much progress it *has* made."

It is important, thought Peter to himself, that at least the Central Committee should really know the *truth*. He said aloud: "I should like to know both answers."

"The only thing it does any good to tell the Proletarians, of course," said Adams, "is that our technological progress has been so great since capitalism that any comparison would be absurd. 'How could there have been any progress under capitalism?' we ask them. 'Nobody then sought anything but profit; and

61

everybody maximized profits by selling the public shoddier and shoddier goods.' "

"Is that true?" asked Peter. "I'm sorry; I mean, what is the *entre-nous* answer?"

"The records kept by the Central Committee for its own guidance, as far as I can interpret them," said Adams, "indicate that the present state of technological progress in Wonworld is the same as it was from about 100 to 120 A.M."

"Under the old calendar," Peter figured quickly, "that would have been in what the bourgeoisie called the years from 1918 to 1938?"

"Yes. In some things—in airplanes, say, and in most direct war weapons, we are probably a little ahead of that period, and in other things a little behind."

"But how could that have happened? After all, the bourgeois world was not finally annihilated until—"

"You are about to say," Adams cut in, "that the bourgeois world continued for several decades even beyond 1938?"

"Yes."

"And may have made technological progress in that period?"

"Yes. And if it did—"

"And if it did— Why did the world's knowledge and technological state actually go backward after that? Well," continued Adams, "what with civil wars, physical destruction, the necessary burning of books saturated with capitalistic thinking, the suppression of some kinds of knowledge in order to prevent dangerous insurrections, and so on, a good deal of theoretical knowledge was lost. Though people were able to make some things simply by copying the old ones, we lost some secrets. It is probably just as well that we did, for some of these were terribly destructive."

"But hasn't there been any progress in more than a century of Wonworld?"

"*Entre-nous,* practically none."

"Why not?"

"That, Comrade Uldanov, is a question I have never been able to answer."

One of Peter's first visits with Adams was to the offices of the *New Truth*. There were two newspapers published in Moscow—the *New Truth,* in the morning, and the *Evening Revelation* in the afternoon. The *Revelation* contained almost nothing but cartoons and comic strips. Its existence was necessary, Adams explained, to interest the Proletarians, who almost never bought the *New Truth.*

Though nominally only the morning newspaper of Moscow, the *New Truth* was in fact the master newspaper of Wonworld. While other cities had a morning and an evening newspaper of their own, each with its own title, every newspaper in Wonworld carried the same editorials every day, all telegraphed out from the offices of the *New Truth.* This applied also to about two-thirds of the news items. The other news items referred to local events. Peter found even here, however, by making comparisons of his own in the files, that the identical story would be repeated in, say, the Moscow *New Truth,* the Berlin *Tageblatt,* the London *Times,* the New York *Times* and the Chicago *Tribune* under local date lines. (Most of these names and newspapers had originally been bourgeois in origin; the Wonworld government had simply expropriated and continued them as communist publications.) The names and addresses of the persons involved would be changed, as well as the locale, but the story otherwise would be exactly the same.

Peter asked about this, and Adams referred the answer to Orlov. Orlov was a round-faced, bland little man. In addition to being editor of the *New Truth,* he was a member of the Politburo and head of the entire Wonworld Press Department.

"Naturally," said Orlov, "readers are most interested in what is happening to people in their own localities."

"But precisely the same thing," protested Peter, "couldn't have happened on the same day to different people with different names in different places."

63

Orlov and Adams laughed.

"Are these stories deliberately *invented?*" asked Peter.

"If you stop to think, Comrade Uldanov," said Orlov, "you will see that, for propaganda purposes, invented stories have every advantage over real ones. There is no objection to *basing* a story on a real incident, but even in that case it will almost always be found to require processing. It will have to be changed from the real event to make it more dramatic, or to point a clearer moral. Suppose nothing real happens on a given day, for example, to point a good communist moral? What would *you* do then, comrade, if *you* were editor?"

"But what about these stories of workers whose output is five or ten times as great as that of the average worker?" asked Peter. "These are true, aren't they? You show their pictures, and I have even heard some of them make speeches about their work, and urge their fellow workers on."

Orlov and Adams laughed again.

"Stop and think a minute, comrade," said Orlov. "Do you really think it would be possible for a bricklayer, say, to lay ten times as many bricks in a day as the average bricklayer?"

"But why—?" Peter began.

"To point out that some worker laid 35 per cent more bricks than the average would be interesting," Orlov went on, "but hardly inspiring. Our idea is to make the workers thoroughly ashamed of their present production rate. This is precisely what our system of creating special prodigies does. Stakhanovite heroes, worker giants, we call them. And we also accomplish another purpose. Workers are not likely to think they have a right to express any dissatisfaction with their lot when you make them feel that they are turning out only 10 or 20 per cent of their potential output."

"But what about B-42? You made a motion picture of him laying bricks. I saw that. It was amazing."

"B-42 is a professional motion picture actor," Orlov said. "He never laid a brick in his life."

"An actor?"

64

"Of course," said Orlov. "You don't suppose that we could get a *bricklayer* to make as eloquent a production speech as that!"

"But he seemed to know what he was talking about—"

"The whole dialogue was written by professional writers."

"But I actually saw him laying bricks."

"Are you sure? When the bricks were actually being laid all you saw was a picture of a man *up to the chest*. Those pictures were taken of a professional bricklayer dressed up exactly the same. They alternated with pictures of the actor from the chest up. As his voice was going on all the time you thought it must be he laying the bricks."

"But the bricks were certainly being laid fast."

"Of course they were. Do you know how long you actually saw bricks being laid in that picture? In three separated takes of less than one minute each. No bricklayer on earth could keep up that speed for more than a few minutes. You don't really think that he could keep it up for the full ten-hour day?"

"The final thing you ought to tell him," Adams added, "is that the bricklaying camera shots were taken in fast motion."

"That picture has had a tremendous effect," said Orlov solemnly. "Tremendous!"

He explained in detail to Peter how the editorials and news items in the *New Truth* were printed simultaneously in hundreds of cities and towns throughout Wonworld.

"It is a wonderful and inspiring thing," he said, "when one thinks that everybody in the world is simultaneously reading the same editorial, imbibing the same views, reaching precisely the same conclusions. What harmony!"

"But why is there, in effect," Peter asked, "only one newspaper in Wonworld?"

"If there were any other newspaper," explained Orlov patiently, "and it agreed with the *New Truth,* it would be unnecessary and superfluous, while if it disagreed, it would be pernicious. Under capitalism, as I understand, there were many competing newspapers. What was the result? Wherever they

65

said substantially the same thing, they were hiring many reporters or editors where they only needed one. That illustrates the enormous wastefulness of competition. Socialism has achieved enormous overhead newspaper economies under unification and mass production."

"But suppose," said Peter, "that the old capitalist newspapers reported different things from each other, or expressed different views of them?"

"When they did," Orlov replied, "the results were even worse. The public became confused and ended by believing none of them."

Peter was troubled by this logic but could not put his finger on the flaw.

"I think we should impress upon Comrade Uldanov," said Adams, "the vital co-ordinating function of the *New Truth.*"

"Yes," said Orlov, "the *New Truth* is the mouthpiece of Wonworld. It is here that the Party members, the Protectors and the people everywhere learn each day what to do and what to think. Of course the major policies are laid down by the Politburo as a whole; I merely carry them out. It is for the Politburo to decide, for example, whether we shall say that the production record is very bad, in order to exhort and sting everyone to greater output; or whether we shall say that it is very good, in order to show how well the regime is doing and to emphasize the blessings of living under it."

"These decisions are sometimes very difficult," Adams put in. "We often find that a zigzag course is best. For example, if goods are shoddy and fall apart, or if too many size nine shoes are made and not enough size eight, or if people cannot get enough to eat, there may be grumbling and complaints—or silent dissatisfaction. We must make sure that this unrest does not turn against the regime itself."

"Therefore," said Orlov, "we must *lead* the complaints. We must ourselves pick scapegoats to denounce and punish."

"This is known," added Adams, "as communist self-criticism."

"It is in the columns of the *New Truth,*" Orlov resumed,

66

"that everyone learns what to think of every new book or play."

"One thing I do not understand, Your Highness," said Peter. "The government publishes all the books, and would not publish any book that it did not approve. And it puts on all the plays. Yet I sometimes see a very unfavorable review of a book or a play."

"That might happen for all sorts of reasons," Orlov explained. "Most high officials do not see a play, for example, until after it has been put on. They may then find it unamusing, or even deviationist. And if the public does not go to see it, we must decide whether we shall denounce the play or denounce the public. And with books, again, the party line may have changed between the time the book was ordered and the day of publication. Or a reviewer—provided he outranks the author or the publisher's reader who passed on the book—may detect some deviation that escaped the publisher's eye. All of which," Orlov concluded, smiling, "explains why we have to change the head of our publishing house so often."

"Publishing is the most hazardous occupation in Wonworld," Adams explained.

"Another important function of the *New Truth,*" continued Orlov, "is to decide who are the heroes and who are the villains. There must be heroes to inspire the people to greater achievement, greater conformity to the party line, and greater relentlessness in tracking down deviationists; and there must be villains as scapegoats and as examples to be shunned. We on the newspaper decide who they are."

"But when you decide, for example," asked Peter, "whether to say that the production of shoes, say, is very good or very bad, or who is responsible for it, why don't you just find out the real facts and say whatever happens to be the truth?"

Orlov looked bewildered.

Adams came to the rescue. "Comrade Uldanov," he explained, "has still not yet learned to make the neo-Marxian logic an

67

integral part of his thinking. As I have already pointed out to you"—he turned to Peter—"the truth is whatever belief works successfully; it is whatever statement has the best results. The truth is whatever is good for communism."

Chapter 11

PETER moved quickly into the Inner Circle. While Bolshe-kov was still away, he was made a member of the Party. Only about one in every ten Protectors, he learned, was so honored.

"I must act quickly," was the only explanation Stalenin gave him.

A week later he became one of the 140 members of the Central Committee of the Party. His promotion was the fastest in the annals of Wonworld. Articles about him appeared in the *New Truth* and were reprinted everywhere. He was credited with all sorts of prodigies he had never performed. Nowhere did he find it once mentioned that he was Stalenin's son.

With Adams he inspected innumerable government bureaus. His principal impression was of mountains of paper work. "Every pin produced in Wonworld is recorded," he was proudly told. It certainly was. At least in triplicate, and sometimes through endless carbon copies. Peter wondered whether the time and expense of recording the pins weren't greater than that of making them.

At the headquarters of the Bureau of State Security—the secret police—Peter walked past miles of steel cabinets. A complete dossier, he found, was kept about every person in Wonworld. There was a vast amount of cross-filing. In addition to every person's serial number, name if any, annual photograph, finger prints, biography, family connections if any, occupation, friends and acquaintances, there was also a notation of what he could be accused of in an emergency.

"Just to keep everybody in line," explained Kilashov. Kilashov was head of the secret police and a member of the Politburo. "This emergency accusation," he said, "isn't necessarily the one used when an accusation has to be made. But it's often a great time saver."

"What evidence have you," Peter asked, "that these accusations are true?"

Kilashov smiled grimly. "There is no better evidence than a man's own confession, and we know how to get that."

Adams took Peter on an inspection tour of shops and stores. There were not many. People often had to come long distances to get to them. "This means a great economy in distribution costs," he was told. He invariably found fewer and poorer goods for sale in the shops themselves than in the shop windows. The latter were mainly samples, he learned, not yet turned out in quantity—things scheduled for the next Five-Year Plan.

No item could be bought, moreover, except with a specific ration coupon for that particular kind of item. There were no proletarian ration tickets for specialties. There were merely bread ration tickets for bread, chicken ration tickets for chicken, shoe ration tickets for shoes. . . .

"Suppose a man breaks a shoelace?" Peter asked.

"Each pair of shoes," Adams explained, "is sold with an extra pair of laces."

"And if he breaks even this second pair—?"

"He can get a third pair of laces by applying for a special coupon and swearing out an affidavit that the breakage was an accident. His application for this special coupon, however, is recorded against him on his passport, his labor book, and in the secret police dossiers."

"Doesn't that procedure rather discourage applications for special shoelace coupons?"

"It certainly does. And it discourages the breaking of shoelaces, dishes, or anything else."

With his eyes sharpened by experience and by Adams' dry comments, Peter became increasingly appalled by the carelessness, waste and chaos in production. The output of one item never seemed to match that of any other. There would be too many suits of one size and too little of another. Whole housing projects would be held up because of a shortage of tar paper. But in the Moscow district there were far more window frames than could be used in the planned new housing because the window-frame makers had proudly exceeded their quota.

"Bolshekov must have read of your promotion in the newspapers, Peter," said Stalenin. "In his last report from Kansas he adds casually that it would contribute to your education to go out there and see conditions at first hand. Of course all he really wants is to have you under his eye. But you should go."

"What does he say about Kansas?"

"A million peasants have already died there this year from starvation and typhoid. At least another million will die before the year end."

"What does he say caused the food shortage?"

"The drought. The worst in history."

"Can't food be brought in from other sections?"

"Into *Kansas?* Which is supposed to feed other sections?"

"But—"

"We simply haven't the transport," said Stalenin. "Practically all the bread being consumed in Moscow now is from wheat from the Argentine. Of course Russia must get priority in everything; and there just isn't any more wheat to be had from the Argentine— But you can get all that from Bolshekov."

"When do you want me to start?"

"Tomorrow. Bolshekov is at Wichita. You are to meet him there. Sergei is making all the arrangements for your trip."

Great Bend, Kansas. Peter was at breakfast in his private car. He gazed out the train window. The station platform was crowded with begging peasants. They stared at him, and at

71

the food still on his table, with hollow eyes. Women held up infants for him to see—deformed little monsters with big heads, horribly swollen bellies, and skeleton limbs dangling from them.

He got up and went to the train kitchen. "Something must be done for these people!"

"We have only enough for ourselves, Comrade Uldanov," said the chief cook. "And I am under absolute orders not to give—"

"Then at least let the rest of my own breakfast be given to them!"

"We are under absolute orders from Moscow not to permit that either, Comrade Uldanov. Whatever you leave untouched is eaten by members of the train crew."

Beaten, Peter returned to his seat. He was ashamed to look out again until the train started to move. At the edge of the platform men and women were lying prone, staring up out of expressionless eyes. A mass funeral procession went by.

The whole trip had been a nightmare. He had taken off from Moscow on a large bomber. He could not now remember the number of dreary stops for refueling and repairs—in Siberia, Alaska, Canada, CVA. They had had to land first at a forced labor camp in Siberia, where Peter had seen hundreds of scarcely human creatures, mostly women, filthy and in rags, working in complete silence, many of them up to their knees in muddy water. Armed guards watched their every movement.

The plane had come down twice in Alaska, in clearings in the wilderness.

Because of Peter's curiosity, they had flown relatively low when they got to the remote district of CVA. A guide had pointed out to him, every now and then, a herd of elk or bison roaming the prairie states; but there were few signs of human habitation.

The original plan had been to fly direct to Wichita, but the plane had had to make a forced landing at a place that had once been the site of the proud capitalist city of Denver. For a whole day Peter, accompanied by a member of the plane's crew, had wandered among the crumbling and deserted ruins.

72

Peter tried to imagine what Denver must have been like in the days of its glory, when the barbarian capitalist chiefs held court. The only sign of life he found now was a lizard.

It had finally been discovered that the plane would have to wait for new parts from Moscow, and Peter had been forced to finish the journey to Wichita on this single-track railroad.

They passed one more station—Hutchinson—without stopping. He was grateful for that.

At Wichita he was conducted to Bolshekov's waiting automobile. Bolshekov stood just outside, looking taller, gaunter, more green-complexioned than ever. He looked Peter up and down. "Congratulations on your amazing promotion!" His tone was bitingly sarcastic.

A crowd of starving peasants and workers stonily watched them drive off.

About fifteen minutes later, in the open country, the chauffeur had to stop to change a tire. Everyone got out. Peter noticed thick weeds along the roads and vacant fields full of wild sunflowers. All the seeds had been picked out of the blossoms.

They started off again.

A light rain began to fall. Peter felt his first wave of hope, almost of elation. "Rain!" he shouted.

Bolshekov stared at him as if he had said something stupid.

"But doesn't this break the drought?" Peter asked. "Won't this mean relief?"

"It's nothing."

"But I thought your whole trouble was caused by the greatest drought on record?"

"True."

"But what has the comparison actually been? How much rainfall did Kansas have in the last six months or so? How does that compare with the second worse year?"

"Am I being cross-examined?" asked Bolshekov coldly.

Peter dropped the subject. What was really wrong? Was this the greatest drought on record, or wasn't it? Or—it occurred

73

to him suddenly—was it a drought at all? Was it merely government propaganda—the "official" explanation of the famine?

They arrived at a collectivized farm, the first Peter had seen. Broken-down tractors were rusting in the rain. Not a single tractor was in working order.

Bolshekov sent for the director. "The last mechanic on our state farm who knew how to fix tractors died of starvation last month, Your Highness," explained the director. "We filed an application through the regular channels for a replacement, but so far not a word from Moscow. We have also filed applications for the replacement of broken tractor parts."

"How long ago?"

"Two months."

"And *nothing* has happened?"

"Yes, Your Highness. Yesterday we received a reply saying that our application had been made on form S–27–Q, which has been obsolete for three months, and that we must obtain new forms from the Central Printing Office."

"And have you acted?"

"We have been searching, Your Highness, for the proper form on which to apply for forms to the Central Printing Office. The central office doesn't seem to have furnished—"

"Arrest that man," ordered Bolshekov.

"You see," Bolshekov said to Peter as they drove off, "how hopeless the whole problem is. The same story everywhere. The collectivized farm directors blame the tractor parts makers for delays in deliveries. The parts makers blame *their* suppliers in turn, or tell us that the state farms are careless in handling the machinery. . . ."

After inspecting three more collectivized farms, with much the same results, Bolshekov called it a day. They drove back to the hotel Broadview in Wichita.

"Dinner will be brought up to your room at six," Bolshekov told Peter. "Come to my suite at eight."

Peter decided to go for a walk, but the moment he stepped out of his hotel he was besieged by starving beggars. Men and

74

women, more dead than alive, were lying on the sidewalks. He had nothing to offer but nontransferable ration coupons. He bought the local newspaper, *Humanity,* and immediately returned to his hotel room to read about the famine.

On the front page was a prominent story about a young coal miner who during his six-hour shift had cut one hundred and two tons of coal instead of the usual seven tons. The story sounded vaguely familiar, even to the figures, but the name and place were new to him. There was also a picture of two well-fed, laughing young peasant girls carrying a banner. The leading editorial denied that there was any distinction between Marxism and Leninism.

He went carefully through the whole paper.

There was not a word about the existence of a famine.

In the evening, Bolshekov explained to Peter the economic system under which the state farms operated.

"Just before I was put in charge, the system was for the State to take everything that each collective farm produced over and above what was necessary for the sustenance of the workers on the collectives. That system broke down. The collectives would raise only enough for their own sustenance, and leave little or nothing for the State. So I reversed the rule. My system was to set up first a minimum quota of grain, vegetables or livestock for each collective to turn over to the government. Only when *that* was filled was the collective allowed to retain the quota for its own sustenance."

"But suppose," Peter asked, "that the quota you took away from a collective left its workers without enough to live on?"

"They starved, of course. And though they probably deserved to, we were later forced to change the formula again, to our present formula. . . . Our government investigators now figure first what ought to be the normal production of grain, livestock, and so forth, of each State farm. This assumed 'normal' yield isn't the maximum possible, but it is better than the expected average, for it assumes good weather, good growing conditions, good management and hard work. Then we deduct from this total 'normal' yield the amount needed for the sustenance of the workers and managers of the collective itself. This is called the Sustenance Quota, and the balance is called the Government Quota."

"Suppose, Your Highness, that the total yield of a collective farm in a year is only 75 per cent of its calculated 'normal' yield?"

"Then the government only gets 75 per cent of its normal quota, and the collective gets only 75 per cent of its Sustenance Quota. Nothing could be fairer than that, could it?"

"Can the workers on a collective live on only 75 per cent of their Sustenance Quota?"

"Barely. But that is why they will try to make sure of reaching their full quota the following year."

"How do you know, Your Highness, that the quotas have been fairly assigned to each collective?"

"A government investigator who assigns too small a quota is simply liquidated."

"And if he assigns too large a quota—too big a quota for the collective to be fairly expected to reach?"

"Oh, that is what the collectives are always contending! That's their stock excuse for every failure."

Peter thought it wise not to press this particular question further. "But suppose," he continued, "that a collective farm exceeds its set normal production quota?"

"The surplus above the Sustenance Quota all goes to the government, of course."

"Why, Your Highness, doesn't the government apply the same rule in reverse? That is, if the collective produces 110 per cent of its total quota, why not increase the State's share only 10 per cent and allow the collective's own share to increase 10 per cent?"

"But what would the collectives do, in a socialist society, with a surplus above their own needs? Withhold it? Waste it? Wonworld needs every bushel of grain it can get."

"But if you allowed the collectives to keep the surplus above the quota to be set aside for the State, or even a proportional percentage of the surplus," said Peter, thinking out loud, "wouldn't that give them an incentive to produce more?"

"Merely *for themselves?* In an equalitarian society?" asked Bolshekov. "And just what do you mean by *incentive?* That sounds to me like the language of capitalism. Are you talking of private profit?"

Peter confusedly apologized for the suggestion.

Chapter 12

PETER kept his own notes on the Kansas trip. On the day of their return Bolshekov reported his findings to a special meeting of the Politburo. That evening Peter was called in to give an independent account to his father.

"There are a lot of things in your report," said Stalenin, "that Bolshekov did not tell us. I like your thoroughness. Perhaps you weren't completely miseducated after all."

He started to wander off into reminiscences, and talked of the weekly reports he used to receive about Peter from Bermuda. For the first time Peter saw clearly what until now he had sensed only vaguely. At each meeting his father was a little less brutal, a little more human, a little less sure of himself. This was a symptom, Peter now concluded, of the old man's physical deterioration.

Stalenin suddenly broke off his reverie. "How are you coming on with my handwriting?" he asked.

Peter wrote several Stalenin signatures.

"They are still not perfect," said his father, "but they'll do as a start. Here!" He pushed several legal decrees at Peter: "Sign these with my signature. . . .

"We'll begin now," Stalenin continued as Peter was signing, "to alternate the imitation with the real thing. After a while I'll have you sign my name to all decrees. Then if anything happens to me your forgery will already have established its authenticity." He grinned.

He got up and closed and locked the door which, like all the doors in his office, consisted really of two doors with an air space between, to prevent eavesdropping. Then he led Peter over to the safe, turned the combination, and opened the heavy steel door. He took a key from his breast pocket, opened a little steel drawer in the upper left-hand corner of the safe, and carefully drew out two phonograph records. He carried one over to a phonograph by the wall, and turned it on.

It was Stalenin's voice.

"Comrades and citizens of Wonworld," it began. "I told you on my last public appearance on May Day that the mounting pressure of work upon me would prevent me from making any further public appearances. This pressure has now grown to a point where I am forced to deputize more work than ever. I have therefore asked my son, Peter Uldanov, to sit as my deputy in meetings of the Politburo and on other occasions, and to make public announcements in my name of whatever new policies or decrees I find necessary. I shall, of course, be more active than ever as your leader . . ."

The record went on for about fifteen minutes. It ended in a rousing appeal for more work, more loyalty, more austerity, and more sacrifices.

"I have marked this Record X," Stalenin said. "It is to be broadcast immediately on the entire Wonworld network . . . if I should get a stroke that incapacitates me. Here is the announcement to precede it." He handed Peter a script. It began by declaring that His Supremacy, Comrade Stalenin, No. 1 Citizen and Leader and Dictator of Wonworld, had a most important announcement to make. . . .

"And here," said Stalenin, more solemnly, "is Record Z. It is to be broadcast immediately . . . in the event of my death. You would have to act quickly, before Bolshekov got the news."

He put it on. It announced that his doctors had warned Stalenin that a continuation of his work would destroy his health; that he was therefore resigning as Wonworld Dictator, and that he had appointed Peter Uldanov to succeed him, under

79

the title of Stalenin II. He urged all his supporters and every citizen of Wonworld, including every member of the Politburo, to rally round Stalenin II. He was glad to announce, he continued, that he had the loyal support of Bolshekov in this plan, and that it was, in fact, Bolshekov who had originally suggested to him that Peter Uldanov would be the ideal successor. "The next voice you hear," concluded the record, "will be that of your new Dictator. The Dictator has abdicated; long live the Dictator!"

"Did Bolshekov really suggest that?" Peter asked, astonished.

Stalenin stared at him incredulously. "Of course not. That was put in to forestall any effort by him to unseat you."

Peter looked at him admiringly. "You think of everything."

Stalenin put the records back carefully in the drawer, locked it, and locked the safe. "Burn this combination into your memory," he said to Peter. "You will be the only one to know it besides myself: 8—2—7—5 . . ." He made Peter try it three times, first repeating the numbers to him as Peter turned the knob, then making Peter open the safe twice from memory. "Here is a duplicate key for the small safe drawer. Guard it with your life. I have left orders with Sergei that you are the first one, and the *only* one, to be notified in case either of these things happens to me. I think Sergei is trustworthy: I saved his mother from one of Bolshekov's firing squads.

"And now," he continued, "about your living quarters. The only safe place for you to live is right in this building. I have had the apartment below mine prepared for your occupancy. One room is being soundproofed, like this one, and in that you may have a piano."

"That is wonderful of you, father—"

Stalenin cut him short. "You are never to use it for more than an hour a day. The room will be ready within a week."

He took his pipe from his desk and began leisurely to fill it. "Tomorrow we have a hurdle to take. I am going to arrange your election to the Politburo. It may not be easy. The Politburo has to vote on it. You remember No. 7—Petrov? He is sixty-nine; his health hasn't been too good. I have persuaded him to hand in his resignation tomorrow on the promise that he can retire in grand style in the country. He is to propose you as his substitute. Of course he will vote for you. I will recommend that you be admitted only at the bottom—as No. 13. That means that everybody below Petrov would automatically be promoted one number. Counting mine, that ought to mean eight votes for you. And we can certainly count on Adams. Even Bolshekov may not think it good politics to vote against you. . . ."

Chapter 13

H IS election to the Politburo had a mixed effect on Peter. Though he felt guilty about it because he had done nothing to earn it, the deference now paid to him increased his confidence, even in his talks with Bolshekov. He became bolder in his questions.

"Though I have now inspected any number of factories and collective farms," he said at their next meeting, "I am still not clear how our economic system as a whole works. For example, how do you decide—"

"Very simply, No. 13," cut in Bolshekov. There was heavily sarcastic emphasis on the *No. 13*. "We decide everything on communist principles. These principles were laid down by Karl Marx. The chief one is: *From each according to his abilities; to each according to his needs."*

"Does everybody in Wonworld have what he needs?"

"Is that a hostile question?" asked Bolshekov sharply.

"But from what I've seen—"

"You're interpreting Marx too literally. Of course everybody can't have everything he needs unless we first collectively *produce* enough for everybody's needs. That's why we have to send so many Social Unreliables to concentration camps and shoot the rest—to force them to produce up to their abilities. Unless people produce up to their full ability they can't have everything they need. But until then, of course, we try to distribute equally what there is. The great principle is that of no economic class differences. The great principle is that of equal distribution."

"How do you get equal distribution?"

"Simple. First of all, the Commissar of Production—that's *me* —determines how many calories people need to live on, how many yards of clothing they need, how many square feet of shelter, and how much and what kind of amusement. Then he gives orders for all that to be produced. *His* subordinates assign quotas of production to particular industries. *Their* subordinates assign quotas to particular factories. *Their* subordinates assign quotas to particular workmen. And then each industry, factory, manager and workman, down the line, is held responsible for producing its or his quota."

"Suppose these quotas happen to be assigned unfairly?"

"Remember, *I* am in charge. That never happens."

"But suppose your *subordinates* make mistakes? Suppose they try to be fair, but just don't know what a particular industry, factory, or workman is capable of producing?"

"Of course we can't *entirely* eliminate mistakes. But if a subordinate makes a serious mistake, he is sent to a concentration camp—or shot. That reduces mistakes to a minimum."

Peter had seen this system in operation. He was still not convinced of its efficiency.

"Are you always sure," he persisted, "that you are shooting the right man? For example, suppose one factory—not maliciously, or intentionally, but because somebody has made an honest mistake—is assigned twice as big a quota as it can possibly fulfill, and a second factory only half as much as it could easily fulfill? Even if you shoot the workers in the first factory for falling below their production quota, the workers in the second factory will still be producing less than their best. Or, if they exceed a quota which has been fixed too low, they will be applauded when they do not deserve applause."

"Even if you are a member of the Politburo, No. 13—in fact, precisely because you are now a responsible member of the

83

Politburo—you will have to guard your tongue. Such things do not happen under our system."

"My questions are purely hypothetical," Peter hastened to say. "I'm just asking them to learn how you meet these problems—I must know how to answer subversive critics."

There was just a touch of sarcasm in Peter's voice. He smiled slyly. He was learning how to handle himself with Bolshekov.

"We have several ways of dealing with this problem," said Bolshekov, less hostilely. "The quotas are usually based on the previous production record of each industry or factory or workman—"

"But that might mean, No. 2, that some factories and workmen were penalized for their own good production record in the past while other factories and workmen were rewarded for their bad past production records—"

"We are also guided by *averages* in assigning the production quotas. For example, if nail factories on the average turn out a thousand nails per man per—"

"But suppose one factory, with old machinery, turns out only 500 nails per man per—whatever period—while another factory, with new machinery, turns out 1500 nails per man in the same period? Then the average rate of the two factories is, say, 1000 nails per man. But it isn't the individual worker's or the individual manager's fault in the old factory—"

"All these are questions of detail," said Bolshekov impatiently. "My subordinates have mathematical formulae to deal with all these problems."

Peter was not convinced, but decided to shift the subject. "Let's assume, then, that you solve your production problem. How do you solve your distribution problem?"

"Simplicity itself. We issue ration tickets for everything we produce. People apply to the RTB—Ration Ticket Bureau—for ration books or individual coupons. And that's that."

"But suppose—"

"Suppose it's suits or shoes. Each number is entitled to a new suit of clothes or a new pair of shoes every three years. He applies for and presents his ration ticket and gets outfitted."

"But suppose a person—a number—tears or wears out his suit before the end of three years?"

"That's his lookout. But in shoes he is entitled to one resoling a year—provided he can prove that the soles were worn out in the course of his regular work and not by abuse."

"Why is proof necessary?"

"Why? The resoling is done for him at public expense; it's a drain on collective resources. The shoes are merely a form of public property that he holds in trust, and—"

"What about food?"

"Food is handled the same way. In the ration books there are bread coupons, margarine coupons, potato coupons, bean coupons, and lamb or chicken coupons. In spite of Wonworld crop conditions, due to the worst drought in history, every number in Moscow still gets either lamb or chicken once a week." There was a touch of pride in this announcement.

"What about coffee? Or cigarettes?" asked Peter.

"Coffee or cigarette coupons have to be applied for separately. Every proletarian adult is entitled to a package of cigarettes a month."

"And if he doesn't smoke?"

"He doesn't apply."

"If he doesn't smoke cigarettes, can he get something else instead?"

"Why should he? He's entitled to the cigarettes. If he doesn't apply for them, Wonworld saves just that much diversion of productive resources."

"What's to prevent him from applying for cigarette coupons and exchanging these for, say, somebody else's lamb coupons?"

"Only the concentration camp." Bolshekov smiled grimly. "I'm astonished to learn that you didn't know this. Every ration coupon has stamped upon it not only the number of the coupon itself but the number of the male or female to whom it is issued. Undetected exchanges are impossible."

85

"But what would be the harm, say, in allowing one man to exchange his cigarette coupons for another's margarine coupons?"

"All sorts of harm. One number would consume double the number of cigarettes he really needed. The other would consume twice as much margarine as he really needed. It would force us to increase production both of cigarettes and of margarine. It would create speculation in ration tickets. It would throw all our productive plans out of kilter. As it is, if X doesn't smoke cigarettes, he doesn't apply for ration tickets and we don't have to make cigarettes for him. But if those tickets had an exchange value he would apply for them. We would have to make the additional cigarettes. And then he would exchange his cigarette ticket for a ticket for the coffee that Y didn't drink. So we would have to make more coffee too and—"

"How do you decide how many cigarette coupons to print?"

"We base it on the last five years' demand."

"Suppose you make more cigarettes or grow more beans than are applied for?"

"That seldom happens. First of all, we usually issue just a few more ration coupons than the amount of goods we produce."

"But then some persons must find that their ration coupons are no good!"

"True—but it's better than having an unused surplus of something, which is sheer waste. However, the real problem is not surpluses; the real problem is always not having enough to go round. If we are to be able to give 'to each according to his needs,' there must be enough to go round. We can't produce enough to go round unless each produces according to his ability."

"What's your system, No. 2, for insuring that each person does that?"

"First of all, he is taught from his earliest childhood that it's his duty to do it. Every year, month, week, day—one might almost say every hour of his life—he has dinned into his ears this one message: Work! *Work!* WORK! Production! *Pro-*

86

duction! PRODUCTION! He hears it in every speech. He hears it on every radio program. He reads it in every issue of the *New Truth*. He finds it in every novel and play. And he sees it on every billboard. WORK! THIS MEANS YOU! PRODUCTION DEPENDS UPON YOU! And there is a picture of Stalenin—or me—or even a picture of a pretty girl worker—with his, my or her finger pointing right at him!"

"And the net result?"

"Appallingly disappointing!" confessed Bolshekov. "No, we cannot depend upon exhortation alone. That is why we have to use threats and force. That is why we have to have enormous concentration camps, and why I have to have so many people hung, guillotined or shot. You don't think I *like* to order people shot, do you?"

Peter was eloquently silent.

"And yet I can't understand it," Bolshekov went on. "I don't know which baffles me most—the masses' lack of mass consciousness or their lack of intelligence. With all the conditioning our people get from their earliest years, with all the exhortation, all the propaganda, you would think everybody without exception would *want* to produce to the peak of his ability. They no longer have any capitalist masters! The fruits of their labor are no longer expropriated by somebody else! They now collectively own everything! Wonworld and everything in it is their collective property! You would think they would want to increase this property. Everybody is now working for everybody else! And yet everybody complains about the bad quality of goods and about how little he gets! Why can't he understand that it's *his* shoddy work that makes goods bad, that it's *his* lack of production that leaves so few goods to go around? Why can't everybody understand that whether or not there is a great aggregate production to be distributed depends upon *his* contribution to that aggregate?"

"Maybe because it isn't so," Peter suggested.

"What!"

Bolshekov's eyes seemed to flash green fire.

"Well, of course," Peter continued, "everything you say is perfectly true when you look at the problem *collectively*, as you do. But it isn't true for the *individual* (if I may coin a word), when he looks at it from *his* point of view. You say that everybody is now working for everybody else. Isn't that just the trouble—that nobody is now working for *himself?*"

"For daring to express one tenth of such heresy, any other man would be sent to a concentration camp," warned Bolshekov. "Does No. 1 know that you hold such views?"

"Just bear with me a moment. I am trying to help you solve a problem that you admit baffles you," said Peter with conscious courage. "The individual is told that if he increases *his* output he will, other things being equal, increase *total* output. Mathematically, of course, he must recognize that this is so. But mathematically he senses, also, that his own contribution can have only an infinitesimal relationship to his own welfare. He knows that even if he personally worked like a galley slave, and nobody else worked, he would still starve. And he knows also, on the other hand, that if *everybody else* worked like a galley slave, and *he* did *nothing,* or only made the motions of working when somebody was watching him, he would live like a commissar—I mean, like a king. . . . I have been reading about kings in the histories you recommended."

"But he knows, No. 13, that if *everybody* stopped working he would starve. He knows that if *everybody* only made the motions of working, and then only when being watched, there would be universal starvation, while if *everybody* worked, even when no one was egging him on, there would be plenty to be shared among all."

"I know all that, No. 2," persisted Peter. "And *he* knows all that—as an abstract proposition, or when he looks at it from *your* standpoint as Commissar of Production—or when he looks at it collectively. And apparently some people do. But not, I fear—from what I have observed—the majority. When we consider the majority, I'm afraid, each person tends to look at the matter most of the time from his *own* standpoint. Maybe he can make occasional sacrifices for the good of the whole for brief intervals. But year in and year out? Well, let's figure it. What is the population of Wonworld?"

"About a billion."

"A billion. Then say I am a worker and by backbreaking work I *double* my production. If my previous production was average, I have increased Wonworld's *total* production by only *one billionth*. This means that I personally, assuming equal distribution, get only *one billionth* more to eat, in spite of my terrific effort. I could never even notice such an increase. On the other hand, suppose, without getting caught, I don't work at all. Then I get only one billionth less to eat. The deprivation is so infinitesimal that again I would be unable to notice it. But think of all the work I would save!"

A tiny cloud of doubt seemed to drift across Bolshekov's brow.

"This talk of billionths is unreal," he said finally. "It assumes that we could make a mathematically exact distribution of goods throughout Wonworld."

"Then let's reduce it to a smaller scale," said Peter. "Suppose you had an isolated collective farm with 100 workers. You assigned each worker a particular segment of land to work on, and they raised an average of 100 potatoes per man per year. They would then collectively produce 10,000 potatoes a year, and each worker would receive a ration of 100 potatoes a year regardless of his particular production. That wouldn't be enough to live on; so they would all urge each other to work twice as hard and raise twice as much. Now suppose conditions are such that there is no constant or effective way of supervising a particular man's work or measuring his particular contribution to the total output. And suppose each man knows that his particular contribution cannot be calculated or checked by a supervisor? Yet suppose one worker—let's call him A—because of his social conscience doubles his number of hours or intensity of work and increases his own production from the 100 potatoes previously raised to 200 potatoes. The others, however, let us say, raise the same 100 potatoes as before. At the end of the year there are now 10,100 potatoes to distribute—equally—'according to need.' So instead of getting 100 potatoes, A, as a result of doubling his own output, now gets 101 potatoes—just one more potato."

"You assume an impossible situation in which only one man in a hundred has any mass consciousness."

"All right. Let's reverse the situation. Suppose *everybody else,* through mass consciousness, doubles his output of potatoes but that A, realizing that the others are going to do this, can loaf undetected and produce no potatoes at all. Then the total number of potatoes produced on the farm is 19,800. And when these are equally distributed, 'according to need,' A—who has now produced nothing—none the less gets 198 potatoes, or almost twice as many as when he was working."

"And your conclusion?"

"My conclusion is that under these conditions a man's output, or the intensity of his effort, will be determined not by some abstract, overall, collectivist consideration but mainly by his assumption regarding what *everybody else* is doing or is going to do. He will be willing 'to do his share'; but he'll be hanged before he'll break his back to produce while others are loafing, because he knows it will get him nowhere. And he is prone to be a little generous in measuring how hard he himself is working and a little cynical in estimating how hard everybody else is working. He is apt to cite the very worst among his co-workers as typical of what 'others' do while he slaves. All this may be why your exhortations based on collectivist considerations are so ineffective."

Bolshekov looked troubled. He seemed to have no immediate answer. Peter pursued his advantage: "Let's say I'm an unusual person, a sort of worker genius, and that if I strained all my faculties I could actually turn out ten times as much production as the average worker. But I turn out only 50 per cent more than the average, and yet get praised for doing it—because I am above average. Why should I be so foolish as to show the authorities what I could really do? I wouldn't live any better. I wouldn't get any more ration tickets than the next man. But once I had shown my capacity, my superiors would hold me up to its continuation —on the principle of 'from each according to his ability.' Therefore I find it wiser never to reveal my ability. Therefore nobody ever discovers that I am not producing according to my ability. Never having put it to a strain, in fact, I never even find out myself what my real ability is."

"This is heresy," said Bolshekov. "I shall turn over as a full-time assignment to one of my subordinates the task of drafting an answer to it. The answer will be, of course, for my and your eyes alone."

"Why such secrecy?"

"We are never foolish enough to answer criticisms that no one has yet thought of. We merely prepare such answers ready for use."

"But what of the problem that's worrying you?" persisted Peter. "Maybe my criticism goes deeper than we started by supposing. Perhaps—perhaps the aim 'to each according to his needs' is the very thing that prevents us from ever getting 'from each according to his abilities?'"

"But everyone, No. 13, *ought* to work to the peak of his abilities! It's his *duty* to work to the peak of his abilities! Why shouldn't he? He's no longer being exploited by a master class!"

"But what he really fears under our present system, No. 2, is that he is being exploited by the slackness or malingering of his fellow workers. And perhaps his suspicions of others arise from his knowledge that he himself is secretly trying to exploit them by his own slackness or malingering—"

"Your subversive arguments prove what I have always contended," said Bolshekov; "that unless everyone is conditioned to communism from infancy, such skepticism and heresies are bound to arise. It was a dangerous thing No. 1 did when he allowed you to get this miseducation!"

Peter felt it wise to shift the subject again. "There is something that puzzles me about your description of our system of distribution," he resumed. "You speak of equal distribution. But I haven't noticed this equality. The Protectorate, for example, to which I now have the honor to belong, gets more—"

"I did speak of equal distribution," said Bolshekov, "but I also spoke of 'to each according to his *needs*.' Now wherever there isn't enough of something to go around, it's this second principle that governs. We can only turn out a few automobiles, for example, and all of these are needed for the commissars and other members of the Protectorate. They need these to get around; they need these to do their work properly—to fulfill their functions. We may think of these as capital goods rather than consumption goods. They are the tools that we members of the Protectorate need to carry out our functions properly."

"But since I have been a Protector," said Peter, "not to speak of conditions since I have been a member of the Politburo—*I* haven't been getting just the food stamped on these ration cards. I have been getting much better bread and beans, incomparably better coffee, and—"

"Except when there is a very severe shortage," said Bolshekov, "we can try to distribute equally in *quantity*. But it's impossible to have equal distribution in *quality*. Some beans or chickens or what-not will inevitably have a better flavor than others. The Protectors may as well get them."

"But the Protectors get broccoli and beef and caviar," said Peter, "and the masses, the Proletarians, never get them at all."

"We simply can't produce enough broccoli and beef and caviar for everybody. We can only produce a limited amount. And that amount necessarily has to go just to a small group. We can't distribute one cubic inch of beef or a single tiny caviar pellet to everybody just to make a fetish of equal distribution. So why not reserve it for the Protectors, who need to be kept in full health and vigor and whose morale needs especially to be kept up, so that they can carry out their especially arduous directive functions? For the same reason the Protectors get the best living quarters and more and better suits, of a distinctive color. We must encourage people to want to get into the Protectorate. We must provide . . ."

"Incentives?" asked Peter shrewdly. "But that's just what I'm trying to say. Why can't we provide incentives for *everybody?* Why can't we provide *graded* incentives, so that each man within his own abilities, however high or low in the scale those abilities might be, would have a direct incentive for putting forth *his* best efforts? Suppose his abilities were such that he could never hope to be a Protector, but that he *could* hope to be just a little better off if he put forth his best efforts—"

"I think, No. 13," interrupted Bolshekov sarcastically, "that before suggesting all these reforms of our system you might wait until you have at least learned how the system works. After all, it is the product of our best minds. All our arrangements are passed upon by the Central Plannning Board and by the Supreme Economic Council, both of which I head, and by the Congress of Co-ordinators, over which I also preside. And yet you, who did not even know what the system was a few short months ago—"

Bolshekov's words were much milder than the threat in his voice.

"I'm sorry," said Peter humbly. "I will strive to learn."

Chapter 14

THE pounding on the door grew louder.

Edith woke up, her heart racing. She pulled on her slacks in the darkness, then turned on the light. The pounding was repeated, this time apparently with the butt of a revolver. She opened the door.

Three members of the Security Police stood outside.

"L—92?" asked the officer.

Edith nodded.

"You're under arrest."

Maxwell had come to the door.

"EN—57? You're under arrest."

Neither asked why. No one ever asked why.

"Have I time to shave?" asked Maxwell.

"You have five minutes to dress."

From behind the curtain on the other side of the room, Edith noticed the white frightened face of the three-year-old boy.

As she put on her one luxury, a wrist watch, she noticed the time: quarter of three.

They were led down the dark stairs to the street. A Black Maria stood waiting. As they sat on its hard benches they were blindfolded with black kerchiefs. It started off.

They could not see each other; they dared not speak. But each knew what the other was thinking.

They were thinking of Edith's mother, Helen. She had been a teacher in a nursery. One day, two years ago, she had not come

94

home. No one at the nursery would tell them anything; no one could even remember whether she had been there that day or not. The police told them nothing, and marked it against them that they had asked.

After the first few days they had never spoken to each other about Edith's mother. Speculation about her fate, if she was still alive, was more self-torturing than the assumption that she was dead.

The Black Maria stopped. Edith was led out, still blindfolded. She heard the Black Maria start off again. She was led up some steps, and apparently through two doors. She was aware of light underneath her blindfold. The blindfold was taken off.

She found herself in a woman's jail.

She was registered, fingerprinted, and taken to a cell. It was about six feet by nine, with a single narrow bed. There were five women in the cell, three of them crowded on the bed, the other two lying on the floor. Several wakened when the light was switched on, and looked sleepily and angrily at the new prisoner who was going to crowd them up still more. The matron pushed Edith in, locked the iron grating door, and switched off the light again.

As Edith's eyes grew accustomed to the darkness she could notice that her five cell mates had gone back to sleep. Cautiously she felt her way to the floor, and tried to stretch out and join them. She stared into the darkness.

Chapter 15

IN another five minutes the Black Maria stopped again, and this time Maxwell was led out. When his blindfold was removed, he found himself in a sort of reception hall before a desk. On the wall in front of him was a sign: RUTHLESS EXTERMINATION OF WRECKERS. The man behind the desk ordered him to empty out his pockets. Maxwell took out his ration books, passport, workbook, pencil, watch, and laid them on the desk. They were all he had. A guard felt his pockets.

He was registered, fingerprinted, blindfolded again, taken on an elevator, and pushed out. His blindfold was removed.

He found himself in a large white cell, with not a single piece of furniture in it but a stool. The whole ceiling was covered with blindingly bright electric lights. A steel cell door clanked behind him.

There were no windows—no way of telling whether it was night or daylight outside.

When he had been sitting on the backless stool, as he judged, half an hour, he tried to lie on the white stone floor and get some sleep. The floor was cold. The light, reflected from all sides and from the floor itself, was inescapable.

After a while he got up again and paced around, then tried to lie down again. How long this went on—three, seven, ten hours—he could not have said. At last two silent guards opened his cell door and motioned him to come along with them. He was so tired mentally that he found it difficult to concentrate.

With an effort he told himself that what he was going to need most now was courage, fortitude, strength.

He was led before a police captain at the same desk where he had been registered.

"You know what you're charged with, of course?" asked the captain.

"I have no idea," said Maxwell. "I've done nothing against the laws."

He had no sooner said this than he realized it was not strictly true. The laws were so drawn, so numerous and so all-embracing, that it was virtually impossible for any denizen of Wonworld to avoid technical violations every day.

"I may as well warn you now," continued the captain, "that you will save yourself considerable trouble by confessing immediately."

"I have nothing to confess. I do not even know what I am charged with."

The captain turned to a uniformed clerk next to him. "Read it to him."

"The charge, or the confession?" asked the clerk.

"Oh, the charge."

The clerk read the charge in a rapid, slovenly monotone. Maxwell had difficulty in following, but it appeared to accuse him of deliberately misdesigning the proposed new Lenin super-dam—designing it in such a way that it would break in a crisis—and specifying materials, such as types of steel, types of concrete, and types of electrical machinery that he, Maxwell, knew to be in short supply and unobtainable, though they were no better than other materials that he knew to be in ample supply. The charge also accused him of conspiring with other people, yet unknown, to insist on these specifications, to follow bourgeois engineering formulae, and to demand unobtainable skills on the part of workers.

"Well?" asked the captain.

"All this is untrue," said Maxwell. "Of course I had to specify

97

materials that would be sure to stand up under the maximum stresses and strains—"

"You refuse, then, to sign the confession?"

"What confession?"

The captain turned wearily to the clerk. "Read the confession."

The clerk began to read in the same rapid and unintelligible monotone.

Maxwell broke in. "I can't even understand what he's saying!"

With an air of weary patience, the captain turned to the clerk. "Hand him the confession."

Maxwell read it. "I, EN—57, sometimes known under the name of John Maxwell," it began, "being of sound mind and body, have been driven by my conscience to make a clean breast of . . ."

It went on to say that the charge didn't begin to measure the real scope and degradation of Maxwell's crime. It described the careful cunning with which he had begun to lay his plans. It told of the bourgeois ideology that had corrupted him. In the confession he repeatedly debased himself, repeatedly insisted on how low he had sunk, repeatedly emphasized the greatness and goodness of Stalenin, and especially the greatness and goodness of Bolshekov, one sight of whose glorious face had once made him hesitate in his determination to carry through his dark scheme.

"It's my duty to inform you," said the captain, "that if you confess there will be considerable mitigation of your punishment. You will be sent to a concentration camp, no doubt, but for a maximum of eight years. And nothing will happen to your daughter."

Maxwell turned pale. "What will happen to my daughter if I *don't* confess?"

"I'll leave that to your own imagination. . . . Well?"

Maxwell stood silent.

The captain prompted him. "You hear about a lot of people who confess, don't you?"

Maxwell nodded. He read these "confessions" every day in the *New Truth*.

98

"Ever hear of anybody who *didn't* confess?" The captain was smiling grimly.

Maxwell never had. He knew of many people who simply disappeared, without explanation from anyone. These must have been the people who refused to "confess."

A new key to the system suddenly opened something in his mind. There were terrible consequences for weakness, but still more terrible consequences, and no corresponding reward, for strength. If you "confessed" to crimes that you did not commit, you were disgraced, shunned, despised, condemned to a life of utter wretchedness and horror. But if you stood up with superhuman courage against all threats to yourself or even to those you loved, nobody ever heard of your courage, nobody ever learned of what you had withstood. You had not even the satisfaction of setting an example to inspire others. A known martyrdom was one thing: a known martyrdom was something for which a man might gladly give up his life, allow himself to be put to torture— yes, even sacrifice those he loved more than himself for the greater final good of humanity. But an unknown martyrdom? . . . A meaningless martyrdom? . . .

"Well?" asked the captain.

Maxwell stood silent.

The captain wearily pressed a button on his desk. Two guards entered.

"Take him to the Second Degree Room."

He was led down a corridor into a chamber that might once have been a big cell. It was illuminated only by three giant spotlights. Behind them as he entered, Maxwell could dimly make out a police official behind a desk, another on a chair to the left.

He was led so that he faced into the three spotlights at the exact point on which they were concentrated. They were blinding.

The questioning came from a voice behind the desk. "Number? . . . Name, if any? . . . Address? . . . Occupation? . . . You are charged with . . . What have you to say in answer to . . ? Do you deny that . . ?"

99

He heard himself answering mechanically. He could think of nothing but the blinding lights. The questioning went on and on. His legs and back became like lead. . . .

His questioner stopped. Maxwell heard him get up and say something in a low voice to someone who had just come in. How long had Maxwell been standing there? Two hours? All morning? *Was* it morning?

He heard footsteps behind the desk again. His interrogator, he supposed. But the voice that began to question him now was a new voice. Maxwell dimly realized that his first interrogator had been relieved. The second took up where the first had begun. Had no attention been paid to Maxwell's answers?

The questions rolled on.

His voice became husky and his throat unbelievably dry. He pleaded for a drink of water. He explained that he had phlebitis and asked to be allowed to sit down. These requests were treated as if they had never been made.

The second interrogator was relieved by another, and he in turn by a fourth. The questions were barked at him, mounting in savagery of tone.

The room began to spin. . . .

He fainted.

He was at last brought back to consciousness by violent slaps on the face, and finally pulled to his feet again.

"Before we resume," said his examiner, "we should tell you that your daughter Edith, in another prison, is undergoing the same sort of examination that you are. She has already confessed, but they are asking for more details. They will keep at it until you also confess. . . ."

The questioning began again. But he was not thinking now either of the questions or of his answers. He was thinking of Edith. . . .

The lights began to spin again. He was retching. There was an excruciating pain in his bladder. He was overcome with a longing to have everything over with, to learn the full extent of his punishment, to begin serving it. He sank to the floor.

"Bring me the confession," he said. "I'll sign it."

As he signed, he thought, Now they will let me have peace. How many hours had passed? How many days?

He heard an order: "Take him to the Third Degree Room."

The cell-like chamber to which he was now brought was much like the former one. Again they stood him before a battery of dazzling lights. Two inquisitors took part in questioning him.

"We can get the rest of this over with quickly now, Maxwell." The voice came from the questioner on the right. "You would like that, wouldn't you?"

"I have already confessed. They promised me that if I confessed they would tell me my punishment and let me sleep!"

"You have merely confessed your own part in this treason. Now we want to know exactly who was involved with you. Tell us the whole plot. We want the names of everybody involved in it. Who gave you your orders? To whom did you report?"

"I have signed the confession you asked me to sign," said Maxwell. "I am willing to take my punishment. Let me go."

The reply was several sharp blows on his face.

He was ordered to stand facing the wall, just far enough so that he could touch it at arms' length with the longest finger of each hand. Then he was ordered to move his feet back about twelve inches, keep his heels touching the floor, and maintain his balance only with the contact of one finger of each hand.

"Now tell us. To whom did you report?"

"I've already confessed. I'm ready for my punishment. Send me to a concentration camp. Shoot me! But don't force me to accuse innocent people!"

The questioning went on relentlessly. For the first few minutes his two fingers could support the leaning weight of his body. But the area around the two fingernails soon became flaming red; the area below them was yellowish-white. He tried to substitute his index fingers. He was slapped violently for doing so. His two long fingers bent more and more beneath his weight. The upper part of his arm, then his shoulders and legs began to tremble. He was drenched in sweat. His head began to swim.

"I can't talk this way," he gasped. "I can't think. I can't hear your questions. I don't know what I'm saying!"

They let him stand straight on his feet for a few minutes and then took him again before the brilliant lights. "All right. Tell us now. There were others, weren't there?"

"Yes. There were others."

"Who were they?"

Maxwell did not answer. His arm was twisted until he shrieked out in pain. The questioning continued. "No generalities. We want details!"

He mentioned a couple of invented names and numbers, and was forced to admit that they were invented. He pleaded with them again: "Kill me! But don't force me to accuse innocent people. Let me die with some vestige of self-respect!"

Tired and dulled as his mind was, he had a nauseating realization that this was precisely what they were out to destroy—his self-respect. They did not care about his body. They were torturing that only enough to torture his mind. They were even eager to keep his body alive until they had destroyed his last trace of dignity as a human being.

They forced him to stand again in the same position against the wall, resting on his finger tips until he cried out in agony.

His whole frame was quivering. . . .

Chapter 16

YOU'VE come to arrest us?"

The O'Gradys seemed not only resigned but relieved.
"We'll pack immediately."

It had been Peter's first opportunity to call on the Maxwells
since his election to the Politburo. He gathered finally from this
couple, with whom the Maxwells had shared the room, the appalling news that Edith and her father had been arrested in the
middle of the night two weeks before.

That was all they knew. Ever since that night they had expected to be arrested themselves—for the crime of not having
reported to the police the "treachery" of the Maxwells (whatever
it may have been) before the police themselves suspected it. In
Wonworld the guilt of any man disloyal to the state was shared
not only by his family, but by anybody billetted with him who
had failed to betray him in advance.

Through some oversight the O'Gradys had not yet been arrested.

Peter returned to his limousine. "To Security Police Headquarters," he ordered.

The files at Security Police Headquarters revealed nothing.
They did not even record the fact that Maxwell or Edith had
been arrested. The arrest, Peter concluded, could only have been
ordered secretly by Bolshekov.

He told the chauffeur to drive to his father's office. When he
got there he found the secretary pale and grave.

"I've been trying desperately to reach you," said Sergei. "His Supremacy has just had a stroke. The doctor is with him now."

Peter was led into the bedroom. His father was in bed. His eyes were closed, his cheeks puffed out, his face flushed; there was froth around his lips.

The doctor was bending over him.

"How serious is it, doctor?" Peter asked.

"Very."

"What do you think will happen?"

"In a few hours he may come out of this. But even if he does, he may remain paralyzed on his right side. I'm not sure he will have control of his tongue muscles—or, in fact, that he will be able to speak at all."

The dreaded moment had arrived. Peter must act, and now.

Bolshekov, he knew, had spies everywhere. Perhaps he had already learned of the situation.

Whom could Peter trust?

The sense of his immense responsibility fell on him like a ten-ton weight. Blessed are they without responsibilities. Blessed are they who do not have to make decisions, who have all their decisions made for them. No wonder so many were content to have no liberties. Liberty meant responsibilty. It compelled decisions. Liberty was compulsion. To be *free* to decide meant that you *had* to decide. And you had no one to blame for the result of bad decisions but yourself.

He turned slowly and heavily to Sergei.

"Find Adams," he ordered. "Get him over here immediately. Tell him it's urgent—but don't tell him why."

The record!

That was his first duty. If he lost time on that, he would lose everything. He must postpone even the effort to discover and release Edith and her father until the record had been broadcast.

He ran back from the bedroom to his father's office. His hands were trembling slightly as he turned the combination of the safe. He took the closely guarded key from an inside pocket, opened the small inside steel door, and carefully drew out the record marked X.

Sergei entered. "His Highness Comrade Adams is on his way over."

Peter told Sergei about the arrest of Edith and Maxwell. "Find where they are, who is holding them, and who ordered their arrest. And send a message down for my car to stand by."

He paced nervously up and down. The wait seemed interminable. At last Adams arrived. Peter rushed him immediately down to the car.

"To the Central Radio Station," he called to the chauffeur.

He had the record and the script in his brief case. On the way over he told Adams what had happened.

Adams looked stunned. "Yet I *had* noticed something wrong with No. 1's health," he said.

"I am trusting you completely," said Peter. "I'm lost without your help."

"You can count on it. You know I'm an American anyway, and haven't a ghost of a chance of ever becoming Dictator of Wonworld myself. That job is a Russian monopoly. The real danger is Bolshekov. If he becomes Dictator his first act will be to slit my throat. You can count on me absolutely."

They mapped out what their procedure would be when they got to the radio station.

Once inside the building Peter had double cause to congratulate himself on his decision to take Adams. Everyone recognized Adams immediately, but in spite of the worldwide publicity attending Peter's promotion to the Politburo, very few seemed to recognize Peter or know who he was.

"Interrupt the program," Adams ordered the announcer. "Introduce me."

Adams was brief: "I am speaking to you from the Central Radio Station of Moscow. With me in the studio are His Supremacy, Comrade Stalenin; and his son Peter Uldanov. His Highness Comrade Uldanov, as you know, was elected a member of the Politburo three weeks ago. His brilliance, and the conse-

105

quent speed of his advancement since his return from America, have created a Wonworld sensation. And now you are about to hear a message of the utmost importance from His Supremacy, Comrade Stalenin, No. 1 citizen and Leader and Dictator of Wonworld. . . . His Supremacy!"

Record X was turned on:

"Comrades and citizens of Wonworld," it began. "I told you on my last public appearance on May Day that the mounting pressure of work upon me would prevent me from making any further public appearances. This pressure has now grown to a point where I am forced to deputize more work than ever. I have therefore asked my trusted son, Peter Uldanov, to sit as my deputy in meetings of the Politburo and on other occasions, and to make public announcements in my name of whatever new policies or decrees I find necessary. I shall, of course, be more active than ever as your leader, working silently, often alone, late into the nights, working for you, the proletariat, working as one of you, as your vicar, as your spokesman, as your servant, working for you, the dictators of Wonworld. For the security of Wonworld depends upon the dictatorship of the proletariat, which must be maintained at all hazards, and I, as your vicar, as your deputy, representing you, mean to maintain it.

"But I cannot do this without your help, without the help and support of every man and woman in Wonworld. Comrades, the future depends on you. We must work harder than ever before. We must all work longer hours. We must all tighten our belts one more notch. The Era of Abundance is before us. But this abundance will be possible in the future only by our further sacrifices in the present. The land of socialist plenty, as you have been told for more than a century, is to be reached only by the path of socialist austerity. There are only a few steps more along that path. We cannot risk or throw away all that we have won by refusal to take those steps now! And through my son, my deputy Peter Uldanov, I will from time to time announce those steps. Meanwhile I can only urge all of you once more to put your shoulders to the wheel. And tonight I ask you, around your

106

tables, in your homes, to drink with me a toast to the Global Union of Soviet Socialist Republics—to Wonworld Forever!"

When the record had finished, Peter stepped up to the microphone:

"Thank you, Your Supremacy. Thank you, my father. I promise you solemnly and faithfully, to the utmost of my ability, to carry out your instructions as your deputy. Every act I take will be in your name and at your command, and I will need the loyal and unquestioning support of every comrade in fulfilling the great trust and responsibility you have placed in my hands."

A recording was put on of the music of "Marx Save the Dictator."

Adams stepped before the microphone once more: "A recording of this entire program will be put on a Wonworld hookup at eight o'clock this evening. At the time when His Supremacy's speech is being rebroadcast, I urge all of you, in your homes, in offices, in factories, in barracks, on farms, in correction camps—wherever you may be—to join me in a solemn toast to Our Great Leader and to his newly appointed Deputy."

The program was over. Some recorded music was put on. Adams turned to the announcer and the technicians in the recording room.

"We have carried out this program at the orders of His Supremacy. A critical situation came up at the last moment which required his urgent presence elsewhere, so he made this recording. You are all to observe the strictest secrecy about the fact that he was not personally present. This is the beginning of the policy which he laid down in his May Day announcement. You will announce tonight's forthcoming rebroadcast at half-hour intervals. For the eight o'clock Wonworld hookup, you will order all the direct-wired loud speakers throughout the Global Union of Soviet Socialist Republics to be turned on full blast."

On Adams' advice, Peter called an immediate special meeting of the Politburo, in Stalenin's name. As customary on such occasions, Sergei did the telephoning. This time the members were called in the reverse order of their priority. Bolshekov was notified last, and late. Each member as he arrived was asked whether he had heard the afternoon's Stalenin broadcast. Giraud, who, Adams knew, disliked Bolshekov, arrived early. Adams took him aside for a few moments.

Adams and Peter declared that they had just spoken with Stalenin and that he would be in at any moment. But when everyone but Bolshekov had arrived, Sergei by prearrangement came in and said that Stalenin had been detained and had asked that Peter conduct the meeting in his absence.

Adams proposed a resolution endorsing the new arrangement. It was seconded by Giraud, and passed just a few minutes before Bolshekov arrived.

Peter excused himself, turned the meeting over to Bolshekov, and said that the only other business His Supremacy had wanted conducted was a reading of the report of a special commission on the causes of the new famine in the Argentine. Adams read the report.

It had all come off perfectly. Peter felt a new admiration for Adams' shrewdness. The meeting, as Adams had pointed out in advance, would validate the new arrangement before there was time for anyone to plot to overthrow it. It incidentally kept every member of the Politburo, and especially Bolshekov, under Adams' eye while Peter and Sergei, in the next room, confirmed the new situation over the telephone with the heads of the Security Police and the armed forces, apart from Kilashov and Marshal Zakachetsky themselves, who were both at the meeting.

"Where are the Maxwells?" Peter asked, the moment the most essential telephoning had been done.

Sergei shook his head. "I've been able to learn nothing."

Peter went in again to his father's bedroom. The doctor was still there. His father's condition had not changed.

PART TWO: GROPING

Chapter 17

WHEN Stalenin regained consciousness he was, as the doctor had predicted, almost completely paralyzed on his right side. His talk was reduced to monosyllables: "No—yes—it —he—she—that—who—where—what?"

Particularly "what?"—asked in every connection, and sometimes without any apparent connection at all. Peter had constantly to guess what it was that Stalenin was asking about. His father seemed to understand a good deal that was said to him, and to be able to indicate his wishes. But his wishes, with the passage of time, became constantly more passive, except in things that concerned his immediate animal comforts.

But the stroke had brought about something far more remarkable than hemiplegia. It had completely transformed Stalenin's character. The strength, the hardness, the brutality, the cynicism, melted away. He became gentle, childlike, affectionate.

For ten days after Stalenin's stroke Peter spent every evening at his bedside. They were dreary vigils. At the same time that Stalenin's supper was brought in, his food-taster would enter, hollow-cheeked and expressionless, and take a little something from everything on the tray, to make sure it was not poisoned.

When Stalenin was sitting up again Peter cut his visits down to three evenings a week. He found his father astonishingly easy to manage now. He discovered that he could get approval for almost any course of action he proposed, merely by the tone and manner in which he proposed it.

Peter's first task, he was convinced by Adams, was to strip Bolshekov of any real power over the political and economic life of Wonworld and to assume it himself. But he felt it would be dangerous to do this in so pointed a way as to humiliate Bolshekov publicly. So he relieved him (by forging orders signed *Stalenin*) of his duties as Commissar of Production, Chief of the Central Planning Board, Chief of the Supreme Economic Council, and Chief of the Congress of Co-ordinators. Peter turned all these offices over to Adams, with the understanding that he himself was to make all the really crucial decisions.

To save face for Bolshekov, and to pacify him, Peter decided to appoint him Chief of the Armed Forces, and to announce in the name of Stalenin that this position was so important that it would occupy all of Bolshekov's time.

"That is the worst thing you could do," warned Adams. "Bolshekov will make the armed forces loyal to himself, not to you."

"I have gone as far as I safely can for the present," Peter said.

"There is only one safe course with Bolshekov," said Adams. "You must liquidate him. Arrest him quickly and quietly; have him shot immediately; make no announcement unless you have to; if you do, accuse him of treachery; arrest everyone friendly to him, everyone capable of leading a revolt; wring confessions out of them that they are Bolshekovites, and plotted—"

"I'm not going to have anything to do with such methods," Peter said. "If my mind is clear about any one thing today, it is that brutal and degraded means inevitably lead to brutal and degraded ends."

"With Bolshekov in power, or even with Bolshekov alive and free, you are in danger of achieving nothing but your own downfall. And mine—if I may be permitted to refer to so minor a consequence. It's his life or ours."

"I'm not going to begin my deputized rule with a murder," Peter answered. "I intend to strip Bolshekov of power, and I've gone as far as I can at the moment."

"Will you do at least one thing?" pleaded Adams. "Make Bolshekov head of the Army and Navy, if you must, but at least turn over the Air Force to someone else."

"Whom would you suggest?"

"Why not take that portfolio yourself? Just sign a decree by Stalenin appointing yourself to the job. You could design a very dramatic uniform for yourself."

So Peter signed two new decrees, one appointing Bolshekov head of the Army and Navy and another appointing himself head of the Air Force. He forgot about the uniform.

He began to take up with Adams the problems that had been troubling him increasingly since his arrival in Moscow.

"I'm going to ask your advice," he said, "on every important problem. I hope you won't simply approve whatever I suggest. If you do I'll make some fantastic mistakes. Can I count on you to be completely outspoken and candid with me?"

"Candor is what I like most. You can count on me absolutely."

"We ought to be on a less formal basis," said Peter. "It's obviously so awkward for us to call each other 'Your Highness' that we practically haven't been calling each other anything at all. What *is* your first name?"

"My full name is Thomas Jefferson Adams. It's my real name too. I never took a party name, like Stalenin or Bolshekov. Most people that know me well just call me Adams."

"I'll call you Adams, then. Will you call me Peter?"

Adams nodded. But he apparently felt awkward about it. He took to calling Peter "chief," in a half-ironic, half-affectionate way, as a sort of compromise.

Peter began to speak about the poverty, misery, inefficiency, waste, tyranny, servility, and terror of Wonworld.

"Surely it is possible, Adams, for mankind to devise a better system than this!"

"I agree that it is possible, chief. But I should like to remind you that the best minds in Wonworld had been working on this problem ever since the triumph of communism. Successive reforms only seem to substitute one set of evils for another. . . . This, of course, is only what a few of us in the Party have been saying to each other. Stalenin and Bolshekov are two of those to whom I have never dared to say it."

"But haven't changes brought any increase of knowledge, any progress?"

"We always officially announce that they have. Every experiment we make must of course be pronounced a success, even when we abandon it. But personally—and *entre nous*—I have never noticed any progress in *my* lifetime."

"But before that?"

"Well, of course, if you believe the official histories—"

"Well, let's put all moral, political and economic questions on one side for a moment," Peter said, "and take merely technical and scientific progress."

"I've gone into that question, chief, out of personal curiosity. So far as I can figure, in the whole century and a quarter since the founding of Wonworld we have on net balance made no technical progress whatever. We have improved a few practical things—or rather, we have applied what was already known in a few new directions. But in theoretical knowledge, as I told you once, we are actually far behind the level that the bourgeois scientists had reached in the last throes of the capitalistic world. Our official histories pooh-pooh it, but it seems to me that there is strong circumstantial evidence for thinking that the bourgeois scientists of the capitalist world had actually succeeded in splitting the atom. There are even grounds for believing that the bourgeois scientists had used this knowledge to invent an appallingly destructive bomb, and had actually used this. When I was a youngster, my father—the only American up to that time who had ever got to be a member of the Central Committee of the Party—once repeated whispers to me that the Soviet scientists stole the secret from the capitalist countries, with the help of bourgeois scientists and bourgeois fellow travelers, and that Russia got the jump on the capitalist world in using it. Some whispers went on to say that this, and not—as our histories have it—the inner technological decay of capitalism, was the real reason for the communist triumph. Apparently after our victory was complete, all the scientists who knew the atomic secrets were liquidated."

"But surely," said Peter, "nobody believes any of this melodramatic nonsense!"

"Oh, I'm not saying I *believe* it, chief— My father didn't *believe* it; he merely cited it to show how fantastic the anticommunist lies could become."

"It certainly shows what childish minds these anticommunists had," Peter said.

"Yes, chief. We inner-circle communists have named this sort of thing 'Buck Rogers' stuff, after a notorious capitalist liar of that name."

"Who was Buck Rogers?"

"He was the richest man of his time, and invented such tales to keep the masses in subjection."

"Let's get back, Adams, to this question of technological progress."

"Well, my best guess, chief, as I've said, is that we are now technologically in the state of the capitalist world in the capitalist years circa 1918 to 1938, just before the outbreak of the Second World War."

"Didn't capitalism make any technological progress in the decades after that?"

"Personally, I think it did," said Adams. "One hears stories of airplanes propelled by jet power that went faster than the speed of sound—"

"More Buck Rogers stuff?"

Adams shrugged his shoulders.

"Anyway," announced Peter with determination, "there is going to be progress now."

Adams nodded a loyal but skeptical assent. "Where do we begin?"

"That is the question that has been bothering me for some time," said Peter. "There are so many places to begin. . . . But the first thing that needs to be done is to free the people from terror, to free them from servility and groveling. . . . We must give them freedom from fear."

"From fear of what?"

"From fear of *us*, of course. From fear of the government."

"But fear is the only thing that keeps people in line! If people didn't fear the government, if they didn't fear our police, how would we be able to keep them from committing every sort of crime?"

"Crime would continue to be made illegal," said Peter, "and people would be punished for it by penalties graded according to the seriousness of the crime. But crime must be carefully defined by law."

"It already is."

"Maybe. But we should change the laws so that nobody can be arrested unless he is charged with a definite crime. He should be told what that crime is. He should be allowed to confront his accusers and to answer them. These accusers should present real evidence. The man accused should be assumed to be innocent until he is proved guilty and not, as now, the other way round. And maybe—I haven't yet thought this out—the accused ought to be entitled, if he wants, to have someone else who knows the law better than he does, and who knows better than he does what his rights are, to defend him. Maybe the government itself ought to provide him with such a defender."

"I shudder to think what would happen, chief, if the cards were stacked so much in favor of the criminals. You would practically never be able to find anyone guilty. The criminals would certainly be freed from fear—"

"I think it can be made to work," Peter said. "Anyway, I'm going to try. . . . Don't misunderstand me. Crime will continue to be illegalized. But each crime will be carefully defined, and nobody will be punished unless he is guilty of an act that had *already* been defined as a crime *before* he did it. We are no longer going to have acts declared to be crimes *retroactively*."

"But suppose somebody does something that is clearly antisocial, that is clearly against the interests of the State, and we have merely neglected beforehand to define that act as a crime?"

"Then that will be our fault, Adams, and we will have to define it as a crime so that we can punish it in the *future*. But we will not punish anybody for having done it before it was defined as a crime. If I may invent a term, we will not pass any *ex post facto* laws."

"It seems to me, chief, that you have thought of a most ingenious way of tying the government's hands in advance. How can we guess ahead of time every crime that anyone can think of committing? And what's the use of having prosecutors and judges if we are not going to allow them to exercise any discretion?"

"The discretion of the judges will be exercised," replied Peter, "in interpreting and applying the existing body of law. The judge will have to decide whether the evidence presented by the prosecutor or the plaintiff is substantial enough to show that the accused actually did the act with which he is charged. But first the judge will have to decide whether the act with which a man is charged would fall within the pre-existing definition of a crime."

"How are you going to get a judge to act with all this impartiality and self-retraint?"

"We'll remove any judge who doesn't."

"In other words, chief, we'll remove any judge who doesn't act the way we should like him to act. Stalenin has been doing that already."

"But the government until now, Adams, has been removing judges for being too merciful or too impartial. *I* will remove them for being too harsh or too biased."

"This arrangement then, chief, will last only as long as your own power lasts—certainly no longer than there is someone in power who feels exactly as you do."

"Well then," said Peter, reconsidering, "we will have to make the judiciary *independent* of the whims of the government."

"Won't the judges be *part* of the government?"

"Well, independent of the *executive arm* of the government."

"Pardon me, chief, but aren't you contradicting what you just said a minute ago? You were going to remove any judge who did not act with impartiality and self-retraint, and did not conscientiously apply the law as it stood. If you make your judges independent of you, how are you going to discipline them and make them carry out their duties and powers without abuse?"

Peter lit a cigarette.

"You're right. I'll have to give all this more thought. . . . But what I am trying to do is to establish what we might call a *rule of law*. The only way, as I see it, in which we can free the people from constant fear of their own government is to set up a definite code of rules, a definite set of laws, and then say to them: 'As long as you live in accordance with these rules, as long as you stay within these laws, you are free to do whatever else you wish without fear. You need no longer be in terror of being sent to a concentration camp or being shot just because you have incurred the personal displeasure of the judge, or of some government official, or of someone higher up than yourself. If you are accused, your accusers must definitely prove your guilt, instead of forcing you to try to prove your innocence. And above all, no so-called "confession" will be wrung from you by threats or fatigue or force or torture. As long as you stay within the pre-established code of laws, you are free to do as you like.' Such a rule of law, as I see it, is the only thing that will free the people from terror and from the arbitrary decisions of those in power."

"That's a very pretty picture, chief, but the problem isn't quite that easy. For example, what things are you going to legalize and illegalize?"

"Well . . . I will illegalize murder, and assault and theft, and other forms of injury to other people—"

"*I* have something more fundamental in mind," interrupted Adams. "How are you going to get people to work? How are you going to get them to do the unpleasant tasks rather than the pleasant ones? How are you going to get them to do their best on the tasks to which they have been assigned? These, and not

116

the comparatively infrequent crimes you have just mentioned, are the problems that come up every day with everybody."

Peter sighed, and thoughtfully put out his cigarette stub. It was six o'clock, and he was due for dinner with his father. "That, Comrade Adams," he said wearily, "is a problem we will have to solve some other day."

Chapter 18

PETER knew it would be futile to try to get anything out of Bolshekov himself. But he had every top official of the secret police, from Kilashov down, report to him individually in his father's office for cross-examination. All professed to have no knowledge whatever of what had happened either to Edith or to Maxwell. There was no record to be found in any file of their arrest. Kilashov protested that if they had been arrested it had been without his orders and without his knowledge. And he swore to Peter that for an arrest to take place without a record of it somewhere in the secret police files was impossible. Peter must remember, however, that there was always a chance that private gangsters and wreckers might pose as secret police. . . . Such things happened. These impostors, for reasons of their own, may have done away with the Maxwells. . . . At any rate he, Kilashov, had ordered the Security Police to make the most thorough search. Naturally he was just as much concerned about the mystery as was Peter himself. . . .

In his spare time Peter began to make personal systematic visits to all the women's and men's jails in the Moscow district. In each jail he ordered the prisoners lined up before him. Gray, listless, burned-out faces without end that filled him with pity and horror; but among them he did not find the two he was so desperately looking for.

"Of course, Adams—coming back to the questions you raised the other day—of course people ought to consider it a privilege

118

to work for the State, because when they work for the State they are working for themselves; they are working for each other . . ."

Peter stopped. He found that he was mechanically repeating the arguments of Bolshekov.

"I agree that people ought to feel this way," said Adams, "but our experience shows that they just don't. The hard fact is that some people simply have to do more unpleasant chores than others, and the only way we can get the unpleasant chores done is by compulsion. Not everybody can be a manager, or an actor or an artist or a violin player. Somebody has to dig the coal, collect the garbage, repair the sewers. Nobody will deliberately *choose* these smelly jobs. People will have to be assigned to them, forced to do them."

"Well, perhaps we could compensate them in some way, Adams—say by letting them work shorter hours than the others."

"We thought of that long ago, chief. It didn't work. It unluckily turned out that it was only the pleasant jobs, like acting or violin playing, that could be reduced to short hours. But we simply can't afford to have people work only a few hours on the nasty jobs. These are precisely the jobs that have to be done. We couldn't afford to cut our coal production in half by cutting the hours in half, for example; and we just haven't got the spare manpower to rotate. Besides, we found that on most such jobs a considerable loss of time and production was involved merely in changing shifts."

"All right," agreed Peter; "so under our socialist system we can't have freedom in choice of work or occupation. But couldn't we provide some freedom of initiative—at least for those who direct production? Our propaganda is always urging more initiative on the part of commissars or individual plant managers. Why don't we get it?"

"Because a commissar or plant manager, chief, is invariably shot if his initiative goes wrong. The very fact that he was using his own initiative means that he was not following orders. How can you reconcile individual initiative with planning from the center? When we draw up our Five Year Plans, we allocate the production of hundreds of different commodities and services in accordance with what we assume to be the needs of the people. Now if every plant manager decided for himself what things his plant should produce or how much it should produce of them, our production would turn out to be completely unbalanced and chaotic."

"Very well," Peter said; "so we can't permit the individual plant manager to decide what to produce or how much to produce of it. But this is certainly a big disadvantage. For if someone on the Central Planning Board doesn't think of some new need to be satisfied, or some new way of satisfying an old need, then nobody thinks of it and nobody dares to supply it. But I have in mind something different from that. How can we encourage individual plant managers to devise more efficient ways of producing the things they are ordered to produce? If these plant managers can't be encouraged to invent new or better consumption goods, at least they can be encouraged to invent new methods or machines to produce more economically the consumption goods they are ordered to produce, or to produce a higher quality of those consumption goods."

"You're just back to the same problem," Adams said. "If I'm a plant manager, and I invent a new machine, I'll have to ask the Central Planning Board to get somebody to build it, or to allocate the materials to me so that I can build it. In either case I'll upset the preordained central plan. I'll have a hard job convincing the Central Planning Board that my invention or experiment won't fail. If my invention does fail, and it turns out that I have wasted scarce labor and materials, I will be removed and probably shot. The member of the Central Planning Board who approved my project will be lucky if he isn't shot himself. Therefore, unless the success of my invention or experiment seems absolutely certain in advance, I will be well advised to do what everybody else does. Then if I fail, I can prove that I failed strictly according to the rules. . . . Now take your other suggestion, chief. Suppose I devise a more economical method of making the product assigned to my factory. I will probably need different proportions of labor and materals, or different kinds of labor and materials, than I would with the old method. And in that case I will again be upsetting the central plan."

Peter sighed. "That doesn't seem to leave much room under our system for initiative, improvement and progress."

Adams shrugged his shoulders.

Peter lit a cigarette and thoughtfully blew some smoke rings.

"Very well then, Adams. So under our socialist system we can't have freedom in choice of work or occupation; we can't have freedom of initiative. But can't we at least give people more freedom in the choice of what they consume?"

"How are you going to do that?" Adams asked. "We issue ration tickets for everything we produce, and we try to distribute them evenly—at least within each of the Four Functional Groups. We can't let people have ration tickets for more than we produce. They complain about that already."

"No, Adams; but some people like cigarettes and others don't; some like beer and others don't; some prefer spinach to potatoes, and some like it the other way round. Why not permit everyone his choice?"

"Well, maybe we could work out something better than the present rationing system, chief, but the fundamental problem remains. People can consume only what is produced. We must draw up our production plans in advance, on the basis of the known needs and assumed wants of consumers. And then . . . well, I repeat: people can consume only what is produced. So how can they have freedom of choice?"

"I think there are two answers to that," said Peter, after blowing a few more smoke rings. "We could still give consumers considerable freedom of choice *individually,* even if they did not have much when considered *collectively.* In other words, out of the stock of goods already produced, we could devise some method under which one person could get more spinach if he preferred, and the other more potatoes, instead of each having to take the exact proportion in which the total supplies of spinach and potatoes were raised."

"Well—maybe, chief. But I still insist that the fundamental problem would remain unsolved. Considered collectively, how can consumers have any freedom of choice? They have to take what there is."

"But can't we find out in advance what it is they really want, and then make that? In other words, can't we guide production to anticipate the wants of consumers, instead of merely obliging consumers to take what we have produced?"

"We are always trying, chief; but it isn't so simple. Suppose, for example, that in relation to the wants of consumers we turn out too many peanuts as compared with pins? Then we will run out of pins sooner than we run out of peanuts. In other words, people will use up their ration tickets for pins before they use them up for peanuts. They will then start taking peanuts because they can't get any more pins—"

"Oh, come!"

"Well, change the illustration— They will start taking more spinach, for example, because they can't get any more potatoes. But because they are entitled by their ration tickets to the entire supply of *both,* and because their need for goods exceeds the entire supply of goods, they will end by consuming the entire supply of spinach as well as of potatoes."

"But if people consume all of one product before they turn to another," asked Peter, "don't we know that we are producing too little of the first or too much of the second?"

"Usually we do, chief. But we can't know from that just *how much* more of the first we should have produced and *how much* less of the second."

"Can't we tell from the preceding *rate* at which the two products have been consumed?"

"No. Because if people begin to think that soap is going to run short before salt, they will all scramble for soap. Therefore soap will run short in the state commissaries sooner than otherwise. The relative rate at which soap is taken by consumers while it lasts will be faster than if people thought that both soap and salt were going to last them throughout the consuming year."

"But can't we keep making readjustments in the relative amounts produced, Adams, based on this experience, until we get consumption of soap and salt and everything else to come out even?"

"That's what we are always trying to do, chief. But I still haven't got to some of the real problems. The trouble is that very few things are consumed evenly throughout the year even if we should get the relative production of each thing exactly right. People don't burn coal evenly throughout the year, but only in winter. And if they have the storage room, they ask for the entire supply they are entitled to as soon as the ration ticket permits it. Yet the fact that three-quarters of the whole supply of coal is asked for in the first week of the consuming year doesn't necessarily mean that the coal supply is short or is going to run short. Again, ice is consumed mainly during the summer, and all sorts of other things are wanted only seasonally. The only reason people turn in their coupons for new clothes evenly each month throughout the year is that we stagger the validity dates on the clothes coupons in the first place so only one-twelfth become due each month. . . . And still again, some things, like vegetables and fruits, are consumed entirely within a few months of the year for the simple reason that that's when they come on the market, and they won't keep. In short, trying to figure relative shortages and surpluses by relative rates of consumption throughout the year is a tough problem. In most cases we who direct the economy have to solve it by pure guesswork."

"Couldn't we figure it out by mathematics?" asked Peter.

Adams grinned and shrugged his shoulders. "How are you going to find the mathematical formula for somebody's wayward desires? How are you going to find the equation for when I want a cocktail—or whether I want a Marxattan or a Stalini? . . . And I haven't even mentioned one problem. Suppose there is some product, or some potential product, which is not produced but which, if it were invented or discovered or produced, people would want in great quantities? How are you going to find by mathematics that people would want such a product *if* it existed? Or even that such a product is missing?"

Peter sighed. "It's all pretty discouraging. We seem to be reduced to the conclusion that under our socialist system we can't have freedom in choice of work or occupation and we can't permit freedom of choice for consumers. Is that right?"

"People are free to use or not to use their ration tickets," answered Adams.

"In other words," said Peter, "they are free to consume what we tell them they can consume. They are free to consume what we, the rulers, have decided to produce."

"Right, chief."

There was a long pause.

"Well, I can think of one more kind of freedom," Peter said, "and I am determined to create it. That is the freedom to criticize the government."

Adams started. He seemed to waver between incredulity and alarm. "You mean that you would permit people to criticize the actions of the government, and perhaps even denounce the government, and go unpunished?"

"Exactly!"

"Why, chief, you and I would be destroyed in a few weeks! If we allowed people to criticize us with impunity they would lose all fear of us—all respect for us. There would be an explosion of criticism that would blow us out of our seats—out of Wonworld. And what would we accomplish? Our successors would, of course, immediately suppress criticism again, for their own survival. If we are going to make reforms, let's find out for ourselves what's wrong. Let's make our reforms quietly, not under pressure. . . ."

But Peter concluded that Adams was wedded to the status quo and would argue against any innovation whatever. He was determined to go ahead with at least this one great reform.

He issued a proclamation inviting criticism of the government. It promised that there would be no punishment if this criticism was constructive, truthful and responsible. The proclamation was published in all the government newspapers, broadcast on the radio, even published on billboards.

"This young idiot will soon hang himself," Bolshekov confided to Kilashov, when he heard the news. "Maybe it won't be necessary for us to lift a finger."

Chapter 19

PETER eagerly looked forward to the results of his reform. There weren't any. None of the things happened that Adams had predicted. On the other hand, none of the consequences followed that Peter had hoped for. There was simply an intensification of the kind of criticism that had already been going on. People in superior positions continued to criticize people in subordinate positions; they continued to put the blame for failure on people who were not in a position to protect themselves; they continued to accuse people in minor positions of being deviationists and wreckers.

This was what had always been known as communist self-criticism.

Peter put out still another proclamation. He ordered a stop to this sort of criticism. For a while it greatly diminished. But still no subordinate criticized his superior, and no one criticized the Politburo, the Party, or the government itself.

"What happened, Adams? Or rather, why didn't anything happen?"

Adams smiled. "I should have foreseen this, chief. It should have been obvious. All that happened is that nobody trusted your proclamation. They thought it was a trick."

"A trick?"

"Yes—a trick to smoke them out. A trick to find out who were the enemies of the government, and to liquidate them. Everybody waited for somebody else to stick his neck out, to see what would happen to him. Nobody wanted to be the first. So nobody was."

"Should we secretly order a few people to start criticizing the government, just to prove to the others that it is safe?"

"You seem to have a will to political suicide, chief. Besides, that would certainly be a trick. Why can't you leave well enough alone?"

"But why didn't anything happen?" persisted Peter. "I still can't understand."

"The truth is," said Adams, "that you were protected by the policy of Stalenin and his predecessors. They have quite properly created an atmosphere of terror that is not easily dissolved. Besides, what actually happened—and I should have been bright enough to foresee it—was inherent in the situation."

"How so?"

"Because you have absolute power, and absolute power includes unlimited power to punish."

"But I publicly promised, in a self-denying proclamation, not to use that power against honest criticism!"

"That doesn't matter. You still have the power. And as long as you have the power, people will fear that you are going to use it."

"But if they find me adhering to my promise?"

"It still won't matter. You have power over the economic fate of every man in Wonworld. You—or what is the same thing, the economic hierarchy over which you preside—have absolute power to decide what job a man shall have, or whether he shall have any job at all. You can decide whether he shall have a brilliant career, or an obscure one, or a horrible one. You can decide whether or not food ration tickets are issued to him—in other words, whether he can live or die. Now suppose someone publicly criticizes you, and that his criticism is really telling? Pride may prevent you from publicly repealing your own proclamation, or from openly violating it. But are you sure that you won't be tempted to punish this critic on some other ground—on the ground that he is a negligent workman, or a bad manager, or a saboteur or traitor? And even if you are above such a temptation, are you sure that your critic's immediate superior, or someone else along the line, won't punish him on some such ground in the hope of gaining favor either with *his* superior or directly with you? And even suppose that everybody in the hierarchy is so angelic as to be above this temptation? Do you still think anybody would be foolish enough to take the chance? Suppose your critic really were guilty of negligence or incompetence or treachery, and were punished for it? Isn't it likely that everyone would leap to the conclusion that he was really being punished for criticizing you, and that the actual charge against him was merely a frame-up? Suppose your critic were not promoted and did not deserve promotion? Wouldn't he be certain none the less to attribute his lack of promotion to his criticism of you? . . . To be perfectly candid—and it helps to enforce my point— I'm not sure I'm not taking a big risk myself even in saying these things privately to you."

He smiled in a way obviously meant to be winning.

"And what is your conclusion from all this?" asked Peter.

"My conclusion, chief, is that control over a man's livelihood, over his means of support, over his economic career, means in effect control over all his actions and all his speech. To deprive him of economic liberty is to deprive him of all liberty. Where the State is the sole employer, each man must not only refrain from doing or saying anything that will offend his superiors who constitute the State; he must go further, and exert himself to do or say anything and everything calculated to please his superiors who constitute the State. And that is why there has been all this incredible fawning and abject adulation of Stalenin —if you will pardon the liberty of my saying so."

Peter got up and paced the room. "Very well. You win. So, to sum up: Under our socialistic system we cannot have freedom of initiative; we cannot have freedom of choice of work or occupation; we cannot allow consumers' freedom of choice; there cannot be any freedom to criticize the government . . ."

He stopped suddenly and stared at Adams. "But this is the

opposite of everything in our socialist textbooks! I'm frankly bewildered. What did Friedrich Engels mean, anyhow, when he said that 'Socialism is an ascent from the kingdom of necessity to the kingdom of freedom?' "

"He was talking only of what conditions would be when the socialist heaven had finally been reached," Adams answered. "He was obviously not talking of the transitional period from capitalism into socialism. That period, as Marx very distinctly pointed out, would be marked by the 'dictatorship of the proletariat.' And when Marx said 'dictatorship' he meant *dictatorship*."

"How long was the transitional period supposed to take?"

" 'Until the resistance of the capitalists has been completely broken,' as Lenin said. Until the capitalists have disappeared, until there are no classes."

"How long was *that* supposed to take?"

"A few years . . . maybe even a few decades . . . I don't know."

"But we completely defeated the capitalists and the bourgeoisie more than a century ago!"

"I suppose Marx and Engels would argue, chief, if they were alive today, that the transitional period would go on until the last remnants of capitalist mentality had been stamped or educated out of people's minds, until each wanted to work for all and not for himself."

"But we have now had more than a century of daydreaming, pep talks, exhortations, denunciations, forced labor, shootings and torture—and we still don't seem to have brought about that transformation in human motives!"

"Human nature, chief, seems to be a little more stubborn than Marx and Engels supposed. They argued, of course, that it was not human nature that created human institutions, but rather that it was human institutions that created human nature."

"Doesn't that sound, Adams, like putting the cart before the horse? . . . And even under capitalism, if a man really wanted to work primarily for humanity, instead of primarily for himself and his family, wasn't he free to do so?"

"But under capitalism, chief, he got the highest rewards by

working for himself; therefore his biggest incentive was to work for himself and not for others."

"That's begging the question. If a man is not already selfish, he is not stimulated by selfish incentives. If he finds his greatest reward in advancing the welfare and happiness of others, that is what he will do; and selfish incentives will not divert him, because he will not feel them."

"Then I suppose the answer is, chief, to set up social institutions so as to harness even the self-regarding motives in such a way that when a man pursues his own welfare he will do most to promote the welfare of society."

"But socialism begins precisely at the other end, Adams! It argues that it is only by pursuing the welfare of society that a man can promote his own welfare. The appeal is still primarily selfish. But the argument, judging by results, appears to be unconvincing. . . . Let me put it this way: 'I want to get rich,' said the individual in the Dark Ages. 'Go ahead and get rich,' answered capitalism, 'and you will find, to your surprise, that you have also incidentally enriched society.' 'I want to get rich,' still says the individual today. 'Devote yourself to enriching society,' says socialism, 'and you will find, to your surprise, that this is also the surest way to enrich yourself.' "

"Isn't that the nobler appeal, chief?"

"I don't know. But it seems to me that the real question is which system actually works best."

"You started by asking me, chief, what Engels meant when he said that socialism was 'a leap from the kingdom of necessity to the kingdom of freedom.' "

"Ah, yes . . . and what *did* he mean?"

"He meant, I take it," answered Adams, "that under capitalism the individual was not free but enslaved, because one class was dominated and exploited by another; one man was dominated and exploited by another; the worker had to obey the orders of his employer or starve. And socialism means freedom from all this."

"I don't quite see it," Peter said. "Under any system of production whatever, there has to be social organization. There have to be those who direct the work and those who are directed; those who give orders and those who follow them; those who boss and those who are bossed. There has to be, in other words, a managerial hierarchy. If it is merely a question of building a single house, there has to be someone to decide that the house is to be put up, and what kind and where. There has to be an architect to design it, a builder to interpret the plans and to decide what workers to use and what to tell them to do—"

"But under socialism, chief, unlike capitalism, there is no exploitation of the workers for the profit of the employer."

"Under socialism," retorted Peter, "the State is the sole employer. If the worker fails to please the powers that be in the State, or if he arouses their active animosity, there is no one else to whom he can turn. A far greater tyranny may be exercised over him under socialism than I imagine was even possible under capitalism. For if a worker failed to please a particular employer under capitalism, I imagine he was free to go to another. And the fear of losing his exploited workers to some other employer must have mitigated the exploitation practiced by each employer. . . . But under socialism, if a worker falls out of favor with the powers that constitute the State, he can be forced to starve; there is no one else to whom he can turn."

"What I think Engels meant, chief, is that under capitalism the workers were exploited by the capitalist class, and crises and depressions seemed to come like visitations apart from anybody's wishes; while under socialism, society takes its destiny into its own hands and is in that sense free."

"I see," said Peter sarcastically. "And in practice, who constitutes 'society?' Who *is* 'society?' "

"Society is everyone."

"Oh, come now! *Everyone* can't make the decisions. No two persons' decisions would ever agree."

"Well, by society I mean the State."

"And by the State—?"

Adams grinned. "I mean us."

"Exactly. The hierarchy momentarily headed by me," said Peter. He had a sick feeling as he thought once more of his appalling responsibility. "What it comes down to is this, Adams. Society consists, and consists necessarily, of a small body of rulers and a large body of ruled. And this body of rulers itself consists of a hierarchy, finally topped by one man with the power to resolve disputes and make final decisions. So when we say that 'society' does this or that, we mean that the State does this or that. And when we say the State, we mean the ruling hierarchy. We mean the Protectors; we mean the Party; we mean the Central Committee; we mean the Politburo; we mean merely the Dictator himself—or," Peter grinned, "the Dictator's Deputy."

"But under socialism," protested Adams, "the State reflects not the will of the exploiters against the proletariat, but the will of the proletariat themselves. The State is just the mechanism by which the People express their will. It is a dictatorship of the proletariat—"

"Or a dictatorship *over* the proletariat? Let's face the real facts. Under our socialist system a few people—say the Central Planning Board—make the economic plan, and the rest of the people are ordered to carry out the plan. All initiative must come from the center, and none can come from the periphery."

"It *has* to be that way, chief. There would be no point in having a master overall plan, deciding just what goods should be produced, and just how much of each, and by just whom, if anybody anywhere were free to decide to make or do something else. That would be chaos."

"But isn't there any productive system that would allow more liberty, Adams? Isn't there any system that would allow more centers of initiative? What actually happened under capitalism? Were workers free to change from one job to another that they liked better? Was the individual capitalist free to decide to make what he pleased, and in the way he pleased? Was the consumer free to consume what he preferred, and to reject what he didn't like?"

"I don't know what happened under capitalism, chief. Nobody

132

knows. And we destroyed the capitalist literature so completely that I don't see how we are going to find out. But surely we are not going to turn back to that discredited and vicious system—which the world got rid of at the cost of so much blood and sacrifice—to take lessons in how to improve socialism!"

"All right," agreed Peter, "let's forget about capitalism. But I still don't understand what Engels meant when he called socialism 'the kingdom of freedom.' I still don't know what Marx meant when he said that under socialism the State would 'wither away.' For it seems to me that it is above all under socialism, where the State owns all the means of production, does all the planning and assigns and controls all the jobs, that the State is and must be closest to omnipotence. . . ."

He gazed unseeingly out of the window.

"Adams, you have convinced me. It is precisely under a socialist State that the least liberty can exist. Under complete socialism, in fact, liberty for the individual is simply impossible. And if I had really succeeded in encouraging it, which fortunately I did not, I would simply have brought on chaos."

Adams looked satisfied. He took a pinch of snuff.

"I've thought of one additional reason, chief, why you did not succeed in your campaign to encourage criticism. The State owns all the printing shops, all the book publishers and all the newspapers. You can appoint or remove the heads of any of these, not to speak of the subordinates. You can even order them shot. Naturally none of these dear comrades was eager to die or suffer for the mistake of printing somebody else's criticism. They would probably not have printed any criticism except on your direct orders."

"All right, all right! Don't rub it in, Adams. My education proceeds slowly, but I am making progress."

133

Chapter 20

PETER and Adams were in Stalenin's office, holding their regular four o'clock conference.

The intercom buzzed. It was Sergei's voice: "Bolshekov's secretary is on the telephone, Your Highness. He says that No. 2 would like No. 13 to come to his office."

Peter made a grimace at Adams. This was what he had feared and expected. This was now his biggest hurdle.

"You can't blame him," said Adams. "After all, he does outrank you, and it's protocol for the lower number to come to see the higher—when and if invited."

"Why can't I simply refuse to see him?"

"You'd better see him and get it over with. If he thinks you're afraid of him—"

"Tell Bolshekov's secretary," said Peter to Sergei through the intercom, "that No. 1's Deputy will be pleased to see No. 2 here at No. 1's office at quarter to four sharp tomorrow afternoon."

Adams' raised eyebrows expressed a mixture of admiration and misgiving.

It was fifteen minutes before the intercom buzzed again. "There was considerable difficulty, Your Highness," Sergei announced. "No. 2 wishes me to say that he regards this whole procedure as a complete violation of protocol, but that the matter is so urgent that he will waive his prerogatives and be at this office at approximately the time you suggest."

"He said 'approximately?'"

"Yes, Your Highness."

"Thank you, Sergei." He flicked off the intercom, smiling grimly, and turned to Adams. "I shall consider it a favor if you will also be here at 'approximately' the same time. Have you any advice as to how to handle him?"

Adams offered some advice.

The next day Adams arrived at Stalenin's office at exactly quarter to four.

"I knew Bolshekov would purposely be a little late," said Peter.

Bolshekov arrived a little after four. "I think it's about time I knew the meaning of all this," he began immediately. "Why can't I get to see No. 1?"

"You heard the radio announcement. You read the newspapers," replied Peter. "You know that No. 1 wishes to be in seclusion to concentrate on major problems of policy, and that he has appointed me his Deputy and liaison man to act for him."

"That may be a good enough line for the proletariat," said Bolshekov, "but it isn't good enough for me. What's wrong with Stalenin? Has he had another stroke? Is he incapacitated?"

Did Bolshekov really know, or had he just made a lucky guess? Peter tried to remain poker-faced. "You seem to know so much. Why do you ask me?"

"He's had a paralyzing stroke," Bolshekov said. "Either he should resign, or the Politburo should announce that he is incapacitated and that I, as next in line, have succeeded him."

"That would be very convenient for you."

"I intend to bring the matter up at the next meeting of the Politburo!"

"At your own risk," Peter warned. "No. 2 is not a bad position: you should be very content with it."

"I beg to remind you that No. 2 doesn't tolerate anything like that from No. 13—especially—"

"That does remind me," said Peter. "I wanted you to be on time so that you would not miss the 4:15 broadcast. It's 4:15 now."

135

He turned on a radio by the wall. The smooth sonorous voice of an announcer was already in the middle of a sentence:

". . . that His Supremacy has promoted his son and Deputy, Peter Uldanov, from No. 13 to a newly created number, 1A. No. 1A will rank just below No. 1 and above any other number. It is to be so treated in all matters of precedence and authority. His Supremacy is especially happy to add that this move has the wholehearted endorsement of His Highness No. 2, Comrade Bolshekov; of His Highness No. 3, Comrade Adams; and, in fact, of the whole Politburo. . . ."

Peter turned off the radio and smiled sardonically at Bolshekov. "You wouldn't want to go back on your publicly pledged word, would you?"

"I'm told also," remarked Bolshekov drily, "that Stalenin never made that broadcast appointing you as his deputy. It was simply a record." There was a quietly smoldering green fire in his eyes.

"Why can't Stalenin make a record if he pleases?" Peter said at length. "Does he have to go personally to the broadcasting station in order to satisfy *you?*"

"For a completely miseducated young man," replied Bolshekov, "you seem to be learning fast." He jerked his head sidewise in Adams' direction without deigning to look at him. "This little broadcast was probably *his* plan. . . . I confess that I have been a little slow to see something that is now obvious. Your father, in fear of becoming incapacitated—and in fear of me—groomed you as his successor. That was a major error. It would be an unparalleled disaster if an ignorant young amateur like yourself, still wet behind the ears, should become Dictator of Wonworld. Fortunately that can't happen. A mistake that successful doting fathers used to make under capitalism was to assume that their beloved sons inherited their ability. It is particularly strange that Stalenin should have made this error. Every Marxist knows that ability is determined entirely by environment and education— and you were brought up ridiculously. You will never be Dictator, because you haven't the ability to hold on to your seat. Even"— this time he looked disdainfully at Adams—"with No. 3's advice."

"I must admire your candor and outspokenness," said Peter. "I will be guided accordingly. . . . And now, if you are quite through, you may go."

"I should like to warn you," said Bolshekov as a parting shot, "not to try to have me liquidated. You would find the enterprise much too risky."

"What did I tell you?" asked Adams, as soon as Bolshekov had left. "You should have had him liquidated immediately. Now it is probably too late. It was foolhardy to make him head of the Army and Navy. He wouldn't talk as he does unless he were already sure of his power."

"He thinks I am going to play his game of intra-Party intrigue, and that he can beat me at it," said Peter; "but I am going to do something so novel that it will throw him off balance."

"What?" Adams looked suspicious and faintly alarmed.

"It will not be a struggle between Bolshekov and me for power, for the simple reason that I am going to put the ultimate power into the hands of the people."

"What do you mean?"

"I am going to hold elections."

"But we already hold regular elections!"

"We call them elections," said Peter, "but they are absolutely meaningless. We put up only one candidate for an office. The individual voter has no choice. He must either vote for that candidate or against him. And he must vote in public. And he *must* vote. He knows that unless he votes for the candidate we choose he is as good as dead."

"You don't mean to say," said Adams, now really alarmed, "that you are going to let people vote *secretly!* They would vote to undermine you; they would vote against the government candidate—and you wouldn't even be able to find who the guilty ones were."

"I intend to do precisely that. I intend to make the ballot secret and to protect that secrecy. For unless a man votes secretly, his vote cannot be free. Unless it is secret, it is an intimidated vote. He now votes for the government's candidate because he knows that is the only healthy thing to do. Public opinion cannot be known—it cannot even be said to exist—unless it is free."

"I always said you had a will to political suicide," replied Adams, with a sigh. "What date have you set for your death—and mine?"

"This time I am going to be a little bit more cautious, Adams, than in my futile free criticism order. I'm going to try the experiment on a small scale. About a month from now, the regular elections are due in the French Soviet Republic. I'm going to try out the plan there."

He telephoned his orders to France. For each office no fewer than two candidates were to be nominated, and more if any more wanted to be candidates.

A deluge of letters, telegrams and telephone calls poured into the Kremlin. They were all pleas, requests, almost demands for instructions. They were from the local district commissars appointed by Moscow or from the local district councils. All contained the same question. Which candidate or candidates did the Kremlin want them to name? Always in the past the Kremlin had picked the candidate, or had left the choice to the central government commissar on the spot or to the local council. But in the latter case the commissar or council had merely recommended the candidate and waited for the Kremlin's approval before actually naming him. Now they did not know how to proceed. Naming *more* than one candidate was bewildering. All professed that they were loyal Communists, and passionately devoted to the Kremlin. But how could they carry out the Kremlin's wishes unless they knew what its wishes were? How could they name the candidates that the Kremlin wanted named unless the Kremlin told them who they were?

Peter replied to all requests that they were to be completely free in naming the candidates and, for that matter, anybody could run as a candidate on his own initiative, provided only that a nominating petition was turned in signed by at least 4 per cent of the adult inhabitants of the district. He didn't care, he said, whether the candidates named agreed in their views with the Kremlin or not; in fact, one of the Kremlin's purposes was to develop an intelligent opposition.

The local authorities were even more bewildered. For years, for generations, the Kremlin had devoted itself to stamping out any vestige, shadow or possibility of opposition. Why did it wish suddenly to *create* an opposition?

The local authorities arrived at the same conclusion. This was simply a new Kremlin trick to smoke out any opposition and annihilate it. None of them were going to be victims of *that* obvious dodge, though most of them were willing enough to co-operate with Moscow energetically in helping to perpetrate it on others.

But they wanted instructions, and they moved guardedly.

The pattern that evolved became pretty uniform. The local authorities would name a single government candidate, citing his record of loyalty, devotion and zeal, and would wait for approval of this candidacy by the Kremlin before taking any other step. Peter approved all candidates automatically. Then the local authorities would look for an opposition candidate. Their usual assumption was that this opposition candidate was to be chosen as a victim. When his name was sent into the Kremlin it was accompanied by a dossier giving reasons for suspecting his loyalty. Peter informed the local commissars that the Kremlin would not take sides and would not interfere: it would approve all candidates automatically.

The opposition candidate, after being named, invariably declined the nomination. He was then ordered to accept it, and to make a campaign. His campaign invariably consisted of advocating the election of the government candidate, and of asserting his own complete devotion to the government.

Even so the local authorities asked the Kremlin to tell them which candidate to support. They apparently wanted this as part of the record.

When it came to the secrecy of the ballot, the local authorities invariably assumed, also, that what the Kremlin wanted was not real secrecy but only the appearance of secrecy, so that unwary disloyal voters might be trapped into voting for the opposition candidate under the impression that their vote would go undetected.

When the great election day arrived, the voters were not to be trapped. They voted 100 per cent for the government candidates. The local authorities sometimes reported this 100 per cent, and sometimes reported only 98 per cent and some fraction for the government candidate, in order to show that there was still a group of deviationists and wreckers to be stamped out—and meanwhile to act as scapegoats for governmental failures.

After the French elections, the Kremlin was deluged with more letters, telegrams and telephone calls. What punishment, they asked, was to be meted out to the unsuccessful opposition candidates?

Peter was completely disheartened.

"You see, Adams," he said, "what generations of suppression and terror have done to the people. I cannot even *force* them to make their own choice; I cannot even *impose* democracy upon the people!"

"Frankly, chief," said Adams, "I don't understand what you are trying to do. We already *have* democracy. As all our textbooks have told us for generations, we have the only real kind of democracy, a people's democracy, a socialist democracy, a communist democracy. I understand that under the old capitalist regime they had a pretense of democracy, a mock democracy, but everybody had to vote the way his capitalist boss wanted him to vote or he would lose his job. They used to have the pretense of an opposition such as you tried to set up in France; but as the capitalists owned both of the supposedly competing major parties, it didn't make any difference which party was in power."

"The capitalists seem to have mismanaged the business fantastically from their own point of view, Adams, judging by the final results."

"Well, chief, I suppose the capitalists finally lost control, and that the bourgeois governments finally were marked by real dissension. . . . But surely you can't set up political opposition and dissension as an *ideal!* The political ideal is harmony, loyalty, unanimity. This is what our socialism has achieved. And mankind having at last accomplished this after years of blood and sacrifice, you want to restore dissension all over again!"

Peter lit a cigarette. He was not sure how to answer this.

"I suppose we do want harmony and unanimity," he said at length. "But we want harmony and unanimity based on free and uncoerced agreement, and not merely the *appearance* of unanimity based on force and threats and fear. Maybe free unanimity is the ideal, and maybe mankind can gradually approach it. But can it ever achieve it—in the absence of universal omniscience and universal self-renunciation?"

"Chief, exactly what *is* your concept of democracy?"

Peter tried to clarify his ideas as he smoked.

"Democracy as I conceive it," he said slowly, "exists when the government depends upon the uncoerced will of the people in such a way that it can be peaceably changed whenever the will of the people changes."

"Whereas now—?"

"Whereas now, as you know perfectly well, Adams, the government can be changed only by death, assassination or violent revolution."

"And how could you secure this possibility of peaceable change, chief?"

"By leaving decisions to an uncoerced majority."

"And do you believe that this majority will always act wisely, or will know what is good for it?"

"Of course not. I would not base majority rule on any such nonsensical belief. I would base it merely on the assumption that this is the best way to preserve internal peace—that it is the best way to avoid violence and civil war."

"Then you mean, chief, that there should be an arbitrary agreement always to have things decided the way the majority wants them decided, regardless of how wrong or stupid or dangerous the majority's wishes are?"

"I agree with you, Adams, in supposing that the minority—or at least *a* minority—will sometimes be wiser or more nearly right than the majority. But who would decide between them, and how would the decision be enforced?"

"That is simple, chief. *We* would. As we already do. *We* do the deciding and *we* do the enforcing—and we are certainly more competent, and immensely better informed, than the majority."

"For all practical purposes, Adams, I myself have only been included in this 'we' for a few months, and then not by ability but only by the accident of birth or—shall we say?—of filial affection."

"But you are an exception."

"Thank you," said Peter. "But if I'm not mistaken, this is the way kings and the ruling nobility were selected in the pre-capitalist era, and I'm not sure that it isn't an inevitable long-run accompaniment of rule of minority. A minority, it seems to me, can hold on to power only in one of two ways. The first is to get control of all the guns and to be more expert at force and violence than its opponents; in which case it can stay in power— like our own Party—only by constant suppression of the majority, by arrests, purges, concentration camps and a continuous reign of terror."

"And the second way?"

"The second way, Adams, is for the ruling minority to get at least the passive support of the majority. It can do this by convincing the majority either that the minority is inherently superior or that, at all events, allowing it to continue to rule is the best way to keep the peace. The institution of inherited royalty seems to have met both these requirements at once. When everybody agreed that the next ruler should always be the eldest son of the reigning king, regardless of the ability or even of the normality of that eldest son, it at least prevented a civil war for the succession every time the reigning king died—not to speak of civil wars during his reign. But in addition to this, the ruling dynasty and nobility accomplished a trick that looks at first glance impossible. They convinced everybody else, including even

142

the most brilliant men, that they, the existing rulers, were inherently superior, by the sheer accident of birth, to everybody else."

"If the trick of minority rule is so easy," said Adams, "why are you so eager to have majority rule?"

"Because minority rule seems to me to rest either on continuous force or continuous fraud," replied Peter. "The kings were actually, on the average, very commonplace men. Many of them were outright idiots. Their alleged superiority did not exist. They often led their countries to disaster. They started wars easily and often because they could get somebody else to fight them. Their policies were based purely on their own narrow interests."

"But you still haven't explained the advantages of majority rule."

"The majority may not be brilliant," said Peter, "but at least it knows its own wishes better than anybody else. And when a policy is adopted that meets the wishes of the greatest number of people it is likely, at least in the short run, to produce the greatest amount of happiness—or the least amount of dissatisfaction."

"The majority may know what it wants, chief, but not how to get it. It is not hard for a man to know what he wants, but it takes intelligence to know what are the proper ways and means for him to get what he wants."

"True; but it certainly helps if the majority is permitted to try to get what *it* desires rather than what the minority desires."

"But you haven't yet told me, chief, how majority rule promotes internal peace. Isn't a minority likely to start a fight if the majority tries to force something upon it that it doesn't want?"

"Maybe it would, if it were a minority of 49 per cent—in which case the majority would be well advised to proceed cautiously. In fact, it would always be a good rule for the majority not to try to impose on a large minority any policy to which the latter would too strongly object. Moreover, a member of the majority on one issue never knows when he will be a member of the minority on another. For that reason, majority rule, as I see it, would tend to be less tyrannical than any other kind of rule. And finally—to answer your question, Adams—majority rule is the best way of keeping the peace. Because in the event of an insurrection or a civil war, the majority usually wins, and the larger the majority the more probable is its victory. Therefore, if we decide issues by counting heads or noses, the minority will recognize in advance the futility of resorting to violence in order to get its way. The less vital the issue is, the less disposed the minority will be to start trouble. And once majority decision becomes accepted as the proper way of preventing or settling disputes, it should tend to become the most peaceable and stable of all systems."

"Very well," said Adams. "Suppose I agree with everything you have said. I still maintain that majority rule is impossible under socialism—and vice versa."

"Why?"

"We have just seen why. You say your experiment in democracy failed in the French Soviet Republic because the people have been terrorized for generations by communism and must be educated out of their terror. But you have also pointed out that they will never be educated out of their fear because their fear is inherent in the socialist system. And you have finally convinced me that this is true. Under socialism the State controls all the jobs. Under socialism everybody's career, everybody's means of livelihood, depends upon the minority, the hierarchy, already in power. That hierarchy holds economic life-and-death powers over everyone. Therefore nobody's opinion is free. Nobody has the impartial information to form an intelligent opinion, even if he had the courage to form or express one. Because the State, the ruling hierarchy, prints and controls all the newspapers, all the books and magazines, all the sources of information. It owns all the meeting halls. And nobody has the courage or even the means to express his opinion in public. Under such conditions, not only is public opinion not free, which is the only way in which it could be meaningful, but it cannot be said even to exist."

Adams is now stating my own arguments better than I stated

144

them, thought Peter. He said aloud: "But can't we allow private individuals to start their own newspapers, publish their own books and pamphlets, and so on?"

"You mean, chief, to become employers; to hire and exploit printers, reporters, writers and other people for profit; to own printing presses and plants, to own the means of production? All that would be the very negation of socialism."

"Well, maybe we shouldn't permit private individuals to own and run these things for a profit, Adams, but just at their own expense and on their own time."

"Where would they get the capital to start such projects, chief? How long could they stand the loss? Out of what would they pay the expenses? And if their newspapers criticized the government, how long would they hold the particular jobs, the means of livelihood, that the government had assigned to them?"

"The government would have to promise them immunity from punishment," said Peter.

"Oh, come now, chief, we've been through all that! That's what you promised them in the elections, and they didn't believe you. For the basic situation remains. You have the *power* to punish them. You have economic life-and-death power over them. The only thing to prevent you from exercising that power would be self-restraint—a quixotic determination to keep your own promise. And that wouldn't be good enough for a cautious man. He would doubt its reality or its permanence."

Whenever Peter was stuck for an answer to Adams, he either gazed out of the window or lit a cigarette. This time he did both.

"You confront me with a bleak outlook," he said at last. "The other day you convinced me that socialism is incompatible with democracy, incompatible with the expression of any free, uncoerced majority will. You are forcing me to admit that the reign of slavery and terror imposed by my father and Bolshekov is not an accident, not some monstrous perversion of the socialist ideal, but merely *the logical and inevitable outcome of the socialist ideal!* You are forcing me to admit that complete socialism means complete deprivation of individual liberty and an absolute government dictatorship."

Adams looked almost appalled by the extent of his own victory, but he continued: "I'm sorry to seem so negative and disheartening, but I haven't even mentioned some considerations. For example, once we adopt a Five Year Plan we've got to adhere to it; we've got to follow it. We can't have some new transitory majority constantly upsetting, reversing and disorganizing our planned economy—"

"All right, all right," broke in Peter. "I've had enough discouragement for one day."

This way of terminating my conferences with Adams, he thought, is becoming a habit.

Chapter 21

ADAMS was nearly a full hour late for the daily conference with Peter.

He arrived pale and shaken. "Some of Bolshekov's men just tried to assassinate me!" He was breathing hard.

"Where? How?"

"A few minutes after I left the offices"—he paused to catch his breath—"of the Central Planning Board to come here. . . . I was in my car. . . . Another limousine whisked by. . . . A man in the rear machine gunned my car . . . aiming at me. . . . I crouched on the floor. My chauffeur was killed. . . . The car plunged up on the sidewalk and crashed into a building."

"Are you hurt?"

"Miraculously, no. But I had a very close call. I don't mind admitting that my nerves are on edge."

"What have you done?"

"I've called the police, and they say they are going to have the bullets extracted from the chauffeur's body and examined. I don't think I'm going to get much information from *that.*"

"Did you get the car's number?"

"No. And no witnesses."

"What kind of car was it?"

"Exactly like the one I use—I used—myself."

"You say this was done by Bolshekov's men. How do you know?"

Adams stared incredulously at him. "Who else? Who else has

the motive? Who else could get the equipment, hire the assassin? Who else would dare? The worst of it is, we don't know how much support he has, how deep his control goes over the police themselves. Now do you believe me when I tell you that it's his life or ours? You *must* have him liquidated immediately!"

"I'm not going to have any man shot, or even tried, on mere suspicion," said Peter. "First, we must have evidence."

"Moral certainty isn't enough!" Adams was bitter.

"We can never achieve good ends except by good means," Peter said. "I want to do everything to protect you, but I told you I am determined to stop lawless violence on the part of the government itself. I mean it."

"How long do you think you're going to *be* the government when you allow Bolshekov to try to have us assassinated without any risk to himself?"

Peter did not answer.

"You know if it's me today, chief, it's going to be you to-morrow."

Peter gazed out of the window.

"You're not even going to *remove* Bolshekov?"

"I'm not sure that wouldn't be the most dangerous course of all," Peter replied at length. "He's still too strong, too widely and foolishly admired, and has too big and fanatic a personal following. I must first of all discredit him—or rather, let him discredit himself."

"How? By introducing 'democracy' and 'freedom?'" Adams' tone was contemptuous.

"No," said Peter. "By showing the people that we can get far more production than he could."

Adams stared at him as if he could hardly believe in such irrelevance. He finally took a pinch of snuff to calm himself. Then he seemed to decide to play along. "And how do you think you are going to do that?"

"Well," said Peter, "we certainly couldn't get *less* production. I've just been studying the latest reports, which you must also have received, on the agricultural situation, on the famine in

148

Kansas, and on the new outbreak of famine in the Chinese, Indian and Argentinian Soviet Republics."

Adams stared at him again. His expression said: Isn't there going to be any more discussion of the fact that I have just had a narrow escape from death? Peter remained stony-faced. Adams finally relaxed into a sardonic smile. "The famine is very serious, but I don't see what can be done about it. We have signs all over every Soviet Republic: *Work! Work! Produce! Produce! Production Is The Answer!* We have even sent in trained speakers to whip up popular fervor. None of it does any good. The peasants in the American Republic, especially, need to be taught our Russian know-how."

"Let's take a look at our system of incentives," Peter suggested.

"Our system of incentives is very good," replied Adams. "Each collective farm is assigned a minimum quota of wheat, rice, beans, or what not, that it must turn over to the State. In addition it is allowed to retain a maximum fixed amount of its own production for its own consumption."

"How much is that fixed maximum?"

"That depends on the particular collective. But what we allow the collective to retain, after it has met its full quota, averages about 5 per cent of what it must turn over to the State."

"Suppose a collective produces more than the minimum quota for the State?"

"We take it, of course. What else could be done with the surplus?"

"But that doesn't seem to give any incentive, Adams, for the collective to produce an excess."

"The collective has the satisfaction of knowing, chief, that it is adding to the supplies available for everyone."

"Very noble. But it doesn't seem to act as much of a production incentive with most people. I had a long discussion of that with Bolshekov."

"Well, if the collective farm's total production falls below its assigned quota, chief, then both the quota reserved for the State and the quota reserved for the collective's own consumption are cut by the same percentage as its total production has fallen short. In other words, if a collective produces only one-half of its total production quota, then the State set-aside is reduced by one-half, and collective's reserve for its own consumption is reduced by one-half."

"But even if the collective met its full quota, Adams, the reserve for its own consumption has been calculated to be just about enough to keep the workers on the farm alive, hasn't it?"

"Practically . . . yes."

"So under the illustration you have just given, they would be allowed only half enough to keep them alive?"

"True; but Wonworld consumers would have suffered correspondingly."

"Oh, no. What happened to Wonworld consumers generally would depend upon the change in the total production of all the farms considered together, not of any one farm. And it would depend also on how accurately or fairly the expected 'normal' production of an individual farm had been figured. And if this arrangement is made to apply one way, Adams, why can't it be made to apply the other? If the collective produces *more* than its quota for the State, in addition to a minimum reserve balance for its own consumption, why shouldn't it be allowed to keep the excess for itself?"

"What would it do with that excess, chief? The members of the collective are already entitled to enough over for their own consumption, if they produce it. What could they do with more than they need? Hoard it? And why should any surplus be withheld from the Wonworld consumers who need it?"

"What I am getting at is this, Adams. It seems to me that we would get much more production if workers were rewarded in proportion to their production."

"That would be a direct violation, chief, of the Marxist platinum rule: 'To each according to his needs.' "

"Perhaps," agreed Peter; "but it might help to make real instead of merely rhetorical the first part of that rule: 'From each according to his ability.' "

"Chief, how are you going to reward workers in proportion to their production? How would you go about it?"

"It seems to me that it ought to be simple."

"It seems to me that it would be impossible."

"Why?"

"Well, in the first place, chief, how would you determine what the production of any individual worker actually was? Let's take the simplest possible case. Let's take a collective with 100 hands. Let's say it produces 2500 bushels of wheat. How many bushels has each worker produced?"

"Are we back in kindergarten, Adams? Each worker has produced 25 bushels."

"Wrong," said Adams. "The *average* production of 100 hands was 25 bushels each. But some of these hands were sick and produced nothing at all. Others were ignorant, inept or careless, and actually on net balance destroyed part of the total production that would otherwise have been achieved. Some hands worked two or three times as hard as others, and presumably produced two or three times as much wheat—if there were any way of measuring their individual contribution. But there isn't. All we can say is that the *average* result of all the work and machinery and rain and sunlight applied to those acres was 25 bushels of wheat for each hand employed. But you can't assign any particular production to any particular hand."

"I concede your point," said Peter. "We couldn't reward each worker in the collective in proportion to his individual production. But we could at least reward the *group* according to their total production, and let them divide it up evenly among themselves. If one collective turned out 25 bushels of wheat per man per year, and another collective 50 bushels, then those in the second collective should share twice as much among them as those in the first."

"Why, chief? What would be the justice in that?"

"We would be rewarding workers—or at least groups of workers—in proportion at least to their group production."

"We wouldn't be doing anything of the kind," said Adams.

"Not only would it be impossible to tell what any individual worker had contributed to the total production on a collective, but it would be impossible to tell what the workers had produced collectively."

"But certainly we would know that, Adams!"

"No, we would not. All we would know is that the workers, their animals, their tools, their land, insects and the weather working or acting in combination had produced a certain total net result. But we wouldn't know what to attribute to any one factor."

"We would know that—"

"Let's begin with the weather, chief. If the collectives in the Southern Hemisphere got the right amount of rain and the collectives in the Northern Hemisphere had a drought, then those in the North might produce only half as much wheat per acre or per hand as those in the South. But it would be through no fault of their own. And for the same reasons the wheat yield on any one collective would fluctuate from year to year. It would be merely a matter of luck."

"I concede the element of luck," said Peter. "But your argument seems to be stronger against the system we already have than against the system I propose. The minimum production and collection quotas that we assign to the individual collectives don't take account of this mere luck. Moreover, it seems to me that this element of luck is confined largely to farming. It doesn't exist in manufacturing, for instance."

"I have only begun," replied Adams. "Let's consider the land, now. The soil conditions are different on every collective. With poor soil the hands on one collective can produce, say, only half as much wheat per man per hour of work as the hands on a collective with good soil. Or, putting the matter the other way, the hands on a collective with exceptionally good soil could produce twice as much wheat per man per hour of work as the hands on a collective with average soil."

He looked at Peter for confirmation. Peter nodded.

"Then it isn't the fault of the workers on the poor soil, chief, that they produced only half the average production; and it isn't the merit of the workers on the very good soil that they produced twice as much as the average production."

Peter nodded again.

"Very well," Adams continued. "Now let's go on to the animals and tools and machinery. If one collective has horses and the other hasn't any, or even if one collective has better horses than the next, the first will, other things being equal, produce more wheat per man than the second."

Peter nodded.

"And if one collective has a few crude hand tools for the workers and the other has more tools or better tools, or if the second has tractors and the first has none, or if the second has more tractors per man or per acre or better tractors than the first, or if the first has a tractor that has broken down and the second has a tractor that works, then the second collective, other things being equal, is going to produce more bushels of wheat per man than the first."

Peter agreed again.

"So the net of all this is," Adams concluded triumphantly, "that we cannot attribute the collective production even to the workers collectively. The production is the *combined* result of the workers and the weather and the land and the animals and the tools and tractors collectively, and you can't separate the contribution of one of these factors from the contribution of another."

"I'm afraid you're right," sighed Peter.

"And this doesn't apply just to agriculture," Adams continued, pressing home his point. "The same thing applies even more in manufacturing. The output of the workers in a factory depends entirely upon the amount and kind and quality of the machinery with which they have to work. The output of a factory with the best shoe machinery may be 100 pairs of shoes per man in the same time a worker with only a few hand tools could turn out only one or two pairs of shoes."

"When did you think of all this?" asked Peter.

"I thought of it just now, chief, in answer to your proposal."

"That's what I suspected. It seems to me, Adams," Peter said with pretended severity, "that you are a violent deviationist. You have been flatly contradicting Marx."

"Where?" Adams asked. He seemed seriously alarmed.

"Marx declared in the first volume of *Das Kapital*—I have been doing a lot of studying in the last few months—Marx declared that labor is the one and only factor that produces value. He doesn't say anything about the contribution of tools and equipment to production. He contended that the workers were being robbed of whatever part of the value of the total production they did not get—even though it would have been impossible for them to turn out this production without the help of the tools and machines with which somebody else provided them."

"Oh, I'm sure, chief, that Marx couldn't have said anything so foolish as that machines don't contribute anything to the total of production! I'm sorry that I can't cite the relevant passages off-hand, but I assume that he just took the contribution of machines for granted and averaged it out. . . . Or perhaps his point was that labor had originally built the machines anyhow."

"Now don't try to edit or revise Marx," said Peter tauntingly. "Revisionism is a serious crime in Wonworld."

Adams still looked anxious about this.

"Within the privacy of these four walls," Peter quickly assured him, "you have entirely persuaded me that you are right, whether Marx agrees with you or not. Production is the *joint* achievement of labor and capital, land and nature. And I'll admit I don't see how we can find which factor contributes which percentage."

"I'd like to point out," said Adams, "that our present editions of Marx are all expurgated to prevent anyone from knowing what capitalism was really like and so prevent any efforts to restore it. Now perhaps the original editions of Marx did admit that capital contributed to production and to what Marx called *value.* . . ."

"Well, we'll have a search made for all the relevant passages,

Adams. Meanwhile I'm afraid all your criticisms of my proposal are right."

"I wasn't through, chief."

"Go ahead."

"Your proposal, you remember, was to reward workers in proportion to their production—I suppose by giving each of them what he himself had presumably contributed to production?"

Peter nodded.

"Then you would give the wheat grower a certain amount of wheat and the shoemaker a certain amount of shoes. But what would you give the roadmaker? Part of the road? What would you give the sewer worker? Part of the sewer? What would you give the telephone girl? Part of the wire? What would you give the barber? Part of the hair he cut off? What would you give the surgeon? Part of the patient?"

Peter was silent under these taunts. He had no answer. He lit a cigarette and fell back into his own thoughts. Hadn't he been a presumptuous fool for supposing that he could solve offhand all the problems that had obviously baffled all the best minds in Wonworld before him? If there were such easy answers as he supposed, wouldn't they already have been made? Conditions in Wonworld were horrible: that he knew. But you couldn't reform them simply by rushing in and demanding hysterically that everything be changed. He had been self-complacent and priggish to assume that he was the only man of good will. Reform was something that was possible only after the deepest study. . . .

"You haven't answered my questions," Adams at length reminded him.

"Have you any more criticisms?"

"Yes," continued Adams. "Let's pass over the insoluble problem of how you are going to give his own production to each worker when he has merely contributed, say, to the production of some single great unit, such as a locomotive, or to the construction of things like sewers and roads and waterworks that can only be used by the community as a whole. Let's pass over, also, all the workers that perform some intangible service. Let's concentrate on the simplest possible problem—the workers that do turn out something, like wheat or shoes, that they might individually consume themselves. If you give the wheat growers the wheat, they will have enormously more than they can personally consume, and the rest of the world will starve. If you give the shoemakers the shoes, they will have more than they can possibly wear, and the rest of the world will go barefoot—"

"Wait a minute, wait a minute!" shouted Peter, suddenly struck with an idea. "Of course, of course! Why didn't I think of it before! *Let* the wheatgrowers keep the wheat they grow. *Let* the shoemakers keep the shoes they make. But let them exchange their wheat and shoes with each other to whatever extent they wish! Let everybody have what he makes and let him exchange the surplus above his own needs for whatever he wants of what somebody else makes! Then everybody will have to produce something in order to get something else for it. Everybody will be rewarded in proportion to his own production. That will give him an enormous incentive. And to be able to do this he will have to produce what somebody else wants. Then we won't have to coax or exhort people to work any more. We won't have to denounce them for shoddy work. Not only will everybody wish to produce all he can, but he will try to make it of as high quality as possible, so that somebody else will want it enough to give *him* what *he* wants in exchange for it. And then he won't have to take the shoddy goods that the State hands out to him. He can pick and choose, and take only the goods he wants from the people who make them well—"

"Hold on there!" protested Adams. "What would become of our planned economy? It would be completely disorganized. Production would fall into chaos!"

"Why?"

"Why? Because each individual would start producing for himself. He would produce the things for which he could get the most other things in exchange that he personally wanted."

"But in order to do that," replied Peter, "he would have to produce precisely the things that other people most wanted."

156

"Who would build the roads, chief? Who would repair the sewers? Would each worker be assigned part of a road or part of a sewer as his own presumptive production to exchange with someone else? And who would take over part of a road or part of a sewer in exchange for his own product? And whom would the iron miners exchange with? They could only exchange their crude material with the steelmakers, who are the only ones who would want the iron. And the only things the steelmakers would have to offer in exchange would be steel. Would you personally like to take home a couple of steel rails or an I-beam? . . . It's just impossible."

"Maybe that could be solved by a series of exchanges," suggested Peter. "It's true that only the steelmakers would ultimately want the product of the iron miners, but the steelmakers might be able to offer the iron miners food that they in turn had got in exchange for their steel."

"Or part of a railroad that they had exchanged for their steel rails?" Adams' tone was heavily sarcastic. "No; I haven't even mentioned yet the real trouble with your idea. At present the Central Planning Board decides what things the population needs, and in what proportions. When you think of the hundreds of different consumption goods and services, that's a tremendously difficult problem to solve. That's a major headache all by itself. But when we've done this, we've only started. For then we have to decide how many factories to build, how many machines to build, how much of each raw material to produce, and how many workers to allot, to produce each of these consumption goods in the right proportions. And *then* we have to decide how much of each raw material to produce to build the factories and machines themselves."

"But the Central Planning Board," said Peter, "is always making terrible mistakes. We always find ourselves, at the end of every year of our plans, with embarrassing surpluses of this and appalling shortages of that. And when we have a shortage in one thing—for example, our present shortage of nails—it makes a great deal of the rest of our production pointless. We can't finish

157

our housing program until we get more nails. Meanwhile our production of window frames and doors, shingles and roofing, sidings and washstands, is all perfectly useless. . . . We have all these things rusting and rotting out in the rain."

"How do you expect us *not* to make mistakes, chief, when we are faced with such a horribly complicated problem? We constantly have the best mathematicians working on the problem of getting the right proportions. Marx forbid that I should defend Bolshekov, whose mess I've just taken over, but I must concede—"

"Let's not go into that now."

"But the point I started to make," said Adams, "is that if we cannot avoid such terrible mistakes even with our expert overall planning, where we are at least *trying* to match the production of each thing with that of all the rest, then we can't even imagine the chaos that would follow if we let each man decide *for himself* what to produce. Then nothing would match anything. We would die off like flies!"

Peter lit a cigarette and looked out again at the squalid city. "Well," he said at length, "you've successfully disheartened me once more. But I'm not through, I'm not through! I've got a real idea by the tail, and I'm going to hang on. I'm going to work it out. We haven't seen the last of economic progress—"

"For Marx's sake, chief! First things first! I was nearly *murdered* a couple of hours ago—remember? *What* are you going to do about Bolshekov?"

Chapter 22

PETER stood before the full-length mirror and admired his brilliant new Air Force uniform.

He had finally succumbed to Adams' argument that he must build himself up as a public figure to counter Bolshekov's influence, and above all that he must solidify his relations with the Air Force. So he had ordered this afternoon's air maneuvers over Moscow and arranged to review them in the Red Square from the top of Lenin's Tomb. Following Adams' advice he had declared a half holiday and ordered all the factory heads of the Moscow district to march their workers to the square to insure a huge audience.

The uniform was pure white, the only pure white uniform in Wonworld with the exception of his father's. Adams had arranged to have it covered with ribands and medals. Peter hadn't the slightest idea of what any of them stood for, but in addition to the uniform they made him look so glamorous that even he himself was impressed. Forms, flash, ostentation, pomp, ceremony, distort the judgment of everybody, he thought, even those who pride themselves most on their realism or cynicism.

Sergei entered. "Colonel Torganev and your escort wait upon you, Your Highness."

"I'll be right out, Sergei." He took one last look in the mirror, put his cap on at a rakish angle, and left.

Centered among his air officers, at the top of Lenin's Tomb, with a sea of faces as far as his eye could reach looking toward him, Peter raised his arm. The band blared forth, and the air maneuvers began. . . .

"How much are we producing, Adams?"

Adams looked bewildered.

"How much is Wonworld producing?" repeated Peter.

"Of what?"

"Of everything."

"That's a meaningless question, chief. I can tell you how much we are producing of iron, of wheat, of cotton, of shoes, of whisky, or of any other single thing— At any rate, I can telephone the Central Planning Board and ask them to look up the statistics. But I can't tell you how much we are producing of 'everything.' That question doesn't mean anything."

"I ask you how much we are producing," said Peter, "and you offer to tell me how much we are producing of thousands of different things. I could read tables and tables of such figures and be completely groggy at the end, and know no more than I did before. All I want is one figure: the total."

"But, chief, how can you possibly have such a figure? What is 200,000,000 pairs of shoes added to 1,000,000,000 bushels of wheat added to 1,000,000 quarts of gin? It's 1,201,000,000—of what? You can only add things of precisely the same kind— otherwise the total is meaningless."

"Let's take the shoes," said Peter. "Those shoes are of different sizes and qualities, aren't they?"

"Of course."

"So if you have a pair of bad baby shoes, made for Proletarian children, and a pair of the best men's shoes, made for the Protectorate, you add them to get two pairs of shoes?"

Adams nodded.

"And it's by adding all different sizes, types and qualities of shoes that you get your total, say, of 200,000,000 pairs?"

Adams nodded.

"And again, Adams, your 1,000,000,000 bushels of wheat represents wheat of all different grades, quality and condition?"

Adams nodded.

"So," concluded Peter, "even your totals of individual commodities are rather meaningless, aren't they?"

"Perhaps they are, chief; but you're only proving my point. That would make the total of 'everything,' if you could figure it, still more meaningless."

"And you prefer thousands of different meaningless figures, Adams, to one single meaningless figure?"

"But when these totals consist of the same commodities, chief, they do at least have some definite meaning. If you started breaking down shoes to subtotals in accordance with different sizes and qualities, you might end with 200,000,000 different classifications of shoes alone, for I suppose there are no two pairs of shoes exactly alike. You've got to be reasonable about these things. To know that we make, say, 200,000,000 pairs of shoes a year, no matter how they vary in size and type and quality, is good enough for practical decisions."

"It is precisely enough knowledge for making practical decisions that I'm trying to get," said Peter. "Suppose somebody in the Central Planning Board thought that we needed more shoes. And suppose we could make them only by taking more labor away from the production of leather belts, or even away from the production of wheat. Suppose we increased the production of shoes from 200,000,000 to 250,000,000 pairs a year, but only at the cost of reducing the production of wheat from 1,000,000,000 to 800,000,000 bushels a year. Would we be better off or worse off?"

"That's hard to say. We could only judge from the volume of complaints."

"The complaints of the people who would be shot for complaining?"

"No, chief; but from—from the judgment of members of the Central Planning Board."

"Well, suppose you and I were two members of the Board, and that *you* thought we were better off as a result of the change and *I* thought we were worse off. How would the decision be made between us?"

"Well, you're the boss," said Adams, grinning.

"Let's skip that. Suppose I couldn't make up my *own* mind. Is there any way I could decide the point? Would there be any *objective* guidance?"

Adams shrugged his shoulders.

"If we were producing 250,000,000 pairs of shoes and 800,000,000 bushels of wheat," Peter continued, "would we be producing *more* on net balance than when we were producing 200,000,000 pairs of shoes and 1,000,000,000 bushels of wheat—or would we be producing *less?*"

Adams shrugged his shoulders again. "I suppose it would depend on the relative urgency of our needs."

"And who would decide that?"

"Perhaps we would have to interview the entire Wonworld population, man by man, woman by woman, and child by child—assuming we could get honest answers free from fear."

"So when we compare the hundreds of different commodities we produced last year, Adams, with the hundreds of different commodities we are producing this year, with some totals up and some totals down, there is no way of knowing whether, on net balance, our total production has gone up or down, or how much?"

"Our overall production this year is 14.3 per cent higher than last year," replied Adams, deadpan.

Peter stared at him. "But I thought—"

"That is the official figure of the Central Planning Board, chief. That is the official figure of the Five Year Plan."

"How was it arrived at?"

Adams' face slowly broadened into a grin. "*I* arrived at it. By divine revelation, by direct communion with the spirit of Karl Marx."

"You mean you just pulled the figure out of the air?"

"For propaganda purposes. It's part of our indispensable statistical demagogy. If it weren't precise, people would begin to think it was a mere guess." He smiled shrewdly.

"But seriously then, Adams, strictly between you and me, we

haven't the least knowledge of whether total overall production has gone up or down?"

"Not the least."

"And no way of finding out?"

"Can *you* think of any, chief?"

"But the question has to be answered," said Peter. "Otherwise we are planning completely in the dark. Otherwise we are flying blind. Our resources of labor and land and the tools of production are strictly limited; we simply must know how to apportion the production of thousands of different commodities and services in order to provide most satisfactorily for everybody's need. And we can't even begin to solve that problem unless we have"—his mind groped for the concept—"some common . . . some common unit of measurement. If we find that we want to produce more overcoats, and that we can do so only by producing fewer trousers, or shoes—or even cigarettes—we have to find which commodity we can afford to produce less of. And therefore we have to find out how many overcoats are equivalent to how many cigarettes, or how many cigarettes to how many—clarinets, or what not. And we can only do that by finding some quantity or quality common to all of them."

Adams thought a moment. "How about weight?" he suggested. "You are trying to measure the quantity of production. Very well: we measure the quantity of coal produced by the number of tons. We measure the production of pig iron and steel by tonnages. We can convert wheat production and all other production into tonnage figures—and so we can get the total overall tonnage of production."

"That doesn't seem to me to be any better than adding bushels of wheat to pairs of shoes and quarts of whisky," said Peter. "How does *weight* matter? Are we going to add a ton of fine watches to a ton of coal? If you add a ton of gravel to a ton of binoculars you get two tons—of what? Would such a total mean anything? Wouldn't such information be entirely worthless for practical guidance—or even as an abstract figure?"

"But what other standard have you?" asked Adams. "Would

163

you like volume better than weight? Would you like to measure production by the cubic foot?"

"A cubic foot of feathers, I suppose," said Peter sarcastically, "to count for as much as a cubic foot of platinum?"

"Well, weight and volume are the only common units I can think of, chief."

"For our purposes they are meaningless," said Peter. "There's no difference in weight between coal still unmined in the earth and the same coal in the furnace of this building. If tonnages are what matter we may as well count them in the earth itself, without going to all the trouble of digging the coal up, breaking it, washing it, sorting it by sizes, loading it on freight cars, unloading it into trucks, delivering it to houses and factories, and so on." He thought of another gibe: "And what is the weight of a haircut? What is the volume of a shoeshine?"

"Maybe we could measure production by energy, chief! By kilowatt hours!"

"Worse and worse," said Peter. "You can measure electrical power by kilowatt hours, and then you have to stop."

"Maybe we could find certain equivalents, chief."

"Well, find them. A bushel of wheat is equivalent to how many kilowatt hours? Maybe," Peter added in an even more ironic tone, "we could measure production in triangles!"

"Well, you raised the problem, chief. I didn't."

"I apologize for my sarcasm, Adams. You have no more responsibility for solving this problem than I have. But we've *got* to solve it. Otherwise our boasted planning is meaningless—except on the basis of supplying people with their most primitive and obvious needs as *we* estimate those needs. We've *got* to have some common unit to measure *all* our production. Otherwise, I repeat, we're working completely in the dark."

He lit a cigarette. Adams took a pinch of snuff, and got up and walked back and forth. He began warming up to the subject.

"I've got it—now I've really got it!" he shouted finally. "It's incredible that I didn't think of it before, chief! I went a few

164

weeks ago to the Politburo's private library and took out the master copy of Karl Marx's *Das Kapital*—the one unexpurgated copy—at least they claim this one's unexpurgated—and I've been studying afresh all these weeks since you accused me of being a deviationist. And here I'd already forgotten that Marx raised and *solved* that very problem in the first pages of the first volume. It's solved, it's *solved!* All our work has already been done for us! The greatness of Marx was beyond bounds!"

From Adams such enthusiasm was amazing.

"What's the solution?" asked Peter skeptically.

"I think it would be better if I didn't depend on memory, chief, but gave it to you exactly in Marx's own words."

"All right." Peter glanced at his wrist watch. "It's already nearly six, and I'm due for dinner at my father's apartment. Bring that master copy tomorrow."

Chapter 23

SO far as I can gather, chief," began Adams, "it seems that people under capitalism were allowed to exchange commodities with each other—you can imagine the chaos!—and the question that puzzled Marx was what determined the ratio in which these commodities were exchanged? So he goes about it this way—"

He opened his master copy of *Das Kapital* at a bookmark he had slipped in it. "Here's the passage:

> "Let us take two commodities, wheat and iron, for example. Whatever may be their relative rate of exchange it may always be represented by an equation in which a given quantity of wheat is equal to a given quantity of iron: for example, 1 quarter wheat = 1 cwt. iron. What does this equation tell us? It tells us that there exists a common factor of the same magnitude in two different things, in a quarter of wheat and a cwt. of iron. The two things are therefore equal to a third which is in itself neither the one nor the other. Each of the two, so far as it is an exchange value, must therefore be reducible to that third.

"And then Marx, in searching for this common factor, does it first of all by eliminating what it is *not*. And, just as you have been doing, chief, he says it 'cannot be a geometrical, physical, chemical or other natural property of the commodities.' And, to make a long story short, he eliminates other things, such as 'value-

166

in-use'—whatever that may have meant—and he concludes that there remains to commodities 'only one common property, that of being products of labor.' "

"Did he mean," asked Peter, "that everything people wanted or used, and everything they exchanged with each other, had to be a product of labor?"

"Yes, I suppose he did."

"But that just isn't so, Adams! Suppose you and I are lost in the woods. We are starving; but finally one of us finds a tree with nuts on it and the other a bush with berries. Both the nuts and the berries have value to us, and we may share them or swap them in certain ratios. But both are products of nature, not of our labor. Or suppose oil is discovered on one hectare of land and not on another. Other things being equal, the first will be worth a great deal more than the second, but no labor has gone into it."

"But the first piece of land would not be worth any more than the second until the oil was not only discovered, chief, but pumped up, refined, transported where it was wanted, and so on. And all that requires labor. Before it were put in a form to be *used*, labor would have to be embodied in it."

"The labor, if well directed, would of course *add* to the oil's value, Adams, as it was brought from one stage of value to another. But the value would be there before the labor was added! Oil land is worth more than land without oil even before anyone has touched it. When the well has been sunk it is of course worth still more. The oil is worth still more after it has been refined, and still more after it has been transported to where it can be used. The point I am making is that products of nature, even before they have been transformed by labor, have *some* value to us, and different values from one another. Therefore being products of labor is *not* the *only* common property in the physical things people want or use—which I suppose is what Marx meant by 'commodities.' "

"Well, chief, I suppose Marx simply took the contribution of nature for granted, and started from there."

"But another thing that occurs to me," said Peter, "is that simply being the product of labor doesn't necessarily give a thing value. Suppose the labor has been misapplied in producing something entirely useless? Or in producing something actually harmful? Or suppose the labor is so incompetent that it actually spoils something? . . . As I don't need to tell *you*, this is happening every day. In this morning's *New Truth*, for example, there's a story of the ruining of a whole herd of cows by incompetent dairy hands who overmilked them or didn't know how to milk them. And a couple of days ago careless painters in calcimining the ceiling of the public library got a lot of the stuff on the books. And a week ago, a worker called into the Kremlin to repair a fine table drove a nail in the leg and split it down the middle."

"I don't recall, chief, that Marx anywhere says anything about *incompetent* or *careless* work, or work that results in more injury than improvement, but he does allow for *misdirected* or *inefficient* work— But you'd better let me explain."

"Go on. "

"I began by quoting Marx to the effect that commodities have only one common property—that of being products of labor. Well, he goes on to explain that it is this that determines what he calls their 'value,' or the ratios in which they exchange. Let me read: 'The value of one commodity,' he wrote, 'is related to the value of any other commodity as the working time necessary for the production of the one is to that necessary for the production of the other. As values, all commodities are only specific quantities of crystallized working time.' For example, chief, if a unit of one commodity required five hours' work, it would be worth, and it would exchange for, five like units of another commodity that required only one hour's work to produce each unit."

"And if a man dawdled over the first commodity so that he took ten hours to produce it, Adams, would a unit of it be worth ten units of the second commodity?"

"No, chief; that's just what I'm coming to. Marx was very

168

shrewd about this. He specified that it was only the *socially necessary* working time that counted. That's what I meant when I said that he allowed for and discounted misdirected or inefficient work."

"Did Marx ever define what he meant by 'socially necessary' labor time?"

"Yes. Let me read you his definition. The socially necessary working time is—'the working time required to produce a value-in-use under the normal conditions of production, and with the degree of skill and intensity of labor prevalent in a given society.'"

"As I understand that, Adams, by the 'socially necessary' working time Marx means merely the *average* working time that prevails in any society."

"Right."

"So if bricklayers on the overall average lay 60 bricks an hour, he considers that the socially necessary number, even though the highest third among them lay 120 bricks an hour, and a brick-laying genius can lay 360 bricks an hour?"

"Right."

"So by 'socially necessary,' Marx does not really mean what is demonstrably *necessary,* but merely the average?"

"I suppose your interpretation is correct, chief."

"For if, with proper training and skill and spirit, men can be taught to lay 360 bricks in one hour, then it really isn't *necessary* for anyone to take six hours to do it?"

Adams thought a minute. "No-o-o-o," he drawled, "but maybe Marx just used an unfortunate term there. For by an hour's labor he really meant nothing more than an hour's *unskilled* labor, and an average hour of unskilled labor is, I suppose, even less than an average hour of all labor."

"Suppose," put in Peter, "that one man in one hour produces six times as much as the average man in one hour. Surely the product of his hour's work isn't worth as little as the average man's product! Or suppose a highly skilled or endowed man produces something in an hour that the average man hasn't the skill to produce at all?"

"You must give me a chance to answer that, chief. Marx doesn't say that the product of skilled labor equals merely the product of the same amount of hours of unskilled labor. Let me read you what he does say. When he talks of working time, he tells us, he is talking of 'simple average labor.' 'Skilled labor,' he continues, 'counts only as concentrated or rather multipled unskilled labor, so that a small quantity of skilled labor is equal to a larger quantity of unskilled labor.' "

"That doesn't make any sense to me, Adams; because—"

"You'd better let me continue with his explanation, chief." Adams read:

"That this reduction is constantly made, experience shows. A commodity may be the product of the most highly skilled labor, but its value makes it equal to the product of unskilled labor, and represents therefore only a definite quantity of unskilled labor. The different proportions in which different kinds of labor are reduced to unskilled labor as their unit of measure are fixed by a social process beyond the control of the producers, and therefore seem given to them by tradition."

"Let's go back to the point where I interrupted," said Peter. "It seems to me that Marx is arguing in a complete circle. Under capitalism, I gather, people were permitted to exchange commodities with each other, and it was found that these commodities exchanged with each other in certain ratios. Now the problem that Marx set himself to solve was: What determined these ratios? And he answered: the amount of working time embodied in each of the commodities. But then he found, say, that one man, A, worked one day to produce a given unit of commodity X, and another man, B, worked one day to produce a given unit of commodity Y; but that as a matter of fact this one unit of X did not exchange against one unit of Y, but 'experience showed' that it took *ten* units of X to exchange for one unit of Y. So Marx then said that one day of B's work 'counts as' ten days of A's work."

"Yes," replied Adams; "because B's work is skilled and A's work is unskilled."

"But all that comes down to in plain Marxanto," said Peter, "is that Marx isn't measuring the value of the commodity by the working time, but by the relative skill embodied in it—or rather, by a complex measuring rod of working time multipled by skill."

"He *reduces* skill to working time, chief."

"But how does he discover, Adams, by what multiplier or divisor to make the reduction? He does it by looking at the actual ratios in which the commodities produced by the labor actually do exchange. So his explanation is wrong; and he tries to justify it by arguing in a complete circle. He tells us that commodities exchange in proportion to the relative working times embodied in them. But then he is forced to admit that ten units of X commodity, for example, in which *ten* days' work have been embodied, exchange in fact for only one unit of commodity Y in which only *one* day's work has been embodied. And he glosses over the contradiction by blandly telling us that one day's labor of Comrade B, who made commodity Y, 'counts as' ten days' labor of Comrade A, who made commodity X—because, forsooth, 'experience *shows*' that it does! But what experience really shows is that the exchange ratio of commodities was *not* measured—certainly not exclusively measured—by the hours of working time, but by other factors, one of which is relative skills."

"But isn't it true, chief, that skilled labor does count as concentrated or multiplied unskilled labor?"

"But if it does, Adams, Marx should have explained *why* it does. This was the real problem that he had to solve. He simply said that it does—because 'experience shows' that it does. As a matter of fact, experience shows that commodities *don't* exchange in relation simply to the working time embodied in them. Experience shows that Marx is wrong."

"But Marx didn't say," persisted Adams, "that one hour of

171

skilled labor actually *was* two or five or ten hours of unskilled labor, but merely that it *counted as* that in fixing exchange relations."

"It's wonderful what you could do with that phrase 'counts as,'" replied Peter, "once you got fairly started. For example, you ask the manager of a collective, 'How many chickens have you got on your farm?' And he answers, 'I figure we have a hundred and fifty.' So you go around there and count them, and you find they have only fifty chickens. 'But,' says the manager, 'we also have a cow.' 'What has that got to do with it?' you ask. 'Surely,' says the manager, 'you will admit that one cow counts as a hundred chickens!' Or suppose you want to prove that commodities exchange in accordance with their relative weight in pounds. You find, as a matter of fact, that one pound of gold exchanges for 30,000 pounds of pig iron. But you were speaking, you say, emulating Marx, only of 'common, average' pounds, and the pounds in gold 'count as' concentrated or multiplied common average pounds of the kind found in pig iron. In fact, you continue triumphantly, each pound in gold 'counts as' 30,000 pounds in pig iron, because 'experience shows' that it does! A mysterious 'social process beyond the control of the producers' shows that it does!"

"I think I do have an explanation, chief, though Marx doesn't explicitly give it."

"What?"

"Well, we've got to take into account the length of time it takes a man to acquire a skill. For example, an unskilled bricklayer may lay only 60 bricks an hour, and a skilled bricklayer may lay 180 bricks an hour; but it may have taken him two hours to acquire his skill for every hour he works."

"Ingenious of you, Adams, but not convincing. If you think a few minutes, you will find that your explanation raises more problems than it answers. You don't seriously believe that a skilled bricklayer devotes two-thirds of his working life merely to acquiring his skill while producing nothing in the process! You don't seriously believe that he lays no bricks at all during the time he is learning to lay bricks! You don't seriously believe that he lays all his bricks in the last third of his life! Yet that is what your example supposes. You would have to prove that, on the average, skilled workers, merely to acquire their skill, have had to devote a percentage of their working life exactly proportionate to their present increased rate of production over unskilled workers. For example, you would have to prove that skilled workmen who produce twice as much in a day as unskilled workmen have devoted the whole first half of their working lives merely to acquiring their skill—that skilled workmen who produce five times as much in a day as unskilled workmen have devoted four-fifths of their working lives merely to acquiring their skill, and so on. As a matter of fact, there is no reason whatever to suppose that any such proportions hold. All experience, in fact, refutes it."

Peter stopped to light a cigarette.

"And here we come to a crucial point," he continued. "Neither Marx's theory as it stands, or as amended by you, makes any allowance for the enormous differences, not only in training but in *native* gifts and endowments, between individuals. A good bricklayer, with no more training, may lay twice as many bricks a day as a bad one. And he will lay them so that they won't have to be broken off and relaid by somebody else. But the work of an inspired architect, who designs the building that the bricklayers work on, is worth many times as much as the work even of the most skillful bricklayer. And this doesn't depend on the greater length of time that the architect has taken to get his training. His value, if he is a first-rate architect, will be many times as much as this greater training period. And if he is incompetent, uninspired, without sense or taste, his work will have an actual *negative* value, regardless of the length of his training period."

Adams thoughtfully took a few pinches of snuff. "I wish Marx were here to answer you," he said at last. "I can't."

"I have only begun," said Peter, warming up. "I am an apt pupil, and I am now going to use against Comrade Adams the same arguments that Comrade Adams recently thought up against me. For, as so often happens, it seems that in the heat of argument we have reversed our positions. It was *you* who pointed out to *me*, when we were talking of collective farms and manufacturing, that it wasn't labor alone that produced crops, but the *combination* and *co-operation* of land and nature and farm implements and nature. So the same man, for example, could produce twice or ten times as much with a mechanical tractor as with a simple hoe. And the same man with machinery could produce a hundred times as many pairs of shoes as he could if he had only a few hand tools."

"I will have to admit that I was right, chief."

"You convinced me that you were. But if you were right, Marx must be wrong. It is *not* 'simple average unskilled' labor time that determines either the quantity of production or the value of that production to the community; it is the co-operation of a complex set of factors—of labor time, labor skill, land, nature, and the tools of production."

Both sat for a time in silence. Peter tried to blow perfect smoke rings.

"Well," he said finally, "supposing Marx had been right in holding that the quantity or value of production could be measured solely by the labor time necessary to produce. What could we have done with his theory, anyway?"

"You were looking, chief, you remember, for some common unit of measurement for different commodities, so that we could find out how great our total overall production was, compare it with previous totals, decide whether it was better to produce more of commodity A at the expense of producing less of B, and so on."

"That's right."

"Well," continued Adams, "it occurred to me that if labor hours were the right unit of measurement, we could stop issuing ration tickets to workers for particular commodities, and pay them instead in *labor certificates*. Let's say, for example, that we paid them one certificate for every hour worked. If a worker put

174

in the customary twelve-hour day, he would receive twelve labor certificates per day. Then a value would be put upon each commodity depending upon the number of working hours it took to produce it. Then each worker, at the end of the day or week—or, for that matter, whenever he pleased—could turn in his labor certificates for whatever commodities he most wanted."

"Very ingenious," said Peter. "But what would be the advantages?"

"The great advantage would be, chief, that we would get the freedom of consumption you recently spoke about. The individual consumer would not have to take goods in the proportions in which the government allotted them to him, but only in the proportions that he himself preferred. We would therefore be satisfying more needs or desires, and presumably we would be producing goods with a greater total value to the community. . . . That was what we wanted, wasn't it?"

"But I'm afraid it wouldn't work, Adams. This freedom of consumption, as you yourself pointed out to me not so long ago, would totally destroy our central planning. We wouldn't be able to decide in advance what things to produce and in what proportions. We would have to depend upon the whims of individual consumers, and start to produce what these consumers asked for. And it isn't difficult to see what would happen. Let's say that out of every hundred workers, sixty-five are unskilled, thirty have fair skills and five have exceptional skills. Each would get the same amount of labor certificates for his week's work. But everybody would demand first of all the product of the highly skilled or exceptionally endowed workers. And there just would never be enough of this to go around."

"Why not first come, first served?"

"But then people would be rewarded solely in proportion to their luck or patience in being the first on queues to get the limited supply of fine products, while those who worked too hard to get in line on time would suffer."

In reply Adams simply shrugged his shoulders.

"I get more disheartened every day," said Peter at last. "We seem

175

to be up against a stone wall. We must, of course, have socialism and central planning. Anything else is unthinkable. But we have been forced step by step to one depressing conclusion after another. We have been forced to conclude that under socialism and central planning we can have no economic liberty for the individual and therefore no liberty of speech or thought; that under socialism and central planning we can have no free, informed and unintimidated public opinion, and therefore no meaningful democracy. And *now* we are forced to conclude that we cannot even figure under socialism; we cannot even calculate; we do not know how to produce goods in proportion to human needs and wants; we cannot tell whether or when or how much we are misdirecting and wasting labor and materials and other precious resources. . . . We are working completely in the dark, by guess and by goosestep."

Chapter 24

"COME in!"

He had learned to recognize the timid little knock of the waitress bringing his tray.

On most of the evenings when he did not have supper at his father's bedside, Peter had established the custom of having it brought to his desk in the office. It had been his father's former habit to eat his supper at this desk and to work late into the nights. Stalenin had explained to him that this in effect forced all the commissars in Russia to work at the same hours and to adopt the same habit. This got more work out of them, kept them out of mischief and did not give them time to conspire against him.

Peter had adopted the custom chiefly because he found it impossible otherwise to get through his work.

He watched the waitress, a plain-looking woman, as she spread the large napkin on the desk and placed the tray on it. She was dressed in a neat white uniform with a starched cap. She worked in a quiet, timid way, obviously trying to attract as little attention as possible. He noticed consciously for the first time her thin white hands and wrists, her drawn face, the pallor of her cheeks.

He sat down to his lonely meal in a despondent mood. His mind turned again, as it had every night now, to Edith and her father. What step could he take to find them that he had not already tried?

His thoughts stayed with him when he went to bed, and he tried to grapple once more with the dismal conclusions to which he had felt forced to arrive in his talk with Adams that afternoon. He felt almost smothered by multiple layers of despondency.

But toward morning, as he kept turning the social problem over and over in his mind, he suddenly saw a light.

It was with real eagerness that he launched upon his talk with Adams at their four o'clock conference the next afternoon.

"We decided, you remember," he began, "that Marx was wrong in concluding that labor was the only factor capable of producing value. We decided that production was the result of the co-operation of at least *three* main factors—land, labor, and tools. Now as I thought this over last night I was more and more struck by the immense importance of the tools and machinery, their enormous effect on both the quantity and quality of production, and therefore the stupendous importance of improving the quantity and quality of the tools of production themselves. . . . Let's take the three main factors that go to determine the volume and value of production. Let's begin with land. I include in this, of course, natural resources and all other free gifts of nature. It's obvious that we can't do anything to increase these. All we can do is to try to make the best use of them. We are strictly limited, also, even concerning what we can do about labor. We can of course increase manpower by increasing the population. But it is doubtful whether that would make us collectively or individually any better off. For if we increased the population we would also increase the number of mouths to be fed, the number of persons to be clothed and housed, and so on; and we would have less natural resources per capita than we had before—"

"You may be right there, chief. Our statistics don't show it—they were either suppressed or never collected in the first place—but several of us in the Politburo privately suspect that it has been the series of famines and pestilences since the triumph of Communism that has helped us to solve our problems even as well as we do. The population of Wonworld today is estimated at

178

only about a billion. But just before the final Communist-Capitalist War started, the world's population was estimated at about two billions. Now every time there is a famine it leaves fewer mouths to feed with the amount of food that remains; it leaves more square feet of floor space per inhabitant, and so on. So our constant famines are, in a way, part of the solution of our difficulties."

"It is the continuance of just that kind of horrible 'solution' that I am trying to stop," said Peter. "And that brings me to my hopeful conclusion. True, we can't do much about land or labor. But it has just struck me that the quantity and quality of the tools and machinery of production are indefinitely expansible and improvable. If that is so, the economic lot of mankind can be constantly bettered without assignable limit. . . . Such a conclusion opens a new window on the world. It means a new dawn for mankind!"

"Your conclusion may be very important, chief—but haven't we already been trying to multiply and improve our tools of production?"

"In a way, I suppose we have," conceded Peter. "But our emphasis has been in the wrong place. Under the teachings of Marx, our emphasis has been on labor and labor efficiency. But what we have overlooked is that the right tools and machines can multiply labor's productivity far more than added hours of daily work or individual industriousness, however desirable these may be."

"But how do you suppose that a man with so powerful a mind as Marx would ignore or belittle the tremendous contribution to production of tools and machinery?"

"I suppose, Adams, it was because in Marx's day the tools of production were privately owned, that the workers were powerless without these tools and had to come to the owners of them for work, and therefore the owners exploited the workers. Or at least Marx thought they did, and he was so angered by this that he ended by ignoring or denying the tremendous role that the tools of production played in creating goods. He admitted that

179

they were *necessary* for production—he had to do that to explain why the workers who used the tools were forced to come to the employers who owned them. But he refused to admit that the tools *added* to production, and that part of the production must be attributed to the tools—instead of the whole of production being attributed to labor alone."

"You may have something there, chief. I'm going to study Marx some more. . . ."

At their next talk Peter was even more enthusiastic.

"I think I've hit upon a brilliant reform, Adams! It hasn't got much to do with Marx's theory of production at all, at least not directly. It really grew out of my thinking about your own suggestion of using labor certificates instead of ration tickets. You remember I didn't think that would work, and I still don't think it would work. But something occurred to me that would do precisely the same thing that you had in mind. Why not permit people to *exchange* their ration tickets with each other?"

"But that would lead to chaos!"

"How?"

"How? Under present conditions, chief, the Central Planning Board decides what each worker, what each consumer, ought to have. It tries to provide him with a well-balanced ration all around: each person gets his daily quota of bread, and his weekly quota of beans and turnips. Everything is based on giving each person his proper number of calories—or at any rate the same number as anybody else. Then each person gets his yearly allotment of clothing, or of such luxuries as cigarettes and beer. Now if we allow people to start exchanging ration tickets, some of them would not get enough to eat, or would get too many luxuries that they didn't really need—"

"But no one would *have* to exchange his ration tickets, Adams. If he found that he got too little to eat he would very soon cease to make exchanges."

"We simply can't depend on the people, chief, to exercise their own discretion regarding what is good for them."

"You mean that we commissars will have to make that decision for them?"

"That's what a commissar is for."

"Well, Adams, I don't agree. On the contrary, each person knows his own needs best. At least he knows his own desires best. And if one man wants fewer beans and more cigarettes, while another wants fewer cigarettes and more beans, that is the business of each of them. They should be free to seek each other out and make the exchange. . . . Moreover, we will satisfy far more needs that way than we do now. It ought to be the very purpose of an economic system to satisfy as many needs and wants as possible. Under a system of free exchange of ration tickets, each person will be freer to take goods in whatever relative proportions *he* wants them—and not merely in the proportions that someone else, like you or me, thinks is good for him. This freedom of exchange will mean that more wants will be satisfied than now. And ultimately we have no other way of measuring 'production' than by its capacity to satisfy wants."

"What ratios of exchange are you going to establish, chief?"

"What do you mean?"

"Well, how many bread coupons, for example, would you specify as the legal exchange ratio for how many cigarette cou pons?"

"I wouldn't specify *any*. Coupons can exchange in any ratio that suits both parties to the transaction."

"This brings us right back to the chaos I was talking about," Adams said. "If no legal exchange rates are set, some people will start to take advantage of others."

"How?"

"It is bound to happen. If Peter gains by the exchange, for example, Paul must necessarily lose by it. In fact, Paul must necessarily lose exactly as much as Peter gains."

"Not at all, Adams. You are missing the whole point. There is no *inherent* exchange ratio between bread coupons and cigarette coupons, or between bread and cigarettes. The relative value of a loaf of bread and a package of cigarettes will be different in each person's mind, depending upon his own relative desires and wishes. No exchange can or will take place unless each party to the exchange feels that he gains by it."

"But won't one of them necessarily be deceiving himself?"

"Not at all. The gain from the exchange occurs in each case not because of some inherent difference in the relative objective value of the goods themselves, but because each party to the exchange more fully meets his own desires by making it. *Both* parties to the exchange gain, because *both* are better satisfied— otherwise the exchange would not have been made."

"But Marx's labor theory of value—"

"Marx's labor theory of value was wrong, Adams, among other reasons, because it rested on the assumption that values were measured by some *objective* unit, whereas values are only measured *subjectively*. The value of a commodity doesn't reside in the commodity; it resides in a *relationship* between somebody's needs or desires and the capacity of that commodity to satisfy those needs or desires. . . . Marx looked for some objective standard of value because he assumed that two commodities that exchanged for each other must do so because of some 'equality' between them. But if two commodities were exactly equal, in the opinion of two persons, each of whom held one of them, there would be no reason for any exchange to take place at all. It is only because Peter, who holds potatoes, thinks that a certain amount of prunes, held by Paul, would be more valuable to him, that Peter would want to make an exchange. And only if Paul placed the opposite relative value on a given amount of potatoes and prunes would he agree to make the exchange."

"I still contend," insisted Adams, "that your system would lead to chaos. For example, we issue cigarette coupons to every adult. But we find that only two-thirds of these coupons are ever turned in for cigarettes, because some people just don't care to smoke. Under your proposed system, the people who don't present their cigarette coupons under our present system would exchange them for bean coupons, say, offered by people who wanted more cigarettes. And then all the bean coupons and *all* the cigarette coupons would be presented—and there simply wouldn't be enough cigarettes in which to redeem them."

"It would be our business, then," said Peter, "either to increase the production of cigarettes or to reduce the number of cigarette ration coupons to bring about an equality."

Adams shrugged his shoulders in despair. "We're simply going to have to produce more goods which we don't really need to produce. I hope you're at least not going to permit people to exchange the actual commodities *themselves* with each other! That would make the chaos greater still. The government would have no way of tracing who was consuming what. That's precisely why we have always forbidden people to exchange goods with each other. Some people would have unbalanced diets; others would drink too much Marxi-Cola—"

"All right; for the present we'll simply permit the exchange of ration coupons, and see how *that* works."

Adams sighed. "Try it if you like, chief. Maybe it will work. But I must tell you in all candor that if *I* were running affairs I wouldn't fool around with all these economic theories until I had taken care of more immediately important things first!"

"What do you mean?"

"Well, take this parade that Bolshekov has called for tomorrow afternoon—"

"Parade? Bolshekov?"

"Great Marx, chief! Hadn't you even *heard* about it? He announced it on the radio this morning."

Peter was dazed.

Adams stared at him incredulously. "I thought it was bad enough, chief, when Bolshekov announced the parade in his own name, announced that he had called it and that he would review it, and never even mentioned you or even Stalenin! But I assumed that at least he had had your consent, and that you had encouraged him to do it. This move is pretty ominous!"

"I'll soon stop this," said Peter. He flicked the intercom and asked Sergei to get Bolshekov on the wire.

"What is the meaning of this parade, No. 2?" demanded Peter.

183

"It means that I have ordered a parade, Uldanov, and that I am reviewing the armed forces." His tone was one of quiet contempt.

"Well, Bolshekov, I am ordering you, in the name of Stalenin, to call off the parade."

"I am *giving* orders, not taking them, Uldanov. Do *you* want to call off the parade? Try it. See what happens!"

Peter hung up. He turned to Adams.

"I heard him," said Adams.

"You were right," Peter said. "I've been a fool. I should never have appointed Bolshekov head of the Army and Navy. I should have had him liq— Well, I should have done something else than I did. He wouldn't be challenging me the way he is unless he were sure that he and not I had the loyalty of the army."

"The army knows Bolshekov; it doesn't know you, chief. And Bolshekov has been building up his own personal machine ever since Stalenin began to lose his grip. It's too late to try to remove him by a simple order. . . . I'm afraid, chief, that you and I are now the ones in grave danger not merely of losing our jobs, but our lives."

Peter got up and walked around the room.

"Why have you been sticking along with me, Adams?"

"I thought I'd already made that clear, chief. I didn't have much choice. Not being Russian, I haven't the ghost of a chance of becoming Dictator myself. I knew that if Bolshekov came to power his first act would be my liquidation. What did I have to lose by lining up with his only possible alternative?"

"Were those your only reasons?"

Adams paused. "I happen to like you," he said at length, and as if reluctantly. "Your sincerity . . . your disinterestedness . . . your innocent and naïve idealism. . . ."

"You say that almost as if you were ashamed of it."

"These are not the things that a good Bolshevist ought to like," said Adams. "He ought to be strong; he ought to be hard; he ought to be cruel; he ought to be devious. . . . I have been all these things, or I would never have got to be No. 3. Maybe I

184

got to be so cynical that I finally became cynical about cynicism itself."

"I want you to know, Adams, that I trust you completely. And I want you to know also that I'm not licked yet. I've been a fool, yes; but there's still time to act. Thanks to your advice, I think I still have the loyalty of the Air Force. We must and will continue to consolidate that. And now that I've had my ears pinned back, I'm humbled, and I'm asking you for more of your practical advice. . . ."

Chapter 25

AN hour before Bolshekov's parade was due to start, Peter, acting on Adams' advice, went on the radio on a world-wide hookup. The loud speakers were turned on full blast in every street. Peter declared on the radio that he had instructed Bolshekov to order and review this parade (this was Adams' fabrication) in order to signalize and mark the day on which he, Peter Uldanov, acting in the name of Stalenin, was announcing one of the greatest economic reforms put into effect in the history of Wonworld.

And then he announced his ration coupon exchange scheme. Beginning at midnight, anyone was free to exchange any ration ticket in his possession—regardless of the fact that it bore his own personal serial number as well as the serial number of the ticket itself—for anybody else's ration ticket. Ration tickets for cigarettes, for example, could be exchanged for ration tickets for bread or shoes or anything else, and at any ratio mutually agreeable to the parties to the exchange. He went on to explain how people with different needs, tastes and preferences would all be able to satisfy them better now than under the old system. He had ordered Bolshekov to call this parade, he said in conclusion, in order to celebrate the fact that the battle of the ration tickets had at last been won.

This time Peter was determined not to depend merely on second-hand official reports to know how his reform was working. He frequently put on his old Proletarian uniform, and a pair of horn-rimmed spectacles, to wander around and see the reaction of people at first hand.

At first there was no reaction at all. Nobody exchanged ration coupons, in spite of the fact that Peter's broadcast had been published in every newspaper in Wonworld. By his own discreet inquiries and those of his agents he soon learned the reason. Everyone knew that all his own ration tickets were stamped with his personal serial number. Everyone feared a new sort of trap.

On Adams' advice, Peter decided to dramatize the reform. He ordered the following week to be celebrated as Ration Coupon Exchange Week. Outstanding members of the Protectorate were ordered to stand in line on either side of the Red Square at noon each day. They would march towards each other, to the strains of the *International,* meet in the center, and there exchange their least valued ration ticket for another.

The result of this was again unsatisfactory. People now began to assume that it was *compulsory* to exchange at least a few ration tickets. They tried to learn from the Central Planning Board how many they were supposed to exchange and at what rates.

But after a few months these fears began to quiet down. Repeated instructions in the government press began to give people the idea. Genuinely voluntary exchanges of ration tickets began to take place, and at varying rates.

And now it was Peter's turn to make a few surprising discoveries.

At first individuals or families merely exchanged ration tickets with other persons or families living in the same room with them. Then in the same house. Then in the same neighborhood or factory. The rates at which the ration tickets exchanged was a matter of special bargaining in each case. They at first revealed no describable pattern whatever. In one tenement or barracks someone would be exchanging, say, one shirt coupon for five bread coupons; next door one shirt coupon might exchange for fifteen bread coupons.

But gradually a distinct pattern began to take form. The man

187

who had exchanged his shirt coupon for five bread coupons would learn that he could have got fifteen bread coupons from someone else; the man who had given up fifteen bread coupons for one shirt coupon would learn that he might have got a shirt coupon for only five bread coupons. So people began to "shop around," * as they called it, each trying to get the highest bid for what he had to offer, each trying to get the greatest number of the coupons he desired for the coupons with which he was willing to part. The result, after a surprisingly short time, was that a uniform rate of exchange prevailed at any given moment between one type of coupon and another.

Throughout all of Moscow, for example—as throughout any district in which people were permitted to move freely without passports—virtually the same rate would establish itself as between any two coupons. For example, a uniform rate would be established of ten bread for one shirt coupon; and when this general rate was established, practically nobody would exchange for any other. For no man with a shirt coupon to exchange would take only nine bread coupons for it from anyone when he knew that somebody else would offer him ten; and nobody with bread coupons would give eleven of them for a shirt coupon as long as he knew that someone stood ready to give him a shirt coupon for only ten.

Then another striking thing happened. People had at first shopped around from house to house and street to street, trying to get the best rate in the kind of coupons they valued most for the kind of coupons they valued least. But soon people anxious to trade their coupons took to meeting regularly at certain places where they had previously discovered that they found the most other traders and bidders and could get the best rates in the quickest time. These meeting points, which people took to calling coupon "markets," tended to become fewer and larger.

Two principal "markets" gradually established themselves in Moscow, one in Engels Square and the other at the foot of

* The reader is again reminded that this is a translation from the Marxanto. The terms used are in each case merely the nearest English equivalent.

Death-to-Trotsky Street. Here large crowds, composed in turn of smaller groups, gathered on the sidewalk and spread into the street. They were made up of shouting and gesticulating persons, each holding up a coupon or sheet of coupons, each asking how much he was bid, say, in beer coupons for his shirt coupon, or offering his shirt coupon for, say, twelve beer coupons, and asking whether he had any takers.

Then shortly there took place a still further development. One enterprising coupon trader, a Deputy, brought along his little girl's school slate, on which he marked the rates at which he was willing to exchange different coupons for other coupons. He would hold this slate up for the crowd to see.

He offered to trade other people's coupons for them, to get the best rates and to save them the time and trouble of doing all this exchanging themselves. All he asked in return was a small fraction of what he got in exchange. If he got twelve beer coupons for a "client's" shirt coupon, for example, he would keep one beer coupon for his trouble. This takeout gradually came to be called his "commission"—apparently because it was his reward for having the coupons committed to his charge.

And more and more people came to find that they could do better, everything considered, by turning their coupons over to him to exchange, than by trying to trade them directly themselves. For the process of trading was often wearisome and complicated. Someone would want, say, beer coupons for his shirt coupon. But he would not find anyone who wanted a shirt coupon for beer coupons, or who was willing to make this exchange at a satisfactory rate. So he might have to trade his shirt coupon first for bread coupons, and then perhaps trade these in turn for cigarette coupons—because he had learned of someone who was offering beer coupons for cigarette coupons. He saved all this tiring complication by turning his coupons for exchange over to the enterprising coupon trader, Comrade N-13, and letting the latter keep for his services a small percentage of what he got. Somebody happily thought of calling N-13 a "middleman."

Others, for more obscure reasons, started calling him a "broker." Both names stuck.

People found that they saved amazing time and work by taking their coupons for exchange to N-13. For if a man came with a shirt coupon, say, to exchange for beer coupons, N-13 would look in a little notebook he carried, which he called a "customer's book," and might find that someone had left beer coupons with him to exchange for a shirt coupon. Or he might find that someone had left beer coupons with him to exchange for cigarette coupons, and that someone else had left cigarette coupons to exchange for a shirt coupon. So he would make the "triangular" exchange himself.

The business of N-13 snowballed. But it was only for a few weeks that he had a monopoly on it. Other coupon traders also got slates, also set up as middlemen and brokers, also took orders from others. One result was that the "commission," or percentage of the coupons that the brokers kept for themselves, gradually narrowed as they competed with each other to get this "business."

Still another result was that the crowds began to diminish instead of growing bigger. They finally came to consist wholly of "professional" brokers (meeting late in the evening after their regular factory jobs were over) who acted as agents for exchanging the tickets left in their care. These brokers would often make their exchanges merely by comparing the orders on each other's notebooks.

And still a third result was that the professional brokers finally put all their slates together to form in effect one great slate, which they hung against the blank wall of a building in Death-to-Trotsky Street, and on which they marked the prevailing "quotations" of different coupons in terms of other coupons.

These quotations consisted of a record of the ratios at which the last exchanges or transactions had been made. There was also often a record of, say, the maximum number of beer coupons being offered by any broker for cigarette coupons, and the maximum number of cigarette coupons being bid for beer coupons.

These latter quotations came to be known as the "bid and asked" prices. If they were equal, or overlapped, an exchange was possible and took place. But the best offer of anyone with beer coupons might be three of them for one cigarette coupon, while the best bid of anyone with cigarette coupons might be one of them for four beer coupons. In that case no exchange or transaction would occur until the highest bid and the lowest offer came together.

Then still a fourth development took place, to Peter the most unlooked for and fascinating of all. The market in ration coupons had become bewilderingly complicated. The immense slate could not begin to hold the bid-and-asked ratios of exchange for everything. For example, the ratio at which beer coupons were offered for exchange had to be stated in terms of shoe coupons, cap coupons, bean coupons, potato coupons, trouser coupons, cigarette coupons, and so on endlessly. But the ratio of potato coupons, in turn, had to be stated in terms of beer coupons, bread coupons, shoe coupons, cigarette coupons. . . . Though this made an infinite network of possible exchange ratios, the exchange ratio of any two items against a third always worked out to be pretty much in accord with their exchange ratios with each other.

When Peter first became aware of this he regarded it as a remarkable coincidence, and then as something of a miracle. But he soon came to realize that it was due to a perfectly natural and virtually inevitable development. Some brokers made it their business to specialize in what they called "triangular" transactions among ration tickets. They were constantly on the lookout for discrepancies in the mutual exchange relationships of any three commodities. As soon as they found any discrepancy from which they could profit, by a triangular exchange, they immediately tried to do so. Their competitive bids and offers continued until the relationships were ironed out, so that no further profit was possible for anybody as a result of a discrepancy.

For the same reason, Peter found, the ratios of exchange in the market at Engels Square were never far out of line for more than a very short period with the ratios of exchange on Death-to-Trotsky Street; for a set of brokers were always running back and forth between the two markets, or sending messengers, and trying to profit from the least discrepancy that arose between the markets in the exchanges or quotations.

A special name—"arbitrage business"—sprang up for this sort of transaction. Its effect was to unify, or to universalize, price relationships among markets between which this freedom of arbitrage existed.

As a result of this amazing consonance within the infinitely complicated pattern of exchange relationships, people took to the habit of saying that these wonderfully delicate market adjustments were "automatic." The word was ingenious; but Peter was shrewd enough to recognize that it was only a striking metaphor which, if taken literally, could be misleading. These market adjustments were anything but "automatic." They took place solely because there was an alert group of people ready to seize upon the slightest discrepancy to make a transaction profitable to themselves. It was precisely the constant alertness and the constant initiative of these specialists that prevented any but the most minute and short-lived discrepancies from occurring.

Of course each of these specialists was doing this, not in order to make a more perfect market, or with any conscious effort to confer any benefit on society, but solely in the hope of making a transaction profitable to himself—profitable in the sense that he would end up with more ration tickets. And as everybody was trying to maximize his own satisfactions by getting the maximum supply of the particular kinds of ration tickets he wanted, his drive to do this, and the devices to which he resorted to do it, might also be called "automatic." But the process was not automatic in the sense that it took place without anybody's initiative or effort or ingenuity or planning. It took place precisely because each individual—or at least each individual who was energetic and enterprising—was devoting his initiative, effort, ingenuity and planning toward maximizing his own satisfactions.

And soon a fifth fascinating development occurred.

The exchange relationships had become too complicated for any blackboard or notebook or for anyone to hold in mind or calculate in their totality. Therefore the practice grew up of quoting other ration tickets in terms of only a few leading kinds of ration tickets, chiefly those for bread, potatoes, and cigarettes. In the course of further time everything came to be quoted solely in terms of cigarette coupons. The quotations on the big blackboard, which came to be known simply as the Big Board, then became comparatively easy to read. The last transactions would be recorded like this:

Beer coupons	=	¼	cigarette coupons
Bean "	=	1	" "
Bread "	=	1	" "
Cap "	=	8	" "
Chair "	=	40	" "
Potato "	=	½	" "
Shirt "	=	10	" "

And so for all other coupons.

This resulted in enormous simplification. It eliminated the necessity for all the complex cross-rates and cross-calculations of any one type of coupon in terms of another. If a shirt coupon exchanged for 10 cigarette coupons and a chair coupon for 40 cigarette coupons, then it was obvious at once that it would take four shirt coupons to exchange for one chair coupon—and so for any other two items. Thus the device of quoting every type of coupon in terms of a single type of coupon simplified the whole task of comparing the exchange value of any type of coupon in terms of any other.

Instead of speaking of the exchange ratios of these coupons, people now began to speak of the "price" of the coupons. And by the "price" of the coupons they always meant the ratio of exchange with cigarette coupons.

How did cigarette coupons come to be chosen as the kind in which all the others were quoted? This was a problem that particularly fascinated Peter. As a result of his inquiries and inferences he concluded that the situation was something like this. Practically everybody smoked cigarettes and wanted cigarettes.

But if anybody didn't smoke them himself, he nevertheless found that cigarette coupons were the easiest to exchange for other coupons. This was so for several reasons. A cigarette coupon entitled the holder to one package of cigarettes. This package did not spoil quickly like many other things. It was compact and easy to handle and carry in proportion to its value. And in case of necessity exact "change" could be made by opening the package and exchanging single cigarettes.

And as soon as people discovered that they could handle and exchange cigarettes and cigarette coupons more easily than other coupons, they were ready to accept cigarette coupons in exchange for the kind of coupons they had to offer rather than demand the particular kind of coupons that they ultimately wanted. For they found that they could make the best and quickest bargains by taking cigarette coupons *first,* and then *re-exchanging* them for what they ultimately wanted, instead of trying to make a direct exchange. A man with a chair coupon who wanted instead an extra shirt, an extra cap, and more bread, for example, no longer had to shop around until he found someone who had and was willing to part with the exact combination that he wanted—and who was also eager for a chair. He found that he could satisfy his wants more quickly, fully and exactly by exchanging his chair coupon for cigarette coupons first.

And then occurred what was to Peter still one more fascinating development. As cigarette coupons began to establish themselves as the chief medium of exchange and "standard of value," people who already had as much as they could smoke, and even nonsmokers, began to demand cigarette coupons in exchange for their own "surplus" coupons of all kinds, for the sole reason that they found it easier in this way to get the particular coupon and commodities that they ultimately wanted. And this *extra* source of demand for cigarette coupons—as a medium of exchange—increased their exchange value—which meant that the "price" of other goods in terms of cigarette coupons began to fall a bit.

But one day, after the new system of free exchange had been in effect about six months, an extraordinary and alarming thing happened.

The "price" of all the coupons on the board began to shoot up simultaneously. Most people were at first delighted by this development. People with bread coupons now found that they could get two cigarette coupons for their bread coupons instead of only one; people with shirt coupons found that they could get twenty cigarette coupons for them instead of only ten; and so on. And as many people had got into the mental habit of measuring their welfare in terms of the value of their coupon holdings in cigarette coupons, they began to feel richer and better off. They were disillusioned, however, the moment they tried to re-exchange their cigarette coupons for the coupons they ultimately wanted. They regarded the "prices" of these other coupons as exorbitant.

What had happened? Why had the price of everything suddenly gone up simultaneously?

Peter soon discovered the reason. A rumor had developed that the government did not have as many actual packages of cigarettes available as the number of cigarette coupons it had issued, and that therefore people would soon not be able to exchange their cigarette coupons for actual cigarettes. As soon as this rumor developed there was a run on the government shops and warehouses for the actual cigarettes, with everyone presenting his ration coupon at once. The rumor was true. The supply of cigarettes was not in fact equal to the supply of outstanding cigarette coupons.

"It ought to be made a crime, chief," said Adams, "for anyone to present his cigarette ration coupons or even to be caught holding actual cigarettes. The people who are now demanding cigarettes for their coupons are only undermining confidence in the government. They are precipitating a panic. Up to now cigarette coupons have always been as good as cigarettes themselves in any exchange. Most people came to want the cigarette coupons only for exchanging anyway. Why shouldn't they be as good now as they ever were? After all, the government stands behind the coupons even if the cigarettes don't; the whole wealth of Won-world stands behind the coupons. People should be forced to . . ."

But Peter took a different view. He promised that all outstanding cigarette coupons would ultimately be redeemed in actual cigarettes as the government had promised. There had been, he explained, a regrettable "inflation" in the number of coupons printed as compared with the number of cigarettes available. But this would be cured by the government's refusal hereafter to issue coupons in excess of the available packages of cigarettes.

Meanwhile he extended the freedom of the market. He now permitted anybody not only to exchange ration coupons but to exchange the actual commodities themselves after they had got them from the government. He felt like kicking himself for not having done this sooner.

A striking development followed. A dual market sprang into existence—one in the coupons, as before, and another in the actual commodities. Usually the quotations for the commodities were close to, or identical with, the quotations on the coupons for them. But whenever any coupon got too close to its expiration date, or any suspicion arose that there might be fewer commodities available than the amount of ration tickets outstanding against them, or that a particular kind of ration ticket might not be honored for some reason or other, the price of the coupons fell in relation to the price of the commodity that they represented.

The most striking development of all was the gap that developed between the quotation for cigarette coupons and the quotation for the cigarettes themselves. The coupons now exchanged at only about half the value of the actual cigarettes.

This expressed itself in an odd way. A dual set of "prices" appeared on the Big Board—one stated in terms of cigarette coupons, and the other stated in terms of actual cigarettes. And the prices in terms of cigarette coupons were about twice as high as those in terms of cigarettes.

"This is a very bad thing, chief, for the government's prestige," said Adams. "People are permitted through the market publicly

196

to express their distrust of the government's promises. Through the whole price system, and through direct quotation of cigarette coupons in terms of cigarettes, there is a discount of 50 per cent on the cigarette coupons. You are in effect permitting people to say without fear of punishment that this is the extent to which they distrust your promise."

But Peter refused to take repressive measures. "It is a good thing to know," he said, "the real extent of public confidence in the government. In that way we can tell what measures destroy confidence and what measures restore it. In fact, it is wonderfully helpful to us to have the exact quantitative measure of fluctuations in confidence that this open market provides. If we suppress the freedom of the market we suppress the very information we need for our own guidance."

And he set about to restore confidence in the cigarette coupons.

He ordered an increase in cigarette output. He extended the period for which the outstanding cigarette coupons were valid. He announced a reduction in the volume of cigarette coupons that would be issued in the next period so that these would not exceed the available supply of cigarettes.

And he had the satisfaction of seeing an immediate rise in the quotations of the cigarette coupons to a discount of only 20 per cent. Within a few months, as people saw that his promises were being kept, the discount on the coupons disappeared altogether.

He had ordered the record of daily market quotations of coupons and commodities published in the *New Truth*. On the day after the cigarette coupons reached "parity," he circled the quotation in red pencil and silently handed a copy of the newspaper to Adams.

He could not resist a feeling of triumph.

Chapter 26

ELIENA BOLSHEKOV is here, Your Highness."
"Show her in, Sergei."
She had called for the appointment a few days before. What could she want of him? Peter had never met her to speak to, and his mind went back to his first night in Moscow when he had seen her at the opera. Her black hair and lovely legs were still vivid in his memory.

He was not disappointed. She was as striking off the stage as on. Her black Protector's uniform was very trim; the trousers fitted just snugly enough to bring out the shapeliness of her hips and thighs. Her dark eyes were inviting.

"It's so good of you to see me," she began. "I've always been a tremendous admirer of yours, Your Highness—of your statesmanship and courage—but I didn't realize till now how young and handsome you are!"

Peter blushed. He had been a great admirer of *hers*, he said.

"I've come to ask you," she continued, "if we could possibly get you to act as a patron—the chief patron, of course—of our new pageant on The Growth of Civilization. It will depict the whole history of feudalism, capitalism, the class struggle, the final triumph of communism—"

"I'd be delighted," said Peter. "You could have put my name down as a matter of course, or just telephoned me—"

"But I wanted to *see* you, and I wanted to enlist your active interest. I *do* wish you could see what we are planning. Wouldn't you like to see the sketches for the costumes and floats? I would *so* much appreciate your suggestions and ideas."

"I really know nothing about these matters," Peter said. "But of course if you would really like me to—"

"That is wonderful of you, Your Highness. The sketches are at my apartment. There are too many of them to carry around. Do you think you could come up some night and look at them?"

"Well, if you wish."

"Oh, that's *really* wonderful. How about tomorrow night? Or how about tonight? That's terribly short notice, I know, particularly for a man as busy and important as you are. But I'm *so* eager to get started."

Peter made a pretense of consulting his desk calendar. He already knew that he had no engagement. It was Leninsday, and Leninsday evening was now almost invariably kept clear for his piano practice. But he wanted to give himself time to decide. He was tempted; but he realized that the very reasons that tempted him were the reasons why he should not go. She was a lure. She had certainly been asked to do this by her father.

"I'm terribly sorry," he said finally (and as he really was, he sounded sincere). "I'm terribly sorry but I have a meeting with the Central Planning Board tonight—"

"Tomorrow, then?"

"I'm jammed up for the rest of the week." He disconsolately thumbed the calendar pages.

"Next week?"

He turned the pages. "Sunday . . . Monday . . . Marxday . . . Leninsday . . . Prolesday . . . Engelsday . . . Stalinsday . . . every one of them crowded. I tell you . . . I'll try to break one of these engagements and let you know."

She concealed her disappointment. "Oh, that's so nice of you. Here is my address." She wrote it on a card. "I'm afraid it's not at all in the best neighborhood. It's a little hideaway that I have all to myself—even father doesn't know about it. But I simply must have a little place alone where I can work."

199

Peter said he understood.

"I have a tiny favor to ask you," she went on. "I don't want too many people to know where my private apartment is. . . . And then besides, if people knew you called, there would be all sorts of gossip linking our names. . . . *You* know how people are. So, would you mind *terribly* parking your car a couple of blocks away somewhere . . . and walking the rest? When you can come, I won't be asking anyone else."

Peter was now sure that the whole thing was a trap. He felt a little sad about it, promised that she would hear from him in a few days, and gave a last glance at her hips as she left the room.

The free exchange of ration tickets, and the free market for consumers' goods, had constituted, even before the return of the cigarette coupons to parity, a great personal triumph for Peter Uldanov. The army was still almost solidly behind Bolshekov, but civilian opinion was now mainly behind Peter. The people had had their first breath of freedom.

Practically everyone was now happier. A man could now get commodities, to the extent that they were available, at the times and in the proportions that he himself wanted them, rather than in the procrustean ratios in which they were originally doled out by the planning commissars.

And many people seemed to value the new *freedom* to exchange as much as the exchanges themselves. With the same overall production more wants were satisfied. Peter began to sense that this was equivalent to a great increase in production itself. For "production," as he began to see more clearly than he had before, was not something to be measured by tonnages or volume, but only by the satisfaction of human wants. A thousand tons of something a man couldn't use was not worth an ounce of something on which his life might depend. A factory "producing" the wrong things could hardly be said to be producing at all.

Peter took care to exploit the political value of this, his first real success. It went against his temperament, but he had decided that not merely his ability to stay in power, but his very life now depended in large part on showmanship. So he conferred more medals on himself, ostensibly in the name of Stalenin; held more air circuses; had himself amply photographed so that his face and figure would become familiar; gave dinners to the high Air Force officers; ordered long editorials written about the benefits that his free exchange system had introduced into Wonworld. Privately he still felt half-ashamed. But as he looked forward to the coming showdown between himself and Bolshekov, between his world ideal and Bolshekov's kind of world, he became a little less fastidious concerning his choice of means.

The free market continued to fascinate him. He learned new lessons from it every day. It had now ceased to quote anything in terms of cigarette coupons; everything was quoted in terms of actual cigarettes. The "price" of anything now meant its price in terms of packages of cigarettes. These became known, in turn, simply as "packs." Thus when somebody asked "40 packs" for a chair coupon, nobody needed to ask "packs *of what?*" On the Big Board the quotation would be merely "40." As there were twenty cigarettes in a package, when people wanted to make a more exact price they would specify, say, 40 packs and 8 cigarettes, or "40 and 8." The Big Board would simply report this as 40/8.

Peter studied the relation of the Moscow market to the market in other cities and places. These markets were local, both because ration tickets were good for presentation only within a given district, and because people were still forbidden, without passports and specified reasons, to cross the boundary lines of these districts. He found that though there was practically an exact correspondence between prices in the different markets within Moscow, this did not apply to a market in a different district. In such an outside market, permanent differences seemed to exist in the relationship of one price to another, as compared with the relationships in the Moscow markets.

Adams also reluctantly learned lessons from the free market.

"Take this, for instance," he said to Peter. "You would think that once people had decided what a fair price was, they would stick to it. In yesterday's market, shirts were selling at 9 and 5; this morning they were 9 and 7; and this afternoon they're 10 packs flat. Why these ceaseless ups and downs? Why can't people make up their minds? If 10 packs is a fair price for a shirt, it ought to be that always."

"Well, Adams, I suppose people's ideas change of what their wants are. Or maybe new and different people enter the market. A man who has been holding a shirt coupon with every intention of turning it in for a shirt, suddenly decides that he would like more cigarettes instead, either for their own sake or to buy something else. So when he comes to the market the supply of shirts offered is that much bigger. This means that shirts are less scarce and therefore less valuable. At the same time there is a still further demand for cigarettes, which means that people who have cigarettes can get more for them."

"I don't quite understand what you mean by these phrases, chief. I notice that you have been using the words 'supply' and 'demand' lately in senses I don't believe I ever heard before. Take this word 'supply.' It means simply the existing stock of anything, doesn't it?"

"Well, no . . . not exactly. In the sense in which I think of it, it means just that part of the existing supply that people are eager or willing to sell at a specified price."

"And 'demand'?"

"And in the same way, Adams, the 'demand' for anything is not simply the amount of it that people desire, which might be almost unlimited, but the amount that they are willing to take at a particular price."

"Then both 'supply' and 'demand,' chief, seem to me rather complicated concepts. Does each mean the goods that people are willing to exchange *at certain given ratios* for other goods?"

"Precisely," said Peter. "There's no use talking about my 'demand' for a shirt unless you find out how many packages of cigarettes I'm willing to give up in exchange for one. And if you're trying to get cigarettes from me, there's no use talking about my available 'supply' of them except in terms of the things for which—and the ratios at which—I am willing to surrender them."

"Whew!" said Adams. "Then one man's 'supply' is another man's 'demand,' and vice versa? My 'supply' means what I've got to offer, and my 'demand' means what I want in exchange for it, while *your* 'supply' means what *you've* got, which may be what I demand, and *your* 'demand' may be—"

"Right."

"Well then, does the word 'supply' refer as you use it, chief, to an actual physical quantity of something, or does it refer only to something that is determined by the different scales of valuation of different people?"

"Well, we needn't get into all these subtleties just now," said Peter, who was not quite sure what his answer to this should be. "The point I started to make in reply to your original question is really a simple one. You asked why prices change all the time. My answer is that these prices depend on the relations of supply and demand, and supply and demand are volatile things, constantly in flux."

"It seems to me that you have been shifting your ground a little, chief. It wasn't so long ago that I was quoting Marx to you, and his theory that the value of commodities depended on the relative working time embodied in them. And we both finally agreed that though the relative amount of working time had something to do with the answer, it was at best grossly over-simplified—because you had to consider the enormous difference in the skills of different workers, and the enormous contribution of land and machinery to the value of the total product. But now you are shifting the base entirely. Now you tell me that the value of different commodities has nothing to do with all the labor and sacrifice embodied in them but is determined simply by the relation of supply and demand."

"That is right," said Peter; "and that is the very problem that is now troubling me. I have a hunch that if we could reconcile those two conclusions we would be on the track of something really big."

"I confess I haven't the slightest idea of what you're talking about."

"Adams, try to be a little patient with me for a moment. The worst part of it is not only that I haven't the answer to the problem, but that I'm not even sure I can formulate the problem itself. I suspect that once we could make the *problem* clear, we would be halfway on the road to its solution. Let's try. . . .

"We have now established, in consumers' commodities," he went on, "what I have called a free market. Now as a result of that, as a result of allowing everybody to express his wishes freely—by allowing people to exchange whatever they have for whatever they want at ratios that are mutually agreeable to them —we have established certain freely arrived at market ratios, rates or prices. We have found, for example, that a shirt exchanges for approximately 10 packages of cigarettes and a chair for approximately 40, which means that directly or indirectly a chair exchanges for about 4 shirts. . . . Now then, perhaps we are on the verge of formulating the problem that is troubling me. The fact that a chair exchanges for 4 shirts means that people considered collectively value a chair at four times as much as a shirt. Why?"

"Because it's harder to get chairs than shirts, chief."

"Correct," agreed Peter. "Because chairs are scarcer than shirts. But why are they scarcer?"

"Because that's the way the Central Planning Board planned it," said Adams.

"Yes and no," replied Peter. "The Central Planning Board did in fact schedule the production of fewer chairs than shirts. But it didn't say, 'We shall create a greater scarcity of chairs than shirts in order to make chairs four times as valuable as shirts.'"

"It scheduled fewer chairs than shirts, chief, because people *need* fewer chairs than shirts. Shirts wear out, get dirty, and have to be changed sooner and more often than chairs. Hence fewer chairs are made than shirts and hence chairs are scarcer than shirts."

For answer Peter picked up a glass ash tray on his desk. "How many shirts do these things change for?"

Adams looked up the market table. "They sell for one pack."

"That means that they sell for a tenth of a shirt," said Peter. "Yet they don't wear out and don't have to be changed. How many do we produce of them?"

Adams telephoned the Central Planning Board. He learned that all the ash trays came from a single factory, and that fewer of them were turned out each year than chairs.

"So you see?" said Peter.

"Yes, chief, but these things take very little labor to produce—"

"So we are back to our problem," said Peter. "But we get at least to this conclusion. Things are not valued merely in relation to their scarcity. They are valued in relation to how much they are *wanted* in relation to their scarcity."

Adams held his head in mock despair of taking in an idea so complex.

"So this leads us closer to the heart of the problem, Adams. And the problem is this: Are we making things in such relation to the wants of the people as to satisfy those wants to the maximum extent possible with the land, labor and machinery at our disposal? In other words, are we creating the maximum value in relation to our existing means of production?"

Adams stared at the ceiling. He seemed to be trying to take in the problem.

"Let me put it this way," continued Peter, trying to help not only Adams but himself. "Are we wasting, are we misapplying, are we misdirecting, labor, land or machinery in making some things or in making certain quantities of those things, when we might be using the labor, land and machinery better in making other things, or greater quantities of other things, that would meet more wants?"

"I'm just beginning to see the problem," confessed Adams.

"But I would have to see the problem itself in a much sharper focus before I would have any notion of the answer."

"Well, let's see whether we can't get it into a sharper focus," said Peter. "Marx assumed that the only thing required to produce commodities was labor-time—or at least that everything required to produce commodities could be resolved into simple-labor-time or stated in terms of simple-labor-time—"

"And we have decided that that was a gross oversimplification," said Adams.

"Precisely," agreed Peter. "But we also decided that the comparative labor-time involved in producing different commodities had at least *something* to do with their relative scarcity and hence with their relative value. We decided that labor-time was at least *one* of the factors that determined this relative scarcity. Now precisely *because* Marx's answer was a gross oversimplification, it may help us with our present problem: we often have to simplify problems even to find out what they are. All right, then. Let's assume for the sake of simplification that Marx was right in contending that all the sacrifices made in producing goods could be reduced to 'simple average labor time.' Very well. We find out that, in a free exchange market, people value a chair at four times as much as a shirt. Now if it took just four times as many labor-hours to produce a chair as a shirt, then we would be making equal sacrifices to produce equal satisfactions, equal values, and we would not be misdirecting or wasting labor. But if, on the contrary, it should turn out that it took the *same* number of labor-hours to produce a shirt that it did to produce a chair, then we would be obviously wasting hours of labor-time in producing shirts, for those labor hours would be producing far more value—in fact, four times as much value—if they were used in producing chairs instead."

"But we have to have shirts," protested Adams.

"So we do," agreed Peter; "but the real question is, *how many* shirts is it economical to produce compared with *how many* chairs? For if it took the same number of labor hours to produce a shirt as a chair, then we ought to continue to take labor away from making shirts and put it into making chairs, until chairs become relatively so plentiful, and shirts relatively so scarce, that they exchange in the market at exactly the same price—that is, at a ratio of 1 : 1."

"But suppose it actually does take four times as many labor-hours, chief, to produce a chair as a shirt?"

"Then labor is not being wasted," agreed Peter. "But if it took only four times as many labor-hours to produce a chair as a shirt, and 6 shirts instead of 4 should begin to exchange in the market for a chair, it would mean that we were then wasting labor in producing shirts instead of chairs."

"I see the problem more clearly," said Adams; "but I am troubled by something. We had already agreed that Marx was grossly oversimplifying when he contended that 'simple average labor time' is the only thing that produces commodities or values."

"Right," agreed Peter. "And therefore our answer must be modified. But suppose we take 'simple average labor time' *symbolically,* to stand for *all* the costs and sacrifices that have gone into production, then it will help to give us the ans—"

He paused, struck by a new approach. "I think we are now in a position to state the problem clearly, Adams. Let me try. On the market we find hundreds of different kinds of consumption goods exchanging at various ratios with each other. At any given moment the ratio of exchange between one kind of goods and another is the same for everybody in the same market. If that market ratio changes, it changes for everybody. These ratios therefore measure the relative values that the consumers, *considered collectively,* put on these goods."

"And these 'collective' valuations, chief, are, so to speak, the net resultant of individual valuations?"

"Right. Perhaps, also, the collective valuations in turn influence the individual valuations, so that there is a sort of reciprocal determination. . . . But we don't need to go into all these complications now. The point is, that if we are not to waste or misdirect labor, land and machinery, we must fulfill several requirements. In the first place, taking any one commodity in isolation, the sacrifices we put into producing it must at least be more than offset by the satisfactions it yields—otherwise at least a part of those sacrifices have been unnecessary; they have been wasted."

"In other words," said Adams, "the value of every commodity we make should be greater than the cost of producing it?"

"Exactly," said Peter; "provided we agree on just what we mean by 'cost.' At bottom, costs are subjective. Costs are equal to the value we attach to the satisfactions we have to forego in order to attain the satisfactions we are creating. The cost of production of commodity X, for example, is equal to the value of the product or products that we can't produce because the labor, time, land, raw materials and so on necessary for their production are used up in producing X."

Adams seemed to need time to take this in.

Peter continued: "Or we could put the matter in still another way: For every product the value of the *output* should be greater than the value of the *input*—otherwise we are wasting resources."

He lit a cigarette, to give himself time to collect his thoughts.

"The next requirement we must fulfill, Adams, is a little harder to state. The respective costs of production of the hundreds of different commodities should bear exactly the same relationship to each other as the respective prices of these commodities bear to each other in the market. Wherever there is a discrepancy of any kind in these relationships it is a sign that productive resources have been wasted, that some factors of production have been misdirected."

"In other words, chief, such a discrepancy means that less labor, land, machinery and raw materials should have been devoted to producing, say, commodity A and more to producing commodity B?"

"Exactly," said Peter. "And now, I think, we are really closing in on the problem. Not only must the total value of our output exceed the total value of our input, but the value of the output of each product must exceed the value of the resources devoted to producing it. And the solution would not be perfect unless

208

for each product the value of the output exceeded the value of the input by the same percentage as for every other product—otherwise we would know that we were producing too much of products A, B, and C and too little of D, E, and F, etc., and that we were wasting productive resources.

"And therefore the problem we face, Adams, may be stated this way. The ideal productive system would be one that produced the maximum overall satisfactions with the minimum overall sacrifices or cost. The hundreds of different consumption goods must be produced in the relative proportions and by the methods that secure this result. Otherwise we are wasting our sacrifices and our resources or failing to obtain the maximum welfare from them."

Adams thoughtfully stroked his nose. "And we didn't even *see* this problem, chief, we didn't even know it existed, we certainly didn't know how to formulate it, until we had developed a market in consumption goods. . . . The problem seemed simple enough when you and I, as the economic dictators, decided what kinds and ratios of goods and services people ought to have. But the minute we gave them the opportunity to put their *own* relative valuations on these goods, the result began to open our eyes."

"And now," resumed Peter, "we can see still another problem that would never have occurred to us before we permitted freedom of exchange. The problem is not merely how to decide *what* things to produce, and in what proportions to produce them, but how to decide what is *the most economical method* of producing each of them. In what proportion, for example, ought we to use labor and machinery for producing shirts? Which would be more economical—hand sewing or machine sewing?"

"Obviously machine sewing, chief, is more efficient."

"It isn't really more efficient, Adams, unless it is also more economical. And when we start to figure on *that,* we have to figure first on the cost and time required to make the machines to do the sewing. And if we have to make the machines before we can start the sewing, then the process of production is obviously more round-about than if we start sewing by hand right away."

Adams held his head again with his hands. "I don't find it easy to deal with these abstractions, chief. My brain is beginning to sag. Do you mind if we put off the solution of this problem for another day?"

"Not at all," said Peter. "We have at least got to the statement of the problem, and as we started out by saying, that is probably half the battle."

Adams left.

Peter's brain, too, was tired. He buried his face in his hands. Whenever he found himself alone like this, with no problem of his office absorbing his attention, his thoughts returned to Edith. Where could she be? Was she even still alive? What had he left undone to find her? . . .

He heard the timid knock of the waitress on the door.

"Come in!"

He sat up.

She entered with the supper tray, spread the napkin on his desk, set the tray softly on it, and went out again with noiseless steps. He hadn't much appetite, but slowly and dutifully ate what was put before him.

Shortly after he was finished, she knocked and came in again.

"I've brought your dessert separately tonight, Your Highness. It's ice cream. I didn't want it to melt before you got it, so I had it kept in the refrig—"

"Ordinarily it would look very tempting, comrade. But I just can't eat anything more tonight."

"It seems a shame to waste it, Your Highness."

"No. Maybe somebody else will like it."

She put the dish of ice cream on the tray, took the tray out and silently closed the door behind her.

A few minutes later he heard a scream.

He flung open the door. It led into a corridor which in turn opened on the kitchen from which his meals were served. Toward the rear of the corridor was a small serving table against the wall. His tray was on this. On the floor by the table the waitress was writhing in agony.

"The ice cream," she groaned. "It was poisoned. Oh, a doctor . . . please . . ."

When the doctor arrived the woman was dead.

Peter noticed again her thin hands and pinched face.

Chapter 27

HE learned that the waitress and the cook had been taking turns in supplementing their meager rations by eating the leftovers from his meals. That night had been the cook's turn, but the waitress had been tempted by hunger and the untouched ice cream.

When Peter reported the incident the following morning, Adams seemed cold-blooded.

"Remember the day Bolshekov's men tried to machine-gun me? I told you your turn would come next. Well, it came. We have both had miraculous escapes. It would be too much for either of us to expect to repeat the miracle."

"What can we do about it?"

"The first thing you must do, chief, is to change the cook and everyone who had access or could have had access to the kitchen. Everybody should be thoroughly screened by Stalenin's guard. You have been amazingly careless. Stalenin used to have a special food taster at his desk."

"Yes; he still has him at his bedside for meals."

"I keep a dog," Adams continued, "that nobody but myself is allowed to feed. He gets a little taste of everything before I try it."

"How long have you been doing that?"

"As far back as I can remember. Practically every member of the Politburo has to take similar precautions. I'll send a dog over to you, if you want. It's better to have an ugly one, so you don't get too fond of him."

So this, thought Peter, is the life that everyone else in Wonworld envies.

"Of course, the only real remedy, as I advised you long ago, chief, was to throw Bolshekov out; but he has since made his position so solid with the army that you couldn't remove him now without unleashing a civil war. . . . A war which, I think frankly, you and I would lose."

"Then what can I do now?"

"Your only choice is to do to him what he has been trying to do to you. You had better beat him to it!"

"Have him assassinated?"

Adams nodded.

Peter shook his head. "I've told you time and time again, Adams, that I just can't resort to such methods. I don't believe in them. Means determine ends. We are trying to make a better society. A society founded on violence, bloodshed, trickery and murder would be certain to be loathsome. It would not be worth creating. It would not be worth living in."

"Well, if you don't follow my advice, chief, you won't be living long in *this* society, I assure you."

Peter was beginning to find the subject too uncomfortable.

"Let's go back to where we left off yesterday, Adams." There was just a touch of command in his tone. "How are we going to solve the problem of economic calculation? How are we going to determine just what commodities to produce, just how much to produce of each of the hundreds of different commodities, and just what means and methods of production are in each case the most economical?"

Adams looked at Peter incredulously, then seemed resignedly to decide to go along with him.

"Isn't there any way of solving the problem directly, chief? Just by deciding, for example, what things are probably most needed, and how many men, how many machines of different

213

kinds ought to be used in producing each of them—just as we *have* been doing?"

"We have already decided, Adams, that we are working completely in the dark. You simply can't add things that are unlike each other. Or subtract, or multiply, or divide them, or even, in any meaningful quantitative way, compare them. You can't add pigs to pears, or subtract houses from horses, or multiply tractors by toothbrushes."

"I'll try again, chief. How about comparing things in relation to the average labor-time necessary to make each of them?"

"We've already been over all that ground, too," said Peter. "We found that the labor-time of an expert or a genius is incomparably more important than that of a bungler. We found that all sorts of other things besides labor go into producing goods —such as raw materials, machinery and land. And we found, finally, that unless we have some common unit—and that common unit is *not* labor-time!—we can't measure the relative amounts of raw materials, machinery and land that go into producing different commodities."

"Then why not just find out by *trial and error*, chief, whether or not we're making the right things in the right proportions and by the most economical methods? Trial and error! That's the human method of learning. That's the method of science."

" 'Trial and error' doesn't mean anything, Adams, unless you have some definite way of recognizing and measuring the extent of the error. Otherwise you don't know what to correct for in your next trial. If I'm shooting at a target, and my shot falls approximately a foot below the bull's eye, I try to raise my next shot by a foot; if my shots are going too far to the left, I aim more to the right. If a chef broils a steak and finds it overdone, he leaves the next steak over the fire a shorter time. And so on. But what standard have you got for error in the problem we are trying to solve? How do you *know* that the production of some particular item is costing more than it is worth? How do you *know* whether or not you are adopting the most economical method of making that item or any other item?"

Adams was silent for a while. He thoughtfully took a few pinches of snuff. Peter resorted to a cigarette, and blew the smoke toward the ceiling.

"I have it! Adams, I have it!" he said suddenly. "I don't know why we didn't think of it before. You're right. Trial and error! We can use the method of trial and error—and *combine* it with a price system!"

"Now *that* sounds interesting, chief. Just how would you do that?"

"Well, let's think it out. We allowed people first to exchange their ration coupons and then to exchange their consumption goods. And as a result a market was established. Certain exchange ratios, certain relative market values, established themselves. And now we know, for example, that people considered collectively value a chair by four times as much as a shirt, and so on. So we now know how much consumption goods are worth. But we still don't know how much it costs us to make them. But suppose we knew how much *production* goods were worth? Suppose we knew the *exchange* value, the *market* value, of each piece of land, of each tool or machine, of each hour of every man's labor-time? *Then* we would be able to calculate costs! *Then* we would be able to know, for each particular commodity, whether or not the value of the finished product exceeded the value of the costs that went into it—whether or not the value of a given *output* exceeded the value of a given *input.*"

"You've got hold of something there!" said Adams, almost eagerly. Then his countenance slowly fell. "But I don't see how we can work it out!"

"Establish a market in production goods!" exclaimed Peter. "How?"

"At present, Adams, the Central Planning Board decides how much shall be produced of hundreds of different commodities. It allots production quotas to each industry. The heads of these industries in turn allot production quotas to the individual factories. Then, on this basis, so much raw material is allotted to each industry and each factory and so many workers are allotted

215

to each industry and each factory. And so on. Now, let's change this. Let each industry *bid* for raw materials and *bid* for labor, as people do in the consumption goods market, and let these raw materials and this labor go to the highest bidder!"

"At what prices, chief? At what wage rates?"

"Why, at the highest prices and the highest wage rates that are bid!"

"In what would these prices and wages be payable?"

"Why . . . in cigarette packages, I presume."

Adams looked dubious. "Have we got that many cigarette packages?"

"We wouldn't have to exchange *actual* cigarette packages," suggested Peter. "We could just cancel debts and credits against each other. In other words, cigarette packages would not be so much a—medium of exchange as just a—a standard of value. They would enable us to keep accounts, by supplying a common unit of measurement."

Adams still looked dubious. "You say that raw materials and labor would go to the industry managers who bid the highest prices or wage rates. What would prevent prices and wage rates from soaring to the skies?"

"Why, Adams, if a manager bid too high for raw materials or for labor, then his production costs would exceed the value of his product; his input would exceed his output."

"So?"

"So—he would be removed for incompetence."

"And suppose the manager bid too low?"

"Then he would not get either labor or raw materials."

"And the product assigned to him would never be produced?"

Peter was stumped. "I suppose," he conceded, "we would have to remove him also for incompetence."

"It might be even more effective, chief, to have him shot."

"At that rate our managers would have to be awfully good guessers, Adams!"

"The survival of the fittest, chief."

"Or the luckiest!"

They were both silent again.

"No," admitted Peter after the pause, "I'm afraid my analogy was a false one. We can have markets in consumption goods because these goods *belong* to the people who are exchanging them. Therefore a man will only exchange a given quantity of, say, beets, that he does not value so much, for a given quantity of, say, apricots, if he himself really values that acquired quantity of apricots more than that surrendered quantity of beets—and also if he doesn't think he can get any more than that for his beets. Now it isn't hard for a man to tell whether he himself likes apricots better than beets, or any commodity A better than commodity B. But for a man, a manager, to bid for something he won't really own by offering something else that he doesn't really own . . ."

"I think, chief," put in Adams, "that you're too ready to abandon your own idea. I'm beginning to think it's very promising. Now when your managers bid against each other—"

"By the way, Adams, it just occurred to me: What would these managers have to bid with? What would they have to offer in exchange for the raw materials and labor they wanted?"

He seemed unaware that he was now taunting Adams with the same question that Adams had stopped him with a little while back.

"Well, they will just . . . name figures," suggested Adams vaguely. "Or," he added suddenly, "maybe the Central Planning Board could *allocate* a certain hypothetical number of packages of cigarettes to each industry and each factory manager to use for bidding purposes."

"Then each manager's bids, Adams, would be limited by the amount of cigarettes the CPB allotted to him?"

Adams nodded.

"Then why not save needless complication," suggested Peter, "by having the board continue to allot the raw materials and labor *directly,* as it does now? After all, it would only be doing the same thing *indirectly* by allotting the cigarettes to the managers to pay for the raw materials and labor."

217

"There's a difference, chief. The cigarette allotment system would leave more room for managerial discretion. True, the managers would still be limited in the total resources they could apply to the output of the particular product assigned to them. But at least *they,* instead of the CPB, would decide the *proportions* in which they would use raw materials and machinery and labor, or one raw material instead of another, et cetera."

"Your system, Adams—it's *your* system, now that I've seen the flaws—your system wouldn't work. The labor and raw materials would simply go to the most irresponsible and reckless managers, and the prices would be determined by the most irresponsible and reckless managers."

"But, chief, we have already suggested removal or liquidation of the managers whose costs exceed the value of their output!"

"You are not suggesting any incentives for any manager to do the right thing, Adams, but only the most extreme penalties if he does the wrong thing. And under your system very few managers could help doing the wrong thing. Those who bid too high for their materials or labor would be removed or shot because their input exceeded their output; but those who bid too little for materials or labor would be removed or shot because they would not get enough material or labor to fill their production quotas."

"We could *grade* the punishment, chief. We could shoot the manager for a big mistake but merely remove him for a little one."

"All right," said Peter sarcastically. "So if the value of a manager's input exceeded that of his output by only 1 or 2 per cent, we would simply remove him; but if his input value exceeded his output value by 100 per cent, we would shoot him. Now, at just what percentage of excess of costs over product would you place the dividing line between removal and liquidation?"

"Maybe we could have graduated jail sentences."

"You certainly think of the most amazing ways, Adams, of attracting managerial talent. I suppose you think all the finest young workers will be eager to draw attention to themselves as

218

possible managers—provided, of course, they have sufficiently strong suicidal tendencies."

Adams took a couple of pinches of snuff and paced up and down. "Suppose we abandon that whole approach. . . . Suppose we let the Central Planning Board set the prices?"

"How would they set them?"

"They would just guess at what the prices ought to be."

"At what hundreds of different prices ought to be?"

Adams nodded.

"And how would they know, Adams, whether their guesses were right or wrong?"

"Well," said Adams slowly, apparently trying to think the thing out as he paced and talked, "if the prices were right, then the results would show that the value of the output of each commodity exceeded the costs that went into producing that commodity. There would be a balance between the supply of and the demand for each commodity at those prices. But if the price set by the Central Planning Board for any raw material or machine or worker were wrong . . . then the result would show either that the value of the input exceeded the value of the output, or, on the other hand, that the value of the output exceeded the value of the input *by too much!*"

"But how would you know what was wrong, Adams? How would you know where the mistake had occurred—if there really was a mistake? Suppose, for example, that the value of a particular output exceeded the value of a particular input 'by too much.' How would you know what had caused that?"

"We would know, chief, that one or more of the factors of production was underpriced."

"And how would you know, Adams, which factor it was—whether the labor, the raw materials, the machinery, or the land? Or *which* raw material? Or *which* group of workers. Or if *several* factors were underpriced, how would you know which ones and by how much?"

Adams did not answer.

"And how would you know that the trouble *was* underpricing

of the factors of production?" pursued Peter. "Might it not be just because that manager was particularly efficient, or because a particularly efficient method of production was being followed? Or merely because that commodity, relatively speaking, was being *underproduced?* And conversely, suppose that the cost of the input exceeded the value of the output? You would have the same problems in reverse. How would you know whether that result was caused by the overpricing of the factors of production, or of some particular factor, and which, and by how much—or whether the whole thing wasn't caused by a particularly inefficient method of production or an inefficient manager?"

Again Adams was silent for a time.

"You know," he said at length, "I've just thought of something. There's a very clever Italian fellow in the Central Planning Board with whom I've been discussing planning problems. He's a brilliant mathematician. He's tremendously enthusiastic about the markets you established in consumption goods—fascinated by them. And now that I remember it, he came forward independently a few weeks ago and actually suggested setting up a system of pricing for production goods and factors of production. He claims he can work it all out by mathematics."

"Why didn't you tell me about him before?"

"To tell you the truth, chief, I hadn't the slightest idea what he was driving at, at the time. I couldn't understand his mathematics and didn't want to admit it. And anyway, I just put him down as a sort of screwball."

"And now?"

"Now, I'm just beginning to think that maybe I was wrong. . . . Not until this conversation now did I have any idea of what he may have been driving at."

"What's his name?"

"Baronio."

"Let's talk with him by all means."

Peter glanced at his wrist watch. "I'm due to be at dinner with my father in fifteen minutes. Why not bring Baronio with you tomorrow?"

When Adams left, Sergei came in. "One of the new guards we had taken on to protect His Supremacy, Your Highness, turned out to be an agent of Bolshekov's. He had undoubtedly been sent here to assassinate His Supremacy."

"Where is he?"

"When our guards started to arrest him, he tried to shoot them but got shot himself. It happened in the barracks rooms just across the street. I don't think it wise for us to publish anything about the incident—if Your Highness agrees."

"Does His Supremacy know?"

"I thought Your Highness might not want to upset him with such knowledge."

"Very good, Sergei."

I have been given a weight of responsibility, thought Peter once more, that is just too big.

He was awake most of the night.

Chapter 28

I'M afraid I can't explain my ideas in ordinary language, Your Highness," said Baronio, "but only in mathematical symbols. So I brought along this paper."

He was a small, eager-looking Italian.

Peter took the paper. At least half of it seemed to consist of mathematical equations, with sparse explanatory matter in between. It involved a great deal of algebra and calculus. Peter riffled through the more than fifty pages. His eye picked out a passage at random:

> It may be asked if it is not possible for the Central Planning Board, in exercising the power to vary the individual γ's, subject only to the condition of $\Sigma\gamma = 1$, to arrive at a series of γ's, with the equivalents and the technical coefficients such that not only $\Sigma\Delta\theta$ is zero but also the single $\Delta\theta$'s are zero . . .
>
> In fact, the individual γ's must be a function of the λ's and satisfy the condition that the variation of a λ involves a variation of the γ which makes the former equal zero. The function γ must therefore satisfy the conditions

$$-r_b + X\frac{\partial\gamma}{\partial\lambda_b} = 0 \ldots, \quad q_m - r_m + X\frac{\partial\gamma}{\partial\lambda_m} = 0 \ldots, \quad \gamma Q_s - r_s + X\frac{\partial\gamma}{\partial\lambda_s} = 0$$

Peter realized that he had allowed his mathematics to become a trifle rusty. He decided to start from the beginning. He read for a couple of pages and stopped when he came to this:

6. Let us represent among the data the quantities of the different kinds of capital . . .

"What do you mean by 'capital'?" he asked.

"I am using the word in what I think is the same sense as Karl Marx used it, Your Highness. By capital I mean capital goods of all kinds—including cigarette packages because they are the medium of exchange—"

"What do you mean by 'capital goods'?"

"By capital goods, Your Highness, I mean all the produced means of production."

Peter looked at him quizzically.

"By the phrase 'the produced means of production,' Your Highness, I mean to exclude labor and land, though I include the value of the improvements made on land, and I mean to include all capital goods—that is, all the goods that are used for further production. I mean the tools of production put in the hands of the workers. I mean the machines put at the disposal of the workers, and the factories that house the machines, and the raw materials that go into the finished products, and the railroads that transport the raw materials, say, from the mines to the smelters, from the smelters to the finishing mills, from the finishing mills to the factories, from the factories to the stores. And by the railroads I mean the value of the railroad beds, and of the locomotives and freight cars and depots. And I also include the capital goods and motor trucks that deliver goods, and the roads over which the trucks travel—"

"You mean the same thing by 'capital' as you do by 'capital goods'?"

"Well, yes—practically, Your Highness."

"Don't you think the use of such an abstraction as 'capital' for concrete things like capital goods might prove confusing and misleading?"

"Not if it is used carefully, Your Highness. It's a sort of shorthand. Just as we use the abstract word 'labor' to mean all the workers, or the services of all the workers."

223

"The workers are not the same as the services of the workers?"

"No, Your Highness."

"The services of the workers are a commodity, but the workers themselves are not?"

"That distinction is correct, Your Highness."

"So the same word—'labor'—to cover both, is ambiguous, and might lead to confusions?"

"Yes, Your Highness."

"So perhaps we'd better be equally careful, Comrade Baronio, in using the abstraction 'capital.' Now I like your phrase 'capital goods,' but I have difficulties with it. Take railroads. Take a locomotive pulling a passenger car. If the passenger car contains His Highness No. 3—Adams here—who is going, say, from Moscow to Stalingrad to inspect factories in his capacity as head of the Central Planning Board—then the locomotive and the car are capital goods, that is, goods used to promote production. But if the same locomotive and passenger car are pulling No. 3 to some resort on the Black Sea where he is merely going for a vacation, then they are not capital goods but consumption goods?"

"I suppose that would be strictly correct, Your Highness."

"And if the rooms in a certain house are used as business offices for commissars, that house is a capital good, but if those rooms are used simply for commissars' living quarters, the house is merely a consumption good?"

"Yes, Your Highness."

"And if the rooms are used as offices in the daytime, and to sleep in at night, the house is a capital good by day and a consumption good by night?"

"That is right, Your Highness."

"So 'capital goods' is a rather fluctuating concept?"

"I suppose it is, Your Highness. But perhaps only for a few things."

"How would all this affect your equations?"

"It might make them less exact, but I don't think it would invalidate them."

"I have other difficulties with this same phrase," continued Peter. "You write of 'the quantities of the different kinds of capital.' What do you mean by 'quantities'?"

"Why, eh . . . I thought the word 'quantities' was self-explanatory, Your Highness. You see, I go immediately on to write here: 'Let the different kinds of capital be S T . . . to n terms. The total quantities of these existing in the group will be $Q_s, Q_t \ldots$ '"

"You don't seem to get my point," said Peter. "I am asking you what you mean by the term 'quantities.' By the relative 'quantities' of these goods do you mean the relative *values* of these goods as measured, say, in terms of the value of some homogeneous third product, like cigarette packages? For example, suppose a locomotive is worth 600,000 packs and a freight car 25,000 packs, then does the locomotive count for 24 freight cars in your equations?"

"Yes, Your Highness."

"Then your equations already take for granted precisely the thing we are trying to find out," said Peter. "As I understand your paper, you are trying to work out by mathematics what prices the Central Planning Board ought to put on production goods—in order that costs of production might correspond with values of consumption goods in the market—so that we can be sure that labor and capital goods and land are not being wasted or misdirected in making the wrong things or the wrong quantities of the right things. But if your equations *assume* that we already know the values of the means of production, then they assume that we already know the prices that ought to be put on the means of production. So your equations tacitly take it for granted that we already know the answer to the very problem we are trying to solve. . . ."

Baronio was silent for a while. "I gave the wrong answer to your question, Your Highness," he said finally. "By 'quantities' I simply mean physical quantities."

"As measured by what?"

"By weight."

"You mean that you add so many pounds of abstract or homogeneous locomotive to so many pounds of abstract freight car to so many pounds of homogeneous drilling machines to so many pounds of abstract sand to so many pounds of homogeneous watches?"

"But in my paper I already differentiate between different *kinds* of capital, and I don't multiply any of these by price until—"

"You mean you weigh each 'kind' of capital separately?"

"Yes, Your Highness."

"Then your equations assume homogeneity within each 'kind' of capital?"

"Yes, Your—"

"So an old or defective lathe is considered to be worth as much as a new or perfect lathe—provided it weighs as much?"

"I suppose we would really have to count them as two different 'kinds' of capital, Your Highness."

"But then every lathe would be a different 'kind' of capital, depending on its individual age, state of wear and repair, efficiency, et cetera?"

"I suppose so, Your Highness."

"That would require a lot of equations for the Central Planning Board to set up and solve, wouldn't it?"

Baronio was silent.

"It was very good of you to come, Comrade," said Peter at length, "and I appreciate the ingenuity and zeal with which you have worked on this vitally important problem. You at least realize that there *is* a problem—and you understand pretty clearly what the problem is—and No. 3 and myself have certainly got no further than that ourselves. Suppose you leave copies of your paper with us to study."

Peter studied Baronio's paper carefully that evening.

"I don't know whether I am impressed more, Adams," he said the next day, "by Baronio's cleverness or by his blindness. I'm afraid he doesn't realize that his equations tacitly take for granted precisely the things he is trying to find out. What his equations

226

are really saying is that *if* we knew the value of x and y we could find out the value of z. And then he tacitly assumes that he *does* know the value of x and y—or, as he puts it, that he does have the same number of 'independent equations' as he has of 'unknowns.' "

"I read the other copy of his paper that he left with us," said Adams. "I freely confess that the mathematics of it was over my head. But I noticed that his paper referred to a No. ME-13-742 —otherwise known as Comrade Patelli—another clever Italian in the Central Planning Board whose work inspired Baronio. So I have taken the liberty of bringing Patelli with me. He's waiting in the anteroom, if you should care to see him."

"By all means," said Peter.

Patelli was ushered in. Peter had never seen a more intelligent face. He told Patelli about Baronio's paper and his own difficulties with it.

"I'm afraid your misgivings are right, Your Highness. I've been fascinated by the consumers' goods market, and trying to see whether we could solve by mathematics the problem of finding out the correct prices for producers' goods. I think a system of simultaneous equations *could* be used to explain what determines prices on a market. But I have concluded that we couldn't actually arrive by that method at a numerical calculation of what the correct prices ought to be. . . . Let us make the most favorable assumption for such a calculation. Let's assume that we have triumphed over all the difficulties of finding the data of the problem and that we already know the relative preferences of every individual person as between different amounts of all the different commodities, and all the conditions of production of all the commodities, and so on."

"That is already an absurd hypothesis."

"Precisely, Your Highness; that is just the point I was about to make. Yet even if we went on this hypothesis, it would not be enough to make the solution of our problem possible. I have calculated that in the case of 100 persons and 700 commodities there will be 70,699 conditions."

Adams laughed.

"Actually," continued Patelli, "if we took into consideration a great number of circumstances that I ignored, that figure would have to be increased still further. But on these simplified assumptions, we would have to solve a system of 70,699 equations."

"And could we?" asked Adams.

"No, Your Highness. That practically exceeds the power of algebraic analysis."

"Assuming that we have only 700 different commodities," said Peter, "the actual world population for which we have to plan is not 100 persons but about 1,000,000,000. So how many equations, under your simplified assumptions, would you have to solve to get the correct prices of commodities for this world?"

Patelli threw up his hands. "Oh, well—when you get into the neighborhood of seven hundred billions . . . and even Your Highness' assumption is terribly oversimplified. There are so many different grades of each commodity, and different places—"

"And wouldn't you have to change your equations at least every day," pursued Peter, "because supply and demand and everybody's preferences would be constantly changing?"

"Yes, Your Highness."

"So even if one could really know all these equations, it would be beyond human powers to solve them?"

Patelli nodded.

"I suspect that you can't put millions of different items and the preferences of millions of different persons into any meaningful mathematical equation," said Peter. "And I'll go further. Putting aside the bewildering multiplicity of these equations, I suspect that *all* of them would be purely hypothetical; we could never say with confidence that any *one* of them really described a fact. For we can never in fact know what the constantly fluctuating preferences of any one person will be, even if that person is ourself. So I suspect that, tempting as the idea might be, we can't predict human choice and human action by mathematics. This appearance of precise results is delusory. I believe it was our great Russian mathematical logician, Bertravitch Russelevsky,

228

who once defined pure mathematics as the subject 'in which we never know what we are talking about, nor whether what we are saying is true.' And so all these impressive-looking equations that you and Baronio have put together merely seem to me to say, in effect, that *if* we knew so-and-so to be true, then such-and-such would necessarily follow. But——"

He paused eloquently.

Patelli shrugged his shoulders in resignation.

"Anyway," Peter said, "we are grateful for the light you have thrown on the problem."

Chapter 29

HE walked along the line of haggard creatures, in their filthy rags, and stared intently at each vacant face in turn. He had now seen hundreds, thousands of these faces of what had once been men and women. But neither Edith nor Maxwell was among them.

He had not really expected to find them. He did not know whether he feared rather than hoped to find them here. But anything was better than sitting at his desk and getting negative second-hand reports that he did not trust. At least he was doing something himself. He had slipped secretly away from Moscow for a week, left his responsibilities there in charge of Adams, and visited every slave camp in the region that the time allowed. It had all been in vain. This was the last camp, the last line-up.

"I don't understand you, chief," said Adams when their afternoon conferences were resumed. He had been talking of Peter's "negative attitude" toward the proposals of Baronio. "You have this passion for reform, and yet you reject one proposed reform after another without even trying it."

"Would I have to jump out of this window," Peter retorted, "to find out whether or not I would get hurt?"

"No doubt there are some things, chief, that one does know about in advance without trying them—usually because something very much like them has been tried before. But you can't know *everything* that would happen under a particular proposed reform until you try it."

"That used to be the very thing you objected to, Adams. My efforts to introduce personal liberty and real democracy were both wretched failures. And especially while Bolshekov is around, I can't afford any more failures."

"But your freedom of exchange for consumers' goods was a great success!"

"Well, what experiment would you want me to try now?"

"You criticized me severely, chief, for proposing a system that provided harsh penalties for managers but no incentives. Well, why don't you suggest or try some incentives for managers?"

"Such as what?"

"Suppose a manager of a particular factory turned out an output with a greater value than his input. Why not allow him to keep the difference?"

"All of it?"

"Well, half of it . . . or, say, some fixed percentage of it."

"Suppose the situation were the other way round, Adams, and the manager's input—his cost of production—were greater than the value of his output? Would he have to suffer the loss?"

"Exactly."

"Suppose he didn't have that much for us to take away from him?"

"Then, chief, you would be back to my penalties. Fire him. Or, if the loss was big enough, let him starve. Or shoot him."

"I'm afraid, Adams, that your proposal wouldn't quite work out. Suppose a manager really had a surplus of output over input. How would we know that that wasn't merely the result of his having taken a reckless but lucky gamble? Or how would we know that it wasn't really the workers in that factory, and not the managers, who were responsible for the gain shown? Or—most important of all—wouldn't it probably be true, for the most part, that the gains and losses shown by the different factories had little or nothing to do with their individual management but were caused primarily by the arbitrary prices that the

231

Central Planning Board put on the raw materials or labor that a factory bought, or on the finished products that it sold? In short, wouldn't the gains or losses shown by individual factories depend primarily on prices? And aren't we, then, right back to the price problem?"

"But if you have a price system for consumption goods, chief, why can't you have a price system for the tools of production?"

"For the simple reason, Adams, that consumption goods are owned by individuals who exchange them only at ratios that they consider to their personal advantage, while all the tools of production are owned by the State. The State can't sell to and buy from itself."

"But why not, chief? Why can't one industry sell to another, or buy from a third, even if all of them are State-owned?"

"Because the prices set would be arbitrary, fictional and meaningless. The Central Planning Board, Adams, just can't *play* 'market'; it can't *play* 'price system,' like children playing house. Markets and prices, in order to perform the function they do perform—that of showing us the relative values that users and consumers put on things—must be *real*. Our present system of arbitrary allocations of raw materials and labor, arbitrary decisions concerning how big each industry should be and exactly how much of each product should be turned out—this is at least a controllable plan. It may not give people what they want, but at least it is far better than fixing prices at random and then watching the bizarre and unpredictable things that would happen under them."

But Peter was troubled by Adams' criticism that he condemned proposals without trying them. A few weeks later he came up with an idea that had been maturing in his mind for some time.

"One of our great troubles, Adams, is that we are trying to plan more than any human mind can hold. We are trying to plan *every* industry—and all their interrelations—and all the rest. Why not let the workers of *each* industry control and police their own industry? That would decentralize control and break up the planning problem into manageable units."

"The idea has possibilities, chief . . . but it might lead to results we couldn't foresee."

"Precisely," said Peter; "and that is why we ought to try it out."

"But the results might be bad. They might give Bolshekov just the excuse—"

"Why not try it out, then, only on a small scale? Why not apply the idea, Adams, in only one province—far away from Moscow? Why not throw a censorship around that district, so that no news could get in or out until we were certain that the experiment was a success?"

"Have you decided, chief, who our guinea pigs would be?"

"How about the Soviet Republic of Peru? That's certainly remote enough!"

So Peter arranged to go to Peru personally to supervise his experiment. He kept his trip a public secret, redoubled the guard around his father, had Bolshekov more closely watched, and left Adams again in charge of Wonworld at Moscow.

At the very start he found himself confronted in Peru by a problem of unexpected difficulty. He wanted each industry to be self-governing and independent. But what *was* an industry? Where did each industry begin and end? Did the copper industry consist purely of the copper mines? Or did it include the smelters? Did it include the makers of copper wire? Or were the wire makers—whether they made wire of copper, aluminum or steel—a separate industry? Should the sugar growers be grouped with the sugar refineries or with the farmers? Were the shoe manufacturers part of the leather industry, or part of the apparel industry, or an industry of their own? Was carpentry part of the building industry, or part of the furniture industry—or a separate industry?

These problems of classification were endless. No general principle seemed to apply. Practically every decision finally made,

Peter at length realized, was at least partly arbitrary, and most of the decisions were completely arbitrary.

At the end, when the Peruvian commissars he had appointed had finished their work, they had named fifty-seven different industries. Peter had asked that these be reclassified into an even fifty, but he now recognized that they could be classified into only a dozen "industries" or into several hundred.

A temporary head was named for each industry. Someone jokingly nicknamed these heads the industry "czars." Each industry was told to organize itself in any way it thought fit, provided each worker was allowed an equal vote. The industry could fix its own production, its own prices or terms of exchange, its own hours and conditions of work, its own entrance requirements.

Some Peruvians called the new system "syndicalism"; others called it "guild socialism"; and still others liked the name "corporativism."

Peter returned to Moscow, promising to be back in Peru in six months to see how the new system was working. He left a secret cable code with the three top commissars to keep him informed.

Before two months had passed he received urgent cables begging for his return.

He came back to find a chaotic situation bordering on civil war.

The first thing the workers in each industry had done had been to exclude anybody else from entering the industry. Each industry had quickly discovered that it could exact the best terms of exchange for its particular product by rendering it relatively scarce. There had then developed a competitive race for scarcity instead of for production. The workers in each industry voted themselves shorter and shorter hours. Each industry was either withholding goods or threatening to suspend production altogether until it got the prices it demanded for the particular kind of goods it had to supply.

Peter was indignant. He called in the various syndicates of workers representing each industry and denounced them in blistering terms for the selfish and shortsighted way in which they had "abused" the privileges he had conferred upon them.

But as he studied the matter further he cooled off, and took a more objective view. He was forced to acknowledge to himself that the fault was his own. It was inherent in the system he had set up. He had allowed each industry to become an unrestrained monopoly. The more essential or irreplaceable the product that it made, therefore, the more it could and would squeeze everybody else. Inherent in his system had been the assumption that production existed primarily for the benefit of the producers—whereas, he now saw, its only real justification was what it provided for consumers.

He dismantled the new system entirely, and ordered the restoration of the old centralized socialism under the Central Planning Board at Moscow.

Bolshekov, he later learned, had got wind of the experiment and its failure, but fortunately had had no way of making his knowledge public. Peter thanked his lucky stars—and Adams' foresighted advice—that he still had control over the radio and the newspapers.

But as an economic reformer he felt more frustrated than ever before.

Then suddenly, one night at the piano, when he was playing a Bach fugue, an idea hit him like a bolt of lightning. He stopped midway in an intricate passage. His mind had been returning to a question that Adams had asked: "Why can't you have a price system for the tools of production?" And he thought of his own answer: "Because consumption goods are owned by individuals . . . while the tools of production are owned by the State." Of course, that was the right answer . . . but wasn't there an answer to the answer? . . .

Yes, there was! Why hadn't Adams made it then? Why hadn't he himself thought of it then? He knew the answer! The tools of production didn't *have* to be owned by the State!

It was late at night. But he rushed, hatless and coatless, out of his own apartment, took the automatic elevator to the street level,

235

waved aside the sentries at the main entrance, and ran alone along four blocks of solitary streets to Adams' rooms, using a pass key that Adams had given to him. He routed him out of bed, shook him awake, threw his arms around his shoulders, slapped him on the back, hugged him.

"I've found the answer, Adams!" he shouted. "I've found the answer to all our problems! I've found the key that unlocks everything: *Private ownership of the means of production!*"

Chapter 30

EVEN Adams became cautiously enthusiastic when Peter explained all the consequences he expected from his proposed reform.

"I'll put it into effect immediately," said Peter.

"No, chief; it's too revolutionary. You must consult the Politburo first."

"But Bolshekov is certain to oppose it, Adams! And he would probably swing the whole Politburo with him, with the exception of ourselves. He has every advantage. He would probably argue that my plan was new, untried, untested, revolutionary. . . . He might even say that it was anti-Marxist!"

"Don't you think it *is* a trifle anti-Marxist, chief?"

"I'm not concerned with that, Adams. I'm only concerned with whether it would work. If I were to put it up to the Politburo, they wouldn't let me do it, and so I would never find out. I didn't consult the Politburo when I proposed a free exchange system for consumption goods; but once we put that into effect it was a great victory."

"I must admit it's only because of that, chief, that Bolshekov's been afraid to move in on you. But—"

"Then let's act immediately," said Peter. "This is our trump card. It's so important, so revolutionary, that we should put it into effect with great fanfare. I'll make a thumping radio speech over a worldwide hook-up. I'll draft the speech right away. We'll

237

order the text published in the *New Truth* and every other newspaper in Wonworld for release the instant I start talking. We'll print millions of folders with the full text. We'll develop slogans. . . ."

They started to work. Peter began drafting his speech. It explained the scheme, and what its great consequences would be. The details would have to be worked out. The people must be patient in the meantime. But instead of everybody's owning a theoretical one-billionth of every tool of production in Wonworld, each person would now wholly own either a specific tool or at least a definite percentage of a specific machine or factory. . . .

The draft went on to explain what "ownership" would mean. It would be a system of legal rights, established and protected by the government. Each individual would have the right to use as he saw fit the particular implement or machine to which he held legal title. He would not have to wait for directions from the Central Planning Board for every move he made. He would be able to share his tools or machines voluntarily with others, to "lease" them or exchange them on any terms mutually agreeable. . . .

There was a lot to be packed into a half-hour's talk. As soon as the text had been drafted to his satisfaction, Peter fixed an evening three days off as the time for its radio delivery. It was put on the wires and cables for simultaneous publication throughout Wonworld.

On one consequence, however, he had failed to calculate. One of the mimeographed copies of the proposed speech that went to the office of the *New Truth* was sent immediately to its editor, Orlov. Orlov had been persuaded to go along with the new setup on the argument that Peter was Stalenin's publicly appointed deputy. But he read the prepared speech with mounting horror, and then took it directly to Bolshekov. Bolshekov read it in a cold fury.

"That does it!" he announced. "This young idiot must be stopped!"

238

Peter and Adams were at their regular afternoon conference in Stalenin's office.

"Our next step," said Peter, "is to call in our two Italian economists, Patelli and Baronio, and have them work out the details of the new sys—"

Adams jumped up. "Those were shots!"

"I think I did hear shots," said Peter, rising slowly.

They stared at each other with a wild surmise. Neither dared to put it into words.

Sergei burst into the room, his face livid. "His Supremacy has been shot! He's dying!"

They rushed into Stalenin's bedroom. He was in bed, breathing heavily. Blood was seeping through the sheet above him. Peter stumbled over a body.

"Who's that?" he asked, looking down.

"The assassin," said Sergei. "This guard shot him."

The guard stepped forward. "We found these papers on him, Your Highness. . . . One of Bolshekov's gang."

"I've already called the doctors," said Sergei. "They'll be here in a few minutes, but—" He shrugged his shoulders hopelessly.

Peter bent over the dying man. "Father!"

His father grabbed his hand and looked at him appealingly. He seemed to be making a desperate effort to say something. "Rec—rec—record!"

The record! Peter squeezed his father's hand tenderly and bent down to kiss his brow. He turned to Adams.

"Quick! We haven't a moment to lose!"

They rushed back to Stalenin's office. Peter turned the safe combination, took his key from an inside pocket, and unlocked the little steel door to the compartment containing the two recordings that Stalenin had so foresightedly made. He was surprised to find his hand shaking.

Record Z! Peter drew it out gently and looked at it. This might change the whole history of Wonworld!

Sergei telephoned for an automobile to be waiting. Peter and

Adams took the private elevator down, Peter with the precious record in a brief case.

As they got to the exit their car was just drawing up. Thank Marx!

At the time of Stalenin's stroke Peter had explained to Adams only the history of record X. In the car on the way over he added the story of record Z.

They drew up before the broadcasting station.

A line of troops stood before the entrance. A lieutenant in charge was ordering every one off the sidewalk.

Adams and Peter started to walk through. Two of the soldiers blocked them with crossed guns. The lieutenant came up.

"I have orders not to let anyone in!"

"You fool!" said Adams. "Don't you know who we are? I am His Highness No. 3, and this is His Highness No. 1-A."

"Oh!" The lieutenant was flustered. "But, Your Highness, I have orders to let in nobody."

"Nobody?"

"Nobody but No. 2 or those in his party."

"Whose orders are those?"

"My colonel's orders, Your Highness."

"And in whose name are those orders issued?" asked Adams. "Have you a written copy?"

"No, Your Highness. They're purely oral orders—"

"You got them wrong. If they had been given to you straight, you would have known that they were No. 2's orders issued in the name of No. 1 and drafted by No. 1-A himself. But I commend you for your conscientious zeal. You are to let in no one but ourselves and No. 2 and his party. Has No. 2 arrived yet?"

"No, sir."

"Let him in immediately when he does. Are the men's guns loaded?"

"Yes, sir."

"Good. Order your men to fire a three-shot salute the moment No. 2 and his party arrive. That will be the signal for the affair to begin. Remember, three times!"

"Yes, Your Highness."

The lieutenant looked dubious, apparently afraid either to let Adams and Peter through or not to let them through. Adams went back and murmured a few directions to the chauffeur, who nodded and drove off.

Peter and Adams proceeded into the building unmolested.

"That was a tight squeeze," said Peter. "You showed great presence of mind. I'm afraid Bolshekov has made his preparations against us pretty tight."

"I went on the assumption, chief, that he wouldn't have dared give orders specifically directed against us. He would have been afraid of tipping his hand."

"Why did you ask the lieutenant to order his men to fire a salute?"

"To mislead him—and also to warn us when Bolshekov has arrived."

They took the elevator to the tenth floor. When they had got into the main studio through a series of doors and short halls, they found an announcer talking before the microphone: ". . . remember—at four o'clock sharp there will be an announcement by No. 2 himself of the utmost importance to Wonworld. We regret that there has not been time to arrange for a complete Wonworldwide hook-up. It will be carried, however, by all stations in the European and American provinces."

Adams and Peter silently signaled the announcer to stop.

He looked puzzled and frightened. ". . . We will now listen to some class-struggle music. . . ." He signaled through the glass pane to the technicians in the control room, and waited for the return signal that he was off the air.

"But I was told by No. 2, Your Highness, that no one but he and his party would arrive, and that even if anyone else did he was the only one to talk."

"No, no, no," said Adams; "you must have got it mixed up; or someone along the line got it mixed up. The arrangement is merely for No. 2 to make the closing speech. But the really great announcement—the whole purpose of the program, in fact—is

241

this announcement we have here from No. 1 himself. I am to make the introductory speech, then this record will be put on of No. 1's speech, then No. 1-A will say a few words about it and make a talk introducing No. 2. . . . Let's see. What time is it now?"

He looked at the studio clock. "Seventeen to four. Good. We'll begin the broadcast at exactly three forty-five."

"But No. 2's speech isn't scheduled till four!"

"That's right. The preceding fifteen minutes will be taken up by my introductory speech. No. 1's announcement, and No. 1-A's introduction of No. 2. . . . I'm not blaming you for announcing the wrong time. This whole thing seems to have been badly bungled at the Propaganda Bureau. They must even have given the wrong instructions to No. 2, and that's why he's late—"

"Couldn't we wait till he gets here?" asked the announcer.

"Oh he'll be here in time to speak at four. Look! It's quarter of. Announce me."

The announcer signaled the control room to shut off the music. He stepped to the microphone. Peter tiptoed around the plate-glass partition to the control room. He gave a technician the Stalenin record, with instructions to start it at a signal from Adams. Then he tiptoed back into the studio, and after a reassuring smile to the announcer, stepped out through the series of doors to the main hall.

As he got to the hall he heard shots. One. Two. Three. Bolshekov and his party must have arrived.

He quietly locked the two outer doors to the studio from the inside, and put the keys in his pocket.

When Peter stepped into the studio Adams was talking before the microphone. ". . . and now, my dear comrades of Wonworld, it is my great privilege to introduce our beloved leader, the Dictator of All Wonworld, No. 1 himself, His Supremacy—*Stalenin!*"

A record struck up the opening strains of "Marx Save the Dictator."

And then came the voice of Stalenin.

"My comrades! What I have to announce today is very painful

to me, and therefore I shall be brief. My doctors have warned me that any attempt on my part to continue my present burden of work will undermine my health and end my life. If merely my own personal fate were involved, this would not, as all of you have reason to know, matter to me in the least. But what is above all important is the peace and security of Wonworld. I must make sure, therefore, that there is a peaceful transfer of power into the right hands. I am therefore appointing my son, Peter Uldanov, who in a short time has displayed such ability, to succeed me as Dictator of Wonworld. He will do so under the title of Stalenin the Second. I urge all my faithful supporters, I urge every dear comrade of Wonworld—including, of course, every member of the Politburo—to rally round Stalenin the Second. I am especially proud to announce that in this move I have the loyal backing of His Highness No. 2, Bolshekov. It is he, in fact, who, when I spoke of this matter to him, first put forward the suggestion that my son Peter Uldanov would be my ideal successor. And I wish especially to emphasize this magnanimity on the part of Comrade Bolshekov, because it will dispose once for all of the ugly rumors that he is ambitious of power for himself. . . . And so, as of this moment, I am resigning as Wonworld Dictator. The next voice you will hear will be that of Stalenin the Second, your new Dictator. . . . The Dictator has abdicated; long live the Dictator!"

During these last words Peter could hear the muffled sound of banging on the first outer door to the studio. He heard it only because he had been listening for it. Through the soundproof walls of the studio, he realized, neither the announcer nor Adams were yet aware of it. He pulled Adams' sleeve and gave a sidelong glance in the direction of the sound. Adams understood.

The pounding grew louder. Now the announcer heard it, and looked confusedly toward the door. There was a muffled crash— the outer door had been broken open. Loud pounding began on the studio door itself. The announcer tried to open it. He turned accusingly to Peter: "You locked it!"

But Peter had stepped up to the microphone and was taking up

243

from where his father's voice had left off. There was no music, such as the prepared script had called for, but Peter began:

"It is with a deep sense of humility, my comrades, that I take over the awful responsibilities of Dictator of Wonworld. At the wish and in honor of my great father, I now take the title of Stalenin the Second—"

The studio door gave way with a crash. Two soldiers walked in, followed by Marshal Zakachetsky, next a colonel whom Peter did not recognize, and finally Bolshekov.

"Arrest them!" ordered Bolshekov, pointing.

One of the soldiers seized Peter by the left wrist; the other grabbed Adams.

Bolshekov stepped up to the microphone: "This is Bolshekov talking, your new leader and the new Dictator of Wonworld. You have just been listening to a gigantic hoax. Two traitors, two mad dogs, two of the filthiest vermin ever to live in Wonworld, have just tried to seize power. What you just heard was not Stalenin but merely a phonograph record with a skillful imitation of his voice. Two notorious murderers, masquerading under the names of Adams and Uldanov, have just assassinated your beloved leader Stalenin. They had this phonograph record all prepared, and might even have succeeded had not I, Bolshekov, your new leader, thwarted their plans. You will soon hear the last of this Adams and Uldanov—"

With a lightning twist, Peter with his free hand slipped out the pistol from the open holster of the guard who was holding him, and pointed it into the guard's ribs.

"Let go of me," he ordered.

The guard tried to grab the pistol. Peter fired, and the guard fell heavily. Even before he fell, Peter flashed the gun on the other guard, who was trying to reach for his own pistol while still holding Adams.

"Throw up your hands!" The guard raised them slowly. "Get his gun, Adams!"

Peter and Adams were now trying to keep the other five men in the studio covered. All, even Bolshekov, had raised their hands.

"You can't get away with this, you fools," said Bolshekov. "The whole building is guarded!"

"We'll die fighting," said Peter. "Step away!"

It was Peter's turn to take the microphone. "This is Stalenin the Second talking, your new Dictator. Bolshekov is the real assassin of my father. Of that I have overwhelming proof—"

Adams touched him, and motioned him to back toward the door to the control room. They kept the five men covered with their guns until they had shut and locked the door behind them. Then Adams led the way through the exit from the control room to the hall.

"Follow me, chief. I know this whole building!"

They ran across the hall. Two guards outside the studio door fired at them. Adams fired back as Peter ran to catch up with him. They ran down another hall at a right angle to the first, till they came to a door guarded by another soldier. He raised his gun, fired and missed. Adams fired and hit. The soldier dropped.

"Quick!" Adams motioned Peter through the steel doorway, and they bolted it behind them.

"This is the back stairs, the fire escape!" They ran down ten flights until they came to the street floor. The steel door in front of them was closed.

"This door is undoubtedly guarded," said Adams. "We must conceal our guns in our pockets. Let me handle this!"

He flung open the door. A soldier with a musket standing before the door immediately looked around.

"Who's in charge here?" Adams shouted in a commanding tone. Both he and Peter looked up and down. There was a squad of eight soldiers before the entrance.

"I'm in charge, sir," said one of the soldiers. "Corporal 31."

"Where's the lieutenant?" demanded Adams. "I want the lieutenant."

"The lieutenant is in the front of the building, sir, on Ana Pauker Street."

"Your men are needed immediately by His Highness No. 2 on the tenth floor!"

245

"But, sir, the orders to my squad are to guard this entrance and not let anyone in or out!"

"Who gave you your orders?"

"The lieutenant, sir!"

Adams feigned distress. "This won't do!" he said. "We must get some additional men immediately inside the building. They're needed on the tenth floor!"

"But my orders, sir, are—"

"I'll tell you what we'll do," said Adams quickly. "Leave your squad here for the moment guarding this entrance. But drive around with us immediately to the lieutenant on Ana Pauker Street and let me give him the information."

Peter suddenly realized that his car was in front of them, already waiting. So *that* was what Adams had told the chauffeur! A farseeing fellow, Adams! It was quick-wittedness like this, no doubt, that had brought him, even though an American, to the No. 3 position!

The corporal left orders with one of his men and got in the car with Adams and Peter. The chauffeur started off immediately and had gained amazing speed by the time they reached the corner. But instead of turning right toward the front of the building on Ana Pauker Street, he swung wildly left with the tires screaming.

"Hey!" yelled the corporal. "That's the wrong—"

He felt something pressing against his back and something else against his belly. He looked down to see Peter's revolver.

"Keep quite still," ordered Adams from in back of him. "Take his gun, chief."

Peter took it.

The car raced crazily through the streets, the chauffeur sounding the siren continuously. It was a top official car, and everyone hopped out of the way. Instead of making any effort to stop it, traffic policemen jumped for safety.

Chapter 31

AS the car got toward the outskirts of the city its speed rose to sixty-five miles an hour—to seventy—to eighty-five. They were now in fairly open country.

"Where are we heading?" asked Peter.

Adams pointed meaningfully to the corporal, and then spoke to him:

"Listen, soldier, you have been taking part in a revolt. We could shoot you now and throw out your body. Or we could throw you out alive at this speed—"

"Oh, let's stop and let him out here," said Peter.

"They'd kill me for having fallen into this trap," said the corporal. "I'm lucky if that's the worst they do. If they don't even know what's happened to me, they may assume I've been shot and at least let my family alone."

"Do you want to stay with us?"

"Yes, Your Highness." He had apparently just recognized Peter.

"It's 'Your Supremacy' now," said Adams.

"No, no," said Peter. " 'Your Highness' is as high as I care to go."

He turned again to the corporal. "Can we trust you?"

The corporal nodded.

Adams shook his head. "I think we'd better put him on probation for a while."

They bound his hands and feet and sat him between them.

"Where are we heading?" asked Peter again.

"For the airfield," said Adams.

"Why?"

"It's our only chance. You're head of the Air Force. They're loyal—I hope."

They sped along, the speedometer wavering around ninety. The car lurched and pitched crazily.

Peter felt sick and heavy. He had shot a man. Killed him. Self-defense—the only way to save his own life—to save Wonworld. But he had killed. And he had also killed something in himself. "Means determine ends," he had said repeatedly to Adams; "means determine ends." A society founded on horrible means would be a horrible society. Had he been right? Of course. But suppose there were no choice of means? Reason? Moral suasion? Reason with Bolshekov? At that moment? Preposterous! But how about Peter himself? He had solved a problem with murder. Would he try to solve his other problems with murders? Wasn't it precisely this choice of means that had already made the end-result in Wonworld so horrible? . . .

The airfield came in sight. Two sentries blockaded the road. Peter asked for the commandant.

Colonel Torganev welcomed them with the greatest warmth. "We heard the broadcast, Your Supremacy. You are the legitimate successor of Stalenin the First. The Air Force is completely loyal. We are at your absolute disposal."

Peter thanked him. "What can we do?" he asked.

"I don't know how long we could hold this field against the Army," said Torganev. "I don't know how long any field around here could be held. So far as we can learn, the Army is completely under the thumb of Bolshekov."

"So?" asked Adams.

"My advice would be, Your Supremacy, to order every member of the Air Force to his respective field, including every officer, every conscript, every mechanic."

"And then what?" Peter asked.

248

"All would be ready to flee Russia the moment the field became untenable."

"And go where?"

"To the Polish province. Three-fourths of the Wonworld Army is based in Russia and three-fourths consists of Russians."

"What would we do in the Polish province?"

"We would see when we got there. First of all, we must be out of reach of the Bolshekovites."

Peter issued the orders. They were telephoned, telegraphed and flown. He extended Torganev's idea and invited every worker in an airplane or motor factory to the airfields. Every field was to load each plane with all the personnel, bombs, gasoline and other supplies that it could hold. Each plane was to take off, the moment it was filled, for its assigned airfield to the west.

There were not nearly enough fields in the Polish provinces to hold the planes from Russia. Many planes had to be assigned destinations in the Czech, German, and Balkan provinces.

The Air Force at the Moscow field held out for nearly three days, drawing in men, with supplies, who shot their way into and out of Moscow. Adams himself, without consulting Peter or Torganev, took a jeep with two machine gunners into the heart of Moscow in the dead of night and safely pulled out Baronio and Patelli. "We'll need their brains," he explained.

Peter envied him. He would have risked anything to find Edith and her father and bring them with him. But he did not know where to go; he did not know whether they were still in the Moscow district; he did not even know whether they were still alive. Action at any risk was better than this frustration.

At the end of the third day Bolshekov's men had the Moscow airfield surrounded. They began closing in. The field was running out of ammunition. Peter found they had all the men and supplies they could lift.

He gave the order to leave.

The bomber carrying Torganev, Adams and Peter landed at the Warsaw airport.

The commandant was friendly and loyal. Nearly all the planes, Peter learned, had received friendly welcomes from the air personnel at the fields on which they had landed. But the commandant at the Warsaw airfield warned him that there were still enough army troops nearby to make the field's position untenable, and that in any case Bolshekov would order his army westward till it caught up with them.

For the next few months Peter's forces could do nothing but retreat. From each airfield they would pick up all the additional planes, personnel, bombs and equipment they could carry, and fly further west—to French, Belgian, Dutch, Spanish airfields. The task of finding enough fields became increasingly urgent.

Bolshekov's army rolled slowly but steadily westward, filling up the Balkan, Polish and German provinces, recruiting new men, consolidating its positions.

"Why not bomb Bolshekov's territory?" suggested Adams.

"To what purpose?" answered Peter. "We would only earn hatred. We could never land and take over."

So they bombed and machine-gunned only the concentrations of Bolshekov's men that tried to move in on the airfields.

Torganev warned that the Air Force could not hold out on the continent. "Perhaps we can hold the British Isles," he suggested. "The Channel should make it possible." But their advance planes found there only about a fourth of the number of airfields needed to hold the Force.

"We have only one permanent hope," said Adams. "The Western Hemisphere."

Torganev conceded that even the British Isles could afford, at best, only a temporary base. The Air Force and the islands themselves would be dependent on the outside for food and supplies— and Bolshekov had control of the Navy and the merchant marine. It would be futile for the Air Force to bomb the continent if it could not land. Bolshekov would in time build up another air force of his own. Space and industrial capacity were necessary to maintain and expand Peter's air force. And the only counterweight to Bolshekov's army would have to be a bigger and better army.

Peter's side needed space. It needed a continent. And if Peter didn't soon establish himself on the Western Hemisphere, Bolshekov would.

Peter yielded to the argument.

They prepared to move three-quarters of the Air Force to the Americas. But only their long-range bombers were capable of making the trip. The planes still remaining on the Continent were to stay as long as they could hold out without seizure, and then crowd themselves up in the British Isles. The only long-run solution, they decided, was to have the long-range bombers make continuous back and forth trips until they had transported the whole Air Force personnel and supplies to the Americas.

Peter sent a few advance long-range bombers to the American provinces to find out how they were received.

The advance groups were not only welcomed; they were virtually embraced.

The intelligence reports that came back explained this reception on several grounds. There was practically no army whatever in the Western Hemisphere, except for a token force here and there consisting of American privates but commanded mainly by Russian officers. This arrangement had always been resented. Though no one had been allowed to say so openly, and though every effort had been made to expunge the historical record, the Americans felt that they were still being treated as a conquered people. They felt that they were still being drained by taxes to support the luxurious public buildings of Moscow. Though everyone had now spoken only Marxanto for generations, the Americans could still recognize and resent a Russian accent. They feared Russia. They feared Bolshekov. Peter's introduction of a system of free exchange of consumption goods had given them their first taste of what economic liberty might be like. Though Peter was a Russian, he was now "fighting Russia." And the fact that Adams was an American was found to be an additional reason why the Americans tended to align themselves on Peter's side.

Peter was surprised to learn of these signs of sectional feeling. They marred what he had been taught to regard as the wonderful unity of Wonworld. But as American sectional prejudice was on his side, he was happy to take full advantage of it.

When he landed in New York he got a tremendous ovation. People lined the sidewalks throughout his route. Along Fifth Avenue a sea of faces looked out of windows; thousands of arms waved handkerchiefs. Peter found himself in a snowstorm of confetti and shredded newspapers.

It was his greatest day of personal triumph. It was the end of his retreat. From here he could organize a counterforce, and shape a world to his new ideals.

It could stand a little shaping. The greater part of Moscow was a slum, but it was relieved by a few decent public buildings. But judging from the squalor of Fifth Avenue, New York must be *all* slum.

Could it be true, as the histories said, that this city had once been the metropolis of capitalism?

PART THREE: DISCOVERY

Chapter 32

PETER named the territory over which he ruled *Freeworld*. He was installed in Washington in a decrepit, smelly old building which someone, evidently with a fine sense of irony, had once named The White House. This, he was told, was where the old capitalist emperors used to live.

"Alone?" he asked—"with all this floor space?"

He assigned apartments in it to Adams and other officials.

"I am going to introduce my new economic reform immediately," he told Adams.

"We can't afford any such diversion now," Adams protested. "The first thing to do is to prosecute the war against Bolshekov. We have the planes and the trained aviation personnel; but he still has the factories. He will immediately build up a new air force. What *we* must do is to set up airplane factories, motor works, aluminum smelters. We must build up an army, a navy, a merchant marine. We must expand steel capacity—"

"I know, I know," said Peter. "You are entirely right. But it will take several years for Bolshekov to build up an air force to challenge the one we already have. And it will certainly take years for us to do what you propose. My reforms, instead of diverting us, will enable us to do all these things *faster.*"

Adams shrugged his shoulders resignedly.

Peter delivered his first Freeworld radio speech. He announced his new reform.

But it was one thing to declare that there would be "private

253

ownership of the means of production." It was quite another thing to work out the details. It was all very well to say that the individual worker would hereafter own his own hammer, sickle, plow, saw, or paintbrush. But what about a great machine on which many men worked? Especially if it was an integral part of a whole set of machines constituting a factory? Could each worker own a different part of the machine? Could each worker own a specific part of a whole factory—one a part of the roof, another a part of a floor, another a window? What would happen if one worker quarreled with the others and wanted to take his particular piece of the factory away with him?

"The problem is insoluble," said Adams. "The factories, the railroads, the means of production must be owned in common."

Peter refused to give up. He thought at last of a solution.

A factory, a locomotive, any great machine whatever, was a unit. It couldn't be broken up into pieces to be owned separately. But it could be owned *jointly,* and not necessarily by everybody in Freeworld. It could be owned simply by those who actually had to do with its operation.

"My idea is wonderfully simple, Adams," Peter explained. "Suppose, for example, there are a hundred workers in a textile factory, including the managerial force. Then the ownership of that factory would be divided among the hundred workers. Each would own one-hundredth as his share—"

"Just as I said, chief. The ownership would have to be in common."

"Let me finish, Adams. There would be an enormous difference. These hundred workers wouldn't have to wait for orders from a central point, perhaps hundreds or thousands of miles away, to learn precisely what they could make in their factory. They could do what they saw had to be done by their managers on the actual spot—"

"But if we don't have central planning, chief—"

"We'll come to that later. I've thought of a wonderful way in which *individual* ownership can be reconciled with *joint* ownership, and it combines the advantages of *both*. Our problem is to

254

divide the ownership of a factory into, say, a hundred parts so that each worker can own an equal share. Yet we don't want to have the factory itself broken up into a hundred parts. And we don't want any owner tied to his share for life. He might want to move away, or he might prefer to own something else instead. So what do we do?"

Adams shrugged his shoulders.

"We give each worker," Peter went on triumphantly, "the *right* to share in one-hundredth of all the advantages or gains that flow from the ownership and operation of that factory! And we also give him the right to *sell* that right—to exchange it for anything else he wants instead!"

Adams still looked doubtful.

"And it seems to me that the simplest way to do that, Adams, is to give each worker, say, an engraved certificate, declaring that he has the right to a one-hundredth share in the ownership of the factory. Each one of these certificates would be called a 'share.' Any owner would have the right to exchange his share, if he wanted, for a share of any other factory—or even for consumption goods."

"All that is very ingenious, chief. But I still forsee some serious problems."

"For example?"

"Well, suppose one factory has a hundred workers and a second factory, just as big and just as valuable, has only fifty. You would be giving those in the second factory twice as much value as those in the first."

"We will have to work that out," said Peter. "I suppose we will have to do quite a lot of wild guessing. But we can be thankful that we now have a consumers' goods market."

"Why?"

"Because we may be able to estimate the comparative values of at least some factories by the comparative values and quantities of the consumers' goods they turn out."

"But how about mines, say, turning out raw materials?"

It was Peter's turn to shrug his shoulders. "We can't assure

255

absolute equity. We'll just have to guess. We'll try as far as possible, of course, to give everybody an equal share."

"That's only one of the problems I see," Adams said. "Here's another, just as important. Some people are in factories making shirts. Others are on farms raising tomatoes. Each of these groups, I agree, could form part of joint enterprises that would exchange their products with others. But how about the people who work on making roads? How about the people who repair the sewers? How about firemen? How about policemen? What sort of 'shares' are you going to give *them*, for example?"

Peter thoughtfully lit a cigarette. "Maybe we'll have to work out something special for them. Maybe for the factory that employed a hundred people, for example, we'd print a hundred and ten shares instead of a hundred, and distribute the extra ten among those outside the factory to whom we couldn't assign any other kind of ownership. Let's call in the statisticians from our new Freeworld Supreme Economic Council and dump the whole problem in their lap."

The statisticians prepared a plan. The work of detailed calculation was assigned to hundreds of regional boards, and by those in turn to hundreds of thousands of individual factories, workshops, stores and collective farms. The detailed calculations became mountainous.

Peter wasn't happy about the plan. It was obviously full of guesswork, and on a wholesale scale. But he could think of no way of removing the guesswork. He had to start *some*where, he decided, *some*how.

He approved the plan; and on Adams' advice he put it into operation with a flourish. He proclaimed a Freeworld holiday. There were speeches, bands, parades and fireworks. Every day speakers on the radio, on street corners, in shops and factories, explained the plan. Everyone seemed to tingle with anticipation concerning what he was personally going to own. The general feeling reminded Peter of how he himself used to feel at his childhood birthday parties in Bermuda, to which his mother used to invite his tutors and for which she used to bake a special cake, anyone's slice of which might turn out to contain some special little souvenir or prize.

No sooner was the new distribution made than markets developed in production goods, and even in the "shares" issued to each person. These markets bore a striking similarity to those that had developed in consumption goods when Peter had first permitted freedom of exchange. The shares were traded in on separate "stock exchanges." These began by a few brokers meeting on street corners (nicknamed "curb" markets); but trade soon grew to the point where the brokers met in large rooms with great blackboards on them on which the changing quotations were chalked up.

As with consumer goods, the company shares were at first quoted in terms of the number of cigarette packages for which they would exchange.

Then happened precisely what Peter had feared. He had hoped that all the shares would sell or exchange for approximately the same amounts. Instead, wide discrepancies developed. For some shares people bid two, three or four times as much as for others. Those who had the less valuable shares complained of discrimination.

Peter did his best. He pointed out that nobody was forced to sell, and that every group could make their shares worth more by working harder—or even, if they wished, and if their factories could be converted, by producing different goods from those they were already producing.

One of the first results of the change was a tremendous turnover in managers. Under the communist system, managers were selected for their ideological fervor, for their passion for communism, for their ability to make rousing speeches, for their adroitness in producing excuses for not meeting production quotas, for their docility and subservience, for their meticulous care in making out reports in triplicate or quadruplicate and keeping all paper work neatly in order. But the owner-workers now seemed to care for only one thing. Each group of shareholders wanted a manager who knew how to increase their income and the value of their shares. They threw out every manager who failed—however ingenious his explanation for his failure, or however expert he was in slapping backs and kissing babies—and they chose a manager who they thought knew how to succeed, or who had shown by his record somewhere else that he did know how.

Another result of the private ownership of productive property was that equality of income soon ceased. In the factories, for example, the managers were often rewarded out of all proportion to the rewards of the average worker. The workers in a plant seemed willing to pay their top manager almost any amount—provided only that he could increase the value of their own shares, or the income from their own shares, by an even greater amount. The better the manager, they found, the greater the overall productivity of the plant; and therefore the greater the income to be divided among all of them.

But the quickest and most dramatic results of the new reform were on the land. Here there were few problems of common ownership. The collectives were broken up into smaller units. Usually the land was divided up pro rata, and particular parcels of it were assigned to individual families. It was only where this division would have resulted in individual plots of land obviously too small for economical cultivation that several families would agree to work a larger piece of land in common. But in such cases the plot was usually too small anyway to yield a tolerable living for the several families involved, and in the course of time the others would usually sell their share to some one family. A few former members of the collectives went into the business of owning or working tractors, and renting them out by the day to farms too small to afford to keep them all year round.

The yield per acre of all crops grew amazingly; yet the soil was better conserved than ever. The attitude of the peasants toward their work and toward the land changed completely. They worked as never before. No work seemed like drudgery to them.

258

They took a pride in their land and developed a love of it such as even Peter had not dreamed to be possible.

When he asked one of these new peasant-proprietors about his changed attitude, his explanation was simple: "The more work I and my family put into the farm, the better off we are. Our work is no longer offset by the laziness and carelessness of others. On the other hand, we can no longer sit back and hope that others will make up for what we fail to do. Everything depends on ourselves."

Another farmer-owner put it this way: "The greater the crop we raise this year, the better off my family will be. But we also have to think of next year and the year after that, so we can't take any risk of exhausting the soil. Every improvement I put into the farm, whether into the soil or into the buildings, is mine; I reap the fruits of it. But there is something that to me is more important still. I am building this for my family; I am increasing the security of my family; I will have something fine to turn over to my children after I am gone. I don't know how I can explain it to you, Your Highness, but since my family has owned this land for *itself*, and feels secure in its right and title to *stay* here undisturbed, we feel not only that the farm belongs to us but that we belong to the farm. It is a part of us, and we are a part of it. It works for us, and we work for it. It produces for us, and we produce for it. You may think it is just a thing, but it seems as alive as any of us, and we love it and care for it as if it were a part of ourselves."

"The whole thing is just a miracle," conceded Adams. "If I wanted to coin an aphorism I would say: *The magic of private property turns sand into gold.*"

Meanwhile, fascinating developments began to take place in the new markets for raw materials and for production goods. There was now a market for everything that could be exchanged. There was a market and a price for coal, steel and pig iron, for lead, zinc and copper, for rubber, jute and marble, for cattle,

259

hides and leather, for raw cotton, raw wool and flax, for silver, platinum and gold.

At first the prices of all of these were stated in terms of cigarette packs. But after a few months this system came to seem ridiculous, and broke down. Prices of great quantities of raw materials, and of the precious metals, had to be stated in terms of thousands and thousands of cigarette packs. The demand for cigarette packs as a medium of exchange became far greater than the demand for them for smoking. Cigarette packages began to assume so high a value as a medium of exchange, in fact, that it came to seem criminally wasteful to smoke them—though their use for smoking had been the sole source of their original value.

So people took to using the rare metals as mediums of exchange and common standards for stating high prices or the prices of large-quantity transactions. In some markets silver would be used for this purpose, in others platinum, in still others gold. But it proved troublesome to be constantly translating these prices into each other, especially as the price of each of the metals was constantly changing in relation to the others.

Gradually and almost imperceptibly the habit developed of translating all prices into gold for common comparison. Gold became the medium of exchange for all large transactions. Cigarettes were now used as such a medium only in small transactions. In time the value of cigarettes themselves was commonly stated in terms of gold.

Another curious thing happened. Once gold had established itself as the medium of exchange, it had a higher value in relation to silver and platinum, and to everything else, than it had before.

"How do you think that happened, chief?" asked Adams.

"As nearly as I can make out," said Peter, "the reason is this. The demand for gold as a medium of exchange has now become an *additional* source of demand above that for ornament, teeth filling, or any of gold's other original uses."

"But why, chief, out of all the commodities, should *gold* have become *the* medium of exchange."

"Well, it was obviously an enormous convenience that some one thing should eventually become the common medium of exchange. Such a medium, of course, would have to have certain qualities in order to serve satisfactorily. When you start to think of what these qualities ought to be, as I did the other day, you will find that gold combines them better than practically anything else."

"What qualities are they?" Adams asked.

"Well, before anything can become a medium of exchange, it must have a high measure of acceptability for its own sake. Gold has this. It must have a high value with small bulk, so that it can be easily carried in pockets or easily shipped from place to place. Gold, again. It must not be perishable; it must not evaporate like alcohol, rot like eggs or rust like iron. It must, in short, *keep* permanently. Gold, again. It mustn't vary in quality, like wheat, eggs, meat or a thousand other things. One part must be as valuable, weight for weight, as any other part, provided it is the same material. Gold, again. It must be easily divisible, so that it can be cut into any desired size without losing value, or pass from hand to hand in any standardized size. Gold, again. It must have stability of value. Gold has this because the current year's production is always small compared with the accumulated stock. It must be easily recognized for what it is, so that it cannot be easily imitated. Most people can tell real gold instantly, because there is nothing quite like it. It is beautiful to look at; it has an unmistakable ring; it is malleable and impressible, and takes a sharp stamp. And, if you wish, you can always make a final acid test."

"Then you don't think, chief, that the emergence of gold as the medium of exchange was a mere accident?"

"It looks much more to me, Adams, like the survival of the fittest."

When gold first began to emerge as the medium of exchange after Peter's reform, it was exchanged in small bars weighing a hundred grams each. These were stamped, marked, cut and assayed by people who now made a regular profession of being "goldsmiths." But soon prices of everything were commonly quoted in terms of grams of gold, or "goldgrams." People did not actually exchange anything as small as a gram of gold, but gradually the goldsmiths began to stamp small round disks of gold of as small a weight as ten grams. One of these was known as a "ten-gram piece." These disks came to be called "coins." After a while, people no longer asked what the value of any other commodity was in terms of gold. The value of any other object was simply stated as its "price" in gold. Later this was simply referred to as its "price." Most of the time, when talking of the "price" of this or that object, people did not even stop to think that this meant its exchange value in relation to a gram of gold. They began to talk of a "goldgram" as if it were something by itself, apart from a specific weight of gold. Instead of referring to gold as a common medium of exchange, by which all goods were exchanged in an indirect or "triangular" way instead of being bartered directly against each other, people simply referred to the coins and the goldgram as "money." The "price" of anything meant its price in money.*

All this came about by such a gradual and apparently spontaneous and automatic process of evolution that few people appreciated its full significance. But Peter realized that a sort of miracle had come about. His two inventions—first, freedom of exchange of consumers' goods, and second, private ownership of the means of production and free exchange of the means of production—had solved the problem of economic calculation! Or rather, they had given rise to a free market system, a free price system. And it was *this* that had solved the problem of economic calculation.

* The reader is once more reminded that all these terms are merely the nearest English equivalents to those in the original Marxanto, or Revised Marxanto, text.—*The Translator.*

Chapter 33

"SUMMING up the sense of the meeting, then," said Peter, consulting his penciled notes, "it is agreed that we should increase our production of tanks in the coming fiscal year by 20 per cent, our production of military planes by 35 per cent, and our production of transport ships by 50 per cent. Other military production is to continue at approximately the present rate, with the minor changes recommended by the Secretary of Defense. And we have also agreed, overruling the objections of the Secretary of Economics"—he nodded good-naturedly in the direction of Adams—"that the government will carry on this program by placing orders with private industry rather than by building its own plants, on the ground that we can get more efficient and economical production this way. Next, the period of military training is to be extended from eighteen months to two years. Finally, we have agreed that we need urgently to improve our intelligence and counterintelligence service against Bolshekov along the lines recommended in the report we have just heard from the Joint Chiefs of Staff. Any further comments?"

His glance passed inquiringly to each of the nine faces around the table. There were no comments. The meeting was adjourned.

In this miraculous Freeworld market system, people knew at last whether and when they were wasting resources in making things that other people did not want, or in making too much of one thing and too little of another. They could tell by a comparison of exchange values, or prices—and by profit and loss. It was the reduction of the value of every commodity and service to a common denominator, to gold, to "money," to money prices, that for the first time made all this possible.

A special group grew up, known as "enterprisers." These consisted of the more adventurous persons who found that they could make large profits if they could devise or think of some object or commodity that would fill some want not already being filled, or if they could make some existing commodity in a more economical or efficient way than it was already being made. They found that whoever could serve the consumers best was most rewarded, and that his reward was in proportion to the degree in which he served the consumers.

So an enterpriser would borrow money (if he could find enough other people with faith in him), rent a factory, buy or hire machines, and bid against other enterprisers for the services of workers in turning out products.

An enterpriser was adding to production on net balance by the amount that the value of his input was exceeded by the value of his finished output. His input was measured by its quantity multiplied by the prices or rates he paid for it; his output was measured by its quantity multiplied by the prices for which he could sell it.

The amount by which his output exceeded his input belonged to him. It was called his "profit." Sometimes it was very large. Whenever this happened a lot of people contended that the profit was "unfair," "unreasonable," or "exorbitant." But what these same people seldom noticed was the great number of constant, daily failures. More than half of the enterprisers were losing money and not making it. When an enterpriser lost money he was usually through as an enterpriser. He had no funds to start another enterprise; he could seldom get anybody else to lend him any more.

But while nearly everybody with a smaller income would refer to an unusual profit as exorbitant, unreasonable or unfair, nobody (except the enterpriser directly involved) was ever known

264

to refer to a business *loss* as exorbitant or unfair. The loss was simply ascribed to his incompetence. But only a comparatively few people seemed to have the consistency or generosity to admire the exceptional competence, ingenuity and adventurousness of the enterprisers who made big profits because they were exceptionally successful in meeting the wants of consumers.

All this, however, in Peter's view, was beside the main point. Envy and jealousy, and the tendency of the unsuccessful to attribute all success to favoritism or luck, he decided, were simply a permanent element in human nature. Under the old communist system, he knew, the people who were not members of the Protectorate envied and often hated those who were, but dared not say so. But what fascinated Peter now was the wonderful way in which the market system had solved the problem of economic calculation.

This, he saw at last, was not only a vitally important economic problem; it was the central problem that an economic system had to solve.

Neither Peter nor the Freeworld Supreme Economic Council (which he had set up as the equivalent of the old Wonworld Central Planning Board) now had to decide exactly how much ought to be produced of each of hundreds of different commodities. Prices decided. Costs of production decided. The markets decided. In short, the consumers ultimately decided.

If too many hogs were being raised, their price would fall to a point where it no longer paid to feed them corn; and so fewer hogs would be raised. If too many shirts were being turned out, their price would fall below what it cost to buy the cotton cloth, to rent the factory and machinery and pay the labor that made them. Therefore the least efficient shirtmakers would be forced out of business, and the number of shirts produced would fall. If, on the other hand, there was an exceptionally big profit in raising cotton, more cotton would be planted in the next harvest. This would cause the price of cotton and the profit in raising it to fall back again to a level equivalent to that realized in raising other things. If there was a big profit in making shoes, more

265

shoe factories would be set up, until the relative scarcity of shoes was relieved and their price fell. The cure for a low price was a low price. The cure for a high price was a high price. The cure for an excessive profit was an excessive profit.

And this was so because of the individual decisions of the enterprisers, each of whom was constantly seeking to stop his losses or to maximize his profits. He would halt or reduce the production of the things on which one lost money and begin or increase the production of the things on which one made money.

The enterprisers were constantly thinking up new inventions, devices, gadgets or products on which they might make money. The result was that instead of the few hundreds of drab, shabby, monotonous commodities turned out in Wonworld, there were now *thousands* of different commodities and services, constantly getting better and more varied.

And the result of the effort of each enterpriser to maximize his profits led to a constant tendency toward the equalization of profits. This meant, as Peter began to see, that there was a constant tendency toward a proper balance, as measured by consumers' satisfactions, in the production of these thousands of different commodities. It meant, also, that productive resources could not for a long time be misdirected or wasted in making the wrong products. For when a needless product was made, nobody bought it. The particular enterpriser who turned it out quickly failed. And when too much was made even of a needed product, it did not repay its costs of production, so the volume made would quickly be reduced. This meant that there was a constant tendency for thousands of different goods to be produced just in those proportions in which they gave a uniform and therefore the overall maximum satisfaction of consumer needs. And it meant that there was a constant tendency for productive resources—raw materials, tools and labor—to be allocated among the production of thousands of different things just in those proportions in which they would produce the highest value.

And this was not all. This solution of the problem of economic calculation not only decided just how much should be produced of each of thousands of different commodities, but (and Peter thought this might be even more important) it also pointed out and measured which were the more economical ways of producing each of these goods. And it virtually forced the adoption of the most economical way of production upon everybody once it had been discovered by anybody.

One Freeworld enterpriser, for example, adopted a new type of machine and a new factory organization system that made cotton cloth at half the cost that anybody had made it before. The enterprisers already in the business did not want to change. They had their old machines—which still were good and strong and seemed to have a long life before them—and they were used to their old methods. But the enterpriser with the new machine kept increasing his production and underselling his competitors. The producers with the oldest machines and the least efficient organization were forced out of business by the increased supplies of cotton cloth and the lower price. And the other producers eventually had to install the new type of machine in order to stay in business.

The same sort of thing was happening every day, and in every line of production. New and more economical methods were constantly being superseded by newer and still more economical methods. Old products were constantly being displaced by new products.

"Nothing approaching this process ever went on under the old state socialism, Adams," Peter said, "because the commissars and bureaucrats had no such pressure put on them. They had no competition. They didn't even have a way of finding out what the preferences of consumers were, or what their real wants were. They turned out a stock, drab, 'utility' product, the way they had always turned it out, the way it had been turned out for generations, because the consumers either had to take what the State gave them—or nothing."

But Peter had his difficulties even under the new system. For the owners and managers of the relatively inefficient firms kept sending delegations to the White House demanding "laws" to "protect" them from the "unfair competition" of the more efficient producers. Peter not only refused to give them any such "protection" but was constantly forced, both in his private talks and in his public speeches, to tell them why he was refusing it. In the long run, he repeatedly had to explain, penalizing the most efficient producers, the profit-making producers, doesn't protect anybody; it merely impoverishes everybody.

Even Adams, for a time, was on the side of the inefficient producers.

"But isn't it wasteful, chief, for these people to have to scrap all those old textile machines that still have a good life in them?"

"No," insisted Peter. "Because relative costs of production show that these machines are now worthless. They have been made obsolete. Far greater value—far greater worth—can be produced with the new machines."

But a few weeks later Adams returned to the subject, this time with exactly the opposite criticism.

"Why doesn't your private industry have *nothing but* these new model machines, chief? Why doesn't it scrap, *immediately,* all the old machines? Why not let me issue an order, in the name of the Supreme Economic Council, forcing every enterpriser to change over immediately to the latest model machine?"

"You want to force upon private industry something that socialist industry never did and never thought of doing," retorted Peter. "Under socialism the new machine would never have been invented in the first place, because no one would have recognized the need for it. If it had been invented, it would never have been adopted. You asked me only a few weeks ago whether it wasn't wasteful to scrap the old machines."

"But now I've changed my mind, chief."

"And I'm afraid you are wrong both times, Adams. It seems to me that a market economy, the private enterprise system, adopts exactly the right in-between solution—the solution of *constant* but *gradual* advance. It replaces old machines with new ones, and old models with better models; but it can't make

268

the entire change-over instantaneously, and that would not be economical even if it could."

"I don't get your point, chief. Let's put aside the question whether under our old socialist economy the new textile machine would ever have been invented. It now *has* been invented. It exists. It's available. Surely you must admit that if it were now installed everywhere it would increase the production of cotton cloth, and cut the cost in half. Surely the latest technical improvement should be introduced immediately, everywhere. Surely we want to operate industry at the highest technical efficiency!"

"You don't seem to be aware of all the assumptions you are making, Adams. *If* all these new machines could be produced and installed overnight, without using up huge amounts of labor and machine tools for their own production; and *if* the cost of the new machines to each producer did not exceed the economies in producing cotton cloth that they later brought about; and *if* the new machines in fact represented the last possible word in technical improvement, and we could be sure that they would not in a short time be superseded by still better models; and *if* the cotton textile industry were the only industry in Freeworld—*then* everybody ought immediately to install the new machine."

"Do I understand you correctly, chief? Are you saying that the best technical method of production is not necessarily the method that brings the greatest profits for an individual producer or for an industry, and that therefore we shouldn't use it but should retain technically inferior methods that bring more profits?"

"Maybe I *am* incidentally saying something like that, Adams. But I am saying something broader and much more important than that. I am saying that the best *technical* method of producing any single commodity is not necessarily the most *economical* method of producing it."

"But aren't you looking at the matter, chief, merely from the standpoint of the money-profit of the individual producer? And shouldn't we look at it from the standpoint of the greatest productivity for the whole community?"

"It is precisely because I *am* looking at the matter from the standpoint of *all-around* productivity, Adams, that I make the statement I do. It is you who are looking at the matter from the narrow standpoint of a single industry. What we have to consider is *overall* productivity—not the productivity of a single branch of industry, not the mere production, say, of cotton cloth, but the combined productivity of all lines of industry. Therefore we have to compare *all* input with *all* output. In figuring what *net* economies the new textile machines really bring, we must figure the cost of making the new machines themselves. We must consider the amount of labor, machine tools and time that must be diverted to making these machines. For the productive resources used in making the new machines must be taken from making something else—something else that may possibly be even more urgent. And then we must further consider, not merely what happens in the cotton textile industry, but what happens in every other industry. If we were to turn the whole machine-tool industry over to making the new textile machines, then there would be no capacity left to make new machines for any other industry. Yet some other industry may need new machines even more urgently."

"I think I begin to see your point, chief. Other things being equal, goods should be produced by the methods that are technically most efficient. But technical efficiency isn't the *only* factor to be considered."

"Right, Adams—though I should prefer to put the matter a little differently. What must be kept in mind, in choosing the best or most economical methods of production, is not merely the most efficient technical method of producing one particular commodity at one particular stage of one particular industry, but the most economical use of *all* available resources of labor and time and means of production to achieve the greatest general *all-around* production for a uniform satisfaction of consumer wants. And this doesn't necessarily mean the use of the most perfect technical equipment at one particular point when this

270

can only be achieved at the cost of robbing other industries and making them technically more *inefficient.*"

"So, as you see it, chief, an engineer or other technician wouldn't necessarily be able to decide what really was the most efficient means of producing a product?"

"No. He would only be able to answer the *engineering* question. But the individual enterpriser must take into consideration the most *economical* method of producing that product when *everything* is considered."

"From his own standpoint," said Adams.

"Yes, from his own standpoint," agreed Peter. "But what is most economical from his standpoint happens to be also what is most economical from the standpoint of the whole community. In other words, by what looks at first like an amazing coincidence the individual enterpriser makes the same kind of decision that an economic dictator—if he could take into consideration all the needs of consumers and all branches of production—would try to make. The economic dictator would have to decide how up-to-date and perfect the machines and productive resources could afford to be *at any one point.* The difference is that the economic dictator, as we discovered, would not know how to solve the problem. In fact, he wouldn't even recognize clearly what the problem was. And if he did see it, he wouldn't be able to solve it, because he wouldn't have a free market system and a free price system to enable him to measure his costs of production against the value of his product—to measure his input against his output."

"And he—meaning you and I—didn't have double-entry book-keeping and cost accounting to help him either, chief."

"No," agreed Peter. "And I must admit that it was an inspiration on your part, Adams, to think of bringing Baronio and Patelli along with us to Freeworld. Patelli's invention of double-entry bookkeeping and cost accounting will go down as two of the great triumphs of the human mind. Such discoveries were not possible under Wonworld's socialist system. They enable the individual enterpriser to calculate with the greatest nicety, not only for his organization as a whole but for each department within it and for each product, whether resources are being wasted and misdirected or whether they are being used to produce the maximum return."

Chapter 34

B UT these men, these enterprisers," persisted Adams, "are not trying to do the best thing possible for the community. Each of them is merely interested in maximizing his own profit!"

"That is true, Adams, and that is precisely the great miracle. Each of these men is 'selfishly' seeking merely his own private profit. And yet under this new system we have invented, under this private ownership of the means of production, each of these men acts as if he were being led by an invisible hand to produce the things that the whole community most wants, to produce them in the right proportions, and to produce them by the most economical methods."

"*An invisible hand!*" exclaimed Adams. "What a marvelous phrase, chief! For that phrase alone you deserve to be remembered by humanity."

Peter blushed. "I hope not," he said. "After all, it's only a metaphor, and I only mean it as a metaphor. If people thought I really believed that there was some occult and mysterious and supernatural force guiding the actions of enterprisers and workers —or some inevitable harmony between short-run private interest and long-run public welfare—they might ridicule me for it; and I would wish forever afterwards that I had never resorted to figures of speech. No, the new system that we have invented—"

"*You* invented it," said Adams generously, "over my objections to everything."

"Thank Marx for your objections, Adams. They steered me

away from false solutions and blind alleys and helped us to find the truth. . . . Anyway, regardless of who invented it, the new system of free markets and private ownership of the means of production *is* miraculous. I stand by that. It is a miracle. But once it's been discovered, there's nothing occult or mysterious about the explanation. For under this system every enterpriser, every workman, is under the greatest incentive to do his utmost to please the consumer. He has to make what the consumers want, otherwise he cannot sell it; he cannot exchange it for the particular things that he wants. And not only does he have to make what the consumers want, he has to make it at least as well as most of those who are already making it; and he has to sell it at least as cheaply as most of those who are already selling it. And if he wants to make more than a bare living, or if he wants to make more than an average wage, he has to make a product *better* than others do, or sell it *cheaper* than others can sell it. For that reason, what a man makes in the hope of selling it will have to be even better than what he might make merely for his personal use."

"You mean, chief, that production for profit is even better than production for use?"

"Precisely, Adams; because the man who is merely producing a chair for his own use is not competing with everybody else's production; but if he produces a chair in the hope of selling it, he must compete with the chairs that others are offering to the consumers. Production for profit *is* production for use—for if consumers do not find that a product is good in use, they will soon cease to buy it, and the enterpriser will soon be bankrupt."

"Then the 'invisible hand' you speak about," said Adams, "is really competition?"

"Competition is certainly the palm of it."

"But this means that we in the government, chief, must make sure that competition dominates our economic life."

"Precisely, Adams. We must absolutely forbid coercive monopoly. Perhaps that was the central evil of state socialism. The state's monopoly of power, and its monopoly of production. But we must do more than fight monopoly and encourage competition. We must draft our laws in such a way as to raise the *level* of competition. We must so draft them that a man who seeks his personal profit cannot attain that selfish goal *except* by promoting the public welfare."

"And how are we going to do that?"

"We must forbid him, Adams, to do anything that injures the public welfare. Therefore we must forbid theft, fraud, deceit and all misrepresentation of goods. We must illegalize every form of force, violence, extortion, intimidation, coercion. We must compel men to keep their contractual promises, to pay their just obligations and to fulfill their contracts. The corollary to private property is private responsibility. We must not allow a private industry to thrive at the cost of killing or maiming its workers, or injuring consumers of its products, or menacing the public health, or polluting public streams, or polluting the air, or smudging whole communities with the residue of smoke. We must force every industry to pay the costs of the injury it inflicts on the person or property of others."

"All that isn't easy to do, chief."

"It is extremely difficult to do," agreed Peter. "Especially to do rightly. By our new system we have saved ourselves from the thousand needless headaches of planning. But there is never-ending work to be done in perfecting the system of free enterprise. And it can only be done if, in doing it, we adhere to the principles of freedom. But if we do this, if we make it impossible for people to grow rich by violence or force or theft or fraud or sharp practice, then the only way in which they will be able to succeed in business will be precisely by competition and rivalry in serving the consumers."

"Are you sure that laws will be enough, chief, however good they may be?"

A heavy rain was coming down. Peter went to the window and looked steadily out at it.

"No," he said at last, "laws won't be enough, however good. If the people were so corrupt that they were constantly trying to evade the law, and if the police and judges and government were so corrupt that they made no impartial effort to enforce the law, then even an ideal set of laws would be futile. . . . No, the majority of individuals must be moral. The society must live by a moral code. The individual enterpriser or trader or workman must not only fear the police, or private retaliation; he must himself believe in honest dealing, in fairness, in justice, in truthfulness, in honor. . . . Perhaps the greatest vice of the communist system, worse even than its failure to produce goods, was that it destroyed all sense of justice and truth, and made its only 'morality' consist in absolute obedience to the commands of the dictator. . . . But individual freedom is impossible without individual responsibility."

"In other words," said Adams, "despotism may govern without faith, but liberty cannot."

Peter looked at him with startled admiration. "Now *you* have coined a wonderful aphorism which should earn you the gratitude of mankind."

"People will probably remember the aphorism, chief, and forget the author. Or worse, they will continue to remember the aphorism after they have forgotten its meaning."

"Anyway," concluded Peter, "it sums up perfectly what I have been trying to say. If we want our new system to endure, we must not only create an institutional framework of law and order, but each of us must contribute toward building up a moral code to which all of us will adhere, not through fear of legal punishment, or even through fear of what other people will think of us, but solely through fear of what each of us would otherwise think of himself."

"Could we ever develop such a moral code, chief, would we ever live up to it, unless we revived those very religions that communism has been reviling and despising and trying to stamp out all these years?"

Peter looked out again at the rain. "I don't know. I don't know. . . . We can't just *invent* such a religion. We can't just throw together some arbitrary credo about the supernatural and then try to force everybody to subscribe to it. But your question stops me, Adams. I'll admit this much, even now. I'm not sure that men will accept and abide by a moral code, however rational, based on purely utilitarian grounds. Perhaps the masses of mankind will never abide by a moral code unless they feel a deep sense of *reverence* for something. . . ."

"For the universe itself?"

"At least a deep sense of humility, a recognition of their own littleness in the universe, a profound sense of their own bottomless ignorance before the mystery and the miracle of existence. . . . Perhaps we need at least a conviction, a faith, that beyond the seemingly blind forces of nature there may be, there must be, some Great Purpose, forever inscrutable to our little minds."

"Isn't it an example of the pathetic fallacy, isn't it very unphilosophic anthropomorphism and anthropocentrism, chief, even to use such a term as 'purpose' in connection with nature or the universe as a whole? Isn't it presumptuous, and perhaps meaningless, to say either that the universe has a Purpose or that it has no Purpose? 'Purpose' describes a purely human attitude— the use of present limited means to attain future ends."

Peter was looking at Adams with surprise and admiration. "You sound almost like a trained philosopher!"

"Oh, I used to be quite a student of Dialectical Materialism in my twenties, chief. And then, you know, Hegel was available in the private Politburo library because of his profound influence on Marx, and though I was perhaps his only reader—"

"Well, fortunately, Adams, we don't have to solve every problem now."

"No. We should be considerate enough to leave a few," said Adams with an ironic smile, "for our descendants."

Chapter 35

IN Moscow Marshall Zakachetsky was addressing the Politburo.
"I have the pleasure to report," he said, "that the government
now has as many planes in operation as it had the day before the
Uldanovite counterrevolutionaries flew off with our entire supply.
This is even better than it sounds, for we have twice as many
long-range bombers as we had then. And all our planes are new.
Half of the rebels' planes, on the other hand, were obsolete when
they stole them. They are all now three years older; a good part
have probably been junked; they had to start from scratch in
building their airplane and motor factories and their machine
tools; so it seems impossible—"

"Excellent," said Bolshekov. "But we've got to establish even
greater superiority. One year more, and we'll have a little surprise
for them. . . ."

Peter's economic reforms in the Western Hemisphere had succeeded far beyond his fondest dreams. Though only three years
had passed since the flight from Moscow, Peter's statisticians were
already informing him that the man-hour productivity of Freeworld was at least four times as great as that of Wonworld,
and might be much higher.

Peter did not take these statistics too seriously. It was not easy,
he had concluded, to measure comparative living standards or
comparative human satisfactions. Even in comparing goods, it
was not as easy to measure differences in quality as differences in

quantity. And as there was no trade between the two half-worlds, because Bolshekov's regime would not permit it, it was difficult to compare values. But in whatever could be measured in quantity, the achievements of Freeworld were far beyond those of Wonworld. This was true even in the military field, where Peter's intelligence agents informed him that in ship producing capacity, tank producing capacity, and even in plane producing capacity Freeworld had already surpassed Wonworld, in spite of the latter's great head start.

But even more than by the record of production, Peter was struck by the startling change that had come over the whole spirit of the people. They worked with an energy and zeal infinitely greater than anything they had shown before. Peter now found people everywhere who regarded their work as a pleasure, a hobby, an exciting adventure. They were constantly thinking of improvements, devising new gadgets, dreaming of new processes that would cut costs of production, or new inventions and new products that consumers might want.

Adams was bewildered by the transformation.

"What caused it?" he asked.

"I think two things have caused it," said Peter. "And the first is liberty."

"Liberty may be fine for its own sake," replied Adams, "but what has it got to do with this tremendous release of human energy?"

"You have practically answered your own question, Adams. That is precisely what economic liberty does. It *releases* human energy. Before people had economic liberty, you and I and the Central Planning Board laid down the central economic plan. And from then on nobody else had any function or duty but that of slavishly carrying out, to the last detail, the plan that we bureaucrats had laid down. Now *everybody* can plan. Now everybody is a center of planning. The worker can plan to shift to another employer or another line of production where the rewards are higher. He can plan to train himself in a new skill that pays better. And anybody who can save or borrow capital, or who can get the co-operation of other workers or offer them more attractive terms of employment than before, can start a new enterprise, make a new product, fill a new need. And this puts a quality of adventure and excitement into most people's lives that was never there before. In Wonworld, in effect, only the Dictator himself could originate or initiate: everybody else simply carried out his orders. But in Freeworld *anybody* can originate or initiate. And because he can, he does."

"And the second thing that caused this transformation, chief?"

"The second thing, Adams, is that in our new free private enterprise system—an integral part of which is the right to and the protection of private property—every man gets what he himself produces. And as his reward is proportioned to his product—as his reward is, in fact, merely another name for the exchange value of his product—he knows that it depends upon himself, upon the value of what he creates. Each man is constantly striving to increase the amount he himself creates because it increases his own reward."

"I can't see that at all, chief. I can cite you the case of one fellow, for example—"

"I purposely exaggerated," confessed Peter, "for the sake of clarifying the situation. This is what *would* happen if there were perfect competition, including—if it is possible to imagine such a thing—perfect foreknowledge on the part of producers and consumers. Nevertheless, even under our system as it stands, it is still true, though there may never be an exactly 'perfect' correspondence, that every individual and every group *tends* to get the amount of wealth that he or it specifically brings into existence. Everyone tends to be rewarded by the consumers to the extent that he has contributed to the needs of the consumers. In other words, free competition tends to give to labor what labor creates, to the owners of money and capital goods what their capital creates, and to enterprisers what their co-ordinating function creates."

"If you could achieve *that,* chief, no group would have the right to complain. You would have achieved an economic paradise."

"Whether you call it an economic paradise or not, Adams, this is in fact what we have achieved. We have changed the entire principle on which economic life is based. For Marx's unworkable dictum: *From each according to his ability; to each according to his needs,* we have substituted a new, workable principle: *To each what he creates."*

"But even granting that your new system does operate on this new principle, chief, are you sure that it is in every respect superior to the socialist principle of Marx?"

"It works," said Peter; "and the ostensible Marxist principle did not work. When we attempted to enforce the principle of '*to* each according to his needs' we found that it defeated the whole object of getting '*from* each according to his ability.' But the moment we substitute the principle of 'to each what he creates' we automatically solve the problem of getting 'from each according to his ability.' "

"But you can't consistently apply the principle of 'to each what he creates,' " said Adams. "How do you solve the problem of invalids, the crippled, the blind, the helpless; the problem of mothers bearing children, the problem of children themselves—"

"Let's not mix up two entirely different things, Adams. I'm talking of the principle needed to secure maximum production. You're talking of what I think ought to be called '*secondary distribution*.' Let me explain. Under socialism goods were first produced and *then* distributed. But this is not what happens under our free enterprise and private property. Under this new system 'production' and 'distribution' are merely two names for the same undivided process. When production comes on the market it is already somebody's property. It is merely *exchanged* for somebody else's property; it is not 'distributed.' To say that each worker or enterpriser *gets* what he creates is not necessarily to say that each *keeps* the market value of what he creates merely for himself. He is free to distribute what he creates or what he earns as he sees fit. He may provide for his family, or he may give part of his earnings to the helpless or to charity."

"But what you are saying, chief, is that the helpless or non-productive should be provided for only if the productive are generous enough to provide for them. We can't depend on that. The State should give everyone a minimum."

"What *you* are saying, Adams, is that we are all more generous collectively than we are individually. Or rather, that we are all willing to be more generous with other people's money than we are with our own. Or still rather, that our vicarious generosity, our pseudo-generosity, is greater than our real generosity; and that therefore we should force *somebody else* to contribute to the support of the needy through taxes, confiscation, or what not. What you are saying, and what Marx was saying, is that those who have *not* created the wealth should seize it from those who *have* created it."

"But surely, chief, we ought in our collective capacity to make precisely the provision for the needy and the handicapped that we are unwilling to make in our individual capacity—"

"Let's deal with that question at a later time," interrupted Peter. "We have been slipping off the point we started to discuss. I began by asserting that under our new system each of us tends to get the amount of wealth, income or value that he specifically brings into existence. And you are denying this."

"No, I'm not. I'm merely asking you to prove it."

"Well, let's begin, Adams, with an overall view of the situation. Here are hundreds of different industries. Here is an industry making and selling shoes. Here's another industry raising and processing wheat, baking and selling bread. Let's for the moment consider the bread industry and the shoe industry each as separate integrated units. The shoe industry can sell shoes only if consumers want them; it can sell only as many as consumers want, and it can sell them only at prices that consumers are willing to pay. Therefore the gross income of the shoe industry depends upon how many pairs of shoes it collectively produces and how much it gets for each pair. In other words, the gross income of the shoe industry depends upon the total value of what the shoe industry produces. In fact, the gross income of the shoe industry *is* the total value of what it produces."

"Right, so far."

"This value is measured by consumers who are trying to fill their own needs and wants. They measure this value, in effect, by the value of what they are willing to exchange for it."

"They exchange money for it," said Adams.

"Directly," agreed Peter, "they exchange money for it. But they got this money in the first place by exchanging for the money the products that they themselves made. So indirectly they exchange their own products for the things they 'buy' and consume."

"Correct."

"And neither party, Adams, would be willing to make this exchange unless he thought he were getting at least equal value for what he was parting with—in fact, not unless he thought he were getting *more* value so far as his own personal needs were concerned."

"Correct."

"So each industry, considered as a whole, Adams, therefore gets the total value of what it produces. The shoe industry gets the total value of what *it* produces, the bread industry gets the total value of what *it* produces, and so on."

"I suppose that is true," agreed Adams after a pause, "but what does it prove? Suppose the people in the bread industry found they were not getting as much in proportion to their work, skill or input for making bread as the people in the shoe industry got for making shoes?"

"If these people were investors of capital," said Peter, "they would stop putting money into making bread and put it instead into something else—say, making shoes. If they were enterprisers, some of them would quit making bread—or perhaps be forced to quit—and go, let's say for simplification, into the shoe business. And certainly the *new* enterprisers coming along would not go into the bread industry but into something else—again let's say the shoe industry. And finally, workers would quit the bread industry and go into something else—again, say, the shoe industry, where they were offered more money. And certainly *new* workers would not learn how to bake bread but, say, how to make shoes. As a result of this, in turn, the price of shoes would drop and the price of bread would rise until enterprisers were earning approximately equal profits in both industries, until capitalists were getting approximately equal returns from both industries, and until workers of the same skill and ability were getting approximately equal wages in both industries."

"But suppose there were some *third* industry, chief?"

"The same process, Adams, would apply to all industries taken together. There would be a constant tendency for all of them to come into balance with each other. There would be an equally constant tendency for profits in all lines, capital returns in all lines, and wages in all lines to come into alignment with each other, to equal each other—with allowances, of course, for differences in risks, skills, and so on. There would be a constant tendency for all industry, in brief, to come into equilibrium—for all prices, wages, capital returns, production, and so on to come into equilibrium with each other."

"You are assuming, of course," said Adams, "perfect competition, and perfect mobility of labor and of the means of production—"

"No, I am not," replied Peter. "If I were assuming *perfect* competition, *perfect* mobility, *perfect* foresight and so on, I wouldn't have to speak of a *tendency* toward equilibrium. There would then *always* be a *perfect* equilibrium. . . . I am merely assuming that there is a reasonable amount of mobility and a reasonable amount of foresight and a reasonable amount of competition. Under such actual conditions we will not get *perfect* equilibrium or a *perfect* correspondence between a man's income and his production, but we will get a rough correspondence, a *reasonable* correspondence—with a constant tendency toward a more exact correspondence. Of course the more competition we have, the greater this tendency will be. So the effort of our govern-

284

ment must be to encourage the maximum of healthy competition, to keep every field of competition constantly open to newcomers."

"You speak of 'the shoe industry,' 'the bread industry' and so on, chief. Aren't these really general names for several industries? Doesn't the shoe industry have to buy its leather, for instance, from the leather industry? How can you say, then, that the shoe industry gets the whole value of what it produces?"

"These differences between 'industries,' Adams, are all arbitrary differences. We can classify industries any way we please. It's merely a matter of convenience. One of the shortcomings of central bureaucratic planners is that they always forget this. They try to solve the troubles of *the* X industry, say, in isolation, because they fail to see the X industry merely as part of the overall structure of production. Now whether a so-called 'industry' is vertically integrated, or consists merely of one part of a finishing process, makes no difference in the way rewards are finally determined. The price that the shoe industry gets for shoes is determined by consumers. The price that the shoe industry can pay for leather is determined, among other things, by the price that the consumers pay for shoes. In the same way the price that the leather industry pays for hides is determined largely by the price that the shoe industry is paying for leather; and so on. Part of what the 'shoe industry' gets from the sale of completed shoes it must pay over to the 'leather industry,' for example, for the leather. Nevertheless, the 'shoe industry' considered as a whole gets the total value that it *adds* to the leather in making shoes. Of course we can subdivide the shoe industry, in turn, into the shoe manufacturing industry, the shoe wholesalers, the retail shoe industry, and so on. But each part of this industry gets the value that its own services add to the final value of the product in getting it into the hands—or should I say onto the feet?—of the consumers."

"Very well," agreed Adams. "You have finally proved to me that each industry considered as a whole gets the total value of what it creates, and that each segment of the industry gets the total value which that segment adds to the final value of what it creates. But you haven't yet proved to me that free competition tends to give to labor what labor creates, nor to each worker what he personally creates."

"Let me try," said Peter. "We have agreed that freedom of consumption, freedom of movement, freedom of choice of occupation, and freedom of competition tend to equalize the value in different industries of the product that a worker of a given skill can create. This is even more true as between firms in the same industry which utilize the same skills. Let's assume, for example, that a worker in a given firm adds to the quantity or quality of its production a value equal to 30 goldgrams a week—"

"You mean the worker adds to production a value or a product that the employer can sell in the market for 30 goldgrams a week?"

"Exactly. And let's suppose also that this particular worker could add the same amount of output or value to the product of any other employer in that line. Suppose employer A wanted to pay this worker only 20 goldgrams a week."

"Employer A would want to exploit the worker, naturally."

"Let's say he would. Then Employer B, just as selfish, would offer the worker 21 goldgrams a week. For B would be content to make only 9 goldgrams a week out of the worker, rather than stand by and see employer A making 10 goldgrams a week out of him."

"I can see how B's selfishness would cause him to do that," agreed Adams.

"But we have reckoned without employer C," said Peter, "who is just as selfish, and just as profit-minded, as either A or B. Rather than stand by and see employer B make 9 goldgrams a week out of the worker, C would step in and offer him 22 goldgrams a week. And so on. You can assume as many employers as you want—or, for that matter, as few—as long as there is competition among them. At an open competitive auction the price realized for anything is as high as, or higher than, the second most determined bidder feels that he can afford to go. So A and B alone might bid up the pay of our worker—who produces an added product for either of them equal to 30 goldgrams a

286

week—to 26, 27, 28, 29 goldgrams, or 29½, 29¾, 29⅞ goldgrams, until the profit in employing him all but disappeared. For either A or B would rather make a slight extra profit, however small, than see his competitor make it."

"In other words, chief, manufacturers bidding for workers act in the long run on the same type of calculation as manufacturers bidding for raw materials?"

"Exactly, Adams. Their competition bids up the price of labor's services in the same way as it bids up the prices of raw materials."

"As they pay the market price for raw materials, so they pay the market price for labor?"

"Exactly. We can put this in another way by saying that the worker gets the value that he adds to the manufacturer's total product. Wages are determined by the final or marginal productivity of labor. The worker gets what he creates. He gets the value that his labor adds to production."

"Then it isn't the generosity of the employers, chief, but their selfishness and cupidity that leads them to keep bidding up wages to the point where they correspond with the worker's marginal productivity?"

"That's one way of putting it."

"That's a pretty convincing argument," said Adams finally. "But maybe— Well, for example: there are a lot of workers competing against each other, but only a relatively few employers. Doesn't *that* tend to push wages down below the point of marginal productivity?"

"I've had that question investigated by our statisticians in the Supreme Economic Council," said Peter, "and I find that in Freeworld there is about one employer for every twenty workers. But even if there were only one employer for every hundred workers, or one for every five hundred, the result would still be approximately the same. As I just pointed out, only two employers in an industry, if they are really competing, can push up wage levels to the point of marginal productivity."

"And then if there were only *one* employer in an industry," added Adams, "even if he had a monopoly in that industry, I

287

suppose he would still have to bid labor up in order to keep it from drifting into *other* industries, or perhaps to attract it out of other industries. For he must still compete with other industries as a *buyer* of labor's services, even if not as a seller of his product."

"That is true," agreed Peter. "He would certainly have to compete with other industries at least for *new* labor, or for common labor. He might be able to some extent, perhaps, to exploit his *skilled* labor—provided he did not have to employ any additional skilled labor and provided it would take his skilled workers a long time to acquire other skills. But apart from such exceptional situations, the worker must tend to get what he creates. He tends to get the value of his marginal productivity."

"All right, chief. You've sufficiently convinced me on that point. But I still have a few questions to ask. . . ."

Chapter 36

IN Washington, Adams and Peter sat listening to a short-wave broadcast of one of Bolshekov's speeches in Moscow's Red Square. It was full of the usual clichés of Communist propaganda, but suddenly Peter was pulled up:

". . . I should like in passing to say a few additional words about the two traitors who were hung in the square as part of this morning's program. Their numbers were EN—57 and L—92. The first was an engineer who passed under the name of John Maxwell and the other a young woman—very pretty, like most women traitors—who posed as his daughter under the name of Edith Maxwell. Those of you who were here to witness their hanging were told that they had confessed their crime, but I think you all ought to know that they confessed also that they had committed each of their acts of sabotage and treason at the direct orders of the archtraitor and criminal, Peter Uldanov. . . ."

It was not until several weeks later that Adams could get Peter to discuss once more the larger problems of Freeworld.

"Bolshekov's terrible crime, chief," Adams kept repeating, "only provides a stronger reason for you to try to create a world in which such things will be forever impossible. We can only do that with completely transformed political and economic institutions. And we must be terribly sure that in substituting new institutions for those of Wonworld we are substituting the right ones."

"I suppose you're right, Adams," Peter at last conceded. "The past is irrevocable; what's done's done; the future is the only thing we can do anything about. But I wish I could get this horror out of my mind. I know that they're dead; and compared with my ugliest fears about their fate, and all the tortures my imagination has put me through, that knowledge comes at last as a sort of release. But I wish I knew whether they had *really* 'confessed' or not; I wish I knew whether they had *really* accused me, or whether that is just a pure lie of Bolshekov's. . . ."

"Which would you prefer to believe, chief? That they 'confessed' and accused you of their own free will, for trivial reasons? Or that they did it only after unendurable torture? Or that they *withstood* terrible torture—which they could have saved themselves merely by consenting to accuse you?"

"Don't, Adams. I wouldn't want to believe any of those things."

"Then why not stop torturing yourself? Bolshekov was probably only lying."

"The horrible communist system of Wonworld debases and poisons the existence of everybody, Adams. It becomes impossible under it for anybody to believe in human dignity, decency . . ." He made an effort to pull himself together. "What do you want to discuss?"

"I want to come back to the questions we were debating a month ago, chief. You said the worker in our new system gets the value of what he produces. But how can he, when the owners of capital insist on a share of it?"

Peter passed his hand across his brow as if trying to rub out the distractions that were not relevant to this question.

"Let's begin, Adams, by simplifying the problem. You and I are two workmen. I produce a hatchet. I lend it to you, and you chop down trees with it. Suppose you were paid in accordance with the number of trees you chopped down? Would you say you had done all this yourself, and that I was grasping to expect to be paid for the use of my hatchet?"

"No, chief. Your work in producing the hatchet is as necessary to chopping down the trees as my direct work on the trees. Therefore I would *pay* you for the hatchet, and *buy* the hatchet from you."

"Very well. But suppose you didn't yet have the money to do that. Then you might propose, instead, either one of two things. You might come to me and say that you needed a hatchet for chopping down trees, and that if I would lend you one of my hatchets you would give me, in return, part of what you earned with it."

"That would be only fair."

"So you have already admitted, Adams, that I, as the maker or owner of the capital instrument, have been responsible for, have helped to create, part of the product that you, in turn, have completed by the joint use of capital and labor—that is to say, by the joint use of the ax and your muscles."

"I have admitted it."

"Now suppose I, as the owner of the hatchet, decline your proposal that I get some definite percentage of your earnings. Perhaps I don't want to be dependent upon your particular industriousness or your particular ability to get contracts to chop down trees. I may nonetheless agree to let you *hire* my hatchet for a definite sum each month."

"Such an arrangement would seem to me entirely fair, chief—provided you did not try to charge too much for the use of your hatchet."

"The amount of rental I could get for my hatchet would depend, Adams, on the one hand, on how many tree choppers there were like yourself who wanted my hatchet, and on how high the top bidder was willing to bid for it. And it would depend, on the other hand, on how many hatchet owners there were and for how low the lowest offerer was willing to rent. But the tendency would be for the woodchoppers to bid anything up to the amount by which the hatchets would increase their earning power—and that would depend, in turn, upon how much the hatchets increased their productivity."

"But how could you possibly separate, chief, the production of the hatchet from the production of the worker who swung the hatchet?"

"It might help us if we look at the problem in another way," said Peter. "Suppose I made a hatchet, but that a third man, putting in much more time and work, made one of these portable power saws with an endless chain of whirling teeth. Now suppose that with the ax you could only chop down 10 trees a day, but with the motorized saw you could cut down 25 trees a day. The *additional* productivity of the power saw would be 15 felled trees a day. So if you hired out as a tree-feller and charged for each tree you felled, you could earn 150 per cent more with the power saw than with the ax. And therefore you would be willing to bid anything up to that much more for the rental of the power saw. Being a sensible man, you would know that it wasn't *your* productivity that had suddenly gone up 150 per cent, but that what was responsible for the result was the *joint* productivity of yourself and the power saw."

"Very well, chief. I see all that. I acknowledge that capital instruments and land and labor each contribute towards what is inextricably a *joint* product, and that the immediate naked labor is not entitled to the *sole* credit for that product—"

"And with free competition," said Peter, "each factor tends to get paid the *relative* or *proportionate* share that it contributes to the total value of the product that all the factors jointly produce."

"But what I can't understand is this," said Adams. "If everything is *jointly* produced by tools and labor—by capital instruments and labor—how can you tell which part of the product to attribute to each? An ax can't chop down trees without a worker to swing it; a worker can't chop down trees without an ax to swing. And therefore you might argue that the *worker* does everything, because without him no trees would be chopped down; or you might argue that the *ax* does everything, because without it no trees would be chopped down. But the one thing that wouldn't make any sense at all would be to argue, for example, that the ax chopped down two-fifths of the tree and that

292

the worker was responsible for chopping down the other three-fifths."

"You are entirely correct, Adams, in saying that it wouldn't make any sense to state the matter that way. The proportional contributions, the relative productivity, of the ax and the worker can't be calculated in *physical* terms. But they *can* be calculated in terms of *value*. How much would a power saw increase my earnings? That's a practical question; it has a practical answer; and I can afford to bid up to that amount as rental on the power saw. Or if I own a factory employing a hundred men, I can ask, 'How much would ten more men increase my earnings?'— and I can afford to bid up to *that* amount as wages. Or take a more complicated problem. Fertilizer is only one element contributing to the total productivity of a farm. It can never be used by itself, but only in combination with land, capital, labor and waiting. How much can a farmer afford to pay for a given quantity of fertilizer? This will depend on how much more corn he can grow by using more fertilizer, how much less he can grow by using less, and upon the existing or expected price of corn. So the answer depends upon the *marginal* productivity of the fertilizer. That is, it depends upon the *difference* that a given *increment or decrement* of fertilizer makes to the final product— or more accurately, to the *value* of that product. In sum, with free competition, wages are determined by the marginal productivity of labor; and the rental of land and of capital instruments is determined by the marginal productivity of land and of capital instruments. Each factor gets the amount of wealth or income that it specifically brings into existence."

Adams took a pinch of snuff and looked thoughtful.

"I'm still not satisfied," he said at last. "Take money. People are lending money now, and they are demanding for it what is being variously called use-money, usury, or interest. I can't see the slightest justification for that. I'll admit that a power saw— or land, or a factory, or any kind of machine or tool whatever— adds to a worker's production. All these things are productive instruments; and therefore it is perfectly fair to charge a rental for them, corresponding to their productivity, to repay the people who have made these things or who furnish these things. But money? Money is sterile. Gold is sterile. It produces nothing. Why should anything be paid for the loan of it?"

"There are several ways of answering your question, Adams. Perhaps the quickest would be simply to point out that creditors don't *force* loans or money on borrowers. Borrowers pay interest voluntarily; they even bid against each other in raising interest rates because of their competitive desire for money. Evidently the *borrowers* don't consider money sterile."

"But—"

"Let me put it this way," continued Peter. "What difference is there in principle between your borrowing a power saw from me and paying me a rental on it, or your borrowing from me instead enough money to buy the power saw yourself, and paying me interest on the borrowed money? Is the second process any less 'productive' for you than the first?"

Adams paused for another pinch of snuff. "Well, I can see *one* difference, at least. As soon as your power saw wore out, chief, or became obsolete, I would return it to you. If you wanted to continue renting it out, you would have to take a *diminishing* rental on it. Its rental and its value would keep falling until it was finally worthless. But if you lent me the money, you would expect the same amount of interest on it in perpetuity, and at any time that the loan expired you would expect to get back the full amount of your original principal, undiminished."

It was Peter's turn to think a while before answering. "That is true," he said finally. "But what does it mean? It simply means that if I lent you the power saw or some other capital instrument that would sooner or later wear out or become obsolete, I would have to charge you a rental for it much higher than the interest I could charge you for the same amount of money. Then out of the rental that I got for the capital instrument, I would have to set aside each month a certain sum, so that by the time the capital instrument had become worthless I would have enough money to buy a new capital instrument. And so on."

"But how do you know, chief, that there is in fact such a difference between rental rates and interest rates?"

"Because both the lender and the borrower, Adams, are free to choose either course of action they wish. This freedom of choice, plus competition in borrowing and lending, must tend to bring about precisely this relationship. Look at it now from the borrower's standpoint. Suppose you borrow 10,000 goldgrams at 5 per cent a year interest in order to buy a house for 10,000 goldgrams and rent it out for 900 goldgrams or 9 per cent a year. This gives you an apparent profit above mortgage interest of 400 goldgrams a year. But you must set aside at least part of this 400 goldgrams for repairs, maintenance and depreciation of your house. You would probably allow another part as compensation for the risk of finding your house sometimes without a tenant, and still another part as compensation for your labor and responsibilities as a landlord. And so, as long as lenders and borrowers act with equal foresight, it will become a toss-up whether it is more profitable to lend out money for interest or to build houses with it and rent them. Certainly we won't be able to say in advance that the lender of capital will necessarily be better off in the end because he gets interest perpetually and gets back the full amount of his principal. The long-run tendency must be for rentals minus maintenance or replacement cost to equal interest rates."

Adams took still another thoughtful pinch of snuff. He did not seem to be quite convinced, but appeared to be on the verge of being convinced.

Peter continued: "Suppose we look at the matter in still another way. Lending 10,000 goldgrams to a woolen manufacturer is really selling him the amount of cloth that 10,000 goldgrams, put into his equipment, will bring into existence."

Adams thought about this. "That is a striking way of putting the matter," he said at last; "but I don't think it is correct."

"Why?"

"Let's see what happens, chief. When you *lend* 10,000 goldgrams to a woolen manufacturer you really don't *sell* him anything. True, he uses the money to *buy* 10,000 goldgrams' worth of equipment. Now he's got to pay you perpetual and undiminished interest. In order to enable him to do that, he's got to earn a good deal more in each year with his new machines than he pays you in interest, because he has to put aside each year a certain amount of money—we might call it a *depreciation* allowance—in order to buy new machines out of the accumulated sum when the old machines have worn out or become obsolete. Now if everything works out perfectly, he won't merely produce 10,000 goldgrams' worth of cloth. He will produce a certain additional amount of cloth *perpetually*. And as this would mean an *infinite* amount of cloth, it ought to have an *infinite* value, and not merely 10,000 goldgrams' worth of value. In fact, as the new machines, after proper replacement allowances, produce an infinite amount of additional cloth with an infinite value, the machines themselves ought to sell for an infinite price. And as a piece of land, also, can continue to yield crops infinitely, if properly fertilized, it also ought to sell for an infinite price."

What was the answer to that? Peter lit another cigarette.

Adams finally broke into the train of his thoughts: "You know, chief, I've been puzzled about this matter for a long time. I've been discussing it with Patelli. And he has what seems to me to be an entirely different theory of interest."

"Oh?"

"Patelli, chief, argues that interest *isn't* the price paid for the services of capital at all, but something quite different. He says that interest springs out of the fact that people value present goods more than future goods of the same kind and quality. In other words, future goods are bought and sold at a discount as against present goods. Interest, he contends, is the *ratio* of the value assigned to want-satisfaction in the immediate future and the value assigned to want-satisfaction in remoter periods of the future. It is a *ratio* of commodity prices, not a price itself. In other words, Patelli says that interest arises out of what he calls 'time-preference.' "

Peter blew careful smoke rings as he tried to think this out. "Time-preference! That's a very interesting phrase."

"Patelli," Adams continued, "argues that we prefer a cup of coffee today to a cup of coffee tomorrow; or one tomorrow to one a year from now; or one a year from now to one a century from now. Suppose, for example, you had no other means of sustenance, and you were asked to give up a crust of bread today on the absolute assurance that you would get in return two or even three crusts of bread a week from today, would you make the exchange?"

"All that doesn't necessarily mean," replied Peter, "that I value present goods more than future goods. It may merely mean that I prefer to eat when I am hungry and drink when I am thirsty. Or it may merely mean that I prefer to spread my consumption out evenly over time. If I had seven rolls of bread to last me for a week, I'd eat only one a day."

"Patelli," continued Adams, "argues that we always tend to underestimate our future needs and to overestimate our future supplies."

"Perhaps something like that does happen," conceded Peter. "You know, I've just thought of an interesting comparison between the way we look at time and the way we look at distance. When you stand on a railroad track and look along the track and along the line of telegraph poles beside the track, you *know* that as a matter of fact each railroad tie is the same width as all the others and each telegraph pole the same height as all the others. Nevertheless, to your eye and to a camera, each tie seems narrower and each telegraph pole shorter than the one in front of it, and the last pole that you can see is reduced to a mere point in space. This is what's known as perspective. Now perhaps Patelli is right. Perhaps we value things, if I may put it that way, in a sort of diminishing *time-perspective* just as we see them in a diminishing space-perspective. In other words, the further away a thing is, in either time or space, the smaller it looks to us. Now your telegraph poles, as you look at them, diminish to form a definite triangle. And in the same way a perpetual series of equal added outputs of yards of woolen cloth, or a perpetual series of approximately equal crops from a piece of land, tend, as we look forward into the future, to diminish in value to our mind's eye year by year so that they form, not an infinite value but a sort of measurable triangle of value, like the triangle formed by telegraph poles in perspective. And perhaps that is why we put only a finite value on the machine or only a finite value on the piece of land."

"And we arrive at the same sort of result if we look at the matter the other way round," added Adams. "If people estimated future goods as highly as present goods, then you ought to be obliged to pay 100 goldgrams for the privilege of receiving 5 goldgrams a year for twenty years. But I have been in touch with a friend of mine who has set up an insurance business, and he tells me that as a matter of fact I can buy the right to receive 5 goldgrams a year for twenty years for only 62.30 goldgrams."

"Because the current rate of interest is 5 per cent," said Peter.

"But that is only another way of stating the same thing," persisted Adams. "If people valued future goods as much as present goods, you ought to have to pay an infinite sum for the right to receive 5 goldgrams a year *perpetually*. But as a matter of fact you can buy that right for only 100 goldgrams. Or let's clinch the matter by leaving out annual interest payments altogether. I asked my insurance friend how much I would have to pay *now* for the right to receive 100 goldgrams ten years from now. He tells me that I can buy that right for only 61.39 goldgrams. In other words, 100 goldgrams ten years from today is worth only as much as 61.39 goldgrams today. I also found out that 100 goldgrams *twenty* years from today is worth only 37.69 goldgrams—"

"Just a minute!" Peter took out a pen and wrote some figures on a pad. "Ah, just as I suspected, Adams. At a prevailing interest rate of 5 per cent, a man for 100 goldgrams can buy a twenty-year bond that not only pays him 5 goldgrams a year but returns his entire 100 goldgrams at the end of the twenty years. So he actually buys 200 future goldgrams for 100 present goldgrams. Now your insurance friend tells you that the present value of your 5 goldgrams a year for twenty years is 62.30 goldgrams. And he tells you that the present value of your 100 goldgrams at the end of twenty years is 37.69 goldgrams. Now if you add these you get a total present value of 99.99 goldgrams."

"And if you throw in the extra figures beyond the decimal points you get a total present value of 100 goldgrams," agreed Adams. "So everything totals up correctly. . . . But you interrupted me in the reinforcing point I was about to make. Here are the figures: 100 goldgrams ten years from now have a present value of 61.39 goldgrams; twenty years from now they have a present value of 37.69; thirty years from now a present value of 23.14; forty years from now a present value of 14.20; fifty years from now a present value of 8.72—"

"Which proves?"

"Which bears out your illustration, chief, of the telegraph poles, your phrase about time-perspective; which shows that, other things equal, goods have a constantly diminishing value as they are remote in time."

Peter lit another cigarette. He smoked it in silence almost down to the end.

"I can't seem to make up my mind just now," he said at last. "I can't decide whether time-preference causes the interest rate, or whether the interest rate is caused by the anticipated marginal productivity of capital which in turn causes what Patelli calls time-preference."

"But the diminishing value of 100 goldgrams over time—?"

"Doesn't necessarily prove anything about causation, Adams. To say that 100 goldgrams fifty years from now is worth only 8.72 goldgrams today is merely another way of saying that 8.72 goldgrams invested at 5 per cent compound interest today would increase to 100 goldgrams at the end of fifty years. . . . Maybe the two theories can be reconciled, Adams. . . . Maybe they are supplementary. Maybe the marginal productivity of capital goods is one cause of the payment of interest, and time-preference is another, just as the value of gold, for example, is partly determined by its industrial and ornamental uses and partly determined by its use as a medium of exchange. . . . We haven't time now to straighten out the whole business."

"Perhaps we don't even need to, chief."

"What we are certain of, Adams, is this. Relatively few people would bother to save capital at all if they could get no interest for it, and still fewer would consent to let saved capital go out of their hands without the compensation of interest. And we do know that borrowers voluntarily pay interest and even bid against each other to raise interest rates. For if interest rates are less than borrowers are actually willing to pay, there develops what is called a shortage of funds. This can only be corrected by an increase in interest rates which will cause some people to be willing to lend more and others to want to borrow less. In short, we don't necessarily have to know *why* people are willing to pay interest any more than we need to know why they are willing to pay high prices for whisky or gold or diamonds—"

"—or bad paintings."

"Or bad paintings. People's desires and tastes and valuations are what they are, and they seek to gratify them. And it isn't for us, as bureaucrats, to say that their tastes are misdirected, because posterity may conclude that it was *we* who preferred the bad paintings to the good ones."

"In other words," said Adams, trying to sum up, "market values are the composite result of the valuations of individuals. Just as prices are fixed by the market, so are wages; and just as wages are fixed by the market, so are interest rates. And just as consumers are willing to pay for consumption goods anything up to the amount that the addition of these goods adds to their satisfactions, so producers are willing to pay for labor and capital anything up to the amount that a further increment of labor or capital promises to add to their profits."

"I couldn't have said it better myself," said Peter, grinning. "But now let's see some of the implications of all this. It means that if we forbid the payment of interest rates by law, or set a legal maximum interest rate lower than a free market would set, we are certain to reduce the volume of savings, certain to prevent

300

loans from going into the most productive channels, and certain to reduce seriously the volume of lending. And this is only another way of saying that we will discourage the accumulation of capital, which in turn is only another way of saying that we will put fewer tools, or poorer quality tools, in the hands of each worker, so reducing his productivity and wages and reducing the productivity of all Freeworld below what it would otherwise have been. For it is above all the accumulation of capital, the increase in the quantity and quality of the tools of production, that determines the wealth and income of the whole society."

"All right, chief. I'm completely convinced. Let's have free interest rates. But I still have some questions about other aspects of our new system—"

"Not today, you don't," said Peter good-naturedly. "It's after six. And tonight's my night for practicing by myself. I've discovered another wonderful bourgeois composer, Adams. Name of Chopin. I can't begin to describe to you the intricacy, subtlety, delicacy and tenderness of his music. I need him, especially tonight. And I'd appreciate your company. If you want to come up and just sit and listen, you're invited."

Chapter 37

I'M still not reconciled, chief," began Adams the next day, "to the unfair and unreasonable profits that some of these enterprisers are making. This creates great discontent—"

"Among those who haven't made the profits?"

"Yes. And it doesn't seem to me that such exorbitant profits are necessary to make your free market system work. Enterprisers should be content with a reasonable profit, and it seems to me that we ought to have a law fixing a reasonable profit, a fair profit."

"What is a reasonable *loss,* Adams—a fair loss?"

"A 'fair' loss? Such a phrase is meaningless, chief."

"Not any more than a 'reasonable profit,' a 'fair profit.' "

"But surely—"

"Let's see what an enterpriser is, Adams, and what function he performs. The enterpriser is the man who decides whether a new business shall be started, or whether an old business shall be contracted or expanded, or whether to turn from making one product to another. The enterprisers are the men who decide what shall be made, and how much of it, and by what method. There could be no more crucial function in any economy."

"Isn't it dangerous for any single group of private individuals to have such enormous power?"

"In the first place, they don't have the power. Let me amend my previous statement. The enterprisers are the men who *seem* to decide what shall be made, and how much of it, and by what method. Under our new system the *real* decisions are made by the whole body of consumers. The enterprisers merely try to guess what the wants and preferences of the consumers are going to be. The consumers are the real bosses. If the enterpriser guesses correctly what the wants and preferences of consumers are going to be, if he correctly guesses that too much of one thing is being or is going to be made and too little of another, in relation to these wants and preferences, or if he knows how to make the wanted thing cheaper and better than his competitors, he makes a profit. If his guesses are wrong, or if he is less efficient or competent than his competitors, he suffers a loss. In short, the enterpriser is the man who takes the risk."

"You mean he is a sort of gambler?"

"If you want to call him that, Adams. I prefer to call him the risk-bearer."

"But the promoter is also a risk-bearer. So is the speculator."

"True. The speculator, the promoter, the enterpriser, are various types of risk-bearer. But there is a vital difference, as I see it, between these and the gambler. The gambler deliberately *invents* his own risks. He doesn't *have* to lose money simply because one horse can run faster than another. His risks are artificial. But in economic life *the risks already exist;* they exist *necessarily; somebody has to bear them.* The speculator, the promoter and the enterpriser undertake that function."

"But *why,* chief, do the risks exist necessarily?"

"Because, if we look at the matter from the consumption end, nobody knows precisely what consumers are going to want, or what they are going to want most and what least, or what they are going to be willing to pay. And if we look at the matter from the production end, nobody knows, in farming, what the growing weather is going to be, or the amount of crop damage from storms or pests, or precisely where the storms or pests will strike. And in manufacturing, nobody knows, until it has been tried, whether a new method or a new machine will actually be more economical than an old one. *Uncertainty* regarding the future inevitably exists in human affairs, particularly in economic affairs. And somebody has to bear it."

"Why can't the government bear it?"

"That's exactly the system that broke down, Adams. Bureaucrats tried to get around the consumption half of the problem by not bothering to find out what the consumers really wanted, by not permitting them freedom of choice, but by forcing them to take what the government chose to produce. And when it came to the production half of the problem the bureaucrats didn't have to be as careful as the private enterpriser in estimating their relative chances of profit and loss, because they weren't risking their own capital. They could simply throw their losses on the whole community."

"But don't these private enterprisers ever make mistakes?"

"They do; but there is a crucial difference. First of all, the losses caused by their mistakes fall primarily on the enterprisers themselves. And because they know this in advance, because they have the hope of big profits on the one hand and the fear of big losses on the other, they usually estimate very carefully before they go into a new venture. Therefore their mistakes are incomparably smaller and fewer than those of government bureaucrats. In addition to this, Adams, there is a relentless process of selection and weeding out going on all the time. If the enterpriser's ventures are good, he can use his profits from them for still bigger ventures; if his ventures are bad, his losses prevent him from undertaking new ones."

"And what is the test of whether his ventures are good or bad?"

"The test is whether he has been better able to foresee and satisfy the needs of consumers than his competitors have been able to foresee and satisfy them."

"But don't wage earners and the owners of capital, chief, also take risks? Don't they suffer from the mistakes of the incompetent enterprisers?"

"Yes, and they also gain from the foresight or ingenuity of the good enterprisers. But it is because the enterprisers assume the primary risks that wage earners and those who lend capital at interest are able to minimize their own risks. . . . Let's see how

304

this works out. A man decides to launch a new enterprise. He goes to the owners of capital to raise funds, and if he gets the funds, he has to pay the market rate of interest. He rents a factory and has to pay the market rent. He hires workers and has to pay the rate of wages established by the market. Or perhaps he has to pay more than the previous market rate in order to bid capital and labor away from his competitors—"

"Then it isn't necessarily the *owner* of capital who hires and 'exploits' workers?"

"No, Adams. That is just another Marxist error. It is the *enterpriser* who hires *both* labor and capital. In so far as the enterpriser puts some of his own capital into the business, he becomes both an enterpriser *and* a capitalist. But . . ."

He paused, trying to think his way through the next point.

"But what, chief?"

"Well, all enterprisers, Adams, have to pay the same market prices for the same quantity and quality of money capital, factory and office space, raw materials, labor services, and so on. These prices are formed by the competition of the enterprisers against each other, just as the prices of consumer goods are formed, finally, by the competitive bids of the consumers. And it is the prices of consumption goods that determine how high the enterprisers are willing to bid, and can afford to bid, for labor services, money capital and production goods. Each enterpriser, therefore, when competition forces him to do so, is willing to bid for the factors of production a total price equal to the price that he could get from consumers for what he produces—"

"With some allowance for the sheer labor and headache of being an enterpriser!"

"With some allowance for that, of course. But such an allowance would be the imputed value of his managerial labor, which would really be a sort of wage or salary, and not part of what we might call his pure profit."

"Go on."

"Well, in order that an individual enterpriser may make a profit, Adams, the total income that he can get from the sale of his finished product must be greater than the total income he lays out in paying for the factors of production."

"Obviously."

"But the competition of enterprisers in keeping up the prices of the factors of production means that in order for an individual enterpriser to make a profit, he must have *better* foresight than his competitors in meeting the wants of consumers. If he has only *average* foresight he makes neither a profit nor a loss. And if he has *worse* than average foresight he makes a *loss*."

"What do you think would happen, chief, if all enterprisers had perfect foresight?"

"If everybody had *perfect* foresight no one would make either a profit or a loss. Mutual competition would force up wages, machinery, and raw material prices to the point where the total would just equal the total that everybody got for his finished product."

"And what happens under present conditions, chief?"

"Under present conditions, as I have already pointed out, those enterprisers with the most foresight make the biggest profits. Those enterprisers with less than average foresight pay for their errors with losses."

"And the net result?"

"The net result is that profits and losses cancel each other out."

"You mean that, on net balance, profit doesn't exist at all?"

"Not, on net balance, as an isolated thing. When we have allowed for the wages of labor, the rental for land, the interest on capital and the wages—or presumptive or imputable wages—of management, then there is no net sum left over for profits. Or at least not in a stationary economy. In an expanding economy, in which capital is constantly increasing, there is a transient profit. But even that is constantly tending to disappear into higher wages or higher prices for productive goods or lower prices for consumers."

"Your argument, then, as I understand it, is that profits are not made at the expense of wages."

"My argument, Adams, is that in a stationary economy—that

306

is, in an economy that is neither declining nor growing—profits at one place are canceled out by losses at another. Profits, in other words, are not a net price or cost that the community has to pay to the risk-bearers. The unsuccessful risk-bearers themselves pay that cost. The people who talk of 'unreasonable' profits, as I reminded you a while back, never mention 'unreasonable' losses. Any attempt to take away profits from the successful would destroy the vital function that enterprisers play in the private enterprise system."

"And that function is—?"

"That function, Adams, is to provide the maximum of goods and satisfactions for consumers. That function is to diversify production in accordance with diverse needs and wants, to bring about a balance in the production of thousands of different goods and services. And our private enterprisers perform this function so wonderfully well that I'm even afraid that future generations, who haven't known the horrors of central governmental planning under socialism, will take the performance of that function for granted. They may think it is something that happens 'automatically.' They may even forget that this is a central problem that any economic system has to solve."

"But does the individual enterpriser, chief, or do even enterprisers in general, deliberately try to solve that problem?"

"No, Adams. Yet each of them helps to solve it incidentally and unconsciously by constantly watching his own income account and his own balance sheet. If there is a profit in making shirts, he makes more of them, so eventually bringing down their price and the profit in making them. If there is a loss in making stockings, he makes fewer of them, or is forced to stop making them altogether, so raising their price and eliminating the loss of more efficient producers in making them. It is precisely because each enterpriser is trying to maximize his profits and minimize his losses that he serves the consumer best and serves the community best. It is the 'invisible hand' again."

"And it is this process also, chief, that solves the problem of economic calculation, over which you and I sweated so much?"

"Precisely. It decides what things are grown or made, how much of each is grown or made, and *how* each is grown or made. It is the free price system, the relationship of prices to costs, the incidence of profits and losses, that tells the enterpriser which is the most economical way of making a thing—in other words, which is the way that uses up the minimum value of resources in relation to the value of the product. The enterpriser can't learn this from the engineers and technicians. They can only give him part of the answer. The final answer he gets from his bookkeeper."

"Which is another way of saying, chief, that he gets the answer from the markets."

"Which is still another way of saying, Adams, that he gets the ultimate answer from the free choices of consumers."

"But I'm still bothered, chief, and I'm sure most people are still bothered, by the huge profits made by a few enterprisers. Surely such huge profits aren't necessary in order to get them to produce the right goods!"

"Your trouble, Adams, and the trouble of these people you speak of, is that you and they still persist in looking only at the winners of the biggest prizes. You assume these to be typical; you forget about the offsetting losses of the losers. Let's look at a lottery. Let's say that the man who runs the lottery sells 1,000,000 goldgrams worth of tickets, and hands out 900,000 goldgrams in prizes, keeping 100,000 goldgrams for himself."

"Very reasonable of him," said Adams sarcastically.

"I'm not interested in him for the moment," continued Peter. "I'm talking about the subscribers to the lottery. Collectively they *must* lose money."

"Collectively they lose 100,000 goldgrams."

"Right, Adams. But each individual who subscribes dismisses this collective result from his mind, if it ever occurs to him. He subscribes precisely because he hopes that *he,* individually, will be a winner. He is not interested in the fate of the other subscribers. Now if the people outside the lottery looked only at the winners of the huge prizes and thought these were *typical,* and forgot about the huge mass of losers, and if they began to talk as if these winnings were made at *their*—the outsiders'—expense, they would be talking the same way you are talking about profits under our new free enterprise system."

"But aren't these big profits, chief, at the expense of workers?"

"You will usually find, Adams, that the enterprisers who make the biggest profits pay the highest wages. If the profits of the successful enterprisers are at the 'expense' of anybody, I should say that they were mainly at the expense of the unsuccessful enterprisers who made the poor guesses and misdirected labor and capital. . . . And why should you assume that the high profits of the successful enterprisers are any more at the expense of their own workers than at the expense of the owners of their borrowed capital, or of the consumers?"

Adams seemed lost in thought.

"I'm still interested in that lottery you were speaking of," he said at length. "Considered collectively, the subscribers lost because each nonetheless expected that he would be the exception that would win a prize. May not something like that happen in the case of your enterprisers?"

"It is not impossible," said Peter. "It may be that each enterpriser becomes an enterpriser partly because he is unduly optimistic in nature, and partly because he overestimates his own abilities. If that were so, more people would become enterprisers than conditions would justify; or they would bid higher for the factors of production than the prices and sales of their finished product would eventually justify—and so the enterprisers as a whole, instead of breaking even, might have more losses than profits. . . . That might reflect itself in a sort of concealed way— say in most enterprisers merely getting too small a return, relatively, for their own labor of management. In that case, the consumers and workers, or the community as a whole, instead of having to pay a price for the vital service that enterprisers perform, would get those services, on net balance, for less than nothing."

"Then it wouldn't be very accurate, chief, to call your new system a 'profit' system?"

"Certainly not in a declining or even in a stationary economy. It is, of course, a profit-*seeking* system. But then I suppose there is a sense in which all of us are seeking 'profit' under any conceivable system. We speak of spending a 'profitable' evening when we mean merely that we have enjoyed ourselves. We say that reading a book has been 'profitable' when we mean that we have been instructed by it. 'Profitable' action of any sort is merely action that achieves, or partly achieves, the end we are seeking, regardless of whether that end is self-regarding or not. . . . I can't understand this unpopularity of 'profit' except as envy of the successful. Why should there be any more stigma attached to the word 'profit' than to the word 'wage' or 'salary'? Why should one form of income be considered less honorable than another? Why should the people who are afraid to take risks begrudge the rewards of those who have taken them successfully?"

Adams was thoughtfully silent again. "You have answered all the objections I can think of for today," he said at last. "You are right. You have invented a wonderful economic system—"

"We did nothing more than merely make it possible."

"You have invented, chief—or made possible—a wonderful economic system. And one of its chief merits, I now agree, is that it rewards people in proportion to their foresight and their production—their ability to provide others with what those others want. And this supplies the maximum incentive, I also concede, to everybody to sharpen his foresight and to increase his production. . . . But may not the very virtues of the system finally bring about its undoing? How will we be able to protect this system, for instance, against the incessant criticism of the unproductive and the unsuccessful? For no one is ever willing to attribute his failure to himself. He will attribute that failure to the 'system.' He will never see his own shortcomings, but will find a thousand shortcomings in the system. And if you answer one of his criticisms—no matter how crushingly—he will bring up another, ad infinitum. Always he will dream of a system in which, in the world of his imagination, *he* will be at the top, and the presently successful at the bottom."

"But won't the successful, Adams—or, as I hope, the disinterested—always be there to answer the criticisms of the unsuccessful?"

"I doubt, chief, that there will be a decent balance. Nearly everybody wants to be a writer; and therefore writers will seldom get the monetary rewards of speculators and enterprisers; and therefore the writers will be envious of these rewards; and the writers will always be more articulate, more plausible, than the successful businessmen. . . . And then there's another point. Success is relative. Measured in wealth and income, everybody will be less successful than somebody else, except the one richest man in the world. And therefore even those who have much more than the average wealth and income will be unable to understand why others, surely no more intelligent, industrious or farseeing than themselves, have more wealth and income still. Everyone will be willing to take it for granted that those who have less than himself have less because they have contributed less value to the world. But almost no one will be willing to admit that those who have *more* wealth and income than himself have it because they have contributed *more* value to the world. And so your new system will daily be exposed to the danger that—"

"Oh, come now," said Peter, laughing. "Stop imagining things!"

Chapter 38

ANOTHER year passed. A state of war still existed between Wonworld and Freeworld, but it was still a war without battles and without bloodshed. It consisted of a tremendous barrage of propaganda and of feverish preparations for a resumption of the active war that everyone regarded as inevitable.

Adams contended that this propaganda war was a losing one for Freeworld. The propaganda of Freeworld, he insisted, was heard only by the people of Freeworld. Nobody in Wonworld was allowed to listen to the short-wave broadcasts of Freeworld on penalty of death. And in any case, nobody outside of the Protectorate in Wonworld had a radio set.

"This means that only the people whose business it is to answer us know what our arguments are," said Adams. "On the other hand, more and more of our people are acquiring radio sets, and you allow them to listen."

Peter's chief answer was a tolerant smile. "That's our system," he said, "and I intend to stick to it. Means determine ends. We would end up with as bad a society as Wonworld, if we merely aped their methods."

"If we don't do something soon," retorted Adams, "we will end up with a victory for Wonworld. Bolshekov will start bombing us the moment he thinks he has achieved air superiority. He will have all the advantage of surprise and disruption. We have the planes to bomb him now. If we don't get the jump on him, he will get it on us."

"I won't resort to those methods," said Peter. "I still hope to get peace by convincing Wonworld that our system is better than theirs."

Adams threw up his hands in despair. They had been over this argument too many times.

But he conceded that Peter had been brilliantly right about the advantages of his new free system. Both of them continued to watch its development with undiminished fascination.

It was not merely that it outproduced the communism of Wonworld to the point where there was no comparison. This increase in production was itself merely a symptom and consequence of something more deep-seated.

The whole spirit of the people had been transformed.

Peter noticed this daily even in the attitude of small storekeepers toward their customers. There was none of the indifference and surly boredom that had marked the office-holding storekeeper under the socialism of Wonworld. These people waited on customers not merely with courtesy but with eagerness. It was not only that every sale meant a personal profit to them. Every sale was also a confirmation of their foresight in making or stocking certain goods, in correctly anticipating the wishes of consumers, or in anticipating these wishes better than their competitors did.

Under socialism there had been only one center of initiative, at the top of the hierarchical pyramid. Everybody else had merely carried out orders; he had made what he was told to make or stocked what he was told to stock. When he had filled an order, he had done it as a favor to the customer. It had been always the customer, not the seller, who said "Thank you." The customer was always supposed to be grateful because the commissars of Wonworld had graciously consented to order the making of the rationed goods. Neither the good nor the bad guesses of the commissars were considered to be the concern of the local storekeeper himself.

But under this new free market system every sale was a sort of personal triumph for the storekeeper. The decision what to

313

make or to stock, and the task of persuading the customer that this article was as good as or better than what one's competitors had to offer (a task in the long run impossible unless the article actually *was* as good or better), had all the adventure and excitement of playing a fascinating game. And though success, as in a good card game, might be sometimes due to luck—to the fall of the cards—in the long run it was the result of shrewd anticipation and skill in playing one's hand.

True, the hired salesmen in a store did not, as a rule, show quite the alertness and eagerness of the proprietor. But as they were usually under the watchful eye of the proprietor, and as their promotion and salary depended on their success in selling, most of them were incomparably more alert and accommodating than most socialist jobholders had ever been.

This competition in serving the consumer ran through the whole society. It did not show itself merely at the point of sale. Long before that point, manufacturers, enterprisers and inventors vied with each other in thinking up new products that consumers might want, or ways of making old products better or selling them more cheaply. There was a spate of new inventions such as Peter had never dreamed possible. Some of these, it is true, were mere gadgets, often ridiculed by Bolshekov's propaganda ministry and even by writers in Freeworld; but if they were really useless, if they filled no real and permanent want of consumers, they were soon unsuccessful. Time and the consumers kept weeding out what was merely meretricious and selecting what was best.

There was also competition in advertising; and the sometimes extravagant contentions of rival sellers were also the butt of Bolshekov's propaganda and of writers in Freeworld. But the Freeworld government kept this to a minimum by tightening the laws against fraud and the misrepresentation of goods.

Even without these laws, Peter pointed out to Adams, the mischief of fraudulent advertising would not begin to compare with that under socialism. For under socialism no one was permitted to ridicule or even question the claims of the state. The claims of the state went unchallenged precisely because there were no rival claims. But when manufacturer A announced that his soap was the best, and manufacturer B asserted that *his* soap was the best, and manufacturer C swore that *his* soap was the best, it was clear to the consumers that all three couldn't be right. This competitive advertising bred a healthy skepticism in the consumers and even a remarkable skill in weighing rival claims. It was found that in the long run, in fact, people judged a product by the product itself. For the great majority of products, the most skillful advertising soon proved to be impotent if the product itself was not good.

Under socialism, on the other hand, consumers had no choice between competitive products. The product itself was nearly always bad, because the state had a monopoly of making it and a monopoly of advertising it. No competitor could arise to displace it with a better product. No one could throw doubt on the state's advertising claims by rival advertising of another product. There was no one to restrain the state itself when it misrepresented its products, as the leaders of Wonworld always did.

But in the private competitive system that Peter had introduced, the bad or indifferent product was constantly being supplanted by the good, the good by the better, and the better by the best. No one could afford to rest on his past laurels; for though his product by its merits might dominate the market today, it might be threatened by a better product tomorrow. Even the corporations whose products already led the field maintained research laboratories to keep ahead of possible new competition.

The advertisers contended that they increased the pace of industrial progress by bringing new and better products to the attention of consumers sooner than consumers would otherwise learn of them. They argued that their advertising was essentially an "educational campaign." And Peter, though he knew that the motives of the individual advertisers were not disinterested, and though he personally disliked the blatancy of most of their methods, conceded that the basic contention of the advertisers was ultimately right. Their advertising of production goods helped

315

to reduce production costs; their advertising of consumption goods helped to increase demand and so reduce unit costs of production. Buyers were educated by the necessity of judging among rival claims and by actually comparing and trying out competing products. It was the comparative quality and price of the product itself that ultimately decided which product was bought and survived.

Peter rejected the contention that advertising was merely an economic "waste." Like other costs of production, it had the purpose of increasing demand; and it accelerated the process of selecting the better production methods and the better consumption goods. In fact, Peter found it impossible to separate "selling costs" from other production costs. *All* production costs were in a sense "selling costs," because a product had to be made attractive enough to buy. And for the same reason all necessary selling costs were necessary "production" costs.

And it was the process of continually improving production methods and consumption goods that to Peter was the greatest marvel of all. Life in Wonworld had been appallingly drab and stagnant; but Peter had never realized how drab and stagnant it was until the new free market system had wrought this change.

There was no line in which he did not find one miraculous improvement after another. In food, new vegetables and fruits were constantly being developed; new methods of selling and preparing them, and better ways of cooking them. Peter was particularly fascinated and impressed by the development and rapid progress of frozen foods, which enabled people to eat "fresh" fruits and vegetables all year round.

In clothing, where previously there had been cotton, wool, silk and linen, a marvelous array of new, cheaper, stronger and more beautiful textiles was constantly being developed. The chemists now seemed to be able to make textiles out of anything—wood or glass, milk or coal. The chemists seemed on the verge of discovering, in fact, that everything could be made out of anything.

Constant and bewildering improvements were being made in household conveniences, in fluorescent lighting, in radiant heat-ing, in air-conditioning, in vacuum cleaners, in clotheswashing machines, in dishwashing machines, in a thousand new structural and decorative materials. Great forward leaps were now taken in radio. There was talk of the development, in the laboratories, of the wireless transmission, not merely of music and voices, but of the living and moving image of objects and people.

Hundreds of new improvements, individually sometimes slight but cumulatively enormous, were being made in all sorts of transportation—in automobiles and railroads, in ships and airplanes. Inventors even talked of a new device to be called "jet-propulsion," which would not only eliminate propellers but bring speeds rivaling that of sound itself.

In medicine, marvelous new anaesthetics and new life-saving drugs were constantly being discovered. . . .

"In our new economic system, Adams," said Peter, "we seem to have developed hundreds of thousands of individual centers of initiative which spontaneously co-operate with each other. We have made more material progress in the last four years, more industrial and scientific progress, than Wonworld made in a century."

"That is entirely true," agreed Adams. "But I should like to point out that Wonworld also has benefited by this progress. Bolshekov's secret agents here see to it that his technicians get hold of all our scientific and trade publications, and of course they systematically steal our so-called military secrets. So in theoretical knowledge, if not in volume of production, my guess is that Wonworld has made almost as much progress as we have."

"Whatever progress it has made is purely parasitic," Peter said. "It would not exist if Bolshekov's commissars were not constantly appropriating the successful improvements that our free enterprise system has developed."

"You're right, chief. But they get the benefit of them just the same. And after they have adopted or stolen an improvement from us, their propaganda bureau claims that the invention or discovery was really made by some Muscovite."

But it was not merely in material progress that Freeworld

achieved such amazing triumphs. No less striking were the new dignity and breadth that individual freedom brought about in the whole cultural and spiritual life of the Western Hemisphere.

The contrast, Peter found, was not quite so striking in certain realms—music, dancing, chess, mathematics. This, he concluded, was because these arts, sciences or pursuits "said nothing" —or at least what they said was so abstract and elusive that it was seldom regarded as being directly dangerous to Moscow's ruling clique. There had therefore been a tendency, comparatively speaking, to let such pursuits alone. The brains and genius of Wonworld, whenever they could, had always tried to get into these lines where they could function with comparative safety and freedom.

But in nearly all other realms the cultural and spiritual contrast was glaring. It showed itself in novels and plays, in criticism and poetry, in painting, sculpture and architecture, in political and economic thinking, in most sciences, in philosophy and religion.

And this, Peter decided, was because these pursuits no longer had to cater to the presumed tastes of a particular dictator or of a small group of commissars. The novels, plays and poetry written in Wonworld had been nauseating. They became still more nauseating under Bolshekov. For they were devoted either to the most savage ridicule and denunciation of whatever Bolshekov was not presumed to like, or of the most fawning and abject flattery of Bolshekov and of what he was supposed to have created. Sometimes the authors, playwrights and poets made an ideological mistake, or the party line reversed itself suddenly overnight, and then no matter with what servile and cringing apologies the writers were willing to repudiate or denounce what they had themselves written and to start saying the opposite, no matter how completely they were eager to abase themselves, they and their families were lucky to escape with their lives. Peter saw that this was inevitable under any system in which the livelihood of every author and artist depended on the "planners" at the center, on any one individual or compact ruling group.

The end of this tyranny had been like the lifting of a great weight.

Many of the new writers and artists of Freeworld, it is true, now catered to the presumed tastes of a mass public; and the bulk of what was produced was vulgar and cheap. But all this fell quickly into oblivion. It was not the bulk that counted. What counted, as Peter quickly saw, was that each writer and each artist was now liberated from abject subservience to the state, to the political ruling clique. He was now free to select his *own* public. He did not *need* to cater to a nebulous "mass demand." He could, if he wished, write, build, think, compose or paint for a definite cultivated group, or for his fellow specialists, or for a few kindred spirits wherever they could be found. And plays did have a way of finding their own special audience, and periodicals and books of finding their own special readers.

In contrast with the drabness, monotony and dreariness of Wonworld, the cultural and spiritual life of Freeworld was full of infinite variety, flavor, and adventure.

Chapter 39

I am constantly admiring, chief," said Adams, "the incredible
productiveness of your new system, and the wonderful results of the freedom it permits. But I keep constantly having
doubts about it too."

"So I've noticed," said Peter drily. "What are your doubts this
time?"

"They go very deep. Isn't this system, even conceding that it
is enormously more productive than any collectivist system, selfish and acquisitive?"

"How?"

"Well, certainly it *rewards* selfishness and acquisitiveness."

"Of course it does. And so does any other system."

"But socialism—"

"Socialism above all, Adams. And you know that as well as I
do. Under any economic or political system conceivable, selfish
and unscrupulous people will do the things they think will help
them succeed under that system. They will lie, flatter, defraud,
deceive, betray, seduce, even rob and murder if they think it will
advantage them. If piety is the thing, they will pretend to be
more pious than anyone else. If having a 'social conscience' is the
fashion, they will profess to have a bigger social conscience than
anyone else—"

"Yes, but—"

"The point is," continued Peter, "that self-regarding people
under any system will do the things that are most rewarded by

that system. The real question is—what *are* the actions that are most rewarded by a particular system?"

"All right; put it that way if you want, chief, and my point remains the same. Doesn't your free market system reward precisely the most selfish and acquisitive actions?"

"No. It might just as well be regarded as rewarding the most altruistic actions. To begin with, under this system our government has sought to *illegalize* every action harmful to others that it could reasonably be expected to define and detect. We have illegalized not only theft, assault and murder, but libel and intimidation and coercion of every kind. We have illegalized and penalized fraud, misrepresentation of goods, and the breaking of promises and contracts. And by that means we have made it impossible, so far as it reasonably lies within our power, for any enterpriser to succeed except by one thing—by serving the consumers as well as or better than his competitors do. We have made it possible for him to succeed, not by providing people, I admit, with what they perhaps ought to want, but with what they actually do want."

"But shouldn't a really ethical system supply consumers, chief, not with what they actually happen to want, which may often be harmful to them, but only with what is good for them?"

"A thousand times, No. What your suggested ethical system implies, Adams, is that someone at the top—or some underling bureaucrat, for that matter—knows better what is good for you than you do yourself. It is an arrogant assumption of superiority on the part of the ruling clique. It is the essence of the authoritarian attitude. It treats the people like irresponsible wards of the government. It treats the common man with contempt."

"But to give consumers only what they ought to want, chief, to give them only what is good for them—"

"Those are merely euphemistic phrases, Adams, for compelling them to take only what the bureaucrats permit them to have."

"I'm still not entirely persuaded," persisted Adams. "I concede that your laws prohibit the individual from doing what is harmful to others. But they do not prohibit him from doing what is

321

harmful to himself, such as smoking too many cigarettes"—he looked accusingly at Peter—"or drinking too much or staying up too late; and they do not force him to be *positively* helpful and benevolent to others."

"They certainly do not, Adams. Our laws must seek to give people the fullest liberty possible. And the best way they can do that is to restrain only the liberty of each individual to infringe upon the equal liberty of others. Our specific traffic restrictions are not designed to restrict traffic but to promote and make possible the maximum safe flow of traffic. And our specific restrictions on liberty of all kinds can only be justified insofar as they tend to promote the greatest possible safe enjoyment of liberty for everyone."

"But it still remains true, chief, that your laws are essentially negative: they *forbid* this or that, but they do not *enjoin* generosity and helpfulness."

"If you forbid what is harmful to others, Adams, you have a big enough job for any government to take care of. Moreover, you have definite logical boundaries to that job. But if you begin to *demand* altruism legally, there are no logical limits—until everybody has been forced to give away all he has earned, or all he has earned above those who have earned least—and then you are back again to the point where no one has any incentive whatever to earn or produce anything."

"But how are you ever going to get generosity or benevolence, chief, if you make no legal provision for them?"

"Any society worth living in," replied Peter in a tone of conscious patience, "must of course be infused with a spirit of generosity and benevolence. It can't depend solely on negative virtues—on people's merely respecting one another's liberty or their abstaining from deceit or violence. I concede all that to be true. But it isn't the function of the government to *force* people into these positive virtues. It couldn't do it if it tried, and the attempt would merely lead to horrible abuses. These positive virtues must come from *within* the society itself. And that's merely another way of saying that they must come from *within* the individual.

322

A society to be worth living in must have a morality. That is, the individuals of which it is made up must adhere to a moral code. But this morality cannot be imposed by officials, by the police, by the state's apparatus of coercion. It must come spontaneously from individuals, from families, from the precepts of parents. It must be created, enriched and purified by great moral and religious thinkers and teachers, and above all by great moral and religious examples— But we've already been over all this ground—"

"Then you admit," cut in Adams, "that your new free market system does not *in itself* encourage a positive morality?"

"Compared with socialism it certainly does," Peter replied. "If you make it possible for men to succeed only by competition in serving the consumers—"

"You are always talking of the blessings of competition," Adams broke in again. "But isn't competition precisely the chief evil? Doesn't your 'free market' system promote cutthroat, dog-eat-dog competition, the law of the jungle—?"

"You are not talking about competition," Peter retorted, "but only about *bad* competition. You are talking about a *low level* of competition. Of course we should strive constantly to raise the level of competition. To do this we must depend first on a high general level of morality, and secondly on perfecting our system of legal restraints. We do not want people to succeed by superior chicanery, by more clever deceit, by greater unscrupulousness, by superior ruthlessness. Therefore our laws must do everything possible to close these avenues to success and to create conditions under which people can succeed only by superior zeal and ability in serving their fellows. And this is precisely what we have sought to do in our new system. It provides them with a system of rewards in proportion to their output—in other words, in proportion to their success in satisfying the consumer. Under this system they must compete for the consumer's favor."

"But competition has always seemed to me a form of warfare, chief. A sound economy should be built on the *opposite* principle of *co-operation.*"

"Competition in serving the consumer can be called a form of 'warfare,' Adams, only in a metaphorical sense—and it is a false and misleading metaphor. So far from business competition's being the *opposite* of co-operation, it is actually a method of social co-operation and one of the most important. Personal competition, in fact, is one of the greatest of all forces in bringing maximum progress. Whether a man is seeking to be the richest man in his community, or the most skillful surgeon, or the fastest swimmer, or the best pianist, or the greatest novelist or philosopher or saint, it is his sense of personal competition that drives him to wring every ounce of ability or perfection out of himself."

"Then it all depends, in your opinion, chief, on *what* actions or aims people decide to compete in?"

"Precisely," agreed Peter. "Competition, it seems to me, can be made to perform two main functions. One, as I have just pointed out, is to stimulate everyone to make the most of his innate abilities. The other is to assign each individual to that place in the social system where he can perform the greatest service for his fellows. In a society of status or heredity, everybody is likely to be misplaced—if we judge by the standard of where he could do the most good. We must try to place the greatest industrial leader at the head of the most important firm, and the best conductor at the head of the best orchestra—rather than put the potentially best industrial leader in charge of an orchestra and the potentially best orchestra conductor at the head of a manufacturing firm. And a system which gives free play to personal competition, with judgment by immediate colleagues and peers, is most likely to put men in the places they can occupy most effectively."

"I started out on quite another tack," resumed Adams, "when I was deflected. I started by asking whether your system doesn't reward selfishness and acquisitiveness. Now it seems to me, a perfect system should reward *un*selfishness."

"Why?"

"Why?" repeated Adams, surprised. "Why, to give an incentive for unselfishness."

"That is a contradiction in terms," replied Peter. "If you do something 'unselfish' in the hope of a reward, then you are doing something selfish. If you are doing something 'unselfish' and 'altruistic' under the spur of a material incentive—or even mainly in the hope of being praised for your action—then what you do is really selfish and acquisitive. It is illogical to ask for a reward for unselfishness. Unselfishness consists precisely in doing the things for which you are not rewarded."

"But under your free system, chief, everybody is pursuing his own ends."

"That is substantially true, Adams; but it doesn't follow that the individual's own ends are necessarily selfish or exclusively self-regarding ends. . . . Let me put it this way. In what is called a 'business relationship' I find that by serving your ends I can best serve my own. I find that by performing a service for you I can get the wherewithal to carry out some project of my own. It is true that I perform this service for you not for your sake but for my own. Or more accurately—for my own ends, whatever they may happen to be. And you give me something in return, not for my sake, but in order to get my service for yourself. So each of us co-operates with the other, each of us promotes the other's immediate aim, in order to carry out his own remoter aims."

"I can see, chief, how that promotes wealth and production, and social co-operation, and mutuality of service. And all that is very fine. But still the ultimate aim of each of us in this business relation is self-regarding. Each of us, to put it bluntly, is trying to make money."

"Your argument still misses the point, Adams. Money is merely a means. If we are discussing personal motives, we must go further and ask what each of us is trying to get money *for*. Money is wanted as a medium of exchange for something else. It is one means—though a highly important one—of achieving our ultimate purposes. What do we intend to do with the money when we get it? *This* is the main place where the question of motive comes in. A man may earn money to support his family, to send his son to college, to pursue abstract scientific studies, to contribute to some public cause in which he deeply believes, to found a new charity. Now most working people are unselfish in this sense. Most of them support with their earnings not simply themselves, but others—a wife, children, aged parents, a sister or brother, and so on. A man works for his family—not so that he alone, but that *they* can have more. In brief, he works not merely for himself but for those he loves."

"But socialism, chief, argues that he ought to love *everybody,* and ought to work for everybody."

"But the simple fact is, Adams, that he *doesn't* love everybody, and you can't *force* him to love everybody. And if you try to force him to love and support everybody, you merely kill his incentives and impoverish everybody. Of course under a regime of freedom you can persuade or exhort a man to widen voluntarily the circle of his love or at least his good will. And if a man here or there under our free market system *does* love everybody, and *does* want to produce for everybody and give to everybody, there is nothing to prevent him from doing so to the limit of his capacity."

"Then your point," said Adams, "is that while we may regret that more people are not more charitable than they are, the fault is not that of the free market or of the private enterprise system, but of human nature?"

"Precisely," said Peter. "My point is that the nature of human beings primarily determines the nature and working of the economic and social system under which they live—and not, as Karl Marx supposed, the other way round."

"But wouldn't your argument apply also to communism, chief? Aren't its faults also primarily the faults of the people who adopted and operate it?"

"The people first embraced communism, Adams, under a delusion; but then were held to it by bayonets. I am talking about systems that people are still free to change peaceably. Communism is infinitely worse than the potential human nature of

326

the majority of people who live under it, because no one is free to make his will known, no one is free to act, without risk of torture or murder. Let me put it this way. An economic or political system is always as good as the people who live under it—as long as they are free to change it."

Chapter 40

IT was June 21, just five years from the day when Peter's air force had landed in America. The date was now Independence Day, the biggest holiday in Freeworld. Peter had broadcast a radio talk on a hemispheric hookup at noon.

Now he and Adams were completely alone in the White House.

"I gave everybody here the day off," said Peter. "In fact, I insisted that they take it off. There are only two guards outside, with strict orders not to let anybody in—even Cabinet officers—on any excuse. There are no telephone girls at the switchboard, and my own telephone line is dead. It all gives me a wonderful feeling of peace. At last we can have one policy talk without a thousand interruptions. Sometimes during the last few years I've felt the way a philosopher would feel if he were information clerk at the Union Station and had to develop his system between questions."

A hundred miles east of Nantucket Island, the crew of a Coast Guard ship watched a huge flight of long-range bombers pass above them, headed for the American shore. When the captain trained his binoculars on them, he was reassured to see that they carried the Freeworld markings.

"What do you think?" he asked the first mate.

"I suppose it's got something to do with today's celebrations."

"Hear anything about it in advance?"

"Nope."

"Think we ought to wireless a report of it?"

"We oughtn't to make ourselves look foolish."

"Just wireless, as a routine report: *More than one hundred big bombers, our markings, passed over*—then give our position—*heading west by south.*"

"Very good, sir."

"I have heard you call your new system, chief," said Adams, "by many different names, which you seem to use interchangeably. Sometimes you call it free enterprise, sometimes competitive private enterprise, sometimes the private ownership system, sometimes the private property system, sometimes the profit-and-loss system, or the profit-seeking system, sometimes the price system, sometimes merely the market economy, or the free market economy. Isn't it about time you settled on some definite single name for it?"

"Does it matter?" asked Peter.

"Well, you know what Bolshekov is calling it in his propaganda!"

"What *is* he calling it?"

"He says it's nothing but a brazen revival of capitalism!"

Peter hit the ceiling. "The dirty son of a Trotsky!" He had slipped into the old profanity without thinking of its literal meaning.

"Quite true," said Adams; "but we must have an answer for him."

"Well," said Peter, quieting down, "suppose for the sake of argument that Bolshekov's charge were true? Suppose, in our persistent gropings toward a better system than communism, we had done nothing better at last but stumble into and rediscover the very same old 'capitalism' that we had been reviling for two centuries as the depth of human iniquity and misery? Suppose that were true? How would Bolshekov know it, any more than we do? When we destroyed all the old literature, when our forefathers carefully expurgated even from Marx everything but the mere abuse and left as few hints as they could of how the system actually worked, how can Bolshekov know any better than we what the old capitalism was like?"

"He doesn't," said Adams; "but he's got hold of a powerful propaganda weapon, and we've got to find an answer."

"Well, it's perfectly silly," said Peter, "to call our new system 'capitalism.' We can rightly call it any of the names you just cited, but not *that!* How does the name apply?"

"Well, the system certainly makes use of capital, chief, of capital goods, or machinery and tools—"

"Of course it does. But so does socialism, communism, or any other conceivable economic system. Otherwise mankind couldn't survive!"

"Well then," Adams asked, "how do you suppose the old 'capitalism' ever got its name? Why did our filthy bourgeois forefathers ever call it 'capitalism'?"

Peter thought for a moment. "Maybe they didn't. Maybe this was just a term of abuse that its socialist enemies applied to it. Maybe it was merely Karl Marx himself who invented the term, or made it stick."

"But why was it considered appropriate even as a term of abuse?"

"That would be a little hard to guess," said Peter. "Let's see. . . . Let's assume that the term 'capital' already existed, and that it meant money and the tools of production. And let's say that this capital happened to be privately owned by individuals. Then these private owners might get the name 'capitalists.' Now let's say these capitalists used their capital to establish enterprises and hire workers. If people who disliked this system started to call it 'capitalism,' the name itself would adroitly imply that the system existed primarily for the enrichment of the capitalists—and hence for the exploitation or robbery of the hired workers."

"So if the defenders of the system were foolish enough themselves to use Marx's epithet for it," suggested Adams, "they would begin under a heavy semantic handicap?"

"Precisely," said Peter—"or perhaps not. Perhaps they could

have proudly embraced this intended smear and turned it to their own advantage. They could have said: 'You do well to call our system "capitalism." For it is precisely this system that leads to the maximum accumulation and the most efficient allocation of capital. It is only this system, in short, that makes the fullest use of capital, of the tools of production, and so takes burdens off the back of labor, constantly and enormously increases the worker's productivity and wages and well-being.' . . . Yes, I think we could work out a good propaganda answer to Bolshekov."

"Then let me ask—" Adams began.

"But I might add," Peter continued, "that Bolshekov is entirely wrong in applying the term 'capitalism' to our new system if he means by it that it is necessarily the capitalists who hire the workers. On the contrary, as we see every day, it is enterprisers, often without much or even any capital of their own, who hire both capital and labor at market rates of interest and market rates of wages. They could be just as plausibly accused of exploiting the capitalists as of exploiting the workers, because, of course, each enterpriser is trying to hire both capital and labor as cheaply as he can."

"But isn't it competition among themselves," said Adams, "that forces the enterprisers to pay as high rates for both capital and labor as they actually do?"

"Precisely. . . ."

The bomber flight appeared over Nantucket. Two reconnaissance planes were sent up to have a closer look at it. They were fired upon. The colonel in charge of the Nantucket airfield telephoned the Department of Defense at Washington. . . .

The bomber flight passed over New York, releasing a few bombs. It passed over Philadelphia, and dropped another load. Interception planes were now rising to meet it. . . .

The telephone operator at the Department of Defense reported back to the Under-Secretary. "The White House doesn't answer!"

"Ridiculous! Keep ringing. . . ."

"Have you any other objections?" Peter asked.

"When I bring up objections to your new system," answered Adams, "I bring them up as much to clarify my own mind as for any other purpose. I need not tell you that in spite of all these objections I am, on net balance, lost in admiration of your great discovery."

"You are tremendously generous. But I must repeat that it isn't exactly my dis—"

"I am beginning to think, chief, that it is, in fact, the greatest discovery ever given to mankind. For one thing, it has made possible most of the other discoveries that promise constantly to lift at least the material welfare of mankind—"

"Let's not speak slightingly or patronizingly of material or economic welfare," said Peter. "It is this that makes all cultural progress possible. The highest scientific or spiritual achievements cannot be reached by anyone unless he has rather recently had something to eat."

"I agree with all that," Adams said. "And that is why I am asking you this question. Its enormous productivity is, as I see it, merely one of the consequences of your new system. But what do you consider to be the heart of it? What is its innermost secret?"

"Its secret?" said Peter. The question excited him. He got up and paced back and forth. "Let's see. . . . Its secret, perhaps, is that it protects the right of everyone to keep what he has made. He is allowed to have and to hold the product of his labor . . . the amount of value he has contributed to production. He engages only in voluntary exchanges. This voluntary exchange implies giving value for equal value, or rather, it implies that no exchange need be made unless each party to the transaction feels that he gains by it. Under this system, then, all economic relations are *voluntary*."

"Including that of employer and employee?"

"Yes. Under this system the choice of one's productive role is essentially a voluntary choice."

"But if a man has no capital, chief?"

"The amount of capital a man has or can borrow, Adams, depends usually on his previous productive record—and in any case does not necessarily determine his choice of role. The hired salaried managers of great business firms, or our leading motion picture actors, get huge incomes, but are 'only employees,' whereas the man who sets up his own little cigarette stand or gasoline-filling station, or drives his own taxicab, is an 'enterpriser,' a 'capitalist' or perhaps an 'employer,' even though his income may be very low. I am driven to the conclusion that the Marxist separation of 'employers' and 'workers' into antagonistic and irreconcilable 'classes' is nonsensical. The relationship of the employer to the worker is essentially co-operative; it is basically a partnership in production."

"But won't the employer and the worker often disagree as to precisely how much each should get of the value of their joint production?"

"Of course they will; and so at times will all partners. But it is quite another thing to erect such individual disagreements into a theory of an irresolvable 'class' conflict."

"Then am I to understand that the secret of your system, chief, is that productive relationships under it are essentially *voluntary?*"

"That is certainly part of the secret," Peter agreed, "and one of the great points of contrast with any collectivist system, whether it is called communism, socialism, central planning or what not. Under all these systems economic relationships are essentially *compulsory*. They are dictated from the center, from the top. Under them everyone must take the role assigned to him from the top, or the socialist planners cannot carry out their plans. But—"

He kept pacing back and forth. He was not quite satisfied with his answer. The secret? The secret? Why, of course!

"The secret of our new system," he said suddenly, "if it has any secret, is *freedom!* Simple freedom! You set men free, and each turns to doing what he most wishes to do, or what he thinks he can do best, or what he thinks will bring him the greatest means to happiness. The secret is the freedom of each man to make a living in his own way; the freedom to produce what he

333

wishes; the freedom to keep what he creates, or to share it or dispose of it in accordance with the dictates of his own and not some bureaucrat's conscience; the freedom to associate with whom he wishes; the freedom to consume what he wishes; the freedom to make and to correct his own mistakes—"

"But if your great idea, chief, is at bottom simply *freedom*—"

"*Our* great idea, Adams! *Freeworld's* great idea!"

"But don't you remember, chief, that night you ran through the deserted streets of the Kremlin to my rooms? You thought then that your great discovery was private ownership of the means of production!"

"Well, yes. . . . Private ownership of the means of production, Adams, is certainly *a* great idea. But that is because it is an inescapable corollary, an integral part, of *the* great idea, which is individual *freedom*. It is only when the means of production are privately owned that the individual can keep the fruits of his production. It is only when the individual is protected in his right to retain the fruits of his production that he has the incentive to produce. It is only when the individual has the right to own the means of production that he is free to make his living in his own way. And not unless he has *this* freedom—this economic independence, this liberty to earn his own livelihood without the favor of the state, and without licking the boots of the bureaucratic hierarchy—not unless he has *this* freedom can he have any freedom whatever. For freedom is indivisible. Freedom is like a living thing. Freedom *is* a living thing! You may say, if you please, that economic freedom is only the belly of the whole body of freedom. But remember that the belly carries the legs; remember that the belly feeds the heart; remember that unless the belly is there, unless the belly is alive and healthy and whole, the mind cannot think and the spirit cannot dream—"

"But if freedom is the central virtue of the new system," asked Adams, "isn't it also its central danger? Haven't you granted *too much* freedom?"

"Too much?"

"Yes, chief. You have allowed people to say what they please

334

in speeches, to print what they please in books and newspapers. And what is the result? They are using their freedom of speech continually to criticize your government, to criticize even the marvelous new system that you have made possible—the system that has made their very freedom of speech possible. You allow them to criticize without fear of punishment, without fear of losing their jobs or fortunes or means of livelihood or chance of promotion, and therefore they criticize."

"It does seem a bit paradoxical," Peter said. "Wonworld is a hell; but no one inside dares to criticize it, which is precisely one of the things that makes it a hell. Worse, everyone inside is compelled continually to praise it. And the result is that stupid people, hearing nothing but praise of the system, think they must be living in a heaven, though they are sick and terrorized and wretched. And in Freeworld we have created what is—at least by comparison—a heaven. And one of the very things that makes it a comparative heaven is the freedom to criticize it. But stupid people, when they hear so much criticism, begin to think they must be living in a hell, though no one in our recorded history was ever as well off in material and cultural resources as they are. . . . I confess I don't know any answer to this paradox . . . except, perhaps, still more freedom. . . ."

"Still more?"

"Yes, Adams. Still more. You know how futile, when we were still under the old communist-socialist system, were all my efforts to introduce freedom and political democracy. Now, I think, conditions are at last ripe for the introduction of a genuine and free representative government, in which the leaders will be freely selected by the people, and—"

Suddenly they heard the roar of planes. They rushed toward the window.

There was an explosion. Then another, still louder. Then the ack-ack of antiaircraft guns. Then a continuous roar.

"We're being bombed!" shouted Peter. "Let's go to the switchboard. The War Department must have been trying to reach me. I must call—"

335

"That's foolhardy now," shouted Adams.

Peter started out of the room. He heard a terrific detonation. He felt the floor crunching under his feet. He looked up to see the ceiling crack open and fall. . . .

He lost consciousness.

Chapter 41

HE had been deep under water, far down, and felt himself rising to the surface. . . . He opened his eyes reluctantly, from a sense of duty.

He was in bed, in a bare room flooded with sunshine. Standing at his side was a tall dark-haired girl, dressed in white, beautiful and smiling.

She stroked his head. "You had us all so worried, Your Highness."

"Where am I?"

"You mustn't talk. You're in the Peter Uldanov Hospital. You've been unconscious for nearly three days."

He started to say something, but she put her finger to his lips. "The air raid is all over. They did a lot of damage, but Secretary Adams says there was nothing fatal. . . . Yes, the Secretary is fine. The whole White House fell on you, chief, but Echo—I mean—Adams, was dug out without even a scratch. One of those freak things. . . . Secretary Adams is running the war. He says you're not to worry about a thing. . . . The head doctor insists you're not even to think about the war until he says you can."

"How long . . . will that be?" His voice sounded strange to him. It tore his throat apart to talk.

She put her finger over his lips again. "You shouldn't try to talk, chief. You'll have to be a very good patient. Let *us* worry. All we want you to do is to relax, forget things, and get well."

She turned away from the bed. His eyes followed her graceful movements.

"Now, we'll try to get some nourishment into you. This is orange juice. Does that sound good?" All he could see distinctly was the front end of a bent glass tube that she deftly slid between his lips. His swallowing was painful, but the orange juice was wonderfully satisfying. "Now you're to take a little sip of this." It was some tasteless fluid. He fell asleep. . . .

When he awoke the nurse was bending over him. What a wonderful smile she had!

"I dozed off for a few minutes. . . ."

She laughed. "You've been asleep for fifteen hours! That medicine I gave you did it. The night nurse has been here and gone. We'll get some breakfast into you right away."

She slipped the glass tube in his mouth again. He liked the soft touch of her fingers against his lips.

He glanced down at the bed. His whole body was in plaster casts—head, neck, back, legs. He was moved and turned by ropes and pulleys, like a marionette.

"I look ridiculous."

"You look very nice." She smiled. "And you *shouldn't* talk for a while yet. . . . I'm your day nurse. You probably guessed that. My name is Edith Robinson—"

"Edith?"

"Yes . . . is there anything surprising . . .?"

He finished his liquid breakfast and dozed off again. . . .

Everyone was in a conspiracy of silence. No one told him how the war was progressing. He was kept so continually doped with anaesthetics and sleeping tablets that he couldn't even keep track of his own pains. Every day the doctors, Edith Robinson and the other nurses told him he was doing fine. Every day Adams would call and tell him the war was going along fine and he was not to worry about a thing.

"Nurse Robinson!"

"Yes?"

338

"Do you mind if I call you Edith?"

"I should consider it an honor, chief."

"You know, I'm usually addressed as 'Your Highness.' "

"I know. . . . I heard Echo—sorry, Secretary Adams—call you 'chief,' and it seemed much more friendly. I didn't mean to be disrespectful. You know we're very fond of you, chief."

"*We?*"

"Yes. All of us in Freeworld."

"Oh."

He was silent for a while.

"Did I hear you calling Secretary Adams 'Echo'? "

"I'm sorry, chief. That's a nickname. A newspaper gave it to him. I guess it's only recently. . . ."

"How did he ever get *that?*"

"Well, it's short for Secretary of *Economics*. And then . . . a lot of people think he just echoes your opinions and policies and that he's just acting for you now. I don't really think most people intend to be unfriendly when they use it. Secretary Adams doesn't mind. He jokes about it . . . he's a darling."

"Oh, he is?" He was surprised to hear a touch of resentment and jealousy in his own voice.

Three months went by before the last cast was taken off. He found himself gradually walking again, though with crutches. He was told he could leave the hospital if he agreed to take at least another three months for convalescence.

He consented to be taken back to his home in Bermuda, provided Nurse Robinson went with him. A doctor, two other nurses and three servants went along.

The island was even lovelier than he had remembered it, and the sea more incredibly blue.

His strength came back in little jumps. He found himself walking again, without crutches.

Edith Robinson read to him in the long evenings. He began to taste for the first time some of the cultural fruits of his new system. As his reforms had brought a lessening of terrorism in

339

the Western Hemisphere, a handful of old bourgeois books, saved by a few courageous ancestors and their descendants from the all-consuming bonfires, had emerged.

What had been uncovered so far were the works of only three of the ancient bourgeois authors—a William Shakespeare, a Jane Austen, and a Miguel Cervantes. The books were of course all in dead languages, but scholars had patiently deciphered them, and they were now available in Marxanto—or rather in the re-semanticized Marxanto that was gradually taking its place. Edith Robinson and Peter first went through the novels of Jane Austen and found them fountains of pure delight. To save the works of these authors, Peter reflected, though they carried no particular political message, men and women had risked torture and the lives of themselves and their children, on the bare possibility that these works might one day again be brought to light. Men could not have shown their courage, he felt, in a better cause.

But sometimes, as she read to him, his mind would wander from the substance of what she read, and he would find himself listening to her voice itself, to its soft tone, or watching her graceful movements and her neat figure. He found himself making comparisons. This new Edith was so straightforward, so candid, so sure of herself. What he would have given to see that look of independence in the eyes of the shy, fearful Edith he had lost!

And then he thought: It is not really the difference between two women I am seeing; it is the difference between two worlds!

After ten weeks on the island, Peter was strong enough to sit down to his piano again. As he played Haydn, Mozart, Bach, Brahms, Schubert, Edith Robinson sat entranced. "It seems a pity, chief. A man with your gifts—a man who can play as beautifully as you—wasting his time in politics!"

This peaceful life was almost enough to cause him to forget the war. But never quite. With each new surge of strength he felt also a new surge in his sense of responsibility. At the end of

340

fourteen weeks he said to the doctor: "If you try to hold me here for more than another week, I will no longer follow your orders."

He cabled Adams that he would return the next week to take over.

That evening, after she had finished reading to him, Edith said: "The doctor tells me you want to go back." Her eyes were cast down. For the first time she was not looking straight at him or smiling.

He placed one hand on her shoulder, raised her chin with the other, and looked into her eyes: "I want to tell you, Edith, how much your care has meant to me. You have been a wonderful nurse. . . . You know, you'd make some man a wonderful wife. . . ."

Suddenly he knew that he was in love with her, and that the man he was thinking of was himself.

Adams had conducted the purely military operations of the war with brilliance. Already the forces of Freeworld had regained a foothold in Ireland. They were widening it, and establishing and maintaining air bases. They had captured the initiative.

But at home Peter found the economic situation chaotic, and a threat to further military progress. Prices of most things had nearly doubled. Other prices were at their old level, but in these cases the goods were scarce or unobtainable. Essential war production had actually been brought to a stop at some points because of unbalanced output or bottlenecks. As a whole, war production methods seemed inexcusably wasteful.

Peter tried to find out the reasons for all this for himself, and then asked Adams for his own explanation.

"Let's begin with money," said Peter. "Where are all the gold coins? They seem to have disappeared completely, and now I find only paper certificates 'entitling' the holder to a gold coin which he can't in fact get."

"That came about by a series of steps," Adams said. "I really think the present arrangement is a great improvement. First of all, it seemed to me unsafe in wartime to leave gold coins in the hands of the public."

"Why?"   .

"Well, they might hoard them."

"Did they?"

"No; but they might have started to at any time. Gold is a war resource, and all war resources should be in the hands of the government."

"Go on."

"Well, first of all it struck me as illogical, chief, to have gold coins stamped as to their weight and fineness merely by a private goldsmith. That didn't seem to me to give enough assurance to those who were offered the coins. The reputation of the stamper might be merely local, or not warranted; and the receiver might be compelled to make his own assay—"

"But, in fact," broke in Peter, "wasn't the business of stamping gold coins being done more and more by just a few well-known firms, like Lloyd's and Morgan's? And wasn't that precisely because these firms did have a Freeworldwide reputation for care and integrity, and because their coins therefore had a wider and quicker acceptability?"

"I just don't feel," said Adams, "that the stamping of money can be left to private hands. The maintenance of a sound and uniform currency seems to me obviously a governmental function—"

"Go on."

"So I called in all the coins to be re-assayed, reweighed, melted down and restamped with the government's own stamp. This made a completely uniform—and incidentally, I think, a much handsomer currency. I hired first-rate artists—"

"Go on."

"Well, after I had got the new coins all stamped, it seemed to me ridiculous to turn them all back to their owners, who might only hoard them instead of putting them to use. Gold is a weapon of war, and ought to be enlisted for the duration."

"Go on."

"So it occurred to me that all I really had to do was to let the people who had turned in their gold coins keep the *receipts* for them! The receipts represented the pledged word of the government itself. There's nothing better than that, of course; so all I had to do was to make the receipts transferable—"

"Go on."

"I wish you wouldn't keep interrupting me just to tell me to go on!"

"Go on."

"So what I did was to let the receipt holders turn in their receipts for a freely transferable receipt, payable not to a specific person but to 'bearer.' And I must say, I think I made these receipts very durable and good-looking. They were on an expensive paper, skillfully and beautifully engraved, so that they could not be easily counterfeited—"

"And they promised to pay the actual gold on demand?"

"Precisely! They were just like a warehouse receipt! Only of course I issued an order, chief, that no one could get the actual gold until after the war was over."

"I see. No one was entitled to get his own property back until you said so."

"I am actually protecting that property, chief, better than the owners could themselves. I am having enormous underground vaults built in the middle of the continent, near Winnipeg, which will be guarded by troops day and night."

"In other words, you are putting all your eggs in one basket. So that Bolshekov's paratroopers would only have to go to one place with the assurance of getting all our gold instead of having to extract it from each of 200,000,000 persons, each with his own hiding place."

"I can't accept that argument. I—"

"Go on."

"Well, it didn't take me many weeks to learn that a shooting war is a very expensive business, chief. I needed money and needed it quick; so I hit upon a marvelous way of solving the problem!"

"Yes?"

"I simply issued more of the engraved warehouse receipts for gold!"

"Against what?"

"Against nothing. What did it matter? People couldn't get the gold anyway! And the new warehouse receipts circulated as money just as freely as the old, and at parity with them."

"Particularly as you made their acceptance at that rate compulsory."

"Of course."

"What would happen, Adams, if at the end of the war every holder of this paper money were to turn it in for gold?"

"I don't think he will. Why should he? The paper circulates just as well as gold, and is just as acceptable. And it's lighter and handier to carry. We don't need a 100 per cent gold backing, because there will never be a 100 per cent turn in."

"No doubt if there *were* 100 per cent gold backing," said Peter, "and everybody knew it, you would be right in saying that there would never be a 100 per cent turn in. People wouldn't bother to ask for gold as long as they knew they were certain to get it."

"Precisely!" exclaimed Adams. "Don't you see what a wonderful economy I've achieved? I've hit upon a wonderful new monetary technique, comparable, if I may presume to say so, to your own discovery of the free enterprise system!"

"Just a moment," continued Peter. "It is true that people wouldn't ask for gold as long as they knew they were certain to get it. But they would start asking the moment they felt there was any doubt about their getting it. You yourself know this. Otherwise you wouldn't have forbidden people to ask for their gold, or refused to pay it out. Now the minute you issue, say, 200 claims to goldgrams against only 100 actual goldgrams, and the people know that this is the situation, then every holder will know that only the first hundred claims can be honored; so everyone will rush to be among that first hundred, and your marvelous new technique will collapse."

344

Adams was silent for a few minutes. "I simply had to raise money," he said at last.

"Don't you think it was dishonest to issue claims for gold against nonexistent gold?" persisted Peter. "If a private individual did that, you would throw him in jail as a cheat and a swindler!"

Adams looked deeply hurt. "I don't think the two cases are comparable. The government has the taxing power and can use it to get whatever resources it needs to meet its obligations after the war. We have to win this war, and get money in the quickest way we can. And besides, maybe we could turn this whole gold thing into a sort of fiction. What good is gold, anyway? You can't eat it. Why should people want it instead of paper, which circulates as money just as well?"

"On that argument, you can deprive the people of anything on the ground that they are irrational in wanting it."

"But isn't the desire for gold merely a silly superstition—?"

"I'm not going to waste time arguing the alleged irrationality of other people's wants," cut in Peter sharply. "I'm simply going to point out to you the practical effects of what you have actually done. Prices of goods have nearly doubled—"

"Because of the scarcities of goods brought about by the war," said Adams.

"That's what I thought you would say," Peter answered. "But that's only true of a few specific commodities. It's only a very small part of the *general* explanation. People can't offer more money for *all* goods unless they have more money to offer. Let's get back to what I assumed we had both learned several years ago. What is a 'price'? It is a *relationship* between the value of a commodity and the value of the monetary unit. If the monetary unit is a gram of gold, then the so-called 'price' of an article is the relationship between the value of that article and the value of a gram of gold. If, other things equal, an article gets scarcer, its price will go up. But if the article gets no scarcer at all, but the supply of monetary units increases, then the price of the article will also go up—because the value of the monetary unit, in which the price is expressed, has gone *down!*"

"You mean," said Adams, "that every price really reflects two things—not only the value of the particular commodity priced, but the value of the monetary unit in which it is priced?"

"Exactly," said Peter. "Every price is a *ratio* between two values."

"That's a rather ingenious way of looking at it!"

"It's not ingenious at all," said Peter, spurning the compliment. "It applies to all measurement. When I say that the length of a yard is three feet I am merely talking about a ratio between a foot and a yard, and that ratio won't remain unless *both* lengths remain what they are. Let's say this office is twenty feet wide, and next week you issue an order saying that hereafter the foot is only six inches long. Then the office becomes forty feet wide, though it hasn't grown a bit."

"That's not a bad idea," said Adams, grinning. "It would be a way of making all rooms seem larger."

"And in the same way, cheapening the value of the monetary unit, Adams, is a way of making everybody's income seem larger. And fools are fooled by it. Now look what you've really done. You've about doubled the quantity of money outstanding. And therefore you've about doubled the prices of goods, because the value of the monetary unit is not much better than half its previous level. If you increase the supply of wheat, you lower the value of each individual bushel of wheat. Now there is another way of doing the same thing. You can sell 'short' in the speculative markets wheat that you haven't got to deliver, and therefore you can temporarily increase the apparent supply of wheat on the market and temporarily depress its price. Or you can issue certificates and *call* them the equivalent of a bushel of wheat, and force everybody to take them as such."

"But I've raised money for the government; I've raised money to conduct the war!" protested Adams.

"And you did it in such a way," said Peter, "as to kick around economic relationships, to cheat people dependent on fixed mone-

346

tary incomes, and to reward and penalize people without relationship to their real productive contribution or lack of it. And so you've helped to throw discredit on the profit-and-loss system that we made possible at the risk of our lives. . . ."

He paused.

"What do you intend to do now?" asked Adams quietly. "Do you want to recall all the extra money outstanding? That would bring about a panic in the middle of the war."

"You're right," agreed Peter. "Prices would fall; profit margins would be wiped out; manufacturers would shut down; workers would be asked to take lower wages and wouldn't understand why; unemployment would develop, and resentment and bitterness; new injustices would be created, without necessarily correcting more than a few of the old. . . . No; we couldn't withdraw the extra money from circulation. But that is only another reason why you shouldn't have issued it in the first place!"

"What do you intend to do, then?" Adams asked.

"At least we can stop issuing any more, Adams. At least we can freeze the circulation where it is. We can increase taxation, and float bond issues to be paid for out of people's savings—"

The telephone rang. It was Hamilton, the Secretary of Defense.

"Our forces have just captured the airfield outside of Edinburgh, chief! In a week the whole of Scotland should be in our hands!"

Chapter 42

I'M sorry," said Adams, "but whatever caused the increase of prices, at least I tried everything to stop it. For example, I put maximum price ceilings on the necessaries of life—"

"I was coming to that," said Peter. "Let's take the case of beef."

"I'm glad you pick beef," said Adams, "because I acted with great boldness there. You remember that before the war beef was selling at only 50 cents a pound. I kept seeing it climb till it doubled to a goldgram a pound. Then I acted. I ordered the price rolled back to 50 cents a pound—"

"Why?"

"Because a goldgram a pound is outrageous."

"Why? Because you were used to seeing it at only 50 cents a pound?"

"Well . . . partly that. But the sellers of beef were profiteering."

"Any more than anybody else? On the average, didn't most prices double? Didn't most wages double? Didn't most incomes double—as measured in your new cheaper monetary unit?"

"But beef is a necessity of life! The poor can't afford beef at a goldgram a pound!"

"Now let's analyze that," said Peter. "Let's go back for a moment to the reason why beef went up in the first place. I've looked up the figures and find that until you started to fix its price the production and supply of beef didn't go down. So its price didn't go up because beef was scarcer. It went up be-

348

cause you cheapened the value of the monetary unit by printing more money. You blew up the supply of money, so to speak. You blew it up not with more real value but merely by pumping in more air. So a good name for that process would be monetary *inflation*—"

"That's a good phrase," said Adams, "but it has nothing to do with the particular problem with which I was faced. The poor just can't afford beef at a goldgram a pound."

"Could they have afforded it at 50 cents a pound before your inflation started?"

"Well—perhaps they could."

"But after your inflation started, the poor, on the average, had twice as many goldgrams in their pockets as they had before. The prices of *other* things had also doubled, so the sellers of those things had twice as many goldgrams. And the wages and income of the poor, like the income of everyone else, had also about doubled. Therefore the poor man—if his cash holdings and income had been affected in the same relation as everybody else's—did not have to give up any greater percentage of his cash holdings or any greater percentage of his income to buy a pound of beef at one goldgram than he had had to give up to buy it previously at 50 cents."

Adams looked as if he were thinking seriously about this. He did not answer.

Peter continued. "In rolling back the price of beef to 50 cents a pound after cash holdings and incomes and other prices had doubled, in other words, you did precisely the same thing you would have done if, *before* the inflation, you had arbitrarily cut back the price of beef to 25 cents a pound."

"I was trying to protect people against the consequences of high prices," persisted Adams.

"You were trying to 'protect' the public against the consequences of the very monetary inflation you yourself had imposed upon them," retorted Peter.

Adams was silent again. "I still say that the poor can't afford to pay a goldgram a pound for beef," he said finally. "Only the rich would buy the beef. Why should the rich be allowed to buy all the beef?"

Peter sighed hopelessly.

"Let's try it once more," he said. "You rolled back the price of beef from a goldgram to 50 cents so that more people could buy beef. Right?"

"Right."

"But even at 50 cents a pound there are people who feel that they cannot afford beef, or cannot afford as much as they would like. Right?"

"Right."

"So why didn't you cut the price to 25 cents a pound?"

"But it hadn't *been* 25 cents a pound; it had been 50 cents a pound. I considered 50 cents a fair price."

"Because that was the price you were accustomed to. Is the 'fair' price the price one is accustomed to?"

Adams did not answer. Peter continued:

"And even if you *had* cut the price to only 25 cents a pound, there would probably still have been people who couldn't afford to buy beef, or not as much of it as they would like?"

Again Adams was silent.

"And at any price whatever there would still have been *some* people, Adams, who could not afford beef. So why not order the producers to give the beef away? Why not order all the producers to give everything away? Wouldn't that be the logical corollary of the principle on which you acted?"

"Only for a few selected necessities."

"Then you would order only the producers of necessities to give them away? That would be a wonderful incentive for producing necessities, wouldn't it?"

Adams did not answer. Peter went on:

"I'm not going to stop until I've stripped every layer from this onion. Let's look at another implication of your argument. How does our free enterprise system work, and what makes it work? We decided that in it each person was entitled to the value of his own production—to the value of his own contribution to a

350

completed product—and that each person actually tended to get that through the competition of the market. Well, I produce beef, say, at a market value of 100 cents a pound. Anybody who thinks he can raise, process and sell beef for less than that is entitled to try. Anybody who thinks I'm making a bigger profit at beef than he is at something else is entitled to abandon his own line and take up mine. Now while I'm getting 100 cents a pound for beef you're getting 25 cents a pound for potatoes. So in effect you exchange four pounds of your potatoes for one pound of beef. And presumably this comes about, at least in the long run, because, say, the cost of production of a pound of beef is equal to the cost of production of four pounds of potatoes. But now comes along a bureaucrat and orders me to surrender *two* pounds of my beef for four pounds of your potatoes, or to take only two pounds of potatoes for my pound of beef—"

"Or he could cut all prices equally," said Adams, "and keep the exchange ratio the same—"

"Assuming he could make that work, what would he accomplish? He would then cut the income of the 'poor' as much as he would cut the price of beef!"

Adams was silent again.

"And incidentally," Peter continued, "by trying to keep all prices and cost relationships precisely what they were before the outbreak of war, your bureaucrat would delay or prevent the very changes in the structure of production that are most necessary. For what we are trying to do now is to maximize the production of goods needed in war and to minimize the production of goods needed only in peace. And the way to do that most quickly is to make the profits of war production more attractive and the profits of mere 'peace-goods' production less attractive. That would also quickly bring about a higher wage scale in war-goods production than in civilian-goods production. And all this could be most quickly accomplished under a free and flexible price and wage system, not under an arbitrarily petrified price and wage system."

351

"But all I tried to do, chief, was to fix the price of a few selected commodities—"

"All right, Adams; then let's come back to that. You are trying to force one particular set of producers to sell for less than their previous relative profit margin, or perhaps even for less than their costs of production. You are trying to force them to make an exchange in which they do not get, like other producers, the exchange value of what they produce, but only half the exchange value of what they produce. Are you surprised that you have merely made beef scarce? Are you surprised that it has practically disappeared from the market? You are discriminating against one group of producers—"

"They ought to be patriotic enough—" began Adams.

"They simply *couldn't* go on producing even if they wanted to," retorted Peter. "Losses would eventually force them to quit production. So, with your well-meant efforts, you have been harshest toward the very producers who are turning out the things most needed, and you have forced scarcities of the very things you were trying to make more plentiful. By lowering the price of necessities you have lowered the profit margin on necessities, and encouraged people to move into the production of luxuries where they can get larger profit margins!"

"But everybody ought to be satisfied with a reasonable profit!" insisted Adams.

"Ah, yes," Peter went on. "And that brings me to another point. I see that you have been trying to control profits."

"I certainly have," said Adams proudly. "I'm not going to have anyone profiteer out of this war. I am not going to have anyone profiteer when others are making sacrifices, risking and losing their lives—"

"I would like to impose equality of sacrifice in this war just as much as you would," retorted Peter. "Unfortunately, that isn't the way war works—which is precisely one of the reasons for not having a war if you can help it. You can't have a system of equality and justice within an institution, like war, that rests only on superior violence, force and might. In a war there can

352

be only one commander-in-chief; in a regiment there can be only one colonel; in a company there can be only one captain; in a squad there can be only one corporal. One man loses his life and seven survive: you can't arrange it so that each of them is one-eighth killed. One man loses his leg and five are whole: you can't equalize it by arranging that each shall lose only part of his left foot."

"But profits are something that you *can* equalize."

"Now let's look at the results of trying to do that. The first thing you did when the war broke out was to let contracts that gave the contractor his costs of production plus 5 per cent net profit—"

"Five per cent was plenty."

"And what was the result? The result was that you got tremendous wastes in production. Instead of the utmost economy and efficiency in the allocation of productive resources, you got *deliberate* extravagance, *intentional* inefficiency."

"But how do *you* know that?" asked Adams, amazed. "I allowed nothing to be published about it because I thought it would demoralize the war effort. Who told you about that?"

"No one," replied Peter. "I didn't have to ask. Nothing else *could* have happened. What you did was to reverse all the free market incentives. Instead of penalizing extravagance and wastefulness, you put a premium on them."

"I allowed merely a flat 5 per cent—"

"Precisely. And you overlooked elementary arithmetic. If the contractor's expenses were 100 goldgrams on an item, he made a profit on it of 5 goldgrams. If he could succeed in getting his production costs down to only 80 goldgrams, he made a profit of only 4 goldgrams. In other words, if he increased the efficiency of his production, and so released more scarce capital and scarce labor for *other* war production, he was penalized by having his profit reduced. But if he could succeed in *doubling* his costs of production on each item, either by carelessness or deliberate ingenuity, then he doubled his profits on it. If he could get the item

353

to cost 200 goldgrams, he could make 10 goldgrams instead of 5—"

"But I abandoned that system as soon as we found all that out," protested Adams.

"And what did you substitute?"

"I substituted a system under which the government wins both ways. The contract is first negotiated at a flat price. This puts a ceiling on the contractor's profit, and if his unit costs of production run above the initial contract price he is just out of luck: he loses the difference. Whereas—and here is where I think I was ingenious—if he makes too big a profit margin on the contract we step in and renegotiate it, reducing the price."

"What is 'too big' a profit margin?"

"We won't say in advance, but everybody understands from the record of renegotiation so far that anything above 6 or 7 per cent per unit will be regarded as excessive."

"I grant you that that system is at least less vicious than the first one," said Peter. "But let's see what happens under it. A government contractor finds that he is making 8 per cent per unit profit. What incentive has he to cut his costs of production? What incentive has he to make shells, say, more economically, so that he can either make more of them with his present labor and equipment or release part of his labor to make other war materiel no less urgent?"

"If he is a true patriot—" began Adams.

"If he is a true patriot he will cut costs even though he loses by it. But if he is not a true patriot he will do nothing to economize, because his net income will not be improved by economies?"

"That is correct," conceded Adams.

"In other words, if half your war contractors are true patriots they will constantly search for economies anyway, even if they lose money by them; but if the other half are not true patriots they will continue to produce extravagantly and waste essential resources? In still other words, in order to get economy and efficiency in war production, or to prevent waste, you depend

354

entirely on true patriotism, but certainly not on your own contract system, which makes for the opposite?"

Adams did not reply.

"Tell me," Peter continued: "would you apply this system also to the workers, so that every time an individual worker learned to cut costs or to increase his efficiency you reduced his pay?"

"I'll admit that the new system doesn't give as much incentive as it might to reduce production costs and increase efficiency," Adams said; "but at least it avoids the error of the previous cost-plus system, which put a positive premium on waste."

"Does it? Suppose your manufacturer signs a contract and finds himself about to make a unit profit of 20 per cent before your government renegotiators get around to him. He knows he will be cut back to 7 per cent. But if he puts some of his friends and his nephews and his Uncle Charley, whom he has been having to support anyway, on his payroll, he can get the unit profit down to 7 per cent before the government renegotiators arrive. Or suppose he could economize by getting rid of needless workers but would only arouse the resentment of the union by doing so, and would not make any profit out of it anyway? Aren't these foolish positive and negative temptations to place before him?"

"How big a profit do *you* consider reasonable?" Adams' tone was challenging.

"I never think of the problem that way," Peter answered. "I think only of the deterrents and incentives necessary to get the greatest efficiency and economy and the maximum balanced production. There is no such thing as a flat, uniform, 'reasonable' profit. Such a profit would prevent all the productive adjustments that it is necessary for a dynamic economy constantly to make, whether it is to adjust itself to changing supply and demand, changing tastes of consumers, the change from peace production to war production, or what not. What counts is not *absolute* profits, but only *relative* profits and losses. There is never such a thing as a uniform 'rate' of profit anyway, unless it is imposed by government decree; there is only an average profit or loss which

355

can be roughly calculated by statisticians but which is meaningless for the individual producer. Even a profit of 20 per cent may not seem 'reasonable' enough for him if he can make 30 per cent producing something else. On the other hand, a profit of less than 1 per cent might prove a big incentive to economy and production if the only alternative were a loss."

"What are you going to do," asked Adams, "about public resentment against big individual profits?"

"I can only blame your own speeches and your own policies for helping to stir up that resentment," retorted Peter. "You have to make up your mind. Which are you more eager to do: prevent 'profiteering'—or win the war?"

"We must beat Bolshekov, of course—"

"Then let us make that aim No. One, and subordinate everything else to it. Let profits be whatever they have to be to get the greatest possible war production. Maybe we can get at the thing that bothers you by some form of war profits tax; but that's another story. The point is that if we are more eager to stop so-called profiteering than we are to win the war, we may lose the war and everything with it."

"So your verdict, in brief," Adam summed up, despondently, "is that I have done a wretched job?"

Peter suddenly felt ashamed of himself.

"I'm sorry. I apologize. No: my verdict is that in the field of economic policy you have made some very serious mistakes, which have held up the progress of the war. But on the side of *military* strategy, which I have studied with an equal readiness to be critical, your record has been magnificent. You are a genius as an organizer and an executive. Had I been in charge of military strategy, and the actual day-to-day conduct of the war, I should probably have made an unholy botch of it. . . . And so, if this is agreeable to you, I am going to appoint you Secretary of Defense with complete powers—except that I shall assume charge of internal political and economic policy."

Adams was more than satisfied with this verdict, and Peter bent himself to rectifying all the mistakes he thought Adams had

356

made. His changes caused so deep a resentment by those who were hurt by them, and by shortsighted persons who imagined they were hurt by them, that Peter thanked his lucky stars he had not yet introduced a real democracy, for he was certain that on this wave of indignation, which he hoped was only temporary, he would have been swept right out of power.

Democracy won't always make the right decisions, he thought; its merit will lie in the law of averages.

His biggest difficulty, and his biggest shock, came when he tried to stop the inflation that Adams had begun. He made up his mind beforehand that any effort to *de*flate back to the prewar level would be disastrous. What he did not foresee were the derangements and convulsions that followed even when he tried to halt the inflation where it was. Interest rates soared; stock and bond prices collapsed; confidence fell; firms closed; unemployment set in; commodity prices dropped. Peter only dimly understood why this was so. He decided that a lot of misdirected investment and misdirected production had taken place during the inflationary boom, and that this could not correct itself without bringing disturbance and disruption. But he had neither the time nor the surplus mental energy to think the whole chain of causation through link by link and study every aspect in detail.

He felt forced, in the end, to resume a moderate inflation and postpone the final showdown and readjustment until after the war. The great conclusion that he drew was that an inflation must ultimately force a crisis, readjustment and depression; that this showdown had to come, and that the longer it was postponed the worse it would ultimately be. It was one more reason, in addition to what he had originally supposed, why the government must never start, encourage or tolerate a money or credit inflation in the first place.

But Peter's unpopularity in trying to rectify Adams' economic mistakes was covered by the immense popularity of Adams' military victories. These now began to go steadily forward. And Peter himself proved to be justified, after the first months of crisis, by

357

the immense forward leap in war production. The tanks and planes and ships and munitions began to pour out at an unbelievable rate.

It was the incomparable superiority of Freeworld's production, Adams said in a great speech, that must decide the outcome in its favor.

The whole of the British provinces were soon occupied and turned into an immense network of airfields and a military concentration point. A bridgehead on the Continent was secured, and the troops of Freeworld moved ahead at an ever-increasing rate. For once it was seen, in spite of Bolshekov's propaganda, that the troops of Freeworld were bringing not terror but a liberation from terror, millions of Wonworld troops gave themselves up as prisoners, and whole populations went over.

Peter's troops reached the suburbs of Moscow.

At last came the final break.

Just when he seemed on the verge of capture, Bolshekov shot himself.

What was left of authority in Wonworld surrendered.

The war was over.

Chapter 43

THERE were wild celebrations everywhere. For a few weeks the world was intoxicated with peace and liberty. Orators spoke as if humanity were about to enter the gates of paradise.

Peter shared at first in the general elation. But when he began to realize that everyone else was depending on *him* to justify these millennial hopes, the sense of responsibility fell back on him like a heavy weight.

Before victory it had been easy enough to talk eloquently of the better world to come. But when the problem was actually before one, when it came to the actual task of deciding on the means, spelling out the details, and above all of *doing*. . . . "If to do were as easy as to know what were good to do, chapels had been churches, and poor men's cottages princes' palaces." . . . Where had he heard that? . . . Ah, yes, Edith Robinson had read it to him in that rediscovered bourgeois writer, Shakespeare. How wise! And how simply it called attention to the inescapable scarcity of means to achieve all our ends! If only all the noisy and self-complacent reformers who were now intoxicated by their own rhetoric could be got to take this sobering cathartic! . . .

The tremendous problems he faced now were dominantly political. The world was too fantastically big to be run by any single group from any single center. The only solution was to give self-rule to all the provinces—to England, France, Wales, Texas—and to use the central government only to maintain peaceful and free relations among them. But how could he prevent each of these provinces from falling into the hands of some petty tyrant or dictator? He must first of all put the choice of leaders and the form of government into the hands of the peoples of these provinces. The leaders must be freely chosen, and peaceably removable, by the people.

But how could he consistently ask for this when he himself had never been chosen by the people?

He must begin by making the central government of Freeworld a model of a popular representative government. He must begin by risking his own leadership.

He drafted a provisional constitution. It struck him as a happy idea to guard the freedom of future minorities against the possible tyranny of future majorities themselves by setting self-denying limits, in this constitution, to the power of the new government. He knew that a future majority, if sufficiently determined, could disregard these limits or interpret them away; but their action in doing so, he hoped, would be a clearer warning signal than otherwise that they were embarking on a dangerous path.

Next he decided that the people would have neither the time nor the special knowledge to decide technical problems of legislation for themselves, but only to choose a body of representatives to decide these problems for them.

Even this body, he decided, would be too awkward to initiate a detailed legislative program. It should only be asked to ratify or reject the program submitted to it. The real function of this popular assembly would not be to legislate but to choose and keep an executive. It would select its own leader, and ratify or reject the laws and policies he proposed. If it rejected them, then the rejected leader could either resign and let the popular assembly choose some other leader that it *would* follow, or he could force the legislative assembly to go back to the people for a new election, and go back himself, so that the people could decide between them.

This *de facto* government-policy-maker Peter decided to call the Majority Leader; and because his tenure might be temporary and insecure he decided to create a more permanent head of

360

the government, called the President, also to be chosen by the representative assembly, who would be the titular head but who would perform honorary and ceremonial functions and act as a moderator among political factions.

Peter provided a procedure by which his provisional constitution could be amended by the assembly and a popular referendum.

He set a date for an election three months off, and indicated ways in which candidates might be nominated.

Telegrams poured in from local groups suggesting candidates to support Peter's policies. No one dared to suggest any rival candidates.

There was only one way, Peter decided, to remedy this. He withdrew himself as a candidate for any office whatever, and asked Adams to assume the leadership of a Freedom Party.

Rival candidates began to appear. They represented, at first, all shades of doctrine, but leadership among the candidates who were not adherents of the Freedom Party began to gravitate toward a Chinese, Wang Ching-li, a man of remarkable presence and even more remarkable eloquence.

"I hesitate to predict it, chief," Adams said, "but I'm afraid this fellow Wang, and not myself, will become the first Majority Leader."

"But his ideas are so vague you can't do anything with them," complained Peter. "He has started to talk mysteriously about a 'Third Way' that is neither 'capitalism' nor socialism, but he never says what this Third Way is. I can't believe people will vote for anything as cloudy as that."

"It doesn't matter," said Adams. "It isn't his ideas that are going to elect him."

"Then what is?"

"The Chinese vote."

"You mean people are going to vote on mere racial grounds, after national boundaries have long been broken down, after centuries of indoctrination in our common humanity and the brotherhood of man?"

361

Adams shrugged his shoulders. "Maybe I'm cynical. But there are more Chinese than anybody else, and the whole Orient envies the Occident. We never did succeed in reducing Occidental poverty to the level of Oriental poverty, even under egalitarian communism."

"That's because Oriental impoverishment kept increasing, because the Orientals kept overpopulating—"

"Ah, and now, chief, is when the overpopulation is at last going to pay dividends. Power will now be decided by votes. The Orient has the votes; and it will use them to rule the Occident and share the wealth by taxing the West to subsidize the East—"

"Always the black view," said Peter. "But I don't believe it. People will be convinced by reason. I will take the stump for your party, Adams, and we will defeat Wang by argument."

But Wang proved to be a very skillful as well as eloquent debater. He talked constantly against "monopoly." He talked against "bigness." He was against bigness everywhere and in everything, against congestion, overcrowding, and what he called "proletarianization." He was against giant overgrown cities, giant overgrown buildings, giant overgrown factories. He was against the Cult of the Colossal. He wanted everybody to have a balanced, *human* life; he wanted everybody to have his own house and to work in his own garden.

He said he didn't like factories that employed more than 100 people. He demanded equality of opportunity and education for the children of the poor with the children of the rich. He demanded a stiff inheritance tax.

Peter was kept busy answering him. What did Wang mean by monopoly? he asked. Was it always bad? Everybody had a monopoly of his own peculiar talent or genius. Wherever people or products were not completely alike in all respects, competition could not be perfect. But what did that matter? Wasn't it enough if competition dominated economic life, so that every product or method of production that was inferior was constantly being, or on the verge of being, supplanted by something better?

And did Wang want competition in every field? Did he want

362

half a dozen competing telephone companies in the same city? Half a dozen railroads paralleling each other over the same routes?

Did Wang want to *forbid* the existence of factories or companies employing more than 100 men? Did he know how much such a law might cost the public in preventing the enormous economies of large-scale production?

He himself had always been uncompromisingly opposed, Peter insisted, to *coercive* monopoly, to monopoly built up or sustained by any form of force, fraud or misrepresentation, duplicity or unfair practice, and he had already labored to define these coercive practices in the law. He had already illegalized every form of conspiracy or secret agreement to reduce output or fix prices. Did Wang want to go further than that? And with what measures? Let him be specific!

Peter agreed with Wang, he said, so far as his personal preference was concerned, in not liking big cities. But did Wang intend to force his personal preferences on everyone else? Would he *forbid* a city to grow beyond 50,000 inhabitants, say? Who would select who was and who was not to be permitted to live in a city that had reached its legal population limit?

The biggest debate was on the question of inheritance. Wouldn't a denial of the right of inheritance, Peter asked, or even an abridgment of it, open up the door to a gradual denial or abridgment of all property rights? Private property, Peter contended, was not only one of the great pillars of individual freedom, but the main incentive to the accumulation of capital.

But when the great debate was finished, and the election results rolled in, they gave Wang's Unity Party a thin majority. The Uldanov-Adams Freedom Party ran second.

At the first meeting of the new Parliament next week Wang would be chosen as the first majority leader of the new democratic world. Adams would be named leader of the Opposition.

Peter was crushed. He was even more bewildered by the verdict than resentful of it. It was he, Peter, who by a voluntary abdication of power and even at the risk of his life had given the world freedom. It was he who had set up a system under which the individual was at last freed from terror of the State, at last made secure in the possession of some property of his own; and this system had produced wealth on a scale hitherto undreamed of. It was he, Peter, who had made this very election possible. And the people had used it to repudiate his principles— in effect, to repudiate *him!*

He had failed! The people would use their new power to destroy the system he had given them, to destroy even their own new-found liberties!

But Adams had a different interpretation.

"The result had very little to do with principles, chief. I told you what would happen from the start. You had the solid Chinese vote against you—and the solid Indian vote, and the solid African vote. All these people are tired of being ruled by the West. It was you who gave the East the chance to throw us out. I was always against it!"

Yet the next day an almost unanimous demand arose in the press that Peter Uldanov be named the first constitutional President of the Republic of Freeworld. Wang himself called on Peter and urged him to accept.

"No," said Peter. "I am deeply touched by your magnanimity; but I've disqualified myself by campaigning against you, and I'm already labeled as a partisan."

"But I'm as deeply attached to a free market system as you are," Wang insisted. "There is no real difference of principle between us. We differ only on details. The only problem is, how can we best purify and perfect that system?"

"I'm immensely relieved to hear you talk like that," said Peter. "But I've had my share of public life. You know, I was thrown into it against my will, and my fiancée wants me to give it up—"

"Think it over," said Wang, "and let me know after the week end."

Peter and Edith Robinson spent the week end as Adams' guests at his country home high in the Berkshires. Edith went to bed early on the first evening, but Adams and Peter sat before the open fire—it was April—and talked late into the night.

364

"You ought to accept Wang's offer," Adams said. "It's a tremendous honor."

"No, Adams. You know, when the election results first came in I got a jolt. Then I got depressed. But it's all over in two days. Now I feel immensely relieved. For the first time in my life I'm free. And now that Wang has announced his program, I'm convinced that I did succeed. After all, I wouldn't have discovered much of a system if only one man could be trusted to operate it. I was beginning to get the obsession that only I understood how to keep the system from going on the rocks. The election cured me."

"Tell me," Adams said: "now that we have achieved a free system, do you think mankind will at last be happy? Will people not only be enterprising, but just, generous, kind?"

Peter gazed thoughtfully into the fire. "We can't tell whether man, now that he is free, will turn out to be wholly admirable. No system, I suppose, can be any better than the men and women who operate it. If they are selfish, stupid, unjust, hungry for power at the expense of their fellows, I don't suppose our new system, or any conceivable system, can wipe out such vices or save people from themselves. But under a free system man has the opportunity, at least, to do his best, and to show the moral and intellectual stature to which he is capable of growing. . . ."

Adams put a new log on the fire.

"No," Peter went on, "we can't be sure that man, now that he is free, will use his freedom only for acts that are praiseworthy. He may even begin to develop social theories that present his own shortcomings as the shortcomings of the system under which he lives. He may call his own faults the faults of the system. Free man may come even to blame his own freedom, to blame the very system that makes him free, to imagine that there is some other possible system, some other arrangement or distribution of human rights and powers, under which he might be completely perfect and everlastingly happy."

"That isn't the most optimistic conclusion to arrive at, Peter, concerning your own accomplishment."

"But while we don't know, Adams, whether free men will necessarily be noble and magnanimous, one thing we do know—

that *un*free man has been, and will always be, contemptible and wretched. . . ."

The new log suddenly burst into flame. Both men watched it in silence.

"Tell me," Adams resumed at last: "If you are not going to take Wang's offer, what *are* you going to do."

Peter smiled. "I told you I was free. Edith and I are planning to get married next month—quietly, if that is possible—and then we plan to live in the nearest thing to paradise, and to raise a family. We have found a house in Nantucket on a cliff overlooking the sea—"

"Is that all?"

"Not quite. You know, I was trained as a pianist, and until my father—and Bolshekov—forced me into politics my one ambition was to be a great pianist. It hasn't quite left me. I intend to compose music, and to play the piano."

"Is that all?"

"Isn't that enough? To try to play with perfection, and never succeed, but always to feel one's self getting better; to help to enlarge, if I can, that great manmade world of harmony that seems to be beyond the vicissitudes of nature itself; to walk along the beach, to look out on the sea, to—" he felt embarrassed —"to love and be loved—to raise a family. Isn't that enough to fill out the rest of my life?"

"How old are you now, Peter?"

"Twenty-eight."

Adams smiled. "And so you are old, and wish to retire."

"No: and so I am young, and wish to live. Of course *your* definition of life is politics. But even on that definition you'll have to admit that I've lived a pretty full political life in the last nine years!"

"Tell me honestly. Do you really think it possible that you can ever stop worrying about political problems?"

"I hope so. After all, the better political and economic conditions get, the less interest I will have to take in them. Things have arrived at the point, it seems to me, where I can safely leave politics and economics to those who have a predominant taste for such matters. I will play Mozart."

366

"But suppose there is a crisis? Suppose Wang makes a mess of things, or is voted out of power, and the people turn to you as the Elder Statesman and demand that you return from your retirement?"

"I'll cross that bridge when we come to it, which I hope we never do. You are assuming things will go wrong; I am assuming they will go right. And if they go right, I need have no feeling of guilt for not taking part in them. After all, my new definition of a good society is simple: it is one in which it is possible for a man who loves Mozart to devote himself to Mozart. In other words, it is one in which an artist can feel free to devote himself exclusively to his art. And, you know, I'm particularly blessed in that respect, for Edith not only wants me to be a musician but she herself wants seriously to take up the violin—"

"You know," broke in Adams, "in our old Marxist histories, which may or may not be true, they tell about an emperor who fiddled while Rome burned."

"The story may even be true, Adams. But let's not get mixed up. The real disaster was not the fiddling but the burning. After all, it's up to you politicians not to go around starting any more fires—"

Edith broke into the room. She looked fresh and sparkling, and had on a neat tweed suit.

"Good heavens! What does this mean? Have you two been up talking the whole night long? It's after five o'clock. Haven't you heard the news? It was just on the radio a few minutes ago. Do you know what's happened? *You've won!* The count has just been completed from the Chinese and Indian country districts; the result on six seats in Parliament is changed—enough to give the Freedom Party an absolute majority of two seats!"

"That can't be so—" began Adams.

The telephone rang. Adams answered. "Really? . . . No! . . . Astounding! . . . No, you didn't wake me up. I appreciate your generosity. . . . I'm very grateful for your call.

"You know who that was?" he said to Peter. "Wang. He called up to tell me that the radio reports are right, and that he's conceded our victory! My first act is going to be to ask the new Parliament, when it meets tomorrow, to name *you* as the first President. I'm sure the election will be unanimous. You *must* accept! It's your absolute duty to accept!"

"After all I've just said?"

"After all you've just said. This is your program that we're going to put into effect. You can't walk out on responsibility for it."

"And Mozart?"

"Mozart can wait. Others will play him. So far as that's concerned, there's nothing to prevent you from playing him all you want, in private, in your leisure moments."

"But," protested Peter, "the President's term is ten years!"

"And so you'll be an old man of thirty-eight when you get out," said Adams sarcastically, "all used up and ready to be thrown on the scrap heap!"

Peter looked appealingly at Edith.

"You've got to accept, darling!" she said. "You know you do. Adams is right: it's your duty."

"You too think I'm a better politician than I am a piano-player?"

She laughed. "I know you're a better pianist than I am a violinist. It will take me at least ten years' hard practice before I'm fit to accompany you."

Peter sighed, and then smiled. "All right, Adams, make your announcement. But I warn you—I'm not going to be a mere figurehead. I accept on condition that you promise to ask my advice on all serious matters, and even to weigh it carefully."

"Why do you think I'm asking you to serve?" asked Adams.

Edith kissed them both. "Don't you boys know yet that it's after five o'clock? Look at those streaks of light," she said, pointing toward the picture window, "just above that range of mountains. Come, darling," she continued, taking Peter by the arm, "as long as you've stayed up this long, you're going with me on the terrace to see the dawn."

And they watched the sun come up in all its glory.

The Ludwig von Mises Institute

The Ludwig von Mises Institute, founded in 1982, is the research and educational center of classical liberalism, libertarian political theory, and the Austrian School of economics. Working in the intellectual tradition of Ludwig von Mises (1881-1973) and Murray N. Rothbard (1926-1995), with a vast array of publications, programs, and fellowships, the Mises Institute, with offices in Auburn, Alabama, seeks a radical shift in the intellectual climate as the foundation for a renewal of the free and prosperous commonwealth. This student series is one division of a larger publishing program that offers new and classic works in high-quality editions. For more information and ordering, see mises.org

Ludwig von Mises Institute
518 West Magnolia Avenue
Auburn, Alabama 36832-4528
334.321.2100 · Phone
334.321.2119 · Fax
contact@mises.org